to teachers

ACKNOWLEDGMENTS

In my career as a clinical psychologist, a decade of work was barely enough time for a therapist to be considered seasoned. But in the world of commercial publishing a decade is a long time indeed. Achieving longevity isn't possible without the assistance of many people and my gratitude for all the support I've received seems to grow greater every year.

In order to create *Warning Signs* I relied on guidance and instruction from some dedicated public servants who patiently led me through the specifics of their fields of expertise. My thanks to Jerry Burkhalter, a veteran of the Denver Police Department Bomb Squad, Detective Melissa Kampf of the Boulder Police Department, and Assistant District Attorney Chuck Lepley of Denver County. The responsibility for any damage done to the facts is mine, not theirs.

My wife Rose and my son Xan make all of this possible and worthwhile, and my mother Sara will always be my biggest fan. The Limericks, Patti and Jeff, believed in me at the beginning, and Al Silverman has believed in me ever since. My gratitude to them endures. Adrienne, as always, owes her medical acumen and some of her keenest insights to Dr. Stan Galansky. Elyse Morgan and Judy Pomerantz trained their critical eyes on an early version of the manuscript, and Nancy M. Hall's help was invaluable in assisting me during the difficult task of proofreading. They, too, have my thanks.

Bruce Collamore—the real one, not the fictional one in the first couple of chapters—graciously permitted me to use his name and some of his life story in support of charity. His wisdom might be questioned, but not his goodwill or his generosity. Jane Davis is an unsung hero—with great spirit and unparalleled competence she keeps my Web page humming and insulates me from more daily distractions than I will ever know. Thank you.

Fortunately for all of us, my books don't go directly from my word processor to the bookstore. First, the pages go through the hands of exemplary professionals who tune them, shine them, and prepare them for the light of day. My enduring thanks go to all of those at Bantam Dell and Doubleday whose efforts have been so beneficial to this book—especially Kate Burke Miciak, Nita Taublib, Irwyn Applebaum, Deborah Dwyer, Stephen Rubin, Gail Brussel, and Peter Gethers—and to all the wonderful people who support me year round at Janklow & Nesbit, specifically Lynn Nesbit and Amy Howell.

All women become like their mothers. That is their tragedy. No man does. That is his.

—Oscar Wilde
The Importance of Being Earnest

WARNING SIGNS

CHAPTER

1

Hands nipple high, palms up toward the night sky, Bruce Collamore started talking before the cops were even out of their car.

"I almost didn't call you guys. I was thinking that it was all too much like the O.J. thing. Don't you think? I mean, my dog didn't bark like that dog did, but I was walking my dog when I heard the scream. That's pretty close to the O.J. situation, isn't it? Anyway, that's why I almost didn't call. I'm still not sure I should have called. I haven't heard anything since that first scream. Right now, I think maybe it was nothing. That's what I'm beginning to think."

Two Boulder cops had responded to the 911. A coed team. Both were young, handsome, and strong.

The woman was a five-year vet on the Boulder Police force named Kerry VanHorn. She was a devout Christian who kept her religion to herself; she'd once even confided to a girlfriend that she thought prosely-tizing should be a capital offense. She had dirty-blond hair and a friendly Scandinavian face that put people at ease even when she didn't want to put them at ease. Over the years she'd discovered that if she squinted like she was looking into the sun people took her more seriously.

She was the first out of the squad car and the first to speak to the man who apparently remembered way too much about the O.J. case. She tucked her long flashlight under her arm and grabbed a pen before she squinted up at him—the guy was at least six five—and said, "Your name, sir?"

"Collamore, Bruce Collamore." He was wearing a ragged Middlebury College sweatshirt and an accom-modating smile.

"This your house?" She gestured toward the home closest to where they were standing. Jay Street was high on the western edge of Boulder, in territory that the foothills of the Rockies seemed to have yielded only reluctantly to housing. If there was a boundary between urban and rural on the west edge of town, Jay was definitely on the side of the line that was more mountain than burg. The trees and grasses were wild and haphazard, and the curbs cut into the sides of the roadway fooled no one—this was one part of Boulder where the Rockies still reigned.

"This? My house? No. God, no."

"You live on this street, sir?"

"Here? No, I live a couple blocks over on Pleasant.

I was out walking Misty. This is Misty." He reached down and tousled his dog's ears. The yellow Lab dipped her head and wagged her tail. Bruce Collamore and his dog both seemed eager to please.

"So . . . you were out walking your dog and you heard a . . ." While she waited for him to fill in the blank, she briefly lost her focus as she entertained an unbidden association to a crush she'd had on a junior high school teacher she had thought was cute.

Collamore brought her back to the moment as though he were someone who was accustomed to being in conversations where the other party's attention was wandering. He said, "A scream, I heard a scream. A loud one. Long, too. I mean, I haven't heard that many screams in my life but it, you know, seemed longer than . . . well, a normal scream. If there is such a thing? Jeez, 'a normal scream.' Did I really say that? What's wrong with me? Anyway, I think it came from that house. I'm pretty sure it did. That one. There." Collamore pointed at the gray-and-white two-story house directly across from where they stood on the edge of the road. "I had my cell phone with me so I thought I'd go ahead and call 911. Maybe it wasn't the right thing to do. I don't know. I'm a little nervous. You can probably tell I'm nervous."

She could tell. And she wasn't sure that he was nervous only because she was a cop. That suspicion made her a little nervous, too.

His left hand was balled around the dog's leash, so she couldn't see if Collamore was married. When she looked back up at him she squinted, just in case he was thinking what she was worried he was thinking. "What time was that, sir? That you heard the scream?"

"Nine fifty-one."

She wrote down the nine before she looked up from her notepad and lifted an eyebrow. The expression of incredulity interfered with her squint.

"I checked my watch when I heard the scream. You know, the O.J. thing? I thought somebody might want to know what time it happened. It really was that kind of scream—a somebody's-killing-me scream. So I checked my watch when I heard it." He exhaled loudly and ran his fingers through his hair. "God, this is embarrassing. I shouldn't have called, should I?"

She tried to make a neutral face, but wasn't sure she'd succeeded. She said, "No need to be embarrassed. We appreciate help from citizens. Can't do our jobs without it." But she was thinking that in most cities civilians ran and hid after they called 911. In Boulder they stick around on the sidewalk with their cell phones and their yellow Labradors named Misty. And maybe they keep contemporaneous records of their movements on their Palm Pilots. For all she knew this whole situation was already being tracked live on the Net.

Boulder.

Now she looked at the house he'd identified. The dwelling was an oasis of orderliness at the end of the block, the only home that looked like it could be plopped down comfortably in one of Boulder's more sedate neighborhoods. The owners of the surrounding houses—all of which were shabby in the way old cashmere is shabby—were either celebrating their good fortune at having modest homes in such a spectacular location or they were waiting for land values to escalate even more obscenely before they sold their fixer-upper to somebody who'd scrape the lot clear and start all over. She said, "You know who lives in this house, Bruce? May I call you Bruce?"

"Sure. Here? No, I don't. Like I said, I was just walking Misty. We come this way almost every night about this time. Since we walk late, most of the time we don't see anyone. Certainly don't hear many screams. Actually, we don't hear *any* screams. Before tonight, anyway. We heard one tonight, didn't we, girl?" He lowered his tone at least an octave as he addressed the dog.

VanHorn watched Misty's tail sweep the ground. She said, "And that was at nine fifty-one?"

"Yes, nine fifty-one."

"Well, we'll check that out. You don't mind staying here for a few minutes in case we have some more questions? My partner and I are going to speak to whoever is inside the house."

"No, no. We don't mind at all. Misty and I are happy to stick around."

The other cop, Kerry VanHorn's partner, was Colin Carpino. He had two years on the job. He was built like a bulldog but his creamy skin was almost hairless. VanHorn sometimes teased him that she had female relatives who shaved their upper lips more often than he did. She called him Whiskers.

As they moved up the brick walk in single file, she asked, "What do you think, Whiskers?"

"I buy lunch for a week if this is anything other than a waste of time." He shifted his long Mag-Lite from his right hand to his left.

She laughed. "It's your turn to buy. You're getting lunch tomorrow whether this is the Great Train Robbery or the lady of the house freaking out over a spider."

Carpino hit the doorbell button by the front door. They listened as it chimed like a carillon in a cathedral, and they waited.

He knocked. They waited some more.

He hit the bell again. This time he said, "Boulder Police," right after he heard the bells begin to peal inside the house. His tenor carried in the still air. The whole neighborhood of shuttered windows and closed doors had to know now that the cops were here. VanHorn waited for lights to come on, doors to open. It didn't happen. Collamore saw her looking his way and waved at her. She didn't wave back.

Whiskers reached down and tried the latch on the door. It didn't give.

VanHorn responded by touching her holster with her fingertips. The act was a caress, almost sensual in its carelessness—and it was involuntary, like a man checking for the presence of his wallet half a minute after he leaves the automatic teller machine.

The two cops waited for someone to come to the door and tell them everything was just fine.

After most of a minute had leaked into the void between them, VanHorn said, "I'll check the back of the house." She wasn't nervous yet, but she had definitely crossed over the line that separated routine from everything else that existed on a police officer's planet. The feeling was familiar, and not entirely unwelcome. The wariness sharpened her senses. She'd been around long enough to know that wasn't a bad thing.

"I'll take a look at the windows up front here and over on the other side," Carpino said.

The north side of the house was unlit, making it difficult for VanHorn to navigate the uneven path of flagstones. Spreading junipers clotted the open spaces between the window wells. An avid gardener, she hated junipers, especially spreading junipers. She alternated the flashlight beam between the path in front of her and the windows on the side of the house and noticed nothing that alarmed her. She fingered the switch of the radio microphone that was clipped to the left shoulder of her uniform blouse and said, "Nothing unusual on the side of the house. Just some unimaginative landscaping. But even in Boulder I don't think that's a crime."

Carpino replied, "Yet. Hold on, I may have something up here, Kerry." His voice betrayed no alarm. She waited for him to continue. He didn't.

She stepped lightly into the backyard. A streetlight brightened the rear of the house. She reached up and touched the button on her microphone. "What do you have, Whiskers? Open window?"

"No, I'm on the opposite side of the house from you, shining my beam inside into what looks like the living room. I see a lamp lying on the floor and some broken glass. That's all."

After again caressing the flap on her holster with the fingertips of her right hand, Officer VanHorn spent a moment examining the backyard with the beam of her flashlight. Only when she was certain she was alone in the yard did she take determined strides across a pleasant brick patio, past an almost-new gas grill, and up two steps to the door that led to the house. She grabbed the knob of the metal security door and twisted it. The door opened right up. She locked her gaze on the painted French door behind the security panel and fingered her microphone. "Back door's open. Not just unlocked, but open-open. Why don't you call for backup?"

She waited for his response long enough to inhale and exhale twice. Finally, she said, "Colin?"

He said, "Sorry. I may be looking at a person's foot, Kerry, just someone's heel. Like there's somebody lying on the floor. But I can't see past the heel. If it's a foot, then the rest of the body's behind a sofa."

VanHorn sighed. "We'd better go in. Tell dispatch."

"Will do. I'll call for backup and join you back there."

Kerry VanHorn flicked up the flap on her holster and drew her service weapon with her right hand. Her

Mag-Lite was in her left. Before she took another step she squeezed her biceps against her upper torso to convince herself that she'd remembered to wear her vest. She had.

Within seconds, Whiskers joined her at the back door. He, too, had his service weapon ready. He said, "The living room's in the southwest corner. That's where I saw the foot." She nodded and said a silent prayer before she nudged the French door with the toe of her shoe. She winced as the door squeaked open.

She yelled "Boulder Police" as she entered a big kitchen and family room. Shadowed light from the alley street lamp revealed an expensive recent remodel. Cherry cabinets. Granite countertops. Big double stainless-steel sink. Appliances that disappeared into the cabinetry. One appliance she didn't even recognize. She didn't like that kitchens had developed in such a way that people used appliances she couldn't even recognize.

But nothing was out of place. She could hear Whiskers's footsteps on the hardwood floor behind her. The resonant clap was reassuring. There was almost nothing she liked doing less as a cop than walking into dark houses.

The door from the kitchen led to a short hallway. Again she called out, "Boulder Police," and waited for a reply. Nothing. Carpino repeated the announcement. After she waited for a response that never came, she stepped past a powder room and saw a dining room on her right. She played the beam into the room for two or three seconds. It didn't appear that anyone had eaten in there recently; the table was covered with piles of mail. She gestured with her flashlight to reassure her partner before she turned toward the living room. At the bottom of a staircase she flicked the beam up the stairs. She spotted nothing that alarmed her but noticed an odd device on rails attached to the side of the staircase. She also noted a rhythmic *shush-shush, shush-shush, shush-shush* coming down from the second floor. The sound was familiar to her but she couldn't place it. *Shush-shush, shush-shush, shush-shush*. The rhythm wasn't out of place in a house. She was sure of that. But what was it that she was hearing?

Darn. She couldn't place the noise.

She took two steps into the living room and swept her flashlight beam in a wide, slow arc, looking for the foot that Whiskers had seen, praying that he was wrong or, failing that, that there was at least still a person attached to it.

The first thing that caught her attention was the lamp on the floor—she assumed it was the same one that Whiskers had spotted through the window. Then she saw the broken glass, a lot of it. The glass appeared to be some kind of pottery or ceramic; it must have been a big piece before it was busted.

No foot.

Lights flashed outside on the street. VanHorn looked up and was relieved to see a patrol car slide to the curb in front of the house. Her partner whispered,

"Backup's here." She adjusted the grip on her weapon and, for her own benefit, silently mouthed, "I'm doing fine. I'm doing fine."

EEEEHHHHHHNNNNNN.

A loud, noxious buzzing seemed to fill the house. The sound was bitter and sour, like aural vinegar. It blared for maybe two seconds before it stopped as abruptly as it started. VanHorn's pulse jumped when the noise started and she wheeled around to check behind her. Carpino's eyes were wide as he, too, searched for the source of the sound. VanHorn's service weapon felt heavy in her hand.

She shook her head, announcing she didn't know the source of the sound. Carpino did the same.

The buzzing blared again. *EEEEHHHHHHNNNNN.* Once again the sharp sound stopped suddenly.

The noise had seemed to come from everywhere at once.

What was it? What was it? She couldn't place it.

She yelled "Boulder Police" one more time.

Then she noticed that the *shush-shush* had ceased, and the pieces of the puzzle fell into place. VanHorn smiled. She knew what it was. The *shush-shush* had been the refrain of a tumbling clothes dryer. The buzzer was the notification that the cycle was done. Her boyfriend's dryer made the same awful noise. She exhaled and slowly refilled her lungs. "Whiskers? That was a clothes dryer, I think. At the end of its cycle."

He said, "Oh," and definitely sounded relieved.

Someone had recently started a dryer in this house. How long did a load take to dry? Forty-five minutes? An hour?

Through the side windows she watched another black-and-white slide to a stop at the curb.

She stepped around the lamp on the floor so that she could see behind the sofa at the far end of the room. Behind the sofa was an open door. She thought it would lead back to the family room that she'd seen when she first came into the house, the one adjacent to the new kitchen. She swung the beam toward the floor behind the striped couch.

She saw the foot, paused, and then she took another step.

"Oh Jesus. Oh my God. Oh dear Jesus." If she had a free hand she would have crossed herself with it, an affectation of her Catholic past.

At the sight of the blood and the mangled tissue where the person's face should be, VanHorn felt a sour geyser erupting in her esophagus and she swallowed twice to stem the urge to vomit. She took a step back and stumbled over the broken pottery. When she returned her gaze to the body on the floor, she said, "May God rest your soul, whoever you are."

Carpino said, "What?" His voice came from behind her, maybe ten or twelve feet away.

She said, "You were right, there's a body in here, Colin. A lot of blood. Call for an ambulance, okay?"

She counted to three and told herself she was fine. But she didn't feel fine. She felt as though she should sit down to keep from passing out, but she didn't want to disturb what she already knew was a crime scene. Sequentially, she looked everywhere in the room that didn't have a bloody body. She even looked at the ceiling. For her, the act was like looking at the horizon when she was seasick. Finally, the wave of nausea eased and her neurons resumed firing and she carefully checked the room to make triple-sure she and her partner and the guy on the floor didn't have any company.

She dropped to her knees, stooped over the body, and lowered her head to listen for breath sounds. She heard nothing. To feel for a pulse, she needed to put down either her light or her gun. For a moment she weighed her choice, finally deciding to place the torch on the carpet, and, as she'd been taught, she rested three fingers on the underside of the radial bone of the man's right wrist. She was thinking the body was that of a man. The socks were men's socks. She was pretty sure of that. An exposed inch of calf was moderately hairy.

It was a man.

She felt no pulse. She thought, maybe, the body was cooler than it should have been, but only a little, and certainly not cold. She spent a moment trying to remember the speed at which a body gives up its warmth after death—a degree an hour, was that it?—and wondered if it was possible that this man was the same person who had started the dryer upstairs. He couldn't have cooled down that fast, could he? Maybe her own fingers were hot and that's why the body felt cool. That was certainly possible.

Variables, variables.

Bruce Collamore had said he heard the "somebody's-killing-me" scream at 9:51. She looked at her watch. It was 10:17. No, if this were the screamer, he wouldn't have cooled down, yet.

Hot fingers. Had to be her hot fingers.

Still on her knees, she lifted her Mag-Lite again and simultaneously turned her body to address her partner. The beam of the light danced carelessly off the ceiling and the walls. She said, "This guy's dead, and there's a lot of blood. Call for detectives and have the backup team tape off a perimeter out there. Make it a big perimeter. Tell the tall guy with the dog that he's not going anywhere for a while. We have to do the rest of the house. Get some people in here to help out. Tell them to come in the back door and walk straight to the front of the house, then turn left to the living room. And remind them not to touch anything. We have a crime scene and I don't want to be the one to mess it up."

She said a silent prayer and aimed her lamp directly at the body on the floor, trying to discern the details of the man's face through the severe damage and the copious blood.

For a second or two she thought she knew the man and tried to jar an association loose from her memory. It didn't work. VanHorn then decided that she didn't really know him. Again, she repeated her silent prayer and wondered what in heaven God had been thinking at 9:51 that evening.

She decided that He must have been seriously distracted.

CHAPTER

2

The first pair of detectives arrived about twenty minutes before midnight to find a well-delineated perimeter and a crime scene that was barely contaminated. Sam Purdy, the senior detective, was ecstatic. But he kept his joy to himself.

"Who was first officer?" he asked of the patrol cop who was manning the clipboard and controlling access to the scene.

"VanHorn and Carpino."

"RP?" Purdy was asking who had called in the crime—who was the reporting party.

"Still here."

"Wits?"

"Got one, guy named Bruce Collamore. He's the RP, too. That's him sitting in the backseat of my squad. Has a dog with him. Heard a scream a shade before ten. I talked to him a little bit—he's an interesting guy, teaches high school now, math I think. But he played a little pro football when he was younger, if you can believe it."

Purdy grunted. "That's it? That's all you know?"

The officer shrugged. "The Bengals. He was in camp for a few days with the Bengals."

"I should care where he played football?"

"Hey, it's early, Detective. We didn't want to mess with him before you guys got here. Played tight end, if you really want to know. Isn't built like a tight end now, though; he's tall enough, but he's too skinny, more like a Randy Moss type. He's crammed into the back of the squad like an anchovy in a can."

Purdy said, "I might give a shit about any of this if he played for the Vikings, but I certainly don't care about some guy who didn't last a week with the damn Bengals, that's for sure. Whose house is this?"

"Neighbor says it's a family named Peters, but the neighbor didn't hear anything that came down."

Purdy turned to his partner. "You get that? What else do we have, Luce?"

Lucy Tanner looked at her notepad. She knew he was asking her if the detective's log was current. In these circumstances, it was her job to make sure it was. She said, "We were called by dispatch via pager at ten twenty-six, arrived at the scene on Jay Street at eleven thirty-five. Six patrol officers present, all have checked in with the control officer. Medical personnel have come and gone. Photographers present and waiting for clearance to go inside. Ditto CSIs.

Weather? Clear skies, temp near fifty. One wit at the scene, already isolated. Search warrant has been requested from Judge Silverman. We're waiting on it."

"You get snaps? I want a good set of snaps. Who knows what time the photographers will get to go in."

Lucy held up a disposable camera with a built-in flash. "This side of the house is covered."

"Let's go to the back, then."

Kerry VanHorn walked across the front yard of the house, approaching the two detectives. She was squinting. "Detective? I'm Officer VanHorn. I was first officer on the scene, along with Officer Carpino."

"Sam Purdy. This is Lucy Tanner. Where's Carpino?" Purdy thought he recognized VanHorn from a recent altercation he'd investigated between a bicyclist and a pedestrian on Canyon Boulevard. He wasn't sure he'd ever heard of Carpino, didn't think he'd been with VanHorn that day.

VanHorn nodded a greeting to Lucy before she answered. "We entered the home through an open rear door. He's standing watch there."

"Who's been inside?"

"Just Carpino and me initially. After we found the deceased on the main level, two other officers accompanied us on a search of the rest of the premises. Upon further search, we found a disabled person sleeping upstairs in the master bedroom. When we couldn't arouse her enough to take a statement, we called an ambulance. Two paramedics entered the house and removed her. At my request, one of them walked through the section of the house where I found the deceased to confirm that he was, well, deceased. The ambulance left about twenty-five minutes ago. The disabled woman is now at Community Hospital. You may want to dispatch someone to get her statement, Detective. She was not particularly coherent when I tried to talk with her."

"That's it? Got any names?"

"Yes, sir. That's it. And no, sir. The woman was, like I said, incoherent. I think she said her name was Susan, or Suzanne. I had trouble understanding her. She was not able to give a last name. Neighbor a couple of doors down across the street says the family is the Peters. Only wit is the RP, guy named Bruce Collamore. He's waiting in one of the squads. Heard a scream a few minutes before ten. I don't think he's going to be much more help; he's already told us all he knows."

"Yeah, I've already heard all about Collamore. Got cut by the Bengals during training camp, if you can believe that."

"What?" VanHorn asked.

Purdy ignored her question while he went through a mental checklist and reached satisfaction that things were under control. Then he realized he'd missed something. "Coroner here yet?"

"Haven't seen anyone," she said.

Purdy made a note to have Lucy ascertain that Scott Truscott, the coroner's assistant, had been called. He said, "Good job here, VanHorn. You and Carpino managed this scene like you do it every weekend."

Purdy and **L**ucy followed VanHorn down the path to the backyard. Lucy snapped some photographs of the rear of the house before VanHorn introduced the detectives to Carpino. No one shook hands; Purdy and Lucy were busy pulling latex onto their fingers.

"The yard was like this? Nothing's been touched?"

Whiskers answered, "Just like you see it. No one's been back here but us since we arrived. Only things we touched outside were the doorknobs. We did that before we realized what we had."

The **search warrant** arrived around twelve-thirty.

The crime scene investigators and the police photographers preceded the two detectives into the house. After about fifteen minutes, the CSIs reported to Purdy that they'd finished clearing and vacuuming the path to the living room and that he could enter.

Everyone pulled coverings onto their shoes. At Purdy's request, VanHorn led the way inside and pointed out the direction she had walked to get to the living room before she discovered the body. On this return visit she went no farther than the foot of the stairs, using the beam of her flashlight to direct the detectives the rest of the way to the deceased. "He's there, behind that couch."

"All the lights were off? Just like this?" Purdy asked

as he carefully crossed the length of the room and lowered himself to a crouch a few feet from the body. The detective's feet were in a little clearing in the center of the pottery debris.

"Yes. We touched nothing in this room. I did feel the victim's wrist for a pulse and I tripped over some of the broken pottery when I got back up. The EMT was careful, too, when he confirmed the death. I watched him. That's it. Nothing else was touched down here. Upstairs was different. We tried to watch what we were doing, but moving that lady to the hospital spilled some milk. Couldn't be avoided. I've started making a list of everything I think was disturbed up there."

"Good. Finish the list and get it to me. We'll take it from here."

"Oh, I almost forgot, the dryer was on. Upstairs? There's a washer and dryer. When I first came in the house, the dryer was on. It finished its cycle just before I found the body. Made a loud buzzing sound."

Purdy took a moment to catch her eyes and smiled at her. "Scared the shit out of you, I bet, didn't it?"

She laughed. "Yeah. Scared the shit out of me." VanHorn didn't generally condone profane language. But the phrase seemed to fit the circumstances.

"That was when?"

"Ten twenty-five, ten-thirty, give or take a couple of minutes."

"Got that, Luce?"

Lucy raised her pen from her notebook but didn't look up. "Yeah, Sam. I got it."

"You can go, Officer. Good work."

Purdy stood up straight, took a flashlight from Lucy's hand, and swept the room with the beam, pausing a few times. While he perused the space, he took note of the temperature in the house, inhaled the aroma of the room, and digested how the shadows played with the darkness. He knew Lucy would be doing the same drill. In a few minutes, they'd compare impressions. When he finally stepped forward, he approached the corpse cautiously, noting the position of the lamp on the floor, treading carefully around the pieces of ceramic.

Lucy hung back; she was at least six feet behind him. Purdy could hear her breathing through her mouth.

"You okay, Luce?" he said.

She said, "Sure." But Purdy didn't quite believe her.

"You need a minute? Or are you ready?"

"I'm right behind you, Sam. I'm fine."

Maybe a stranger would have failed to recognize the catch in her voice. But Purdy heard it. "If you're going to puke, puke outside, okay?"

He expected her to curse at him in reply. Instead, she said, "I told you I'm fine, Sam."

Purdy once again lowered himself to a crouch, this time right beside the body. For a few seconds he focused on the injuries and on the blood, not on the dead person. A gestalt thing—figure, not ground. The head and face wounds that had been inflicted were severe. At least two deep crushing blows. Probably more. Blood pooled around the man's head like a lake on a dark night. The blood loss was copious. With the flashlight beam he traced a fan-shaped splatter that extended up the nearest wall all the way to the crown molding. The conclusion was obvious: The victim had been standing when he was hit and had lived long enough to bleed like a broken dike.

"Is he dead, Sam?" Lucy asked the question as though she didn't quite believe it was true.

Purdy didn't bother feeling for a pulse. He knew dead. "He's really dead, Luce. Bashed in the face and head with something heavy and hard. My money's on the lamp or this broken pottery."

She didn't reply.

Purdy asked, "Can you see outside? Has the coroner's van arrived?"

"I don't see it out there."

He thought she sounded funny.

Sam Purdy was a big man. He lowered one knee to the carpet so he could lean over and examine the undamaged part of the man's face. It took him maybe two seconds of focus to identify the victim.

"Holy shit. You know who this is, Luce?"

She swallowed. Her voice was hollow. "I can't see him from here. Just some blood. All I see is the blood."

Purdy said, "Whose house is this, anyway? Do you know whose house this is? Lucy?"

CHAPTER

3

It should have been my first clue.

For the first time since Grace's birth I put her to bed all by myself. Shortly after nine o'clock on Thursday night Lauren had pulled the satiated baby from her breast and handed her up to me, smiling wanly. She asked if I'd give our daughter a bath. I was delighted to comply.

Grace and I moved swiftly over the familiar territory that led from bath, to diaper, to fresh sleeper, to my favorite part—bedtime stories in the big upholstered rocker in the nursery. I had no illusions that my little girl even knew what a book was, but I could find no reasonable argument for postponing her introduction to the wonders of the written word, and I could find a million reasons for not waiting. Each night we read a few books. Each night both of us loved it.

Lauren never jumped into the ritual that particular

night, even when the usually irresistible trill of Grace's laughter echoed down the hall between the two bedrooms. I enjoyed the independence of it all and assumed that Lauren's request that I put the baby to bed was her way of giving me a vote of confidence. I also knew I'd have to get used to it; the following Monday Lauren was returning to work after half a year of maternity leave.

Once I'd kissed our daughter for the last time and placed her on her back in her crib, I stepped down the hall to the bedroom to find Lauren curled away from the door, asleep. A few minutes later I touched my lips to her inky hair before I crawled into bed beside her.

It wasn't long after Grace's birth six months earlier that we'd developed a family ritual that consisted of breakfast out on Friday or Saturday morning followed by errands and grocery shopping. The morning after my first solo bedtime flight with Grace was one of those Fridays where I'd managed to keep my office calendar clear, and Lauren drove us into town on our way to breakfast. We were planning to eat at Marie's, followed by some grocery shopping at Ideal, bagels from Moe's, bread from Breadworks, and wine from the Boulder Wine Merchant.

All without moving our car. Almost like in a real city.

As we crawled up Balsam past the mini-roundabouts toward Broadway, Lauren cursed at an elderly man in an impeccably preserved old turquoise Chevy Bel Air who signaled a left turn and then smoothly pulled right into the driveway of a modest brick ranch that had held its value a lot better than his car.

At the sound of Lauren's profanity, I leaned into the backseat and told Grace to cover her ears.

Lauren didn't laugh.

It should have been my second clue.

The reason I was missing so many clues was, I think, that I was out of practice. From the moment Lauren had become pregnant fifteen months before, she'd enjoyed a sabbatical from her long struggle living with relapsing-remitting multiple sclerosis. Her neurologist had told her that the pregnancy might indeed provide a respite from her chronic symptoms and a brief protection against fresh exacerbations of her illness. It turned out that he'd been right on both counts.

What were the usual signs that something was brewing with Lauren's health? Withdrawal and distraction. She'd sense some sign of change in her functioning—pain, weakness, numbness, vertigo, something—and she'd pull away from me. She'd also display signs of irritability.

But my radar was rusty and I was out of practice. For fifteen months I'd floated along on the gentle sea of denial, buoyed by blind hope that our daughter's birth would be her mother's ticket to prolonged good health.

The selection of breads at the bakery didn't include the multigrain that Lauren coveted. Her disappointment at the news was much too keen. The table at Marie's was uneven and Lauren leaned over to fidget with sugar packets until the wobble disappeared. The waitress brought Lauren coffee, not the tea she'd ordered. Lauren tried to sigh away her uncharacteristic annoyance at the mistake. She failed. When she looked over at me and said, "I'm not up for this, Alan. Can we skip breakfast this morning?" I finally realized that something was wrong.

I lowered my coffee mug back to the tabletop and said, "You're not feeling well, are you?"

For a prolonged moment every sound in the crowded coffee shop was muted. No motion blurred anything in my periphery. I followed Lauren's gaze as she looked at Grace, who was asleep in her infant carrier. Tears formed in Lauren's lower lashes.

"What is it?" I asked, even though I already knew.

She didn't answer right away.

"Are you symptomatic?" I said. With Lauren, I didn't need to be any more specific. I didn't need to reference a specific illness. We both knew I was inquiring about her MS.

She nodded, flicked a poignant glance at Grace. At the same moment, she said, "I don't want to be sick anymore, Alan. I don't."

I covered her wrist with my hand—her hand was balled into a fist—and waited almost a full minute for her to continue. When finally she did, she said, "We can talk about this later, okay? I think I'd really like to go home. But we need to stop at the drugstore first. You know?"

I nodded. I already knew about the drugstore stop. She and her neurologist had decided that Lauren would forego prophylactic treatment for her MS during her pregnancy. But by then, Grace and Lauren had each been fortified by six months of breastfeeding and Lauren was planning on resuming her interferon treatments. The prescription for interferon, which was intended to hold fresh exacerbations of Lauren's multiple sclerosis at bay, was waiting for her at the pharmacy. I was suddenly wondering, of course, whether she was restarting the medicine a week or two too late.

Lauren said, "Why don't you take Grace?" and stood. I dropped a couple of bills on the table and lifted our daughter and her baby carrier while Lauren strapped the diaper bag over her shoulder. As she preceded me out the door and headed toward the parking lot, I examined my wife's gait and her balance, looking for signs of what might be ailing her.

I couldn't discern a thing.

Damn disease.

It was like being surrounded by no-see-um bugs. Couldn't find them to swat them away.

Lauren and Grace, Emily, our dog, and Anvil, our foster dog, all slept away much of the afternoon. I was left to spend the day with gutter cleaning, and car washing, and the most noxious of all chores, worrying. Before she retreated to the bedroom for the afternoon, Lauren had revealed that her new symptoms included muscle spasms in three different locations on her left side, some worrisome new tingling in her left hand, and shooting pains in her right foot. The sum of those signs wasn't cause for alarm. She wasn't going blind in one eye, wasn't paralyzed anywhere, wasn't falling over from vertigo. Maybe it wasn't anything major. Not a big storm, I was hoping, just heat lightning flashing on the horizon.

Then she'd added another detail. She was experiencing what she called brain mud, a general fogginess in her sensorium and her thinking. We both knew that she usually experienced the brain mud either as a prelude to or as a result of an exacerbation of her MS.

The presence of the brain mud meant that Lauren and I would be balanced precariously on the edge of a cliff as that day became night and today became tomorrow.

For the second evening in a row I put Grace to sleep by myself. Lauren's fatigue seemed even more pronounced than usual; I sensed that she was asleep before Grace and I finished the last story of our bedtime ritual.

The morning was warm, almost sixty degrees before dawn. Grace and the puppies were still asleep and I was standing in the kitchen tugging on Lycra, hoping to steal an early bicycle ride, when the phone rang. I jumped at the device like a soldier endeavoring to cover a live hand grenade to protect his platoon. I got to the portable after only half a ring, flicking a quick glance at the clock before I punched the talk button and said, "Hello."

It was 5:38. Early.

"Alan? It's Elliot."

I recognized the patrician voice even before he got to his name. Elliot Bellhaven was one of Lauren's colleagues in the Boulder County District Attorney's Office. I'd met him through Lauren years before when he was new in the DA's office, fresh out of Harvard Law. Over the years Elliot had aged, of course, but I still pictured him in my head as the angel-faced, idealistic kid who'd infused the DA's office with a much needed booster of adrenaline. Recently, though, he'd seemed to become part of the establishment he'd once been so eager to jostle.

"Hey, Elliot," I said. I was waiting for him to tell me the bad news. This wasn't a work call. Lauren hadn't been at work in over six months. This wasn't a social call. It was 5:38 on Saturday morning. Elliot's mother had raised him better than that. Much better than that.

"I'm sorry if I woke you, Alan, but I thought Lauren should hear the news from me rather than someone else."

"You didn't wake me; I was up. What news?"

"Is she awake?"

"Not unless the phone woke her." I tucked the phone between my shoulder and my ear and ambled the two steps to the kitchen television and pressed the power button. The set flickered on to Channel 4, the early local news. A female reporter was doing a stand-up in front of a familiar house—a two-story with a wide lawn and a cheery line of bright yellow crocuses near the street. The graphics on the screen read, "LIVE! Boulder." The reporter was dressed in a maroon turtle-neck and looked uncomfortable in the early spring warmth.

Elliot said, "Would you wake Lauren for me, please? I'd very much like to speak with her. Once again, I apologize. I'll hold." He was using a business voice, the kind of tone he might use to an assistant around the office when the boss was around. The tone was polite and respectful, but instantly conveyed the fact that he expected his wishes to be carried out. If I'd been in another mood, I might have humored him and complied.

I eased up the sound on the TV. "*. . . answered a call at about ten-fifteen last night. Apparently, the body was discovered a short time later.*"

I placed the house in my mind. It was over on Jay Street, near the foothills. The house I was looking at on the TV belonged to Royal Peterson, the Boulder County District Attorney—Lauren's boss. Elliot's boss. I'd been to Royal's home for at least three or four staff parties over the years. Had I been there the previous Christmas? No, his wife, Susan, hadn't been well recently. My last visit must have been the Christmas season before.

What body? My heart jumped. I thought about Susan Peterson. Had she been that sick?

"I'd really rather not wake Lauren, Elliot. She's not been feeling well. What's up?" I thought I sounded as normal as anyone would under the circumstances.

". . . *been able to learn that there are signs of a struggle inside the house. Neighbors reported hearing some shouting—one man we spoke with said 'screaming'—but there are no reports of gunshots.*"

Elliot said, "It's about Royal."

"Yes?"

". . . *Royal Peterson's body was removed by the Boulder County Coroner at around four o'clock this morning.*"

Instinctively, I reached behind me and found a chair. I tugged it below me and almost fell to the seat.

"He was murdered last night, Alan. In his home."

I tried to say "Royal's dead?" but wasn't sure any sound actually came out of my mouth.

The cameraman pulled his shot back and I saw Elliot Bellhaven standing on the front porch of Royal Peterson's home talking on his cell phone.

He was talking to me.

Elliot was wearing jeans and a T-shirt. The shirt was covered by a tight V-neck sweater. Knowing Elliot, I knew the sweater was cashmere. His left shoulder was to the camera. On the television, the reporter was still talking, but I had stopped listening to her soliloquy.

I inhaled and forced myself to exhale slowly. Royal Peterson murdered? "Jesus, Elliot. What happened?"

"He was beaten to death last night. We think around ten o'clock. We don't know much else."

"How's Susan?"

"An ambulance took her to the hospital. I think she's stable. Haven't heard otherwise." His tone wasn't particularly compassionate. On the TV screen I watched Elliot turn and face the street.

"She's not a sus—"

"Susan? No, no, not at all. I'm sure you know that she's been bedridden lately, not well. So not at this point, no. She was asleep when the police got here and anyway she doesn't have the strength to do what was done to Royal."

Part of me wanted to know what had been done to Royal. Most of me didn't. I knew that Elliot wouldn't tell me the details anyway. But he'd tell Lauren. She'd share them with me in a manner I was more likely to be able to stomach.

I said, "The kids weren't in town?" Royal and Susan had three grown kids. None of them lived in Boulder. I thought one of their two daughters—Amanda? Amelia?—ran a successful decorating business in Durango. She'd been at one of the holiday parties I'd attended, had appeared to worship her father.

"No. No one was here but Roy and Susan. And . . . whoever it was who killed Roy."

On the screen, I watched as my good friend, Boulder Police Department detective Sam Purdy,

poked his head out the front door of Royal's house and
said something to Elliot. I could hear what he was saying through the phone line, though the sound wasn't
quite in sync with Sam's lips as I watched them move
on the TV screen. Sam said, "Need you in here,
Bellhaven. Now, if you don't mind."

Elliot and Sam weren't friends. I had theories about
the animosity between them, but couldn't be sure that
I wasn't missing something. If I invested time in trying
to understand why Sam didn't like all the people he
didn't like, I'd have precious little time left for almost
anything else.

Elliot pressed the phone against his chest and said
something back to Sam. Reading lips has never been
one of my fortes. I watched Elliot lift the phone back
to his ear and waited for the sound of him speaking to
me. "I'm at Royal's house right now, Alan, and I need
to go. The police want me for something inside. Have
Lauren page me when she's awake. Why don't you turn
on the news? I'm sure you'll learn something interesting from it. This place is crawling with reporters and
microwave trucks."

"Yeah, I'll do that. Thanks for calling, Elliot. Were
you catching last night? Is this going to be yours?"

"Don't know. Mitchell's on it, too. So's Nora. As far
as politics go, this place is drawing potential candidates like an American Legion hall in New Hampshire
in primary season. Have Lauren page me. Bye." He
was telling me that the posturing to be Royal
Peterson's successor was already heating up. As the

spouse of an insider, I was privy to the roster of likely candidates: Elliot; Mitchell Crest, Royal's chief trial deputy; and Nora Doyle, the head of sex crimes prosecution. And now all three were already hovering close to the murdered body of their dead boss.

I watched Elliot fold the tiny phone he was carrying and stuff it into the pocket of his trousers. He paused outside the door of the Peterson home while he pushed his hair back from his forehead and snapped a fresh pair of gloves onto his hands. Lucy Tanner, Sam's partner, held the door open for him. He nodded an acknowledgment to her before he squeezed past her and disappeared inside the house. Lucy stepped outside and squatted beside a plastic case that was resting on the lawn. She held her gloved hands out in front of her like a surgeon who had just scrubbed for the OR.

She was searching the case for something a detective might need to deal with evidence at the scene of a homicide.

My attention was drawn back to the sound emanating from the TV. "... *the controversial Boulder DA had been expected to announce that he would not run for re-election. Back to you, Virginia.*"

The next shot was Virginia in the anchor chair. I stripped off my Lycra jersey and walked back toward the bedrooms wearing only my padded biking shorts. Grace was just starting to stir. I lifted her from her crib and as I changed her diaper we chatted about her dreams and I told her about the warm morning. The dogs heard us chatting—that was me—and cooing,

which was both of us, and trailed after us as I carried
my daughter to the kitchen.

I didn't trouble Grace with the news that her
mommy's boss had been murdered. She didn't even
know Royal Peterson. He had sent a baby gift, though.
I reminded her of that.

I didn't have a clue what the gift had been.

The night before, just before bedtime, Lauren had
poked a one-and-a-quarter-inch, 23-gauge needle into
the meatiest part of her right thigh. She'd then inject-
ed one milliliter of interferon solution into the long
muscles of her quad.

Why? To tame the lions of the multiple-sclerosis cir-
cus.

To keep the brain mud at bay.

This injection of interferon had been her first dose
in fifteen months, and she knew, and I knew, that the
interferon beta that she plunged into her thigh would
make her sick for the next twenty hours or so. She
would feel like she had the flu. She would have muscle aches so sharp they brought tears, so deep that she
would swear that her bones and her hair hurt. She
would have chills. She would have fever.

That's why I was reluctant to wake her when Elliot
called. But she woke on her own a few minutes after
seven and joined Grace and me in the kitchen. Lauren
was wearing a long T-shirt from a Race for the Cure
that I knew she hadn't run in. I didn't think I had run

in it, either. I embraced her and kissed her on the top of her head.

"Good morning. How are you feeling?" I asked as I handed her the baby. She focused her attention on Grace, shaking her head to tell me she felt pretty much how she looked.

I said, "Let's go sit down someplace comfortable. There's something I need to talk to you about."

She was so intent on Grace that I didn't think she'd heard me. But she turned around and walked toward the living room where she curled up on the sofa with Grace on her lap. The little dog, Anvil, a black minia-ture poodle whom we'd inherited from a former patient of mine, noodled his way into position on the part of Lauren's lap to which Grace hadn't staked claim. I sat beside them on the sofa and took Lauren's free hand. She tried to smile as she said, "Hey, now that I'm back on interferon and I can't breast-feed anymore, I can have real coffee. With caffeine. That's a good thing, right? So what's up? What did you want to tell me?"

I waited for her to find my gaze. The moment she shifted her attention from the baby to me, I said, "Royal's dead, babe."

"What?" Instantly, her eyes began to fill with tears.

"He was beaten to death in his home last night. That was Elliot who called early this morning."

"Roy?"

Involuntarily, she gripped Grace even tighter and began to kiss her as the first of her tears dripped into the baby's black hair. I suspected that Royal's death would not be uncomplicated news for my wife. During Lauren's time in the DA's office Roy Peterson had been good to her in many ways, but a few years ago he'd also been one of the first to turn his back on her when she'd been mistakenly arrested for murder. She'd never forgiven him for his lack of faith, or his political opportunism, or whatever it was that had motivated him to betray her.

The phone rang. She waved for me to get it. I wasn't surprised when I answered to hear the voice of Mitchell Crest, the chief trial deputy in the DA's office. Mitch had been a close friend of Roy's, and I offered my sympathy to him before I gave the phone over to Lauren. She grabbed it eagerly.

She would learn all about Royal's murder from somebody who actually knew the details.

Lauren insisted on going into the office. I argued with her briefly. I thought I had good arguments. It was the weekend, she was sick from the interferon, she was still officially on pregnancy leave, her body was sending out lots of signs that the MS bears might be stirring from their long hibernation, and she should probably avoid stress.

I made my case.

She went into the office.

CHAPTER

4

Lauren didn't return home until after Grace and I had finished dinner. For the third night in a row I put the baby to bed by myself. Lauren was sound asleep by the time the bedtime ritual was complete. I joined her in our bed shortly after ten and tried to remember the last time we'd made love, but I couldn't.

The next morning the phone rang early again. Unlike the previous morning, this time it did wake me. The night before I'd set my alarm for 5:45, so even in the foggiest recesses of my brain, I knew it was real early. I grabbed the receiver and said, "Hello," trying to make my voice sound like I hadn't been asleep. I don't know why I always did that.

"Sorry, Alan," Sam Purdy said. "And, yeah, I do know what time it is."

I glanced at the clock. Four-twelve, God help me. "You want to talk to Lauren?"

"Eventually, yeah, I do. First, let me tell you

something. You don't talk with anybody but your wife about this, okay?"

"Sure."

"I can't believe I'm saying these words, but I just picked up Lucy for questioning for Royal's murder."

"What? Lucy who? Lucy Tanner? Your Lucy?"

"Yeah. My Lucy." The words sounded heavy, as though they weighed him down like an anchor. He sounded so tired. I guessed that he hadn't slept for more than an hour or two since Royal's body was discovered thirty hours before. If that.

"You think Lucy murdered Roy?" The words felt as oxymoronic as "Congress passed campaign finance reform?"

"That's the way it looks. Witnesses, fingerprints, other stuff. It's a mess. A total damn mess."

My end of the conversation was causing Lauren to stir. When I looked over, she was sitting up next to me, her breasts swollen with milk that Grace was no longer consuming. "What's going on?" she asked.

I covered the microphone on the handset. "It's Sam," I said. "He just picked up Lucy for questioning in Roy's murder."

"What? Give me the phone." She did a much better job of sounding awake than I did.

I gave her the phone. She said, "Sam, what the hell are you talking about?"

As Lauren questioned Sam, I heard the first signs of stirring on the baby monitor. Seconds later, Grace started to cry.

Lauren raised her eyebrow and mouthed, "Do you mind?"

I threw back the comforter and headed down the hall. I was almost to Grace's door when I heard Lauren call, "Wait, Sam wants to talk to you again." Lauren and I—both naked—passed in the hallway and I grabbed the phone from our bed.

I said, "I can't believe Lucy killed Royal, Sam."

"Yeah, I know, I know. Listen, taking Lucy in was my last official act in the investigation of Roy's murder. As you could probably have guessed, they wanted me off the case as soon as I told them where this was headed. I had to sell my soul to even be allowed to bring her in myself."

"Conflict of interest?"

"I'd like to think so. It's certainly the public face they're going to put on it. But part of me thinks that the big boys are actually worried I might have been part of whatever came down at Royal's house on Saturday night."

"You're kidding?"

"I wish I was."

"They said something to you?"

"No. They didn't have to. Hey, I didn't roust you out of bed to bitch at you about my bosses. What the brass thinks about me isn't my immediate problem. I need your advice on something else. Lucy was smart enough not to say a word to me after I went to her house and woke her up and told her what was coming down. I didn't really press her to talk on the drive over. Once I got her to the department, though, she asked me to help her pick a lawyer. Said she'd sit tight until she heard from one. So she's sitting mute in an interrogation room on Thirty-third Street waiting for me to find a lawyer to tell her what to do next."

I waited for Sam to go on.

"Anyway, so here's what I'm thinking: I'm thinking about that guy who helped the Ramseys—what's his name, Hal Haddon? Do I got that right? I always get those Ramsey lawyers mixed up. The one I think is Haddon struck me as a sharp guy. Principled, you know. But I keep wondering whether principles are a good thing in these circumstances, and I'm worried that his profile's too high after all the heat he took over the Ramseys. You think? I want some advice."

I thought for a moment before I replied. I didn't want to get into a political discussion with Sam about legal ethics, and certainly didn't want him to go on yet another vertigo-inducing harangue about the JonBenét case. I said, "That's a realistic concern, Sam. Public opinion could be against someone like Haddon right from the start. That could rub off on Lucy. That wouldn't help."

"My other thought was either Cozier Maitlin or Casey Sparrow. Lucy might like to have a woman involved. I'm wondering how you two felt about the help they gave Lauren that time when she was, you know . . ."

"Arrested?"

"Whatever. What'd you think?"

"You ask Lauren for her opinion?"

"I will. But I thought I'd ask you first. You dealt with them more than she did. So what did you think? Would you go that way again?"

My thought was, *I hope I never have to.* "Cozy and Casey were great. An odd team, but professional, and creative, and sharp. But it's a moot question—Casey's not available. She's defending that woman in Wheat Ridge who's accused of killing her husband and his parents. Goes to trial this week."

"Oh yeah. That case is hers? I didn't know. Can Maitlin handle something like Lucy's situation by himself?"

"Sure."

"Should he?"

"Different question."

I listened to him breathe. "I want to go talk with him before he hears about Lucy's involvement in all this from somebody else. Will you come with me?"

I immediately wondered why he wanted me to accompany him to see Cozy Maitlin. "Lauren and I are going to visit Susan Peterson at the hospital at ten o'clock. We have a babysitter coming then."

"Good," he said, totally missing my point. "If we go now, we'll both be back home by the time she gets there. We had better be—I have to get some sleep soon or I'll be no good to Lucy or Royal or anybody else."

I stared at the clock by the bed. "You want to go to Maitlin's house at four-twenty in the morning?"

"Nah, I wouldn't do that. That would be inconsiderate. The way I'm figuring, by the time we get there it will be almost five. You know where he lives?"

I almost laughed. "Yes. Last year he bought a renovated Victorian on Maxwell, a block or two west of Broadway. Lauren and I were invited there for a housewarming. There were women in tuxedos carrying trays of hors d'oeuvres and champagne. That kind of party."

"Girls in tuxedos? Sounds fun." Sam's sarcasm was way too thick for the predawn darkness. "For some reason I'll never understand, I don't get invited to parties like that. Cross-street?"

"Near Eighth."

"You can find the house?"

"Sure."

"Then I'll see you at Maxwell and Eighth at ten to five." I thought I heard him chuckle as he hung up the phone.

I took a quick shower, shaved with an electric razor, threw on some jeans and a cotton sweater, and still I didn't make it downtown until a couple of minutes before five. The air was cool. Sam was standing on the curb leaning against his old Cherokee, three doors down from Cozier Maitlin's house. I found a spot by the curb in front of Cozy's painted-lady Victorian. Sam headed my way carrying a cardboard tray with three cups of 7-Eleven coffee.

"Thanks for doing this," he said. "How's little Grace?"

"She's great, Sam. I can't believe I waited this long to become a father. Simon?"

"Feels like I haven't seen the kid in a week. Actually had to give up our Avs playoff tickets a few days ago, if you can believe it. We did go snowboarding over spring break. Kid's a maniac, I'll tell you. Boards goofy-footed. Perfect for the kid of an Iron Ranger, don't you think?"

"You boarded, too?"

He shook his head. "You don't want to know." He gestured toward the coffee he was holding. "This is nice of you—I know you aren't that tight with Lucy. I appreciate you agreeing to help me out."

I shrugged. I'd lost count of the number of times Sam had sacrificed to assist Lauren and me. "It's what friends do," I said, and pointed at Cozy's pretty house. "Cozy may not think it's so nice of me."

Sam snorted a short, derisive blast of air through his nose. "Way I look at it, you make over two hundred bucks an hour, you should expect to get rousted out of bed occasionally. A necessary part of staying humble."

"Criminal defense attorneys shouldn't be humble, Sam. You want the same traits in defense attorneys that you want in surgeons and airline pilots. You want confidence bordering on arrogance."

Sam grunted. He couldn't comprehend the concept of admirable traits in members of the defense bar.

I said, "Lucy has family money, right?"

He shifted his weight before he responded. I knew he wasn't comfortable talking about money. "She seems to. We've never talked about it much. She doesn't live like a cop. Nice apartment. Nice clothes. Nice vacations. I'd say she has money. Once said something about her father's mother leaving her something. I'd suspect she has enough to pay Cozy, if that's where you're going."

"That's where I was going."

"Don't worry about money. Maitlin's going to be drooling over this case. A Boulder police detective about to be accused of killing Colorado's best-known and most controversial district attorney? He'd pay me for the chance to take this case, if I put the screws to him." Sam paused for a moment. "Which I'm not planning on doing, by the way."

We reached Cozy's front door. Sam pounded five times with the flat side of his fist, waited ten seconds, and then did it again. He explained, "First time, the noise wakes you up but you're not really sure what the heck it was, so you're tempted to go back to sleep. Second time is like an instant replay to help overcome the short-term cognitive impairment." Sam pounded five more times. "Third time is to make sure his pulse stays high. That's what I like to see when they answer the door—I want them awake, with a little bit of adrenaline flowing."

Less than a minute later I watched lights flick on inside the house and then heard the concussion of heavy steps on the stairs. The door flung open and Cozier Maitlin filled the entire entryway.

I thought that, at that moment, he looked like the apocryphal Rasputin on the Russian's fateful night at the Yusopov Palace.

Cozy stood six feet eight inches tall in his bare feet. And right then, he was, indeed, barefoot. Not to mention bare-chested. The lower half of his body was adorned with pajamas covered with art deco fire trucks. The drawstring was so loose that the pajama bottoms were in danger of falling to the hardwood floor.

I prayed that wouldn't happen.

Cozy's hair looked like a failed do from a punk hair-care training clinic. His mouth hung open like a third eye and the expression in his gaze was as close to homicidal as I hoped it would ever get. A full day's whiskers completed the picture and left me with a graphic representation of what might have driven his ex-wife, first, to divorce him and, second, to become a lesbian.

If I had been alone, I think Cozy would have killed me right there on his front porch. But the fact that a homicide detective accompanied me caused Cozy to pause. He closed his gaping mouth and raised his chin a couple of centimeters. With one hand he tried to tame his unruly hair, with the other hand he, thankfully, grabbed the waistband of his pajama bottoms.

He said, "Gentlemen."

I fought a grin.

"Good morning, Counselor," Sam replied. "May we come in?"

Cozy stepped back. "Of course. Where are my manners? I assume you are here at this . . . *hour*"—he spoke the word as though the very sound of it caused him significant pain—"because we're about to be dealing with a matter of some gravity and some . . . urgency. Would it be appropriate for me to steal a moment or two and pull on a robe? Would that be acceptable under the circumstances?"

Cozy had a knack of communicating condescension and sarcasm without revealing too much malice. I'd always admired that trait in him.

Sam nodded. He raised his cardboard tray full of 7-Eleven cups. "I brought coffee. Didn't think you'd have made any yet. Maybe should have got doughnuts, too, but I wasn't thinking clearly."

"That's quite apparent," Cozy replied. He actually tried to smile before he retreated back up the stairs to his bedroom to find a robe.

After the defense lawyer disappeared up the stairs, Sam said, "That went better than I expected."

Cozy was down about five minutes later. He'd taken a quick shower and was wearing sweats.

"Alan, Sam. I must let you know that the two of you make an odd pair standing at my door in the dark hours before dawn. My initial guess when I saw you, Detective, was that this was about Royal Peterson. But Alan?

I don't figure your part. So, please, Detective—is this about Royal Peterson's murder? You've been working that, haven't you? Is that a fair assumption on my part?"

Sam said, "Yes, Mr. Maitlin. That's a fair assumption." Sam rubbed the back of his hand across the stubble on his chin. The grating sound was audible, and kind of creepy. "Earlier this morning I picked someone up for questioning in Royal's murder. We're here to talk with you about whether or not you'd be interested in representing that person."

Cozy had been ignoring the 7-Eleven coffee. I doubted that he'd consumed anything so plebeian in quite some time. But after Sam disclosed the nature of our errand, Cozy reached down and lifted his cardboard cup, flicked off the plastic lid, and took a long swallow. When he looked back up he was staring at me. I was wearing my psychotherapist's face, disclosing nothing.

"This is irregular," Cozy proclaimed.

"That's an understatement," I said.

"It's not often that I'm approached by the lead detective of a homicide investigation asking me to represent someone he's just . . . fingered. Is that a good description of what is occurring here?"

Sam's shoulders had sunk and he was focusing his attention on the liquid in his cup as though the shimmering surface were the glass of a crystal ball. My impression was that Sam had used all the energy he'd had left just to tell Cozy why we were there.

At that moment, I suspected that was why Sam had

asked me to come along. He needed me to be ready to take over.

I said, "Sam's not part of the investigation any longer, Cozy. He was removed from the case a few hours ago, right after he picked up his partner for questioning for Royal's murder. On his way out she asked him to help her find a lawyer. He asked Lauren and me for advice. Now, Sam wants to talk with you about representing her. Her name is Lucy Tanner. Sam thought it would be better for you and him to talk before the media is all over this."

Cozy shifted his eyes from me to Sam and back. It was as though he was waiting for Sam or me to slap a thigh and tag him with a punch line. Finally, Cozy stood up. He had to duck to avoid hitting his head on the light fixture that hung in the center of the room. For a minute or more he stood at the large window that faced Maxwell Street, his back to us.

Past him, in the distance, I could see the first glimmers of morning light on the eastern horizon.

Sam was still staring into his cup.

Cozy turned around. He said, "I'll do it."

Sam raised his head and his eyes narrowed at Cozy.

"Where is my client?" Cozy asked.

"Sam?" I asked. "Lucy would still be at Thirty-third Street, right? She wouldn't have been moved over to the jail?"

"When I left she was still at the department. They wouldn't take her over to the jail unless they had enough to arrest her." He shifted his gaze to Cozy. "You should be able to find her at Thirty-third Street."

The lawyer asked the detective a lawyer question. "Do they have enough to charge her?"

Sam said, "In my opinion, no. It's not my opinion that counts, though, is it?"

Cozy nodded. "I'd like to ask you a few things. You picked her up this morning? Was that at her home?"

"Yeah. About two-thirty."

"Did she say anything to you at that time?"

Sam buried his lower lip in his mustache and shook his head. "You don't know Lucy Tanner. Let me tell you something about her: Your new client's a very smart lady, Mr. Maitlin. She's not going to be talking to anyone."

"Then why pick her up? What's the upside? Why not wait until more evidence was developed?"

"It wasn't my decision. Once things started playing out the way they started playing out, it was decided to bring her in to talk to her. The department has kind of a bad reputation concerning delaying questioning of witnesses in murder investigations. I think that was a major motivator in the decision. They wanted to talk to Lucy before she figured out that she should be talking to you."

Cozy sat back. "She was there with you on Friday night, right? At the Peterson house?"

"She was."

"The whole time?"

"The whole time. We worked the scene together. She kept the log."

I could tell Cozy adored the image he was forming in his imagination. He was already cross-examining witnesses in his head.

"She's had access to the murder book from the start?"

"From the start."

Cozy nodded. Sipped again at his coffee. He looked at Sam over the rim of the cardboard cup. "You want to tell me what you have on her?"

Sam said, "See . . . this is where it gets dicey, Mr. Maitlin."

"Call me Cozy."

"I'm not comfortable with that, yet. I'll try to work through it, though, I promise."

I wasn't sure Sam's sarcasm even registered on Cozy.

Sam continued. "Anyway, I'm here to help my partner. I'm not here to betray the Boulder Police Department. Even though it's not my case anymore, you know damn well I can't reveal the fruits of the investigation."

"But you had cause to pick her up?"

Sam closed his eyes, grimaced, and added a little headshake. "Bringing her in may not have been my idea, and may not have been a good idea strategically, but it wasn't bogus."

I said, "Cozy? Think about this. Sam just turned in his partner—his close friend—for questioning in a very, very high profile murder. Even though he didn't agree with the decision, he's telling you that he's convinced that the evidence warranted it."

Cozy said, "That's the truth, Sam?"

"Yeah. That's the truth."

Cozy said, "I should make a quick call to the detectives who are chatting with my client and inform them of my involvement."

Sam buried his bottom lip in his mustache and nodded his agreement before he stood to leave. I stood, too.

Cozy said, "I'll do my best for your friend, Sam."

Sam didn't respond until we got to the front door. "I wasn't honest with you before, Mr. Maitlin. She did say something to me when I brought her in. She reached up and grabbed my head and pulled it real close to hers. She stuck her lips next to my ear and she said, 'I didn't do it, Sam. Keep looking.' That's all she said."

Cozy said, "You believe her?"

Sam said, "A thousand percent."

CHAPTER

5

I'd told myself that the media was going to be all over this case, but still I wasn't prepared for the breadth of the invasion that had already occurred. It was all so Ramsey-reminiscent. Microwave trucks were all over town—the Public Safety Building on Thirty-third, the Justice Center on Sixth, and of course, outside the Peterson home—and reporters and producers were tripping over each other trying to discover a virgin angle or finagle a reluctant interview.

Lauren and I tried to pick a route from our home to Community Hospital that would shield us from the press. As I stopped at a red light at Thirtieth, I said, "Are you thinking much about what Lucy is going through?" As a rule, Lauren and I didn't dwell on the episode that had landed her in even worse circumstances than the ones that Lucy currently faced. Lauren had actually been arrested and taken to jail, accused of shooting someone.

At first, Lauren just glanced my way and nodded. Finally, she said, "I'm just praying she doesn't have to go through what comes next—those first few hours at the jail—the body search, the booking—were the worst part of it for me after I was arrested. I have to think it would be even worse for Lucy because she's a cop."

"If they arrest her, they'd have her isolated from the general population, wouldn't they?"

"I'm sure they would."

The light changed and we were quiet until the next red light at Folsom. I asked, "What do you think about Sam's choice of Cozy to defend Lucy?"

"There's a number of people in town who could do it, Alan, and a whole bunch in Denver, but I think . . . Cozy's the right one. His profile is high, but not too high. He has a good relationship with our office, but not too chummy. He's experienced with capital cases." She paused. "He's a good choice."

"Your words are more enthusiastic than your voice."

"Probably. I think I'd feel better about it if Casey Sparrow was available to help him."

"Is it too much for Cozy to do by himself?"

"With all the media? It may be. It all depends whether she's charged. These big cases are so consuming. But I'm thinking more about the perspective Casey would provide. Sometimes Cozy's style requires ballast."

I eased the car straight into the intersection but took a sharp left with the conversation. "How are your symptoms?"

"About the same."

"Not worse?"

"Not much worse."

"Is it an exacerbation?"

"I don't know yet. Could just be a series of reruns. That's what I'm hoping."

Lauren and I walked hand in hand toward Community Hospital, chatting about what it was like to leave Grace with a sitter, what it was going to be like doing it every day now that Lauren's maternity leave was ending. Our guard was down, and neither of us saw the ambush developing as we approached the ER entrance to the hospital. By the time I had started paying attention, a reporter from one of the Denver TV stations had a foam-covered microphone in Lauren's face.

The reporter was a young Asian woman. I'd seen her work; thought she was pretty good. "Ms. Crowder? Ms. Crowder? Are you here to interview Susan Peterson? Is she a suspect in her husband's murder? Have the police interviewed her yet? Ms. Crowder?"

Lauren's balance faltered as the reporter closed in. I tightened my grip on my wife's hand and silently urged her to keep walking. After another step or two, Lauren spoke without turning toward the camera. "I'm here visiting a friend who's hospitalized. That's all."

"Is Susan Peterson a suspect in her husband's murder? Ms. Crowder? Ms. Crowder?"

The reporter's voice faded as the sliding glass doors closed behind us. "I wasn't expecting them here," I said. "You handled yourself well."

"Thanks. They're like grasshoppers. Once they show up in one place, it seems they show up everywhere."

We were alone as we made our way up the elevator. I asked Lauren the same thing the reporter was wondering about. "Is there any chance Susan was involved? What are you hearing in the office?"

"When the police found her in bed she was so heavily medicated that she was almost impossible to arouse. Her neurologist doesn't think she would have had the strength to do what was done to Royal. So, no, even though they'll take a close look, no one's taking that possibility too seriously at this point."

The elevator door opened. We got out and paused at the nursing station to get directions to Susan's room. A nurse pointed out the room and said, "Her doctor's in with her right now. I'm sure it will only be a few more minutes. You can wait in the lounge."

Just then the door to Susan's room opened and her doctor walked out, a Palm Pilot in one hand, a stylus in the other.

I said, "Good morning, Adrienne." Adrienne Arvin, a little fireball of a urologist, was our neighbor and close friend.

She stopped in her tracks, looked up at Lauren and me, then smiled. "Hi, guys. What are you doing here?"

I stepped over to give her a kiss on the cheek, then

Lauren did the same before she responded, "We're here to visit Susan. She's one of yours, I take it?"

"Be silly of me to deny it at this point, I suppose. I'm doing a consult."

"She's okay?" Lauren asked.

Adrienne muttered, *"Oy,"* and made a face that aptly communicated that "okay" was not one of the modifiers she would use to describe Susan Peterson's condition. "MS is a tough disease, Lauren. I don't have to tell you that. Susan's is particularly insidious. The stress of having her husband murdered hasn't made it any easier on her."

I asked, "Can we go in?"

"Be my guest. She'll be pleased to see you, I think. She's quite tired. I wouldn't stay long."

"Of course," Lauren said. Adrienne pocketed her little computer and bounced off down the hall.

Susan Peterson's multiple sclerosis was different from Lauren's. Susan had secondary progressive disease. Although she'd been diagnosed years after Lauren, Susan frequently used a wheelchair, and lately was bedridden more often than not. She was virtually blind in one eye, and Roy had once confided in Lauren that the pain she suffered from spasticity was growing more and more severe. Adrienne's presence on Susan's care-team was a clear indication that she was suffering bladder problems as well.

While Lauren could expect periods of remission

between infrequent exacerbations of her disease, Susan was likely to deteriorate progressively, with little or no respite from the assault of multiple sclerosis.

We found Susan on her side in bed, facing away from the door. Her room was full of floral bouquets and the aroma was a cloying mix of hospital disinfectants and nature's perfume. The television was tuned to religious programming, but the sound was so low I couldn't hear the minister's words.

We took a couple of steps into the room and Lauren said, "Susan? It's Lauren and Alan."

"Oh, oh, good," she said. "You came to see me? Come on over on this side so I can lay my eyes on you."

Lauren and I crossed the room. Immediately, Susan said, "My girls came in early before church and helped me get made up. It's Sunday, and I wanted to look nice. It's not the way I would do it myself, but— Do I look okay?"

Lauren told her, "Your daughters did a great job, Susan. You look wonderful. Lovely."

"Thanks. But I don't know about the eye shadow. It's so, so . . . And my hair after three days in this bed . . . what can you do?"

Despite the fact that Lauren had done all the talking since we'd entered the room, Susan addressed her words to me. I'd always suspected that Susan was uncomfortable with Lauren. I thought it was because Lauren, too, had MS. And I thought perhaps Susan's ambivalence was exacerbated because Lauren had the less malignant form of the disease.

I said, "How are you, Susan?"

"Better, better. The nurses are a little—I don't want to say slow, but—anyway, anyway, let's just say they're not the most prompt. You buzz, you buzz and . . . you know. I wish Matthew could have stayed longer. He came in from Phoenix but he's gone again already. Mothers and sons, right? Thank God I have my girls. They bring food at least." She touched her hair with her hand. "You could starve to death in here waiting for something edible to arrive."

I bit the soft flesh on the inside of my lower lip.

Susan Peterson had probably always been a difficult woman—what her children's generation would have called "high maintenance." According to Royal, when Susan's disease was first diagnosed she actually softened a little, but as the insidious myelin destruction progressed in her central nervous system, the underlying flaws in her character seemed to have become magnified.

If a young psychology graduate student I was supervising asked me to describe a narcissistic character disorder, I would have been tempted to introduce the student to Susan Peterson.

"What you've been through, Susan . . ." Lauren said. "We're so sorry about what happened to Roy."

"Thank you," she said, and her chin crinkled and began to quiver. "I'm so frightened. So frightened.

"The other night, you know? When it happened? I was asleep. It sounds awful but what can I say? I usually don't sleep well. I have pain that wakes me up. It's in my feet and my back and my left leg . . . sometimes it feels like an electric shock or being stabbed with a sharp knife. So some nights I let Roy give me a sleeping pill so that I sleep through the night. It's mostly for him that I do it, really. It's so I don't wake him during the night with my . . . moaning. Halcion. That's the one he gives me. I don't like it because it knocks me out so much. But sometimes Roy would give it to me in the evening and I'd take it. That's what happened, Friday. He gave it to me and he looked so tired that I took it. I didn't hear anything until these police officers woke me up. They wouldn't tell me what happened to Roy. I didn't find out until the next morning. A policeman told me. A policeman."

She raised a hand to cover her mouth. She looked right at Lauren and started to cry. "Oh, what am I going to do? Who's going to take care of me?"

Ten minutes later as we walked down the corridor outside the door of Susan Peterson's room, I said, "A saint."

Lauren asked, "What are you talking about? What do you mean 'a saint'?"

"She asked who's going to take care of her. Well, that's who's going to take care of her. The answer is, a saint."

"*Alan*. That's so unkind."

"I'm sorry. Her situation is tragic, sweets. But she makes it tough to be purely sympathetic."

"She does. Dear Lord, she does. She's gotten worse, hasn't she? Since she's gone downhill so fast, I mean. I don't complain like that, do I? Tell me I don't. And please tell me I'm not that myopic about my life."

"You don't. You're not. You could never be."

"You don't resent me the way Roy resented her?"

"Roy resented Susan?"

The elevator door opened. Lauren whispered, "He was no saint," as we stepped into the crowded elevator.

"What?" I asked.

"Later."

We exited the hospital through an open delivery door and walked three blocks out of our way to avoid another ambush from the press.

While we were skirting the eastern edge of the park on Ninth Street, the pager we carried so that the babysitter could reach us vibrated on my belt.

I reached for my hip and said, "It might be Viv." Viv was our babysitter/nanny. She was a young Hmong woman with a heart the size of Southeast Asia. With Lauren heading back to work, we were thrilled that Viv had agreed to continue to watch Grace, who seemed to adore her. While Lauren fumbled in her purse for her phone, I glanced at the number on the screen of the pager. I said, "I don't recognize this phone number," and showed it to Lauren.

"Me neither." She punched the number into her cell phone. A moment later she said, "Cozy? Is that you?"

We took about ten more steps as she listened to whatever Cozier Maitlin had to say. Lauren stopped me with a hand on my shoulder and moved off toward a nearby bench. I sat next to her.

Into the phone, Lauren said, "No, I'm technically off leave until tomorrow. . . . That's right, I'm not officially involved with the case at all. I wouldn't be under any circumstances, Cozy. If Roy's murder doesn't go to a special prosecutor, it's going to be run by whichever member of the triad prevails."

Cozy said something. Lauren nodded. "That's right. Mitchell and Nora. The third player in the triad is Elliot." She listened. "Yes, he has that kind of status in the office. Mitch and Nora are wary of him. That's all it takes. Elliot has his supporters, especially among the younger assistants."

I mimed *"What?"* at my wife. She ignored me.

Cozy spoke for almost a full minute before Lauren said, "Are you kidding? Me? Why?" She listened, and looked my way, widened her violet eyes, then raised her eyebrows. Behind her, the park was vibrant with activity. Joggers, bladers, bikers, kids in strollers, couples hand in hand. The mountains loomed immense to the west and the brilliant sky was streaked with wispy clouds. The plums and cherries were in bloom and the air was fragrant with honeysuckle. I catalogued it all while I eavesdropped.

"Yes, I promise I'll think about it. You don't have to worry about that. I'm not sure I'll think about anything else. I'll call you later today. . . . Okay, okay, I'll call you before dinner." Pause. "We eat around six, Cozy. I'll phone you before then. Good-bye."

"Well?" I said.

She folded the phone with uncommon deliberation. "Cozier Maitlin just made me an offer. He'd like me to assist him in representing Lucy."

"You're not kidding?"

"I'm serious."

"Can you do that? I mean can an assistant district attorney just cross over and be a defense attorney?"

"People do it all the time when they leave the office. Cozy used to be an assistant DA himself. With one phone call to Mitchell, I could extend my maternity leave. I haven't gotten the impression that the workload's been killing anyone, so I don't think there'd be any objections. Then I suppose I could do anything I wanted. Once Mitchell learned what my actual plans were, he wouldn't like it one bit, but I don't think there's anything he could do about it."

I sat back on the bench and gave her an appraisal that, had I given it to a stranger, would have probably earned me a whole peck of trouble. I said, "You're interested, aren't you?"

She smiled at me. A soft, natural smile that I hadn't seen in a few days. "You know, hon, I think I am."

CHAPTER

6

Lauren didn't have an answer for Cozy before dinner on Sunday. In fact, she still hadn't arrived at a decision by the time I left the house to drive downtown to see my first patient of the week early on Monday morning. Watching her decision-making process had reminded me of accompanying her to buy a new swimsuit just a few days before. She'd tried on ten different suits but nothing was exactly what she wanted. I tried to stay neutral and supportive as she found a flaw in each and every style she squirmed into, some of which I'd found quite fetching. The problem, I'd decided that day, was that nothing fit the image she had of herself at the beach.

And being a defense attorney didn't fit her image of herself as a lawyer. What she did all day Sunday was the equivalent of twirling in front of the mirror trying to make her ass appear smaller, or larger, or whatever the right size for her ass was.

I'm happy to go on the record as stating that I thought her ass was just fine.

The first patient in my clinical psychology practice that Monday morning was due at 8:45. I had five more scheduled before the end of the day, the last session ending at 5:15. If my patients behaved themselves, it would be a relatively easy day.

By the time I'd finished the earliest appointment, a woman I didn't know had left an urgent message on my voice mail requesting a return call as soon as possible. I phoned her back between sessions. She begged me for my first open appointment. I offered her 11:30.

She wasn't available.

What about 3:15?

Sorry.

We settled—me reluctantly, she enthusiastically—on 5:15. My relatively easy day was deteriorating before my eyes. I left a message for Viv letting her know I'd be home a little later than I'd thought.

The offices that I share with another psychologist named Diane Estevez have a simple system for greeting patients. When a patient arrives in the waiting room, he or she flips a switch marked with either my name or Diane's, which illuminates a tiny red light in the corresponding office. At the appointed time, Diane or I go out and retrieve our patient. Saves a fortune in receptionist expenses.

The light indicating the arrival of my 5:15 wasn't illuminated at 5:15. I walked out to the waiting room just in case the new patient—a woman named Naomi Bigg—hadn't mastered the system, which happened sometimes. But the waiting room was empty. I returned to my office, made the next move in the game of phone tag I'd been playing with Lauren all day long, and wrote some notes, stealing frequent looks at the clock. At 5:25, I decided to give my new patient until 5:30 before I headed home. No-show first appointments were a rarity, but a nuisance nonetheless. My personal rule in life was that fifteen minutes was a reasonable amount of time to wait for anyone, for anything, in almost any circumstances.

The light flashed on at 5:27. I was disappointed; I'd crossed the line and was hoping my new patient had changed her mind and wouldn't show. I reluctantly returned to the waiting room, where I greeted a woman who I guessed was about fifty. She was slender and tall and was dressed in a blue gabardine suit. I assumed she was a businesswoman.

"Hello," she said, stretching out her hand. "I'm so sorry I'm late. It was chaos at the office. I'm sorry, that's not your problem. Oh, I didn't even ask—are you Dr. Gregory? Please say yes."

"I am," I replied, and shook her hand.

"Thank God. I'm Naomi Bigg."

"Please come on back to my office."

Naomi chose the chair opposite mine and surprised me by pulling a compact from her purse and checking her face before she turned her attention to me. The interlude of vanity gave me a chance to observe her.

For some reason, I immediately focused on her eyebrows. They'd been plucked with a ferocity that was impossible to ignore. The remaining arc of hair was so narrow that it appeared to have been drawn into place with a fine-tipped pen.

She snapped the compact shut and returned her gaze to me.

I always started the first session with new patients the same way. I said, "How can I be of help?"

She pulled her hands together in front of her chest as though she were about to pray. "I'm not sure. I'm confused—I guess it would be great if you could help with that." Her eyes were focused out the window. The redbuds in the backyard of the old Victorian were ablaze with the pink of spring. I knew the brilliant blossoms would disappear with the next snowstorm.

I waited for Naomi to continue. She didn't.

Finally, I said, "You're confused?" My words had a singular intent, akin to freeing a stuck CD.

"In the sense that I don't know the right thing to do, yes. I'm that kind of confused."

I waited again, longer this time. It was apparent she wanted to play this like a tennis match. She hit. I hit. I wondered whether it was wise to oblige.

I said, "And you think I can be of help with your decision?"

"Yes. Do you know how I chose you?" She looked my way for the first time since she'd greeted me in the waiting room.

I shook my head.

"I saw you on the news after that thing that happened last fall in Steamboat Springs. You know, with those girls? That's how long I've been thinking about this, about coming to see somebody for . . . help. For therapy, you know? Since at least last fall. I thought because of that work that you did—I mean helping to find who killed those two girls after such a long time—that you might be the right person to help me, too."

She returned her gaze to the redbuds.

I felt like telling her to get on with it, that I had a baby waiting for me at home, a baby who smelled even better than the flowers on those trees. But I didn't.

As I waited for her to resume, my mind drifted back to the previous autumn's events in Steamboat Springs. Lauren and I had accepted an invitation from a private group of forensic specialists called Locard to participate in an investigation of the 1988 murder of two girls outside Steamboat Springs. The outcome of the investigation had garnered a lot of press coverage, both local and national.

"And then I saw you again on the news last night. You were outside Community Hospital? I think you were with your wife. That's when I decided I was going to call, that it was the right time."

Damn news cameras, I thought.

Naomi Bigg said, "You know what anniversary is this week?"

A crack of sunlight burned through my late-day fog. *Aha! Anniversary reaction.* She wanted to talk about a loss she'd suffered at this time last year, or the year before, or . . .

"No," I said, "I don't know what anniversary is this week."

She crossed her long legs, tugged down her skirt. I noticed that her left ankle was bruised. I filed the information.

I was guessing that she'd lost her husband. Divorce or death? I glanced down to check for a wedding ring, but her left hand was covered by her right. My money was on divorce. My second guess was that she'd lost a child. I really hoped not; I knew my heart would resist hearing that story.

"Columbine," she said.

Had Naomi lost a child at Columbine High School? God.

I instantly started considering which colleague I could refer her to, a colleague without a new baby, a colleague who would be able to listen to her grief without terror filling the part of his own heart that cherished a new life.

She was right, of course. That week was the anniversary of the shootings at Columbine High School. Which meant it was also the week of the anniversary of the Oklahoma City bombing. A couple of tragic days in April and a lot of lives for which the beauty of spring would never be the same.

Never.

She gazed at me briefly. "My confusion? I think a lot about the parents, you know?"

"The parents . . . ?"

"The Harrises and the Klebolds."

I'd been wrong, 180 degrees wrong. I thought she'd been talking about the parents of the victims. Instead, she was talking about the parents of the killers.

She went on. "I think about whether they should have known what was going on. Whether they should have known what was in their children's hearts. Even whether they should have turned their own children in to the police. I think about all those things all the time."

The late-day fog in my brain had finally lifted. Suddenly the sunlight was so bright that I couldn't see for the glare.

Sometimes new patients need prompting, and sometimes their stories have such internal force that the words spew forth like fluid from a cut hydraulic hose. The tennis match between us was over and Naomi needed no further prompting. She'd ripped the lid off the Pandora's box that she had carried into my office and snakes were slithering out unfettered.

"Sometimes parents know when their kids are angry, they do. They see it, they feel it. But it doesn't mean they know the depth of the rage, the sense of injustice their children feel, or what awful things their children might do. How could they even have imagined it? The Klebolds and the Harrises? How could they ever, ever have guessed what evil was in their children's hearts? Even with the clues, the term papers, everything. How could they possibly have guessed what their children were going to do that awful day at Columbine?"

The words were so poignant, so potentially revealing, but the tone was impersonal, distant. My new patient was much more comfortable talking about someone else's struggle than she was talking about her own. I glanced again at her left hand. With her thumb she was twirling a platinum wedding band around her ring finger. Good-sized diamond on the matching engagement ring. Married? Separated? I didn't know. But Naomi was about the right age; she could certainly have kids the age of the Columbine assassins.

She lifted her left arm and focused her attention on her fancy watch. "Oh my, the time. We have to stop already, don't we?"

I looked at the small clock on the étagère behind the sofa. We had only two minutes remaining in the session. "In a couple of minutes," I said. "You were talking about how the Harrises and the Klebolds should or shouldn't have known about what their kids were going to do."

Her eyes closed and her breathing became shallow. "It's a hard question to answer from a distance, isn't it? When the tragedy is so terrible, people are so quick to judge."

"Is that how it feels to you?" I asked.

"Can I come back for another session? Now that I've started, I think I'd like to continue talking about all this," she said.

"Of course. We'll find another time before you go." I was rushing my words, husbanding the few remaining seconds. I forced myself to slow down. "Do you have children, Naomi?"

"Work is . . . difficult. I'd need something late in the day. Or maybe I can get away over lunch."

"We still have a minute or so."

"I need to go."

I considered pointing out the resistance she was demonstrating, but it was too early in the process. Anyway, I knew I was being aggressive with my questions. I checked my book. "Thursday at five-thirty?"

"No, not on Thursday. There's a . . . Never mind. I'm sorry, anything else?"

"The only other time I can offer is twelve-thirty tomorrow."

"That's fine. I'll do a late lunch, sure. And yes, I have two children. A boy and a girl."

I couldn't help myself. I asked, "Are you struggling with some of the same questions?"

She was searching her purse for something, perhaps a pen. She said, "Same as . . . what?"

"As the Harrises and the Klebolds? As the parents of Eric and Dylan?"

Once more she focused on her watch. "You know, I think our time is up," she said, stealing my line. She stood and quickly walked toward the door, pausing only long enough to say, "See you tomorrow."

I didn't want her to leave yet. I needed my questions answered. What were her children planning? What did she know? "We have some paperwork to do before you go," I said to her back.

"Tomorrow, okay? We'll do it then. I promise I'll be on time."

CHAPTER

7

I didn't recall locking up my office after Naomi Bigg departed, nor did I remember climbing into my car.

It wasn't the first time in the past few months that the passage of time had escaped my conscious awareness. I feared it wouldn't be the last.

I knew it wouldn't be the last.

See, the previous autumn I'd killed a man.

I'd used a handgun, a silenced .22, and I'd shot him in the head from a distance of about thirty inches. The little slug had entered the man's cranium through his cheek, just below his left eye. The little round of lead had never exited his head.

My own eyes had been closed when I pulled the trigger.

I don't regret pulling the trigger. The man was intent on killing me, my wife, and my then-unborn baby. I don't regret killing him. That's not to say I didn't relive the moment constantly. But every time I replayed it, I once again closed my finger over the metal wand of the trigger, and every time I squeezed gently.

It never changed with the replaying. Every time, I killed him.

It was the right thing to do.

But righteousness failed to quiet the replays. The chaos of the moment still cascaded into my waking thoughts and continued to infiltrate my dreams.

Pieces only. Fragments.

Not the sound of the .22, though. With the suppressor on the barrel, the surprisingly heavy Ruger made just a heartbeat of a sound. Instead, what I still heard during my private nights was the roar of the man's gun as he tried to shoot me. That night the roar had exploded only four times.

But in my relentless dreams the events of the killing continued to explode all night long.

And his grip. The night that I killed the man, I'd felt his hand close around my ankle as though I were his safety line and he was falling off a cliff. When the dreams came, I found myself shaking my leg in my sleep to free myself from his grasp. I'd wake up and he'd be gone. But the next night, or the one after that, his fingers were back on my leg, locked on my skin like leeches.

And Emily, our big dog—I knew she was barking

even though I couldn't hear her. She'd barked furiously at the man I killed that night, her jaws clapping open and closed, her eyes orange and fierce in the dim, dusky light. Now she visited in my dreams, too, sounding her clarion all over again. Warning, imploring. Fierce, silent.

The morning after the dreams, I would wake knowing in my heart that I'd done the right thing and knowing in my soul that I'd never be the same man again.

As I drove home after my first appointment with Naomi Bigg, I told myself that the intensity I was feeling after hearing her fears was due to the incessant echoes of that night the previous autumn.

The night that I shot a man with a silenced .22.

CHAPTER

8

Cozier Maitlin's black BMW was parked in front of our house. Viv's purple Hyundai wasn't.

Our Bouvier, Emily, greeted me at the door. Inside I found Lauren on the couch with Grace and Anvil sharing her lap. Cozy was sitting on what I liked to think of as my chair. In navy suit trousers, a white shirt that had no business looking as crisp as it did this late in the day, and a solid burgundy tie, Cozy offered a much less maniacal portrait than he had the day before when Sam and I had rousted him out of bed before dawn.

A smile to Grace earned me a smile in return. A kiss to my wife did the same. "So I take it you guys are a team?" I asked.

Lauren's grin told me she was happy with the decision she'd made. "Congratulations," I said. "What does Lucy think?"

"She's thrilled," Lauren said. "Or as happy as someone could be in her circumstances."

Cozy said, "I apologize for invading your home. The media doesn't know that Lauren is on board, yet, so for now we're safe up here. They have my house and office staked out, cameras and microphones everywhere. What do they do with all that equipment in between sieges? I was just asking Lauren—you guys control that little road out there?"

"Kind of. We share ownership of the lane with Adrienne."

Cozy said, "Oh."

He and our friend and neighbor, Adrienne, had been in a hot and heavy romance until Cozy made the mistake of introducing her to his ex-wife and Adrienne decided she preferred to navigate the romantic possibilities with Cozy's ex. So the mention of Adrienne's name was not uncomplicated for Cozy. She represented the second woman in a decade who had chosen to leave him for a chance at the fairer sex. Even to someone as pathologically noninsightful as Cozier Maitlin, that fact caused some considerable dis-ease.

He jerked his attention back to the question at hand. "But if you needed to, you could block off the lane? What I'm getting at, of course, is a way of keeping the press at a reasonable distance, should that become necessary."

"That's an oxymoron, Cozy. 'Press' and 'reasonable distance'—it doesn't compute. But the answer to your question is yes. We could block off the lane anytime we wanted. I'm sure Adrienne would happily go along. You know Adrienne; she loves mischief."

He said, "Hopefully it won't be necessary to involve her."

"What are you guys hearing about the case? What's the mood downtown?"

Lauren responded. "Lucy's been on the police force a long time and apparently she has some loyal friends. It looks like the chasm that already existed between the Boulder Police and the DA's office is in danger of growing into the Grand Canyon over this case."

Cozy smiled at the thought. "Tension between the police and the prosecutor's office has been brewing for a long time. You know that Royal's proclivity for pleading out cases has infuriated the cops. And now the DA's office thinks a cop murdered their leader. The rank-and-file cops are already lining up behind Lucy. The brass, not so much. But the lines are drawn. It can only work to our advantage."

"If this doesn't go to a special prosecutor," I said.

Lauren said, "Before I even asked him to extend my maternity leave, Mitchell told me that he's going to try to keep this one in-house. I don't think there's any doubt that he's going to resist the appointment of a special prosecutor even if we ask the court for one."

I took Grace from Lauren's arms. I was wondering about Mitchell Crest's reaction to Lauren's decision to assist Cozy with Lucy's defense. I was taking my lead from my wife, though. She hadn't brought it up, so I assumed that she and I would discuss it later. I said, "And I take it you and your new partner are not going to press for a special prosecutor, are you?"

"Not immediately, no," replied Cozy. "The conflicts within the DA's office and the tension between the district attorney and the cops will work to our advantage. At least in the short term."

"Witness the Ramseys," I said.

"Exactly," he said. "If I'm wrong, Lauren and I can pick and choose the time to demand a special prosecutor. Certainly we'll wait until after Lucy is charged."

"I'll leave you guys to work. It smells like Grace's diaper needs my attention. You want dinner?"

Lauren answered, "Viv left some Asian noodle thing that smells wonderful. Lots of fish sauce. We'll have some of that later on."

Before Grace and I were out of the room, Lauren asked, "How was your day, sweetie?"

I stopped and looked back, recalling how my day had ended with Naomi Bigg. I said, "Fine. Long. I had a new patient this afternoon that was interesting. Nothing like your day, though."

CHAPTER

9

Naomi Bigg wasn't true to her word. She wasn't on time for her second appointment; twelve-thirty on Tuesday came and went and the red light on my office wall never flashed on. Since the appointment wasn't my last of the day I didn't have to ponder how long I'd wait for her. She had me captive for the entire forty-five minutes, whether she was here in person or not.

It's rare, very rare, that a patient's story interests me. Don't misunderstand—it's also rare, very rare, that a patient *doesn't* interest me. The distinction is crucial.

After doing psychotherapy for as long as I've done it, I've listened to a lot of stories told in a myriad of different ways by an incredible variety of storytellers. Bad childhoods, wonderful childhoods; tumultuous adolescence, silky adolescence; heavenly marriages, devilish divorces. Isolation, attachments, losses. Health, illness, heartbreak, death after death after death. The stories almost always take a familiar form and the facts almost always lose narrative interest except for what they tell me about the molecular structure of the storyteller.

As I listen to the life tales of most patients, inevitably I'm left with the feeling that I've read this book before.

But as I waited for the red light to flick on announcing her arrival, I suspected that Naomi Bigg's story was going to be one of the exceptions. The prologue to her tale had been so provocative that I'd actually had trouble concentrating on anything else during the time between her first two appointments. Grace's charms could capture me for a few moments, but my thoughts would soon drift back to the long shadows cast by Harris and Klebold and my concern—no, fear—that the shadows were darkening the space where Naomi Bigg was standing.

Lauren's obvious excitement about working with Cozy to defend Lucy Tanner sparked my curiosity and distracted me for a while, but I was soon struggling anew with my trepidation about how I'd handle the news that I expected to hear: that Naomi Bigg suspected that her adolescent children might be planning some unspeakable atrocity à la Columbine.

Ten times I reminded myself that she hadn't said so.

Eleven times I convinced myself that that was exactly where her story was heading.

The light glowed at 12:51. I did the math: Our session would last only twenty-four minutes, a few of which we were going to waste filling out forms.

Naomi didn't bother to apologize. She filled out the forms and signed the state-mandated disclosure statement in record time.

She smoothed the fabric of her pink skirt and straightened the sweater of her twinset. The shell beneath the sweater was cut in a slightly less-than-modest V. The tops of her breasts swelled noticeably as she took a deep breath. "Where were we yesterday? My daughter? Is that what we were talking about? Want to help me here? I don't know if I told you, but her name is Marin. She's nineteen."

I wanted to correct her. I wanted to tell her, *No, we were talking about the Klebolds and the Harrises, and the Columbine anniversary and about how parents couldn't know what evil lurked in their children's hearts.*

I said nothing. Naomi and I had only nineteen minutes left to talk about Marin Bigg. One minute for each year of the young woman's life. I inhaled slowly, tasting stale cigarette smoke, and I reminded myself to be patient, to follow this woman, not to lead her.

She said, "You've been in Boulder a while, haven't you?"

In psychotherapy, few patient queries are uncomplicated. Was Naomi checking on my experience? My familiarity with the town? Making conversation? What?

I chose an obtuse answer. "I've been practicing in this office since the late eighties."

"I thought so," she said. "Then you may remember what happened to Marin. Four years ago. She was fifteen." She began spinning her wedding ring with her thumb. "Do you remember?"

I knew that if I said I didn't remember, for Naomi Bigg it would be as if I were failing to recall Pearl Harbor or Kennedy's assassination or . . . the shootings at Columbine.

I said, "No." I said it softly, so that she could uncover a covert apology there if she chose.

"She was raped by a CU student. You didn't read about it?" Her tone was slightly incredulous that I hadn't remembered without her prompting.

"I don't recall it specifically, no." During my time in Boulder the local paper had reported way too many rapes. I usually didn't study the stories. The meager details she had provided didn't separate Naomi Bigg's story from the herd.

She looked away from me. "It would be easier if you remembered. I was hoping that you would have." In that moment, I thought I witnessed sadness, and not just the edgy anger that she'd demonstrated thus far.

"That way you wouldn't have to tell me?" I said.

"Yes."

One of the nineteen minutes crept by.

Naomi said, "The details aren't important. She was raped. They called it date rape. Which means what? That she'd agreed to go to a movie first? Anyway, the police arrested the rapist. To make a long story short, the district attorney decided that the rapist deserved a year in jail and cut a deal with him. Without, I might add, the consent of the victim. Or the victim's family."

I noted that Naomi's breathing had grown shallow and rapid. Her eyes had narrowed and the muscles in her face had hardened into something sinewy. I didn't speak.

"He got out of jail in seven months. *Seven* months. He raped my baby and he got out of jail in seven damn months. She didn't get over the rape in seven months. She hasn't gotten over the rape in four years. She won't get over the rape in another forty years."

She pushed her tongue between her front teeth and her upper lip and left it there for a few seconds. "My husband never got over it. He attacked the rapist after he got out of jail. Ringing any bells yet? The man had transferred to Metro. The college in Denver, you know? My husband waited for him to get out of class one night and attacked him in the parking lot at Auraria. I bet the story's ringing those bells now. People forget about rape; they don't forget about assaults on rapists. What does that tell you about this society's priorities?"

Now I remembered what had happened to Marin Bigg. Her father had beaten her rapist to the brink of death with a cut-off baseball bat that big-rig drivers call a tire checker.

"Leo? My husband? His mistake was that he attacked him in Denver. Want to know why that was a mistake? Because they actually hold trials in Denver. The prosecutors in Denver actually prosecute—they don't plead everything out like they do in Boulder. My husband's trial lasted three days. The jury was out for three hours. Three hours. The judge gave Leo six years. The jury foreman phoned me later, after the trial, and he apologized. Said that the jury thought the judge would be lenient, that they never expected him to give my husband six years. Thought that the judge would slap him on the wrist.

"Yeah, the foreman called and said he was sorry. My husband's in Buena Vista. My daughter's scarred for life. My kids don't have a father. I don't have a husband. But the jury foreman was sorry. At least there's that. Right? God, it was such a relief that the man was sorry."

The sarcasm seeped between us like toxic sludge. I was thinking about what to say. I was trying to trace the connection between Marin Bigg's tragedy—the whole Bigg family's tragedy—and the anniversary of the massacre at Columbine. I was trying to fit the Harrises and the Klebolds into the puzzle. I was trying to think of something to say that might be more palliative than "It's apparent how angry you are."

Naomi interrupted my reverie. "But it's Paul I'm worried about. My son. I haven't talked about him. He's seventeen. He's a senior at Fairview."

The clock showed that we had seven minutes left in the session. Fairview was one of Boulder's two high schools. I watched Naomi's discomfort as thirty seconds ticked away before I pulled her back. I said, "You're worried about Paul, Naomi?"

"Yes, I'm worried about Paul. Of course I'm worried about Paul. He's angry. He's young. He's male. He's big. And he thinks that he's been wronged. Wouldn't you be worried about him?"

Her tone was more than sarcastic. It was slightly snide.

I opened my mouth to clarify that the wrong she was alluding to was his sister's rape and its aftermath, but Naomi was quicker than I. "I can't really afford this," she said. Again, I thought I heard some disdain in her tone.

I wondered whether she was talking about money, or whether her complaint was a metaphor for something else. I was about to ask which when she continued.

"Leo's a physician—an oncologist. That gives you some idea of the kind of income we lost when they sent him to prison." She raised her cruelly trimmed eyebrows. "A lot. Now? I'm working as an office manager; I run the practice of one of Leo's old colleagues. How's that for a state of affairs? Let's say things are tight financially in the Bigg household. And it turns out that you're not even a provider with my managed-care plan."

I could've told her that I wasn't a provider with any

managed-care plan, but I didn't. I got lost for a moment as I tried to remember a session with another recent patient where I'd felt so tongue-tied, but I couldn't.

Finally, I said, "Even with the little you've told me, I'm becoming more and more convinced that you can't afford not to do this, Naomi."

She flashed a quick glance at me, sniffed audibly. The sniff wasn't purely derisive, but close. "Go on," she said.

Softly, I said, "I think you might want to tell me more about Paul. Your concerns."

She softened noticeably. "Paul's a good kid. He's my buddy, my friend. He's polite, responsible. He's never been in any kind of trouble at all. If you met him, you'd like him. Everybody does."

"Yes?"

"High school has been tough for him, especially after what happened to his sister and his father. He's been an outsider all through school, very resentful of the popular kids, you know, the athletes. He wasn't treated well. He saw Dr. Haven for a while for help with his . . . impulses. You know her? Dr. Haven? She thought he was depressed, I think. I was never so sure."

Jill Haven was a psychiatrist who specialized in treating adolescents. She was good. "Yes," I said. "I know her."

"Well, it's not important. He doesn't see her any-more. His grades are better, good even. He has a few friends, dates some nice girls. Paul's settled down now. He plays keyboards—that's really his love—and he works at Starbucks. On the Mall? You may have seen him there. He's one of their best baristas. I think he's the best. He makes a killer mocha."

Hearing the word "killer" from Naomi Bigg's mouth gave me a chill. My office was at the west end of downtown, and I didn't get down to the east end of the Downtown Boulder Mall, where Starbucks was, very often, so I doubted that I'd met Paul Bigg. But it was possible.

I found myself fighting off stereotypical visual images of Starbucks's male employees. I wasn't entirely successful. In my mind, Paul suddenly had a persona; he was a tall, distracted kid with a pierced tongue and a sloppy tattoo wearing a filthy green apron.

I allowed Naomi a minute to find the detour she needed to get around her litany of her son's exemplary qualities. She didn't appear to be making a concerted effort to find an alternate route. Finally, I said, "I don't think you've told me why you're worried about him, Naomi."

"I always worry about my children. That's just me. But right now—well, since last fall—I'm worried about him because it seems . . . that he wants to get even. He wants . . . retribution."

"Because of Marin?"

"Sure. And because of Leo."

I should have paused here and allowed her to read the trail ahead, choose her own path, but I didn't. I said, "Is Paul planning something, some kind of retribution?" I was careful to use her word. My heart was pounding in my chest. It's rare that I ask a patient a question when I don't want to hear the answer. But I didn't want to hear Naomi's answer to my question. I was thinking of Columbine and a dozen other school shootings.

But mostly I was thinking about Columbine.

She was silent for longer than I was comfortable with. Her shoulders sank noticeably. "I don't know for sure. Okay? I don't know anything for sure, but I think sometimes he wants to hurt people. As a way of getting even."

"People?"

"People who he thinks are responsible for what happened. I don't know. He doesn't exactly talk to me about all this. He's a teenager. We have to remember that he's only a teenager."

The clock was ticking down toward one-fifteen, the end of our session. I considered extending the time. On the opposite wall, the red light was lit. My next patient was already sitting in the waiting room. "You think he wants to hurt people? You suspect—"

"I didn't say I suspect anything. I said I'm concerned."

She was right. That's exactly what she had said.

Thirty seconds. Twenty-five. Twenty.

"Naomi?" I said, waiting until she found my eyes with hers. The moment they locked on, I felt another chill.

"Yes?"

In other circumstances I would not have pressed her, especially not this early in treatment. She and I had not yet established an alliance, certainly not one that I felt with any assurance could withstand the assault I was contemplating. I questioned my words even before they were out of my mouth.

"Are your concerns about Paul related to the ones you mentioned during yesterday's session?"

She lifted her left wrist and stared at her watch in a manner that left no doubt that she didn't care that I saw her looking. "You mean what I was saying about parental responsibility? About the Harrises and the Klebolds? My sympathy for the position they find themselves in?"

Her tone was provocative. Obviously provocative. I didn't recall Naomi having said anything about sympathy for the position of the Klebolds and Harrises, but I said, "Yes."

She stood up. "Oh my, oh my, look at the time. I'm going to be late getting back to work." She had a package of Salem Slims in her hand before she reached the door. The appearance of the smokes was like magic; I hadn't witnessed the sleight of hand that produced them.

I lifted my book from the table beside my chair. "I think we should set another appointment, Naomi."

She tapped a cigarette into her left hand and fumbled in her purse for a lighter. "Of course, sure. What do you have? Lunch or after work? It's all I can do.

Maybe this time next week? And we have to talk about money. I don't know how I'm going to pay for all this."

Intentionally ignoring the financial question, I said, "Please sit down, I need to say something."

One sigh later she perched on the edge of the chair.

"Unless I'm misreading your concerns—and I don't think I am—the issues you're raising about your son, Paul, are quite serious. Waiting until next week to address those concerns doesn't feel prudent. You decided to come in to see me this week for a reason. You said that you hoped that I could help with your confusion. You mentioned an anniversary that's occurring this week. Are the consequences of putting off our discussion something you want to . . . contemplate?"

She busied herself fingering the long cigarette. "What are you saying, Dr. Gregory?"

"I'm offering you another appointment tonight to give us more time to explore all this. I'm not convinced we should wait."

"Tonight? I can't, I just can't."

"Tomorrow at five forty-five then?"

She considered my offer, finally saying, "All right. Tomorrow at five forty-five."

Over the years, I'd fallen into the habit of taking most Fridays off. Since Grace's birth, I'd promised myself I'd be even more diligent in protecting my Fridays. Occasionally, I knew, I would have to use the time for emergencies. I'd already decided that whatever was going on with Naomi Bigg and her son Paul qualified as an emergency.

"And again Friday at noon?" I said. "If it turns out that it's not necessary, we'll reconsider."

"See you tomorrow, I guess." She didn't even go through the motions of promising to be on time. "I have to think about all this some more. I'll call you if I change my mind."

I have to admit that I was hoping she would almost as much as I was hoping she wouldn't.

CHAPTER

10

Occasionally, I had days at work when I concluded that my patients had spent the previous evening conspiring to find ways to make me crazy. That Tuesday afternoon—after Naomi Bigg had left my office—was one of those. My one-fifteen had just been fired from his new job at Amgen. His résumé for the past twelve months was longer than mine was for my lifetime. I was certain that his parents had been told repeatedly during his preschool years that their son didn't play well with others.

He and I had a lot of work to do.

My two o'clock was a massage therapist with a phobia of gooseflesh. Not the kind of gooseflesh that geese have, but the kind of gooseflesh that people get. How weird was that phobia? So weird that I'd never even been able to find a name for it. The closest I'd been able to get was doraphobia—the fear of the fur or skin of animals. But that wasn't it. Quite simply, this massage therapist was terrified of goose bumps, and although she'd been symptom-free for months, she'd chosen that day to suffer a relapse.

Unfortunately, gooseflesh phobia is a difficult condition for which to design effective behavioral desensitization. Photographs of goose bumps did nothing to instigate my patient's terror, and finding reliable sources of gooseflesh so that I could design progressive exposures for her proved, well, ludicrous. Although medication and psychotherapy had kept her symptoms in remission for almost a year, she explained to me that she had literally run out of a morning hot-stone session in abject panic.

I listened as patiently as I could while I entertained the possibility that she might be better off in a profession where her clients kept their clothes on.

As soon as she'd left my office a woman I'd been seeing for about three months left an urgent message.

The Boulder Police had arrested both her and her husband after a domestic disturbance. He'd been taken to the hospital with a closed head injury. She'd been taken to jail. The fact that she'd been arrested for a domestic disturbance came as no surprise; her marriage was about as stable as an eight-year-old with matches in a fireworks factory. Nor did the fact that she had apparently won the fight; she was tough. What did surprise me was that she chose to use her sole phone call to get in touch with me, and not to call an attorney.

Did I mention that her judgment sucked? It was one of the items we were addressing in the treatment plan.

I was home before Lauren, and Viv seemed eager for some adult company before she left for the day. We sat outside with Grace and the dogs on the deck off the living room and chatted about how school was going for Viv and how cute my baby was. I sipped a beer; Viv drank tea. The sun ducked behind clouds before it plunged behind the Rockies.

As Viv stood to leave she told me that she'd left some shrimp marinating in the refrigerator—she used a word in her native language that I didn't understand before she fumbled for the English word "soaking"— and that she'd already heated up the grill.

I felt blessed that she was watching over my child and my family and I told her so. She blushed.

Lauren came home exhausted. She'd spent much of the day pigeonholed in a conference room in Cozy's Fourteenth Street offices with Lucy Tanner.

Lauren caught up with Grace. I waltzed out to Adrienne's garden and swiped two huge handfuls of spinach that I wilted in a couple of teaspoons of the marinade while shrimp and vegetables sizzled on the grill. When the food was done, Lauren and I sat down to dinner and Grace amused herself in her bouncy chair. Lauren asked about my day before I had a chance to ask about hers.

Her question was polite, conversational, a simple "How was your day? Anything interesting?"

I lifted an asparagus spear with my index finger and thumb—somebody had once told me that the French ate asparagus that way, so I'd convinced myself it was okay—and tried to mimic the casual tone of Lauren's question as I said, "You remember a case from about four years ago, a date rape involving a young Fairview High School girl and a guy from CU?"

Lauren was eating her asparagus by using her silverware to cut it into bite-size pieces. She thought my rationale about the French eating with their fingers was lame. "My case or yours?" she asked.

"Yours. DA's case."

"Four years ago?"

"Yeah."

She sipped some wine. "Yes, I think I do. Why?"

"What do you remember?"

"Bigg. That was the girl, something Bigg. Marina, no . . . Marin Bigg. Her father went nuts after the boy got out of jail and tracked him down and beat him with a baseball bat. That's the case you're talking about, right? My memory is that the father got some hard time. But that was in Denver or somewhere, it wasn't ours."

Grace was cooing and kicking her legs and generally succeeding in stealing more of Lauren's attention than I was getting.

"Yes, that's the case. Since it was a rape prosecution, it would have been Nora's, right?" Nora Doyle had headed the sex crimes unit at the DA's office for as long as I could remember. Instituting the sex crimes unit had been one of Royal's many noteworthy innovations during his tenure.

"Sure, it was Nora's case. But I helped her on it. You don't remember? That was the period where Roy and Nora had just started thinking about expanding the sex crimes office. I did half a dozen cases with Nora before she hired Erica in to pick up the slack. God, this shrimp is good. We should pay Viv something extra if she keeps cooking for us, don't you think? I'm beginning to feel guilty about all the extra work she's doing. And I think I might be getting addicted to her cooking."

"I agree," I said as I set down my fork and picked up my beer. I'd lost my appetite, but I made a conscious effort to sound normal. "You helped Nora? Were you a big part of the case?"

Lauren hadn't even looked at me yet, so she couldn't be aware that I was almost paralyzed with fear by what she'd just told me. Naomi Bigg had said that her son Paul wanted to "hurt people he thinks are responsible."

I'd just realized that list included Lauren.

"We made an early decision to plead it out. Facts are often messy in date rape cases. Dueling witnesses. He says she consented. She says she was forced. Usually no injuries to use as evidence. Rape kit often doesn't tell you much. DNA and blood typing are useless. You know how it goes."

"And you were involved in the decision to do the plea bargain?"

"Sure."

"Was it a clear-cut decision or was it controversial?"

She glanced at me with slightly suspicious eyes. "You know that Royal and Nora always took date rape prosecution seriously. Always. The outcomes weren't always popular, but the cases were always examined carefully. It's been one of our strengths as long as I've been with the DA's office. You know how I feel about all this. We're good on rape, Alan. We're good."

She hadn't answered my question. I said, "Was the family on board?"

"An effort is always made to include the family. But I don't remember specifically. Given what happened later, I'd assume they never signed off on this one. But that's the way it goes sometimes. Given the evidence, I thought it was a good outcome. Still do. In a lot of jurisdictions the offender would have walked given the exact same circumstances."

I knew she was right. "Who defended the boy? The rapist. Do you remember?"

Between bites, she was playing with Grace. Finally, she looked over at me. "Funny you should ask. I think it was Cozy. Why is this so important?"

"Somebody was talking about the case today at work," I said. "That's all. No big deal."

Later, after Grace was down for the night and the dogs were walked, Lauren climbed into bed beside me, and she said, "Lucy was there on Friday night. At Royal's house."

"She was? She admits it?"

"The evidence is pretty compelling that she was there. A witness saw her car around the corner. It's a bright red Volvo. Her prints are in at least two different rooms in the house. None of the police at the scene remember Lucy being inside without gloves during the investigation of the murder. And there's lots of video—all of it shows her wearing gloves.

"So . . . when she heard what they had, Lucy finally admitted to Cozy and me that she was at the Peterson home, but she maintains that it was earlier in the evening. That she left around eight-thirty, quarter to nine. And she said Roy was fine when she left."

I had a hundred questions.

I started with, "Why was she there?"

"She won't tell us. She says that we just have to accept the fact that if we knew why she was there, we'd be convinced she had a reason to kill Roy. She's absolutely certain that talking about why she was at the house will only hurt her. She says she'll reconsider if she's arrested. But not until then."

"She admitted to you that she had a motive to kill Roy?"

"In so many words, I guess she did."

"What could possibly—"

"I don't know. But apparently she's been to his house before."

"She told you that?"

"She's not saying anything about it. But the witness who saw her car remembers the Volvo. Said he's lusted after one forever. He's noticed it parked in front of his house before. He said it's a turbo." She shrugged her shoulders and rolled her violet eyes as though she couldn't imagine being able to tell a turbo from a non-turbo, and certainly couldn't imagine coveting one.

"Had he seen it frequently?"

"A few times, always in the evening."

I asked, "Why did she park on a different street?"

"Obviously she didn't want to be seen going into Royal's house. Maybe she went in through the back. There aren't any fences that would keep her from getting to Royal's back door."

"Does the witness remember what time the Volvo was gone from in front of his house on Friday?"

"We haven't talked to him yet but the police say no. He told them he was out for the evening, got home after eleven. The car was gone when he got home. Cozy and I have an investigator going out to talk to him and to try to corral more neighbors, see if someone saw the car leave before ten o'clock."

"What's Lucy's connection to Royal? Did they have a case together, something they were working on?"

She made a groaning noise to communicate her frustration with my questions. "We don't know. Even if they did have a case, it wouldn't give Lucy cause to have direct contact with the district attorney himself. If it had to do with an investigation, it would be Sam doing the talking, not Lucy, and he'd be talking to someone like me, an assistant DA, not with the district attorney. I can't think of a single reason why someone like Lucy would be dealing with someone like Roy on a direct basis about a case. It just wouldn't happen."

I thought about the details Lauren had shared with me so far. I wasn't a lawyer, but it didn't seem to add up to probable cause. "There must be something else, babe. So she was in the neighborhood—a lot of people were in the neighborhood that night. I don't think Sam would have picked up Lucy based on what you just told me."

"Sam was following orders, that's why he picked her up. But there is more. Murder weapon was a brass lamp. It had been wiped. But Lucy's latents are on pieces of a ceramic dish or something that was found busted on the floor."

"Jesus. What does Lucy say to that?"

"She seemed honestly perplexed. That's all I can say, that she seemed surprised."

We rolled over at the same time and ended up facing each other in the middle of the bed. I rested a hand on her naked hip. "How are you holding up?"

"Okay, I think. I think I'm doing okay."

"No exacerbation?"

"Not so far."

"How's the brain mud?"

"Not so bad. Maybe a little better."

I felt as much relief as multiple sclerosis ever seemed to permit. I said, "So much has happened since last week. I can't believe it's only Tuesday."

She moved my hand to her waist and slid close enough to me that her nipples brushed my skin.

CHAPTER

11

Naomi Bigg was—finally—right on time for the Wednesday session. I let the red light glow on the wall for a good minute before I walked out to the waiting room to invite her back to the office.

She knew exactly where she wanted to start. "Paul has a friend named Ramp. He's older—I don't know for sure, but he's got ID, so I'd say he's twenty-one, maybe twenty-two. Of course, it's possible the ID is fake." She crossed her legs and smiled coyly.

The little grin caught me completely off guard. I didn't know what to make of it. Had it been seductive? Mocking?

"This would be a lot easier if you'd let me smoke."

I didn't say, *It's not my job to make it easier.* I didn't

say, *It's the law in Boulder.* I didn't say, *I can't stand cigarette smoke.*

I said, "Sorry." But I wasn't.

I'd already realized that I didn't especially like Naomi Bigg. I'd tried telling myself that her message was so frightening that I was unable to refrain from blaming the messenger. For whatever good it would do, I was making a conscious effort to monitor the reflexes that my dislike was generating.

Shrinks call this "dealing with the countertransference."

Naomi went on. "I like Ramp. He's pleasant, polite, has a good sense of humor. But I'm not sure he's the best influence in the world on . . . Paul. They've only been friends for a few months, maybe longer than that. Last summer, actually. Paul met Ramp on the Internet, on a bulletin-board-type thing where they were both complaining about the criminal justice system. Ramp has a family situation kind of like ours. His mother was killed by a man who was released on parole after serving four years for murder. The guy got four years for murder, can you believe it?"

"Ramp lives where?" It wasn't like me to demand a fact like this from a therapy patient, but this bit of data seemed important.

"Denver somewhere, I don't know. The truth is that Ramp is even angrier about the justice system's inequities than Paul is. Maybe even more furious than I am."

"You've met him?"

"Oh sure. They hang out at our house a lot, which I encourage. Keeps Paul from driving to Denver so much, and I'd rather have the kids close by, you know, where I can keep an eye on them."

She repeated the coy little smile. I was still unsure what to make of it.

"Every time he comes to the house, Ramp brings papers. Sometimes magazine articles or clippings from the newspaper. But mostly things he's printed off the Net. Stories from around the country about all the things that infuriate him. Plea bargains, mostly. Psychotic parole decisions. Or absurd sentences, like putting murderers on probation. Or giving rapists a few months in jail or no jail at all. He keeps this binder that he calls his 'Hall of Shame.' It's full of pictures of prosecutors, judges, slimy attorneys, expert witnesses who will say anything to get people off. You know what I'm talking about. Everybody knows.

"The stuff Ramp brings keeps Paul stirred up. Now Paul's started collecting stuff on his own, too. They trade it like Paul used to trade baseball cards when he was little."

"Go on," I said. I shouldn't have said anything but I was an impatient audience. I was aware that there was a possibility that my need to hear this story was getting ahead of my patient's need to tell it. In almost all circumstances in psychotherapy, that was a problem.

Naomi said, "Ramp thinks that Leo is a hero."

I tried to remember who Leo was. After half a week of therapy appointments, I sometimes discovered that all the names I'd heard had blended together like the fruit in a smoothie.

"Paul, of course, thinks it's great that there's somebody who understands what his father did."

That Leo. The one who pummeled the rapist with a tire checker. The one doing hard time in a small concrete room in Buena Vista.

"Most of his friends deserted Paul after Leo was arrested for attacking the . . . scum who raped Marin. With Ramp, Paul has a friend who thinks what Leo did is the absolute coolest thing in the world. Ramp actually wants to go up to Buena Vista and visit Leo." She shifted her gaze from the window, to me, and back to the window and the soft light at the end of the day.

"Yes?" I said.

"Ramp's the one who keeps bringing up retribution. 'Wouldn't it be cool?' That's what he says all the time. 'Wouldn't it be cool if somebody raped the judge's daughter? Maybe then he'd know how it feels.' Or 'Wouldn't it be cool if something bad happened to that lawyer's family? Then he'd know the pain.' Or 'Wouldn't it be cool if so-and-so's house blew up?' That's what Ramp always says."

"And Paul plays along?"

"It's like a parlor game. When I ask him about it, he tells me it's just their version of fantasy baseball."

She sounded skeptical. I stated the obvious by saying, "But you're not so sure it's so innocent?"

"I was." For a moment, Naomi appeared uncomfortable. "I didn't like it, that kind of talk. I mean I don't wish tragedy on any family, especially after what we've been through. And then I heard that Royal Peterson had been killed. Since then I haven't been so sure."

There are rare moments in psychotherapy where my practiced façade is tested to the extreme. I think of those moments as slugs that slam into my bulletproof vest. Usually, the lead doesn't pierce the protective shield, but sometimes the bullets rock me back on my heels. This was one of those times.

"What?" I said, as though I was feigning an acute hearing loss. To a casual observer my state could probably just as easily have been mistaken for a brief interim of idiocy.

"Roy Peterson's murder? The boys won't talk about it. Not a word about it since it happened. That alone made me suspicious. The truth was that I half expected them to be celebrating when they heard that Peterson had a dose of the medicine he was dishing out."

"I'm not sure I understand."

"Peterson was like a drug lord. DAs like him all are. With their plea bargains and sentence recommendations they put scum back on the street just like a drug lord ships crack or heroin into town. They think they're doing the right thing but they're really just making things worse. Do you know what percentage of charged crimes went to trial in the last ten years under Peterson? One percent. That's it. One percent."

"I didn't know."

"Do you know that pedophiles, and I mean active

pedophiles—pedophiles who have actually touched children—have received deferred sentences in this county? Do you know that?"

I didn't answer. Part of me knew that it might be true, though. Some cases kept Lauren up at night. They were the ones I heard about at breakfast. I fought an impulse to defend the DA's office.

"Their good-old-boy networks and their political connections—it's disgusting. The excuses, God. When Peterson died, I thought the kids would be celebrating that maybe he choked on some of his own filth."

What did I want to say right then? I wanted to say, *Holy shit! You think your son may have murdered Roy Peterson?* But I kept my mouth shut until I could think of an alternative that might actually keep Naomi talking and not cause her to keep her mouth shut.

"What I talked about that first day? About sympathy for the Klebolds and the Harrises? I think sometimes that I know how they felt in the months before the attack. Maybe even how they feel now. Are you finally beginning to understand what it is I mean?"

I can't say how much time passed before I spoke again. It might have been only a few seconds, but I'd guess it was most of a minute. I broke the silence with a question: "Naomi? Was Royal Peterson ever the focus of any of Paul's wouldn't-it-be-cool games?"

"They were Ramp's games."

The distinction was obviously important to Naomi. Essential, even, as far as our therapeutic alliance was concerned. "Okay—was Roy Peterson ever the focus of any of Ramp's wouldn't-it-be-cool games?"

"I don't really think they did it."

We both recognized that she hadn't responded to my question. I said, "You don't?"

"No." She shook her head for emphasis. "No, I don't think they did it. But, obviously, I'm not sure, not totally sure. So I'm not willing to say anything to anybody about my concerns."

"You just did. You told me you're not convinced that the games the boys are playing are innocent."

"I meant say anything to the police. Or whomever. The question I struggle with all the time is: How much does a parent have to know in order to turn her child in to the police?

"Do you know that before Columbine, Eric Harris's parents failed to notice that their son had an arsenal in their house, for heaven's sake? And that one of them— Eric or Dylan—wrote an essay that predicted what they were going to do? And sometime before the two kids made their assault, Mr. Harris actually took a call for his son from a gun shop? Well, it wasn't enough for him to do anything at all; it certainly wasn't enough for him to turn his son in.

"And the police?" she scoffed. "The sheriff in Jefferson County was informed that Harris had threatened to kill a student a year before the shooting. They even suspected him of detonating a pipe bomb. And they were aware that he had this violent, awful Web site. Some deputies even wrote a request for a search warrant. But the sheriff did nothing with the suspicions. Nothing.

"So I ask you, what does it take to get a parent to believe that her child is planning something evil? What should it take? Believe me, I've thought a lot about it and I don't know the answer to that question. But I do know that it's going to take a hell of a lot more than I know so far."

Softly, I said, "What do you know so far, Naomi?" I didn't say, *Have you found an arsenal, too?* But that's what I wanted to know.

She glared at me as though my question was a trap. "Nothing. I don't know a thing. I haven't found any smoking guns in my house, and I haven't intercepted any calls from gun dealers, and I've checked my child's Web site and it's nothing but the same kind of stuff I hear around the house. I don't know a thing. I know less than the Klebolds and the Harrises knew. I definitely know less than the Jefferson County sheriff knew."

"But don't you think that the Klebolds and the Harrises and the sheriff all should have said something to prevent that tragedy?"

"The sheriff, sure, of course. But the parents? That's easy for us *now*, isn't it? We know what happened. They didn't know what was *going* to happen. Who could've guessed what those two boys were about to do?"

I tried empathy. "It's a tough place for a parent, Naomi."

For a long interval she stared at me, swallowing once or twice, and then she found a place where her composure was more assured. When she spoke again, she took me someplace else I didn't want to be.

We actually spent the rest of the session talking about Naomi's aging parents in Michigan and her fears about the onset of menopause.

I wanted to scream.

CHAPTER

12

The eastern rim of the Boulder Valley was growing dark as I made the final turn onto the lane that led to our house. My headlights immediately illuminated the side of my neighbor Adrienne's big blue Suburban, which was parked at an angle across the narrow width of the gravel lane, just beyond the permanent tin placard that identified the path to our little piece of paradise as a "Private Road." Taped to the side of Adrienne's huge vehicle was a poster-board sign that read NO PRES.

I recognized the artist, and the spelling. The poster was the work of Jonas, Adrienne's son. I was left with an inescapable conclusion: The kid shared not only his mother's aversion to the media but also her spelling challenges.

I pulled around Adrienne's behemoth and drove through the dry grasses until I could ease back up on the lane. In front of our house I found exactly what I was expecting to find, and I also found one surprise. Cozy's BMW was the expectation.

Lucy Tanner's red Volvo turbo was the surprise.

I said quick hellos to everyone, retrieved Grace from her bouncy chair in the center of the coffee table, and retreated from the living room so that Cozy and Lauren could continue to huddle with their client.

Dinner was in a dozen white boxes that were spread all over the kitchen counter, an amazing variety of take-out Chinese, all courtesy of Cozy. But as attractive as the buffet looked, I wasn't hungry. My appetite hadn't recovered from Naomi Bigg's provocative wouldn't-it-be-cool revelations or from her numbing menopause lament.

I stood with Grace in my arms, contemplating a spring roll, but grabbed only a beer on my way to the far end of the house.

The day after Grace was born, Lucy Tanner had stopped by Community Hospital and dropped off a gift, a charming, developmentally appropriate, black-and-white stuffed Gund musical clown with a garish face. Grace loved having the thing hanging above her crib. I didn't think I'd seen Lucy since that day in the hospital.

Although I'd crossed paths with her from time to time over the years during various misadventures I'd had with Sam Purdy, she and I had never grown close. She was a personable, friendly woman with a quick mind, a gentle wit, and an admirable tolerance of her quirky partner. She knew when to let Sam be the boss and she knew when to draw a line across his nose and dare him to cross it. I didn't recall ever seeing her misstep with Sam Purdy, which wasn't easy. I couldn't say the same thing about my own interactions with our mutual friend.

Lucy was uncommonly pretty. Not remarkably pretty, but uncommonly so. With the exception of her glistening blond hair there was nothing conventionally attractive about her features, but the constellation that the individual stars created was alluring, even magnetic. Many men embarrassed themselves when Lucy was in their vicinity, and Lucy was not at all reticent to take advantage of the phenomenon, either personally or professionally.

Over the years, I'd seen her in leather; I'd seen her in a little black dress; I'd seen her in brand-new Donna Karan, but—with the exception of her hours on the job—I'd never seen her dressed to blend in. Lucy always managed to stand off by herself. I suppose that I perceived her as living her life surrounded by a fence. Not chain link topped with razor wire, but more like a good strong wrought-iron barrier with an imposing gate.

Lucy would let you look into her world and its carefully manicured gardens, but she always made it clear that she didn't welcome uninvited visitors.

I was more than a little surprised when I saw Lucy standing in the open doorway to the master bedroom pantomiming a knuckle rap and saying, "Knock, knock." I'd changed into an old pair of shorts and a white T-shirt. Grace was in a fresh diaper and absolutely nothing else.

What do you say to an acquaintance who is suspected of murder? I tried, "I'm so sorry about all this you're going through. It must be like taking a holiday in hell."

"Thanks, Alan. May I come in? Cozy and Lauren are both on the phone. I thought I'd take a little break and was hoping I could sneak another look at the baby. She's wonderful."

Lucy was wearing a starched white shirt and jeans that fit her like hot wax. No jewelry. Black flats. Very little makeup. Given what she'd been through, I expected she would look tired, but she didn't. She somehow managed to slide her hands into the back pockets of her jeans.

"Of course. You want to hold her? She has a fresh diaper—so it's a rare opportunity. Take advantage of it while you can."

She smiled and lifted her arms. "May I?"

I handed Grace over to her. She took the baby with an awkward motion that spoke of unfamiliarity with infants. She said, "Is she always this good?"

"In a word, no. But she's still a wonderful baby. We've been very lucky."

I gestured toward an upholstered chair by the

western window. Lucy sat and made a cute face for Grace's benefit. She said, "Sorry to take over your house. It's been hard to find a place to meet that's not surrounded by the media. My place is impossible. Cozy's office, his house . . ."

"Don't mention it, Lucy. I'm glad there's a place you can go without being harassed."

For a moment she focused all her attention on Grace, whose face was beginning to scrunch up into one of her pre-distress configurations. "Am I doing something wrong?" Lucy asked.

"No, she may be hungry, or she may be cutting a tooth. Those are my current all-purpose explanations for Grace being unhappy. I'm planning to expand the list as necessary as she grows older. But I am hoping those two will suffice at least until her mid-teens."

Lucy laughed gently. "Were life so simple, huh? I wish those were my only two potential problems."

"I do, too, Lucy. I do, too."

Without taking her eyes from the baby, she said, "I told Lauren she could tell you what's been going on. I assume she told you I was there that night? At Royal's house?"

Grace captured and then started sucking on Lucy's pinky. I reached to the bed behind me, grabbed a bottle, and handed it over to Lucy. Grace started eating. "She *was* hungry," Lucy said.

"Yes, she told me you were at the house."

"The press will probably find out soon."

"They usually seem to discover these things."

"I think it was somebody at the department who leaked the fact that I'd been questioned to the media. That still hurts. Sammy picked me up before dawn so nobody would notice."

"Sam's a sweetheart, Lucy. It could have been somebody at the DA's office who was the leak, couldn't it? It might not have been one of your colleagues."

"I suppose," she said before she grew quiet for a moment, apparently fascinated by the simple act of an infant eating. I guessed Lucy was thirty-two, thirty-three years old. She was unmarried and childless, certainly vulnerable to the gravitational pull of maternal yearnings.

I was about to comment about that when she asked, "Alan? You ever do anything . . . ? God . . . you ever do anything that you're so ashamed of . . . ?" She stared out the window at the lights of the city and the silhouette of the mountains. "So ashamed of that you'd do almost anything to undo it?"

"I don't know," I replied, in a moment of stark ineloquence. "Maybe." I tried to guess what was coming next, but was drawing a blank.

"You've probably already figured it out, but I'm talking about the reason I was at Roy Peterson's house."

Moments like these—when acquaintances or friends begin to open up to me as though we were patient and doctor sitting in my office—are always awkward for me. My practiced instinct was to warn Lucy that she enjoyed no confidentiality here in my bedroom, but a friend wouldn't do that, a friend would just listen.

"I wondered," I said, recalling that Lucy had told her attorneys that if people knew why she was at Roy's house it would only support the contention that she had a motive to kill him. Now she was telling me that the reason she was there filled her with shame.

She said, "There's an old saying about good intentions. A proverb, or an aphorism. Are they the same thing, proverbs and aphorisms? Do you know it? Something like the road to hell is paved with good intentions."

I said, "The reason you were at Royal's house—that's still what you're talking about?"

Did she nod in reply? I wasn't quite certain. Finally, she said, "This one was—paved with good intentions, I mean. Not a whole lot of good judgment maybe, but a whole lot of good intentions."

She lowered her head and Grace almost disappeared in the cascade of blond hair. "Grace's done with the bottle. Should she have more? How do you know how much to feed her?"

"We give her what she wants. That seems to work."

Lucy closed her eyes slowly and left them shut. She said, "It's different for adults, I guess."

"What do you mean?"

She opened her eyes and looked up at me. The corners of her mouth turned up in a wry grin. She said, "Giving people what they want, it's more complicated with adults than it is with babies."

"I'm no expert with babies but my initial impression after six months' experience as a father is that almost everything is more complicated with adults than it is with babies." Grace spit out the nipple and started to squirm on Lucy's lap. "She probably needs to be burped, Lucy. Though she sometimes makes that same face in preparation for fouling another diaper. You want to burp her? Don't be surprised if she releases pressure at both ends simultaneously."

"Love to." She moved Grace gingerly up toward her shoulder. "Did Sam tell you that I got engaged a couple of weeks ago?"

"No, Lucy, he didn't. Congratulations. Who's the lucky guy?"

"He's not a cop," she replied.

An interesting prologue, I thought.

"His name is Grant. He's with the Forest Service. I met him last fall when I was out hiking, if you can believe it."

"That's wonderful. When is—"

"Who could guess? Everything's up in the air right now. You know, because of . . . Royal."

I was about to ask Lucy how she'd come to know Royal Peterson when Cozy's huge frame filled the bedroom doorway. He was carrying our foster poodle, Anvil. Anvil looked content in his arms. Against Cozy's huge frame, the sixteen-pound dog also looked like a hamster.

Cozy said, "Hello again, Alan. Did you get some dinner? Wonderful stuff. There's a tart in the refrigerator for later, too. Almonds. No, I didn't bake it. Lucy, want to join us? We're just about ready to get started again."

"Sure." She handed me the baby and said, "Thanks. That was a nice talk. I really appreciate it."

"No problem," I said.

From the other room, Lauren called out, "Sweetie, if you left your pager in the kitchen, it just went off."

I traipsed into the kitchen with Grace in my arms. I didn't recognize the number on my beeper, so I called my office voice mail to see what the emergency page was about. The message was from Naomi Bigg and it was succinct. "Dr. Gregory? There's something more I need to say about what we talked about earlier. Please give me a call."

I asked Grace if she wanted to hazard a guess about Naomi Bigg's pressing problem.

She didn't. Grace had wisdom beyond her months.

I dialed the number off the screen of my pager and heard a smoker's raspy "Hello."

Although I was pretty sure that the voice was Naomi's, I said, "Naomi Bigg, please."

"Dr. Gregory? It's me."

"I'm returning your page." I made certain my tone was as level as a freshly plumbed door.

"You're prompt. Leo always made them wait. He said it was too reinforcing to call right away."

It was becoming clear to me that maybe Leo Bigg was a jerk in more ways than one. Intentionally keeping cancer patients waiting for return phone calls? While I busied myself closing up the cardboard boxes of Chinese food, I let the ball bounce around on Naomi's side of the net.

She took a whack at it after a few seconds. "I was thinking about how we left things today, and what you must be thinking."

"What must I be thinking?"

"That the wouldn't-it-be-cool game I was describing—the one that the boys play—that it might somehow be, I don't know, related to what happened to the district attorney. I assume that I left you with that impression."

Naomi was right on. That was certainly on the list of things that I had been thinking.

She said, "I'm not naive, okay? I can add two and two as well as you can. But, see, none of the wouldn't-it-be-cool games with Ramp and Paul ever—ever—involved someone being assaulted the way that Royal Peterson was assaulted. The news reports all say that he was beaten, you know, hit on the head with something."

I listened as she sucked on a cigarette. She said, "The boys have never joked about doing anything like that—ambushing someone and hitting them on the head, beating them up. You ask me, I think they're too cowardly to do something that confrontational. That's why I don't think they had anything to do with what happened to Peterson."

The argument she was making wasn't particularly compelling. I concluded that the purpose of her call was to reveal to me the foundation for her rationalization. She was eager for me to sign up to support her psychological defenses; she didn't really expect to convince me that her hypothesis was true.

Not feeling particularly cooperative, I assaulted the rationalization I was hearing. "Had the wouldn't-it-be-cool games you overheard ever concerned Royal Peterson in any context?"

"Well, sure. Paul knows the DA's role in the plea-bargain process. Paul and Ramp talked about Peterson all the time. But Roy Peterson was one of ten wouldn't-it-be-cool targets, maybe more. Most of them were people that Ramp was angry at, by the way, not Paul."

"And since Roy Peterson was beaten and not—what?—you think it's evidence that Paul and Ramp weren't involved?"

"Bombs. The boys always joked about using a bomb."

Without any deliberation, I sat down. I had to consciously inhale a breath before I could say, "A bomb? They joked about using a bomb."

"I don't know whether it was a bomb exactly. I don't know about those things. But an explosive of some kind. It's one of Ramp's little hobbies. He talks about blowing things up all the time. He goes out to some ranch out east somewhere, Limon or someplace, and practices. Paul says that once he went out there with Ramp and they actually blew up an old truck. You know, a wreck.

"Ramp's the one who says things like, 'Wouldn't it be cool if the district attorney's house just blew up one day?' Or 'Wouldn't it be cool if so-and-so's car blew up one day?' Like that. All of that stuff comes from Ramp. Paul never talks like that when Ramp's not around."

"Blowing stuff up is a hobby of Ramp's?"

"I don't know, an outside interest, that kind of hobby."

Silently, I counted to ten. Fortunately or unfortunately, the delay didn't change what I was going to say. "I want to make sure I'm understanding you correctly. Because Royal Peterson wasn't killed by an explosive of some kind, you would like to believe that Paul and Ramp weren't involved in whatever happened at his house, even though they'd made overt threats against him."

"They never threatened him. It was just talk about what they wished would happen. When they heard he was dead, it's not like they celebrated or anything."

How nice. "So there's no chance they followed through on their fantasies?"

"Exactly. It was like they felt guilty because they were wishing for someone to die and then it happened. You know what that would be like. You'd feel guilty, responsible. Anybody would."

I considered her argument before I said, "That's a luxurious position for you to have, Naomi."

"What do you mean?"

"I'm thinking of the Klebolds and the Harrises. Over the months before that day at the high school, they probably made the same kinds of judgments about their children. Saw two here, and saw two there, but never allowed themselves to believe that the sum added up to four."

She sputtered as though she couldn't wait to respond to my words. "And, you know what? A thousand other parents—mothers like me—have done the exact same thing. We've seen things and never told the police. And our children never ended up doing a thing wrong. Not a thing. None of them. Two and two never added up. Ever. I thought you would understand."

"Understand what?"

"What it's like for parents. Aren't you a parent? Can you believe that your child is evil? Do you know how hard it is to cross that line?"

I looked down at Grace, asleep in my arms. No, I couldn't believe that my child was evil. Would ever be evil.

Not a chance.

"Not necessarily evil," I said, "but what about flawed? Troubled?" I added a bonus rationalization for Naomi's benefit. "Or what if the child is influenced by the wrong people? That happens."

"Killing someone isn't a flaw, Doctor. It's evil. And evil isn't in the air, you don't just catch it like a virus. It comes from somewhere, some injury deep inside." She paused. "And, although he's certainly been hurt badly by all that's happened, I don't believe my child has ever been to that place. I'd know it if . . . he had—I'm his mother."

I cushioned my voice, foaming the runway with my next words, trying to give her a soft place to land. "But you're not entirely sure, are you, Naomi? That's why we're talking."

She didn't want to come down gently. She said, "Maybe I shouldn't have called you after all. I'll see you on Friday—if I don't reconsider this whole thing."

Hurriedly, I interjected, "The reason you called tonight? Why is it important that I not misinterpret what you said today during our session? It's my impression that you're angry that I'm still able to see both sides of the coin."

"I don't want you to do anything stupid."

"I don't understand."

"I didn't want you to run off and tell anyone what I said. Send the bomb squad to my house or something. That's all."

"I couldn't reveal our conversation to anyone, Naomi. Not without your permission."

"I bet you could find a way around that."

"Are we talking about trust now?"

"I have no damn idea what we're talking about." She hung up as I was trying to figure out a discreet way to inquire about the other nine or so wouldn't-it-be-cool targets that Ramp and Paul had mentioned.

As the line went dead in my ear, I said, "Is my wife on that list, Naomi?"

13

I went to bed knowing that I needed help. And I woke up the next morning knowing that I needed help.

Although I would've loved to have discussed the whole Naomi Bigg situation with Lauren, and would have welcomed her reasoned counsel, confidentiality concerns and peculiar circumstances made that impossible.

The peculiar circumstance, of course, was the possibility that Lauren was one of the potential targets of Paul and Ramp's wouldn't-it-be-cool games. And the very real possibility that the game was really only a mind game.

The way I looked at it was that my position was simple. I couldn't risk saying anything and I couldn't risk not saying anything.

What I'd decided I needed was what psychotherapists call supervision. In another profession, I suppose the same thing might be called consultation. Basically, supervision means that one psychotherapist invites another, hopefully more objective, usually more experienced professional to review and comment upon his or her work.

On those occasions when I decided I needed some objectivity with my practice, I relied on one of three different people, depending on the specifics of the case. When the issues in the case involved ethics, as this one did, my first choice was almost invariably Raymond Farley, Ph.D. Raymond's capacity to detect prevarication and rationalization was finely honed, and I knew I could count on him to help show me which side of the trees the moss was growing on in the forest where I was lost.

I called his home at seven-fifteen on Thursday morning. His youngest daughter was a junior in high school, so I figured the Farley household would already be humming along.

Raymond's wife answered.

"Cyn? It's Alan Gregory, how are you?"

"Alan, hello. How am I? Not quite as awake as you are. You want my sugar, right? I'm trying to get my daughter out the door. Let me find him. Raymond? It's for you."

A moment later I heard Raymond's baritone. "Alan. Long time. How's your new baby?"

"Grace is great, Raymond. How're your kids?"

He answered me at great length and with great patience. There was little hurry in the blood that coursed through Raymond Farley's veins. No one ever, ever took more care while finishing a story, and no one ever finished a meal after Raymond Farley finished his. "You didn't call to get an update on my kids, though, did you? What can I do for you?"

"I've got a case I would love to run by you. It's urgent, unfortunately. I see this woman again tomorrow evening and I should probably talk to you before her next appointment."

"Outpatient?"

"Yes."

"What's the urgency?"

"Columbine issues, Raymond."

"It's that time of year, I guess. What are we talking, grief? Anniversary reaction? Post-traumatic stress?"

"I'm not referring to the last Columbine, Raymond. I'm referring to concerns about the next Columbine."

"Oh," he said. "Oh."

"Can you squeeze me in?"

"I'm going to be at CU in Boulder doing a seminar on suicidal tendencies from one to three today. Meet me outside of Wardenburg—the student health center—at three. If the weather holds we'll find someplace pretty to sit, and we'll talk."

I rescheduled my two forty-five patient, picked up sandwiches and drinks at Alfalfa's on Arapahoe, and started to wait for Ray on the University of Colorado campus.

The campus is over a hundred years old and the founders had had their pick of prime foothills real estate for the location of the university. They'd chosen wisely. The CU campus is far enough from the vaulting mountains to maximize views, close enough to ensure that the Rockies would never cease to be a dominating presence. The flagstone buildings and red tile roofs of the major buildings on the University of Colorado campus are as distinctive an architectural feature as can be found on any campus in the western United States. The feeling is vaguely Italian, and that afternoon, the brilliance of the April sunshine added to the Mediterranean ambience.

Raymond Farley walked out the front door of Wardenburg a few minutes after three. I held up the bag I was carrying. "Grilled chicken on sourdough. I seem to recall you have a fondness. And Dr Pepper? Did I get that right?"

He rewarded me with a welcome embrace and his wide grin. His rich brown skin glowed in the springtime sun. "You recalled correctly, on both counts. I'm afraid I'm responsible for the demise of way too much fowl. Cynthia says that she thinks I'll have to answer to Saint Peter about that."

"If that's all that Saint Peter has to question you about, Raymond, you'll have a fine day at the pearly gates."

We walked in the direction of the planetarium and

found a bench below a small mountain ash that was just beginning to leaf out. Raymond unwrapped his sandwich and popped the top on his Dr Pepper. "You talk while I eat," he said.

"The patient I'm concerned about is a fiftyish female whom I saw for the first time this past Monday. Tomorrow's appointment will be our fourth session this week. That alone should tell you something."

It told him something: Raymond whistled between chews.

It took about five minutes for me to explain Naomi Bigg's situation—her daughter's rape, her husband's jail sentence, her son's friendship with Ramp and their preoccupation with retribution. All the details I could remember about the wouldn't-it-be-cool games.

His first question surprised me. He asked, "Your patient's white?"

Raymond wasn't. I wondered about the question. "Yes, why?"

" 'Cause, for some reason, black kids don't tend to do these things."

Raymond gave me a moment to digest his remark, then asked me to repeat the part that had to do with Royal Peterson's murder.

I did, finally adding, "Lauren was involved in the plea bargain of the kid who raped Naomi Bigg's daughter."

"Ahh," Ray said. "That explains your tone."

"My tone?"

"My impression, listening to you, is that you don't like this woman you're treating. I'm not accustomed to hearing negative countertransference so clearly from you. But now you say that you fear your wife's in danger—that explains your negative feelings."

"I'm pushing her, Ray. Pushing her hard. Her resistance . . . is intense. She desperately wants to believe her son is uninvolved in anything other than some retribution fantasies. I've known her—what?—three days and already I'm pounding away at the resistance, and the reality is that I don't have the alliance to get away with it. She's getting angry at me."

Raymond chewed methodically, appreciating each mouthful of food the way that I imagined Mozart appreciated each note of a concerto. After Ray swallowed, he asked, "Whose idea was the four sessions this week? Yours or hers?"

A simple question. But one that told me that Raymond Farley already understood the crux of why I'd asked him for supervision on this case.

I sighed involuntarily. "Mine."

"You're trying to goad her into taking some action against her son, aren't you? Confront him, turn him in?"

"I suppose I am. That would protect Lauren. And maybe a whole lot of other people, as well."

"Sure it would. But it's not your job. Here's what I'm thinking: Given your concerns about Lauren's safety, you probably shouldn't be treating this patient at all.

You know that you can't be objective as a psychothera-pist if you're putting your wife's interests in front of your patient's interests."

"Raymond, that's the dilemma. Given my concerns about Lauren's safety, there's no way in the world I'm *not* going to treat this woman. If Lauren's really at risk, I have to be in a position to know what's coming next. If I refer her to someone else, Lauren could be in danger and I wouldn't even know it."

He kissed the last bit of sauce from the tips of his fingers and wiped his hands with his napkin. He said, "If you've already made your decision, what do you want from me?"

He read my reaction in my expression—I imagined I looked as though I'd been slapped in the face—and he grinned at me kindly. "Step back, Alan. You want from me exactly what she wants from you. She wants you to validate her inaction in regard to her concerns about her son. You? You want me to validate your inaction in regard to your concerns about continuing this treatment. You won't do what your patient wants you to do, and even though I've been bribed with an excellent sandwich, I won't do what you want me to do. I'm not about to tell you that you have a 'get out of jail, free' card on this one."

With some effort, I managed to smile back at him. "I actually didn't think you would, Raymond. Help me with something else then. This kid—her son— how dangerous is he? Because of my anxiety over Lauren, maybe I'm misreading the facts. You work with more young people than I do."

"What do you know about him?"

I told him everything Naomi had revealed about her son, Paul.

When I was through, Raymond leaned back and rested his weight on his hands. "There're some concerns there, no doubt about it. I've been on a committee at Wardenburg trying to help the university develop criteria for identifying kids who might be at risk of violent acting out. Your patient's son has some warning signs, that's for sure."

"What criteria has your committee developed?"

"We started with the criteria the FBI proposed and we're modifying them slightly." He held up one of his big hands, flicking out one finger after another as he ticked off the criteria. "One, kids who are on the outside socially and have verbalized their anger at popular kids, or even bullies. That fits this kid. Two, kids who have made overt threats, especially threats to kill. That fits. Three, kids with a prior mental health history. That fits. Four, kids who feel that they've been wronged, that they're victims. That fits. Five, kids with a history of the troublesome triad—fire setting, bedwetting, cruelty to animals. I'm assuming that you don't know enough about his history to confirm that one, do you?"

"No."

He gave me his wide, all-knowing grin again. "You know what they say? With four out of five, you get egg rolls."

"You're not making me feel any better, Raymond."

"Is that my job? Helping you feel better? How about I just give you a massage. That should help."

"Funny."

He touched his watch. "Couple more minutes, Alan. Then I have to hit the road back to Denver. Damn turnpike, you know?"

I knew all about the damn turnpike. I said, "I'm thinking of leaking some of what my patient told me—the part about the boys' plans to use explosives. I have a friend on the Boulder Police Department, and I'm thinking of suggesting he find a way to sweep Royal Peterson's house for explosives."

Raymond's eyebrows rose like a pair of levitating caterpillars. "You're thinking of what?"

"I know it sounds absurd but hear me out. What if those two boys were in Royal's house to plant an explosive device and Royal discovered them after it was already in place and there was a scuffle and they killed Royal? Then the kids ran. The bomb, or device, or whatever, could still be there, right?"

Raymond gazed at me as though he was wondering what psychotropic medicine I needed.

I pressed on. "When I talk to my detective friend, I wouldn't reveal my patient's name, wouldn't even say that a patient told me. I'd just make an oblique suggestion about my concerns, just enough to get my friend to get the police department to look for explosives at Royal's house."

Raymond's face could hardly have been more

skeptical. "I've heard your rationalization. I'm still wondering about your reasoning."

"What if there is a bomb planted there? Somebody could get killed if it went off. Royal's wife, Susan, Susan's health aide—somebody. If it turns out that nothing's there, I just look a little silly. My cop friend is used to that."

Raymond didn't quite smile and he didn't quite start shaking his head. But it was close. "Say there is something there. And the police find it . . . What if your patient's son's fingerprints are on the device? In effect, you've turned him in to the police, based on confidential information you had no right to divulge."

"Lesser of two evils. *Tarasoff* says I have to give a warning if I feel that someone's in danger based on what a patient tells me."

He opened a palm and held it up like a traffic cop. The pink edges of the soft flesh around his palm surprised me, even though I'd seen Raymond's hands a hundred times before. He said, "Not quite right. The court's *Tarasoff* decision says that you have to provide a warning if your patient makes an overt threat against an identifiable person. Based on what you've told me, your patient hasn't threatened anyone, Alan. No one. And regardless, I've not seen any court decision that extends the *Tarasoff* ruling to include hearsay. This isn't your patient threatening anybody. This is your patient talking about what somebody else might be planning." He removed his eyeglasses and blew at one lens. "If Lauren weren't involved—if you didn't think she was at risk—you wouldn't be considering this kind of action and you know it."

I argued back. "But if it were child abuse that I was hearing about, it wouldn't make any difference. Hearsay or no hearsay, right?"

"The child-abuse exception is handled specifically under Colorado law, Alan. This isn't."

I couldn't argue with the point that Raymond was making, so I moved the argument in a different direction, saying, "What if what's going on is that my patient actually wants me to turn her son in? What if that's her agenda with me? She can't stop him herself, she can't bring herself to turn him in, so she wants me to do it for her. She keeps talking about the Klebolds and the Harrises. There's a message there that I can't ignore."

He didn't respond right away, so I persisted. "The parents of the Columbine murderers may have failed their children and their community with their ignorance or their denial of what their children were planning, Raymond. But the Jefferson County Sheriff's Department had enough information, too. The family of a kid that Klebold and Harris threatened told the sheriff's department all about the threats and about the crap that was on Harris's Web site. The sheriff even linked Harris to a pipe bomb that somebody had exploded and went ahead and drafted an affidavit for a search warrant for his house. That was a year before the killings, but the sheriff didn't follow through with any of it."

"And you don't want to be accused of making the same mistakes as the Jefferson County sheriff?"

"No, I don't, Raymond. I don't. One of those two, Harris or Klebold, was in psychotherapy, too. He was seeing a psychologist. What if he actually told the guy he was planning to kill some students at his high school but didn't mention anyone in particular? Are you saying that the psychologist didn't have an ethical obligation to report that?"

"We don't know what that psychologist knew."

"But I know what I know."

"Do you?"

I said, "I don't want people to die when I might have had enough information to prevent their deaths."

"Especially your wife."

"Of course, especially my wife."

"You're not even certain she's been threatened, are you?"

"I can't risk it, Raymond. I can't."

"I suggest you step back and see the parallel process, my friend."

"What are you talking about, Ray?"

"Your patient is struggling with whether or not she has enough information to do what most parents consider unthinkable—turning her own son in to the authorities because she believes he may be planning an unspeakable atrocity. Go ahead and underline 'may.' Remember Styron? *Sophie's Choice?* This is one of those. You, too, are struggling with whether or not you have enough information to do the unthinkable—breaching your patient's confidentiality and turning this woman's son in to the authorities because you believe he may be planning an unspeakable atrocity. Go ahead and underline 'may' one more time."

I said, "The moral obligations are clear for both of us, Ray. My patient should act. Failing that, I should act."

"Are the moral ambiguities so invisible to you? Are you in any position to make that judgment? I think I've made a damn good case that your objectivity is compromised, Alan. The bottom line is that you shouldn't be treating this woman at all. Your motivation as her therapist is not limited to assisting her with psychological concerns. Not at all. That alone should cause you to excuse yourself. Another therapist, an objective therapist, should make the decision about what to do with these supposed threats."

"How can I turn my back on what I know?"

"You know a mother's fears. That's all that you know. I don't think that's enough."

"She's telling me something, Raymond. She's telling me enough."

Raymond stood. He said, "I've not seen you like this before. You seem to want to believe that the rules don't apply right now."

I could no longer keep the intensity I was feeling out of my voice. "What rules? There aren't any rules that apply to this situation. Ethical standards evolve, Raymond, we both know that. There are always new situations developing that the old rules don't address."

"And this is one?" he asked skeptically. "You're sure of that?"

"Before *Tarasoff*, therapists couldn't even warn potential victims that they'd been threatened. Now we can—we must. That's a change. That's an ethical evolution. Circumstances required it."

"And you want the freedom to decide that this is the foundation for another ethical evolution? *Tarasoff* wasn't the result of a rogue therapist rewriting the rules, Alan. It was a California Supreme Court decision."

I scrambled to my feet. "I've never been in a position like this before. You have to admit these circumstances are unique."

His eyes flaring, he countered, "You have a patient who needs an objective outlet for exploring an issue that is troubling her. What, I ask you, is unique about that circumstance? It happens to both of us every day. The only thing that's unique about this situation is that you've decided to substitute your judgment for your patient's. How long do you think our profession can survive therapists doing *that*?"

"You know exactly what I mean. This is . . . different."

He dabbed at one corner of his mouth with the paper napkin. "Then act like it's different, Alan. The way I see it is that you're trying to straddle a high fence and you can't seem to get either foot on the ground. On one side you're making a case that your concerns are so great that they warrant your violating ethical principles that I know you hold dear. On the other side you're apparently not quite concerned enough about any of it to just go to the police and state your case. You have to get off the damn fence one way or another. Either it's a serious threat and you put your judgment ahead of your patient's, or it's not a serious threat and you shut up and help her with her struggles."

I pressed. "How would you get off the fence? If it were Cynthia in danger? Or one of your kids?"

"Is Lauren really in danger? Is Grace? Are you certain of that?"

"No, I'm not certain."

"Then your question about what I would do if it were Cynthia or one of my kids is too facile. I get to answer your question in the abstract. I get to play 'What if?' You? You have to make your decisions in the here and now when your head is full of nothing but I-don't-knows."

He stared at me while I struggled to reply. Finally, he said, "Where the heck did I leave my car?"

CHAPTER

14

Although I'd seen Royal and Susan Peterson's home plenty of times on the local television news in the days since Roy's murder, I hadn't been there again in person until Friday morning as I was parked across the street sitting in the front passenger seat of Sam Purdy's red Jeep Cherokee. The floor mats of Sam's old car were so caked with dried-on dirt and gravel that I couldn't tell whether they were made of carpet or rubber.

Sam had been quiet since he'd picked me up at my office. Now he'd started humming, never a good sign with Sam.

Out of nervousness as much as anything, I said, "It's just like seeing Plymouth Rock."

Two or three seconds passed before he said, "What the hell are you talking about?"

"Years ago, I drove to Plymouth Rock from Boston—it's a long way. The day I was there it was raining pretty good. You make the long drive, you find a place to park the car, you get out, you walk to the shore, you stand behind a little iron fence, you look down, and what do you see? You see a rock. That's it. A rock. Not a big rock, not an interesting rock. We're not talking Gibraltar. It's just a rock."

"Yeah, your point?"

"That's kind of how I feel right now, seeing Royal and Susan's house. I expected—seeing it in person after the murder, all that's happened there—that it would feel different, somehow, than it used to. More important, more moving. I don't know. But . . . it's just a house."

Sam harrumphed.

I continued, eager for him to understand. "It's like finding out Santa Claus is just a guy in a red suit."

Sam yawned. "I don't know. Lawn needs to be mowed. That never would have happened if Royal were alive. I think he was a keep-the-lawn-mowed-and-the-walkway-edged type of guy. I bet he was a regular Friday-after-work or Saturday-morning-first-thing-type yard guy. So that's different, the lawn not being mowed. In the winter, after a storm, I bet he was the first guy on the block out with his Toro, blowing snow halfway to Nederland."

I looked sideways at him. "Not in a particularly philosophical mood, are you, Sam?"

He laughed. "With what you told me to get me to do

this, you're lucky I'm here at all. Don't hold your breath for Sartre."

I cracked open the car door. "I'm going to get the key. You want to come with or you want to stay here?"

"If it's all the same to you, I'll stay here and ponder the Plymouth Rock thing a little bit more. Maybe I'll get it."

As I walked across the street, I retrieved the yellow sticky note that I'd stuffed in my pocket and checked the address. The number matched the house right next door to the Petersons'. I walked up a flagstone path and rang the bell.

The woman who answered the door was young and harried. She had a toddler perched on one hip and another child, a girl around four, corralled between her legs. "Yes?" she asked. Her tone said, *This had better be good.*

"Ms. Wallace? I'm Alan Gregory; I'm a friend of Susan Peterson's. She said she would call you to authorize you to give me a key to her house. She said she left one with you for emergencies."

"Yeah, right. Hannah! You stay put, you hear me? How is Susan doing?" The little girl tried to squirm away. The woman trapped her with a knee and tried to smile at me. The expression ended up looking more like a grimace. "Such a tragedy what happened to Royal. Have to admit, it's scared the whole neighborhood. Hold on, I'll go get the key." She grabbed Hannah's hand, and mother and children disappeared down the hall.

I heard some insipid children's music playing in the background and reminded myself that my day listening to insipid children's music would soon come. I wondered whether the offensive sound was coming from a CD or a video and whether it involved a purple dinosaur or animated Japanese monsters.

I said a silent prayer that Grace would have good taste.

The woman returned with both children and with the key. She handed the fob out the door, and said, "Here you go. Just slip it back through the mail slot when you're done with it. Nice meeting you."

The door was closed before I said, "Thank you."

Sam met me on the road in front of the house. He said, "You never told me, what did you tell Susan Peterson to get her permission to do this?"

"You may not know this, but your friends at the police department only turned the house back over to her yesterday. Since she got out of the hospital, she's been staying with one of her daughters in Durango. I called down there and made up a story about something Royal and I were working on together, said I knew where the papers were in his study."

"She went for that?"

"She trusts me."

"Fool."

"Your guy is coming, right?"

"My guy is a girl and, yes, she's coming." He glanced at his watch. "We're early. She'll be here."

"She's off duty?"

"Way off duty. She's on disability after getting hurt on the job. Like I told you, she trains K-9s now, earns a little extra money."

Just then, a fifteen- or twenty-year-old Mercedes wagon rounded the corner and slowed as it pulled up to the curb. The paint on the car had oxidized to the point where I couldn't even guess at its original color. One front fender was liberally treated with rubbing compound. A young woman hopped out of the driver's side. She waved hello to Sam and walked to the rear hatch of the car. When she opened it, a medium-sized dog with floppy ears and indeterminate heritage jumped out and heeled beside her. She fixed a lead to the dog's collar and together they joined Sam and me on the sidewalk.

The woman limped noticeably.

Sam said, "Dorsey, this is Alan Gregory. Alan, Dorsey Hamm. Ex–Westminster Police Department, and this is her K-9 friend, uh . . ."

Dorsey was a stocky woman. Her skin showed evidence of a lost battle with adolescent acne. Her hair was cut carelessly. My impression was that she had long ago stopped trying to be attractive and that she was absolutely content with her decision.

She said, "I'm pleased to meet you," and held out her hand. "This here is Shadow." As I drew close enough to her to shake her hand, I thought I caught a whiff of cannabis. Involuntarily, I glanced at Dorsey's eyes. Red trails arced across the whites like lightning bolts.

The dog's tail was in nonstop motion. The rest of him was perfectly still.

"What kind is he?" I asked.

"Lab-shepherd mix. Both breeds tend to be good with explosives." She told him to sit, and he lowered himself without delay. On their best days, my dogs weren't as well-behaved as Shadow.

And they didn't have their best days very often.

Sam said, "I'm not going inside, Dorsey. Wouldn't be appropriate, given Lucy's situation." He handed me a pair of latex gloves and told me to put them on. He said, "Let's not complicate things with your prints, eh?"

Sometimes, especially during the height of hockey season, Sam developed an unconscious tendency to affect a Canadian accent. I think it came from watching too many Canadian athletes and listening to too many Canadian sportscasters on television. The affectation tended to fade a week or so after the league awarded the Stanley Cup.

He offered a pair of gloves to Dorsey. She took them and while she snapped them onto her hands, he said, "I appreciate your willingness to screen this place for me; I owe you one."

Dorsey glanced at the house. "Oh, don't mention it, Sam. Shadow needs the work, and unfamiliar environments are great training tools. We'll be in and out of a place this size in ten minutes, max. Probably not even that long. Don't go out for coffee or anything." She shortened the lead, touched the dog, and leaned down close to his ear. "Come on, boy. Come on. Let's go treasure hunting."

I proceeded up the walk, unlocked the front door of the Peterson home, and held the door for Dorsey and Shadow.

Dorsey reached down and whispered an instruction to Shadow that I couldn't quite hear. Her next message to the dog was a simple hand signal.

The dog charged forward, lowered his head, and started searching the Peterson home for explosives. Dorsey held the lead and stayed within a few feet of him.

My dogs could do that. Either of them.

Right.

Seconds after we were inside, Dorsey led Shadow up the stairs to the second floor. I didn't follow them right away; I was distracted. As soon as we were in the house I'd started looking around, trying to identify the precise place where Royal had been bashed to death. I thought the news reports had mentioned the living room and I was curious whether there would actually be a chalk outline to indicate where the body had been found. By the time I had examined the living room pretty carefully—no chalk—and was ready to start up the stairs, Shadow was already preceding Dorsey back down to the first floor.

Dorsey said, "Upstairs is negative."

I said, "Good."

Shadow moved away from the staircase, lowered his snout to the hardwood, took a few steps, circled a spot just beyond the doorway that led to the dining room, and sat. The dog's head swiveled toward his master and back to the floor. Dorsey looked at the dog, then over to me. "That's an alert—a positive," Dorsey said, her voice suddenly swollen with tension. "Is there a basement below that, or a crawl space? Do you know?"

All I saw was the dog sitting peacefully. I expected something different, though I don't know what. "Basement," I said in reply to Dorsey's question. "My memory is that the stairs are in the kitchen." I added, "What do you mean, 'positive'?" Though I knew what she meant by "positive."

She didn't answer. She found the way to the kitchen and led Shadow down the stairs. I fumbled for a light switch, finally illuminating the dark staircase. The basement was nicely finished, but the ceilings were low and the space felt claustrophobic. The large room at the base of the staircase was set up as a home office for Royal. One long wall was lined with shelves filled with an impressive collection of abstract pottery. I counted fifteen large pieces and a few small ones. A prominent space on a shelf that was near the foot of the stairs was empty.

Royal's collection of ceramics had apparently once included sixteen large pieces.

After no more than ten seconds, Shadow moved from a quick sniff around Royal's office to focus on an adjacent utility room. There he immediately picked a spot near the center of the room, raised his snout in the air, circled once, and sat.

Dorsey said, "Wow. That's another alert. He's confirming."

"Confirming?"

"Watch this," said Dorsey with obvious pride.

She moved a six-foot stepladder from the far wall and set it up on the exact spot where Shadow had been sitting. She released him from his lead and, without a moment's hesitation, the dog climbed the length of the ladder, balancing his front paws on the top platform, his back paws on the second-to-last rung.

"Isn't that cool?" Dorsey said. "I didn't even have to teach him that. He does it all on his own."

"Amazing," I agreed. I could barely breathe. It was as though Shadow were stealing all my air.

"It's another positive," she said, as she lifted the dog off the ladder and placed him on the concrete floor. "I think it's the same spot he smelled from up above. I bet something's been tucked up there between the floor joists."

I leaned in and peered up into the dark recess.

She asked, "What do you think?"

"The floor plan is kind of hard to follow from down here, but, yeah, I think it may be the same spot where he sat upstairs."

She pulled a flashlight from an asspack around her waist and aimed the beam up toward the ceiling. "Holy moly, there it is. Wow, wow, wow. I've never found a real one before. I'm just a trainer, you know?"

I reminded myself to exhale. "Are you going to go up there and look at it?"

"Are you nuts? The device could be booby-trapped. Shadow locates the things; that's where my involvement stops. I sure as hell don't examine them or disarm them. I've already given enough of my body to law enforcement, thank you, and I've gotten as close as I plan to get to that device, whatever it is."

"Of course, I wasn't thinking," I said. I was so nervous, I was barely capable of thinking.

Dorsey said, "What do you say we get the hell out of here as quick as we can? It gives me the willies knowing that there are really explosives here."

"You're sure that we're talking . . . explosives?"

"Me? I don't smell a thing. But Shadow's pretty sure. He's been an A student. Most K-9s work at eighty-five to ninety percent accuracy. Shadow's almost done with his training and he's been near ninety-five percent for the last couple of weeks. The fact that he's sure is plenty good enough for me."

"If that's the case, getting out of here as fast as we can sounds like a perfect plan," I said. My throat was so dry I had trouble getting the words out of my mouth. I held my breath for a moment so I could listen hard for the sound of a clock ticking.

Or my heart pounding.

Nothing.

Dorsey wasted no time herding Shadow back up the basement stairs toward the front door. Seconds later, Dorsey, Shadow, and I were all back outside on the Petersons' front porch. When I looked up, I saw Sam pacing across the street.

Dorsey waved to him while she simultaneously slipped Shadow a treat.

"It's positive, Sam," she called out. "Sorry."

Sam buried his face in his hands. I was pretty certain that if I were any closer to him I would have heard him curse me in some imaginative way.

To Dorsey, I said, "I think I'd feel a whole lot more comfortable if we got off of this porch, maybe joined Sam across the street."

CHAPTER
15

At Sam's suggestion I departed the scene, loitering around the corner while Dorsey loaded Shadow into the back of the old Mercedes. Sam wanted Dorsey and the dog long gone before the Boulder Police Department mobilized its assets to deal with the latest crisis at Royal Peterson's home. Sam had already told me that his plan was to tell his superiors that he'd received an anonymous tip, not that he'd finagled a way to get a bomb-sniffing dog to do the initial reconnaissance of the house.

In the three minutes after Dorsey drove Shadow and the Mercedes away, a half-dozen Boulder Police Department black-and-whites arrived, followed moments later by a big rescue squad truck, a pumper from the Boulder Fire Department, and finally, about ten minutes later, a truck and trailer carrying bomb squad members and their equipment. I thought it was an impressive response for a town the size of Boulder.

The Petersons' block was evacuated in short order; many of the evacuees ended up congregating near my anonymous post around the corner. A lot of people gathered; I assumed that the block behind the house had been evacuated as well. Yellow tape seemed to be stretched everywhere. I kept an eye out for Susan Peterson's neighbor, the one with the two little kids who'd given me the key, but they never came around my corner. I wondered if the police had used Boulder's reverse 911 system to alert the neighbors. The program permitted the authorities to use an automated system to phone residents and inform them of an emergency. I made a mental note to ask Sam.

When the first TV microwave truck arrived, I used it as my cue to begin walking away. On foot, if I ambled, I figured it would take me about fifteen minutes to get to my office downtown. If I pushed the pace a little bit, I thought I might have time to grab a snack before I got to Walnut Street and still have about twenty minutes to prepare myself for Naomi Bigg's noon appointment.

Knowing myself, I knew that I'd spend every one of those twenty minutes second-guessing my decision to alert Sam Purdy that there was a possibility that explosives had been planted in Royal and Susan Peterson's home. Although I couldn't quite convince myself that I'd done what was right, the fact that

Shadow had discovered a cache of explosive material brought me close to convincing myself that I'd done what I had to do.

By twelve o'clock, the scheduled starting time of my appointment with Naomi Bigg, only about an hour had passed since Sam Purdy had called in the threat of explosives at the Peterson home. I decided that the odds were long that Naomi Bigg would have already heard about the arrival of the bomb squad and the fire department. She would have had to be watching TV or listening to the news on the radio. Nonetheless, as I waited for the red light on the wall to flash on, I steeled myself for the possibility.

What would I do if Naomi confronted me? I'd already decided not to lie to her. Instead, my plan was to maintain that by tipping off the police the way I had, I had not breached her confidentiality at all.

My argument? As with most rationalizations I'd heard in my life regarding ethics, my reasoning had a structure as complicated as DNA.

First, I planned to argue that the information that I'd shared with the police was the result of deduction on my part. Naomi had not, in fact, told me that I would find explosives in the Peterson home. Yes, she had obliquely raised the possibility that Ramp and Paul may have been planning to place a bomb, but then she had vociferously argued against it.

I could hardly be accused of breaching confidentiality around a topic that hadn't even been specifically addressed in therapy.

The truth was that I could be so accused, but the argument I was twisting into my personal version of a double helix was comforting, nonetheless.

Second, the information that I'd provided to Sam Purdy could not reasonably lead anyone to discover the identity of my patient. The reality of my profession—for better or for worse—is that psychotherapists share information from psychotherapy sessions all the time. If the information does not provide clues that can be linked back to a specific individual, such leaks are usually treated as harmless indiscretions.

I told myself this was one of those.

Third? The third argument was for my ears only, not for Naomi's. It was this: To whom was Naomi going to complain? She could hardly go to the police with her allegations against me. And a formal petition to the State Board of Psychologist Examiners alleging malfeasance didn't seem likely. She'd have a hard time filing the charge without identifying her son. And I'd actually like to watch the ethics board grapple with the information she would provide about him.

I decided that the worst that could happen is that Naomi would storm out of my office and that I'd never hear from her again.

The trouble was this: Given the danger I feared Lauren might be in, not hearing from Naomi again was my greatest fear.

Naomi Bigg was on time for her appointment.
Maybe it was because Dorsey and Shadow and the
package above the stepladder were still very much on
my mind, but my first thought upon seeing Naomi was
that, unlike Dorsey, Naomi would never, ever cease trying to be attractive. Nor, I suspected, would she ever
achieve Dorsey's level of contentment with her appearance.

Naomi's black crepe suit was impeccably pressed.
Since I was congenitally unable to even bend over
without wrinkling my own clothes, I was always
amazed when other people could make it through a
workday looking as though they had a miniature hab-
erdasher with a steam wand stuffed in their briefcase.

I acknowledged her curt "Hello," and then I waited
to discover if she'd learned of the emergency response
that was taking place on Jay Street. I rehearsed my
arguments while she settled herself on her chair and
found a place for the big Vuitton bag. The thing thud-
ded to the floor as though she were transporting
dumbbells.

"You know," she said finally, "you never asked me
what I thought about Royal Peterson's murder. We
talked about the boys, and their reaction, but you never
asked about me and my reaction. After I left last time,
I found that odd, that you hadn't asked me about it."

No, I thought. *Instead of discussing your reaction to
Royal Peterson's murder, we discussed peri-menopause,*

a topic I find so engrossing that it often distracts me from
pursuing more important things, like murder.

"You would like to talk about—"

"I didn't feel a thing." As she trampled over the end of my sentence, I couldn't tell if my words had been superfluous or if she was just ignoring me. "I didn't feel bad that a man had been killed. I didn't feel particularly good that the man who'd released my daughter's rapist was dead. Hearing that Peterson had been murdered didn't move me at all."

I said, "What do you make of that?"

Like "How does that make you feel?" it was one of those questions that made me feel like a caricature of a psychotherapist. Every time I spoke those or similar words, I was secretly embarrassed. But I asked the questions nonetheless, probably more frequently than I would like to admit.

The reason? Sometimes they worked.

And they always bought me time to think.

Naomi's response sounded rehearsed to me. She said, "Vengeance is a funny thing. If you read the final reports about Klebold and Harris—and believe me, I've read everything—and what they did at Columbine High School, their passion for vengeance had deserted them at the end. After fifteen, twenty minutes they'd lost their energy, they'd stopped hunting down kids, they'd even given up trying to explode their ineffective little bombs, and eventually they just turned their guns on themselves. I think when the adrenaline was finally totally depleted they realized that they'd failed to achieve whatever it was they'd spent a year trying to achieve. I wonder sometimes if vengeance is ever satisfying. I discuss it with Leo all the time. Every visit to prison, it seems we talk about it.

"He maintains that what he did that day in Denver wasn't vengeance. He says it was simply an act of self-respect. In his mind, he did what he had to do as a father. That was all."

"And you, Naomi, what do you think?"

"Leo? He's kidding himself. What he did to the rapist was vengeance, pure and simple."

"But he's satisfied? You just said that you wonder if vengeance is ever satisfying."

"Leo's in prison, for God's sake. He'll rationalize anything to survive that. You would, too. Don't feign ignorance, Doctor; it's not becoming." She flipped her hair off her collar with the fingers of her left hand.

As Naomi's admonition filled the space between us like a bad odor fills an elevator, it finally struck me that she and I had not spoken a single word about the bomb squad's arrival at Royal Peterson's house. We were talking about something else: high school slaughter and an imprisoned husband and father and teenage boys with enough vitriol expanding in their veins to explode their spleens.

I stifled a relieved sigh, not unaware of the irony.

"What?" she demanded.

"You didn't actually answer my question earlier. About your reaction to Royal Peterson's murder."

"You were asking me how I feel about not feeling

anything? It's a preposterous question."

I cautioned myself to portray more patience than I was feeling. "What I'm wondering is . . . how you understand . . . your reaction."

Naomi crossed her legs. The toe of the dangling foot rotated side to side as though she were extinguishing an imaginary cigarette. "Don't talk to me like I'm an idiot. What I'm wondering is why I'm sitting here with you. If I understood my reaction to Roy Peterson's murder, why on earth would I put myself through this? You think sitting here with you is fun?"

Fun? No. How about rewarding, at least. Therapeutic, maybe? I suspected she wasn't done. I waited.

Suddenly, her eyes moistened and I thought she might be near tears. My immediate reaction was to consider the possibility that the sorrow I was witnessing was an act. I cautioned myself to be receptive to the possibility that the emotion was sincere. She leaned over and tugged a tissue from the box on the table by the sofa. The gesture was abrupt and fierce, as though she feared someone might be holding on to the other end of the tissue and she was determined to have it.

She said, "God. I don't want to be this way with you."

"What way?"

"This way. Exasperated. Critical. It's how I am at work. It's how I am at home. I criticized the mailman today for putting two rubber bands around the bundle of mail when one would do fine. What's that about? All the time, I'm irritable, I'm critical . . . I'm bitchy. I swear it's my hormones."

"You know, you have been under a little bit of stress, Naomi." I'd intended the comment to sound slightly sarcastic; Naomi's gentle laughter convinced me that I'd hit my mark.

"Yeah, I guess I have," she said.

From those hopeful words of conciliation my worst fears began to materialize. For the rest of the session I followed Naomi as she led me down the rocky path that took us back into the world of peri-menopause.

My kingdom, I prayed, *for some estrogen.*

I usually had no trouble generating empathy for the plight of women struggling with the assault of unbalanced hormones. But these circumstances were anything but usual. My impulse was to insist that Naomi prioritize. And insist that her number one priority should be helping me figure out what the hell Ramp and Paul were up to.

Any relief I might have been feeling that my patient hadn't mentioned the discovery of an explosive device in Royal's home was simmering away in front of my eyes. Now that I knew that a bomb had indeed been stashed in the house, I needed to discuss it with Naomi, whether she brought it up or not.

I batted the issue back and forth, back and forth, as Naomi tried to numb me with tales of mood changes, body temperature regulation problems, and menstrual irregularities. At one point she said, "And don't even ask me what this has done to my sex life."

I didn't ask. Her husband was in prison. I assumed that fact alone should have greatly impeded her sex life. In my mind, Naomi and I didn't have ten minutes to waste, and I figured any expansive gripes about her sex life could easily devour ten whole sessions.

Nor did I ever decide what to do about Ramp and Paul and the wouldn't-it-be-cool games.

Just peri-menopause.

When our time was up, Naomi and I found a time to meet on the following Monday. She composed herself enough to say thank you. I was surprised to discover that I felt that her sentiment was sincere. As she stood to leave, she picked up her big bag and performed whatever sleight of hand she did to produce her pack of cigarettes, and then she started toward the door to my office.

Halfway there she paused and pivoted on one foot to face me. "By the way," she said. "Did you hear the news this morning? About that bomb?"

By the time I was ready to stammer out a reply, she was out the door.

CHAPTER

16

The neighborhood around South Dahlia Street in Denver is an urban oasis, sequestered in relative privacy between the suburb-mimicking big-box sprawl of University Hills Shopping Center and the always-congested multilane ribbons of concrete that comprise Interstate 25, which bisects southeast Denver like a bypass scar on a cardiac patient. Unlike Washington Park, Highland, University Park, and a dozen other old Denver neighborhoods, the area hugging South Dahlia Street had somehow escaped the infectious gentrification that accompanied Colorado's recent high-tech firestorm of population growth.

The block of Vassar Lane that intersected with South Dahlia from the west was lined with modest, unrenovated houses that rested on decent lots and were shaded by mature trees. The home of Brad and Debbie Levitt was an especially nondescript blond brick ranch with a detached garage, a long driveway, and a crowded grouping of linden trees near the front door.

Debbie Levitt had just returned from dropping off her two children at school and had started to turn her four-year-old Isuzu Trooper into the driveway when she thought she felt a fierce, levitating concussion somewhere below her. She was never able to confirm her suspicions about the acceleration taking place beneath her seat because her awareness of the immense force endured for only a few milliseconds before the brain structures that Debbie Levitt needed to process such simple sensory awareness disappeared in the searing flash that blew up and out through the Trooper.

Right across Vassar Lane, Rosalyn Brae was the only witness to the aftermath of the explosion, which she saw in the rearview mirror of her two-month-old Honda Odyssey. Rosalyn had just strapped her toddler into his child seat and was preparing to back out of her garage to take him to preschool when she felt the force of the explosion as shock waves from the disintegrating Trooper rocked her car. The roar assaulted her ears, the concussion shook her bones, and she looked up at the mirror in time to see metal and plastic flying through the air, a billowing cloud of profuse smoke, and, seconds later, a wall of searing flame.

When she'd recovered from her initial shock, Rosalyn could hear her son screaming from the backseat. She hit the switch that closed her garage door before she grabbed her son from his car seat, and she ran inside to call 911.

She told the emergency dispatcher that something terrible had happened to Debbie Levitt across the street but she didn't know what. The dispatcher pressed her for details.

Rosalyn sobbed, "Her car! Her car! It, it . . . Oh my God!"

"What's wrong with her car, ma'am? Has there been an accident?"

"No, no, it's like—oh God—it's just gone. The noise was so loud."

"The car was stolen?"

"No, no, it's . . . it's still there. But there's a fire. It's on fire."

"A fire? Her car's on fire? Okay, the fire department is on its way, ma'am. Was anyone hurt in the fire?"

"I suppose, I mean, I guess she was driving the car, right? I didn't see her . . . but I guess she was driving. It's still burning. I can see it from where I'm standing right now."

"The fire department is on the way, ma'am. As we speak, they're on their way. Are you close to the car, ma'am? The one that's on fire? Because I would like you to step back."

Rosalyn Brae took two steps back and bumped into her kitchen table.

"Now, you think Debbie Levitt—is that her name?— was driving when the car caught on fire? I'll send the paramedics for her. But you hold on, okay? Keep talking with me, stay on the line until someone gets there."

Rosalyn Brae had a sudden insight and told the dispatcher that she knew what it was that had happened: She thought maybe her neighbor's car had been hit by a meteor.

Two days later, when the audio clips of the 911 call hit the local news, Rosalyn Brae was appropriately humiliated.

By Friday noon, the Denver Police had a pretty good portrait of the victim of the car explosion.

Debbie Levitt was a thirty-one-year-old mother of two. She was someone who introduced herself to strangers as "a wife and mother." But the cops soon learned that, in addition to running her household, Debbie worked part time at The Bookies, a children's bookstore a few miles from her house, volunteered at the Barbara Davis Center for Childhood Diabetes at the University of Colorado Health Sciences Center, ran a Girl Scout troop, and coached her older daughter's soccer team. She also coordinated her local Neighborhood Watch program.

Almost everyone whom the police talked to commented about Debbie's size. She was "a whisper of a woman" according to one neighbor. "Four foot ten, ninety pounds, but as big as a redwood," was how the woman who owned the bookstore where she worked described her.

The thought that Debbie Levitt might have had an enemy who was angry enough to blow up her car was absolutely absurd to every single person interviewed by the Denver Police.

Debbie's husband, Brad, the manager of a retail store in Larimer Square, volunteered to allow the police to search the Levitt home and eagerly provided the family financial records to investigators. By midday police detectives had largely ruled out a drug connection or financial retribution as possible motives for the explosion.

Brad Levitt picked up his two children about an hour before school let out that afternoon. He drove them to his parents' house on the Seventeenth Avenue Parkway in Park Hill. That's where he told the children what had happened to their mother.

CHAPTER

17

Sam Purdy and I hadn't had a chance to talk since I'd left him orchestrating the arrival of the emergency response team at the Peterson home that morning.

I'd called him Friday afternoon after Naomi had departed my office and left him a voice mail asking if he'd meet me after work. He called back and left a message that he'd meet me after he got home from the Avalanche playoff game in Denver, but that he had something he'd promised to do for his wife. He said he'd page me when he got back to Boulder.

When **I** left home around ten-fifteen and drove toward the King Soopers on Thirtieth Street, Lauren and Grace were both sound asleep.

I spotted Sam over in the produce department. He already had a cart in front of him. It took me three tries to find a cart without a wobbling or stuck wheel. Part of my general karma in life is that I don't have good luck with shopping carts. The wheels all worked on the one I ended up with, but it had something brown and sticky plastered all over the plastic flap that covered the leg holes of the little child seat.

I didn't want to know.

I walked over to join Sam. He was sniffing cantaloupes and tapping the ends of them as though the aromas and echoes told him something important. I said, "Isn't worth buying them before the Texas crop comes in at the beginning of May, Sam." I pointed at the big pile in front of him. "Those are the early season melons from Southern California."

He didn't look up. "Actually, isn't worth buying any of 'em before the Rocky Fords show up at the end of the summer. Now, those Rocky Fords," he said, pausing for emphasis, ". . . now *those* are melons."

A few feet away from us, a tall young woman, her brown hair piled haphazardly on her head, was busy selecting strawberries. As soon as Sam finished speaking, she turned toward him and smiled, her shoulders retreating and her posture straightening just the slightest bit.

Sam Purdy didn't appreciate the irony. I didn't think he'd even noticed the woman's flirtation. He certainly didn't appreciate the fact that in Boulder—after his comment about the melons—she was three times as likely to have hit him over the head with a pineapple as she was to smile at him.

"I didn't want to say anything this morning, but you really look like shit," I told him.

"Avs lost tonight. Sloppy play behind the goal. They gave up two power play goals. Two. There's no excuse for that, none, not in the playoffs. I ever tell you that I hate turnovers?"

"Pastry? You hate those kinds of turnovers?"

He shook his head at me and stepped away from the cantaloupes. "What about kiwis? I like the way they taste but I've never figured out how to get the damn fuzzy stuff off without throwing away half the fruit. How do you do that?"

"You've lost weight, Sam."

"You gonna buy anything or you just gonna yap?"

"I think I'm just gonna yap," I said.

"I don't know why I agreed to do the grocery shopping again. I hate it. Sherry said it would be a growth experience for me. All I'm growing is another hemorrhoid. I keep thinking maybe I shouldn't be a cop in Boulder at all. I should be a cop in some real town where men don't meet their friends on Friday night to do the grocery shopping."

I laughed. "King Soopers is where the girls are, Sam."

"The single ones, yeah. In Boulder, the married ones all send their husbands. This is probably the place where half of the extramarital affairs start in Boulder. I swear we live in a city of wusses. You ever notice that?" He fingered his list, moving his reading glasses down from the top of his head so he could have a prayer of reading the scrap of paper. "Sherry said I should ask you about garlic. She said you'd know how to pick out garlic. I can't believe I have a friend who can't bait a hook but knows how to pick a bunch of garlic."

I couldn't bait a hook. Not a prayer. "A head of garlic, Sam. But that's not important."

"You got that right."

I led him over toward the onions and garlic.

He fumbled with a plastic bag, but his fat fingers couldn't quite get it open. He said, "In case you're wondering, I don't really want to know about garlic. Don't even think about lecturing me about garlic. Just pick one."

"You've lost weight," I said for the second time. "Are you worried about Lucy? Or is something else going on?"

He tried to separate the folds of the bag with his teeth. "You heard the details about the device we recovered at the Peterson home?" he mumbled.

I'd been waiting patiently for him to get around to it. I said, "I heard what's on the news, that's all."

"It was a pipe bomb, rigged to a radio controller. Just needed a signal and it would have gone off."

"Jesus."

"Nothing fancy about it, apparently. X-ray didn't show any booby traps. Guy who made it wasn't trying to hurt anybody who found it."

"How did they disarm it? Did they take it out of the house and put it in that little round trailer you always see on the news?"

He shook his head in disdain at my ignorance. "The little trailer is called a total containment vehicle, and no, they didn't use it. In situations like that they use a robot with a disruptor on it. Blows the thing apart with water. It's like a little water cannon. That way nobody actually has to get close to the device."

"That's it? Couldn't doing that make the bomb go off?"

"There's a risk of sympathetic detonation but it's more theoretical than real. I've never seen it happen."

"How do you know all this?"

Sam ignored me, instead asking, "You done with your questions? Because my supervisors in the department are curious how I knew that there was a bomb in the house."

"First, tell me how you know so much about the bomb squad."

"I took an FBI course. Now, how did you know it was there?"

"What did you tell your supervisors?"

"I told them I got an anonymous tip."

"They believed you?"

He shrugged. "What are they gonna do?"

"How does this all bode for Lucy?"

We'd moved from the produce department to the back of the store. "Is there a right way to do this?" Sam asked. "Should I go all the way across the back and then do each aisle? Or should I just go up and down each aisle and see a little bit of the dairy case each time? How do housewives do this? It seems to me I should do the freezer part last. That makes sense."

"You're free to improvise."

He made a noise. "Don't know if anyone told you but Lucy's prints are on that ceramic thing. The one that was used to bash Royal in the face? We found it in pieces all over the floor in the living room."

"Lauren told me a few hours ago. When I was in the house this morning with Dorsey and Shadow I saw a collection of fancy ceramics downstairs in Royal's office. There was one space empty on the shelves. I was thinking that that's where it came from."

"We reached the same conclusion. Somebody grabbed it downstairs, carried it upstairs to whack Royal."

"Anybody else's fingerprints on the ceramic?"

"Roy's and Susan's."

"The fact that her fingerprints are on it isn't good news for Lucy. But . . . I thought the murder weapon was the brass lamp."

"The coup de grace was from the lamp, yes. Current theory is that the initial blow was from the ceramic thing."

"And Lucy's prints aren't on the lamp?"

"No. Just some partials from Susan and the woman who comes in to help her with the cleaning. That's it. The theory to explain that little discrepancy is that Lucy wiped it where she touched it. She couldn't wipe the ceramic because it was busted all over the floor."

"And now your colleagues are working under the assumption that Lucy planted the bomb we found?"

"Current theory is yes. They searched her place and her car again this afternoon, looking for evidence from the bomb or residue from the explosive. That's something they didn't cover with the initial search warrant. The thinking goes that she planted the bomb, and Peterson discovered her doing it, confronted her. She picked up the ceramic whatever, climbed the stairs, and bashed him in the head with it."

"Why didn't she just use her gun? Shoot him or hit him with it?"

Sam gave me a disgusted look. "Don't go there. She didn't do it. The reason she didn't choose her weapons carefully is because she didn't choose her weapons at all. It's simple."

I knew about the second search warrant at Lucy's place, of course. Lauren and I had discussed some of the day's events at dinner a few hours before. "They find anything at today's search?"

"I don't know yet. God, I told you—of course not. She didn't do it." He waved at the case in front of us. "Are all these eggs the same? Does it make any frigging difference which box of frigging eggs I choose? Never mind, don't answer that."

I pretended to be interested in the fat content of Philadelphia cream cheese as I said, "I'm sure you heard about the explosion in Denver this morning." This was the real reason I'd agreed to meet Sam at the grocery store so late on Friday evening. I wanted to know what he could tell me about the car bomb that I'd heard about from Naomi Bigg and later, on the news.

"Sure. That woman was killed when her car blew up." Sam was still distracted by the eggs. "Denver," he added, shaking his head.

The tone implied that, as far as random explosions went, Denver belonged in the same category as Beirut or Sarajevo or Belfast.

I asked him, "You think it's just a coincidence that a car exploded the same day we found a device in the Petersons' house?"

Sam rolled his eyes, tugged a cell phone from the back pocket of his jeans, and scrolled through the memory until he found the number he wanted. While he was dialing, he said, "The ATF people are way ahead of you. They've been trying all day to see if there's any evidence the two devices were made by the same person. Chemistry takes some time." A few seconds later, he said, "Walter? Sam Purdy in Boulder. How you doing?"

I couldn't tell how Walter was doing, but describing his condition to Sam took quite a bit of time. Sam spent the time examining a rack that displayed single servings of highly processed cheese spread that was packaged with a wide variety of crackers and pretzels. There were some cookies packaged with globs of white goo that looked like frosting, as well. Finally Sam asked Walter what the Denver Police knew about the car explosion earlier that day. Sam apparently wasn't pleased with Walter's response, which caused Sam to remind Walter that Sam was the one who had located the radio-controlled explosive device in Royal Peterson's home that morning.

As I attempted to eavesdrop, I watched the woman with the strawberries from the produce department choose between vanilla and plain soymilk. In her cart she also had a big bag of Cheetos and some Häagen Dazs.

I tried to guess the parameters of her diet. Couldn't. But I guessed that she would go for the vanilla. She did.

Sam flipped his phone closed. "It was definitely a car bomb. They just got a read on the explosive an hour ago. As I said, ATF's involved. They're still filtering debris to try to identify what kind of initiator or timer was used. By the way, the explosive is totally different from what we found in the device in Royal's home this morning. Walter thinks they'll know something specific about the initiator in the Denver bomb the next day or so."

"Motive?"

"Walter says they're not there yet."

"Who's Walter?"

"Somebody I know."

"He's on the Denver Police Department?"

"He's somebody I know. That's all. And his name's not really Walter."

"Really? But you call him Walter? Who is he?"

"Tell me who tipped you off about the bomb in Royal's house and I'll tell you who Walter is. But I won't tell you his real name."

"You know I can't do that."

"It's a patient, isn't it? One of your patients knew that there was a bomb in Royal's house? You know something that will help Lucy and you keep it from me, I swear I'll find a way—"

"You know I can't tell you anything about my patients. Tell me who Walter is or I'm not going to teach you anything else about groceries."

"Promise?"

We walked down the pet food aisle. Sam was perusing the dog treats even though he and Sherry and Simon didn't have any pets. I asked, "Why isn't Lucy in jail? It sure sounds to me as though your colleagues have probable cause."

He pulled a little ball of tissue from his pocket, unfolded it the best he could, and blew his nose. After he stuffed the tissue back into his pocket, he rubbed his eyes with his knuckles before he replied. "Jeez, do you have allergies? What a pain. It's the only thing I don't like about springtime, the only thing. To answer your question: There're a bunch of reasons Lucy hasn't been picked up. One, in Boulder we have a rather well-known history of crossing every *t* and dotting every *i* before we arrest somebody, especially somebody with a high profile, and especially for a high-profile felony. Two, Lucy's no flight risk. Three, the prosecutors don't want to have to deal with Cozy and Lauren about discovery yet, and if we arrest Lucy then they have to start turning stuff over, and four—the real home-run reason—is that nobody has a clue about motive yet. They'd like to have at least a clue about her motive before they lock up a cop for murder. Especially a pretty, blond cop. PR, you know."

He'd let go of the handle of his cart. I pulled it behind me as I continued down the aisle; I still had hopes of finishing the grocery shopping by midnight. Sam trailed absently behind the cart. He was looking for something.

While I waited to find out what, I asked, "Why was Lucy at the Peterson house that night? Has she told you?"

He waved at the incredible variety of dog treats on the upper shelves. "Do your dogs like this crap?"

"Emily will eat anything. Anvil doesn't eat anything. Answer my question about Lucy."

"That little dog is a weird dog. I like him, but he's a weird dog."

"I'm glad you like him, Sam," I said. I didn't argue; Anvil was a weird dog. I loved him anyway.

"I'm in an awkward place here, Alan. I don't mind telling you what I know, but if you go and tell Lauren and Cozy, then the people who are willing to talk to me so far won't be willing to talk to me anymore. Does that make sense? If Lucy gets charged, Cozy and Lauren will get all the investigators' reports. So everybody just needs to be patient."

"I won't tell them anything, Sam."

He stared at me with rheumy eyes. "Okay. I don't know why Lucy was at Royal's house that night. When Susan Peterson was interviewed by our detectives, she confirmed that a female cop had visited Royal 'numerous times' in the past, but she maintains she never met the woman, says she was always upstairs in bed during the visits. Susan figured the woman who was stopping by had something to do with the prosecutor's office, a case Royal was working on, or something like that."

"Susan's sure it was a cop, not a DA?"

"That's what she says."

"Does Susan have a name for the cop?"

"No. Royal never told her or she doesn't remember. Susan says the voice she heard downstairs was female. That's all she knows."

"But she thinks it was the same cop each time?"

"Yeah."

"Multiple visits?"

"Yeah."

"Lucy never mentioned Royal to you, Sam?"

"Not once that I can remember. Not even casually. That's what's so goofy. But she's private, always has been."

I said, "She suggested to me that the reason she was there that night has to do with something she's really ashamed of."

Sam stopped and grabbed his cart back from me. "She said that to you? Recently?"

I nodded.

He checked all around him for the presence of other

shoppers, lowered his voice to a whisper, and said, "You think Lucy was sleeping with Royal? Is that what she was saying?"

I could tell how distasteful the thought was to Sam. I could also tell that this wasn't the first time in the past couple of days that the thought had crossed his mind. I said, "I don't know. She was just talking about things she was ashamed about. Said one of them had to do with the reason she was at Royal's house that night."

"She's engaged, you know," Sam said. "Just got engaged. Wouldn't wear a ring, though, wanted to keep it private."

"She told me that, too. You know the guy?"

"She's talked about him some, but I've never met him." Sam was exceeding the grocery store speed limit now, not even pausing to see whether the shelves he was passing had anything at all to do with the items Sherry had penciled on his grocery list. I caught up with him only because an elderly man was blocking the aisle with his cart while he tried to retrieve a can of guava juice from the top shelf. I helped the man get the can of juice down and he pushed his cart away. I think Sam's driving was scaring him.

Sam argued, "She couldn't have been screwing Peterson. If Lucy loves her fiancé enough to marry him, why would she be having an affair with Royal?"

"We don't know that she was having an affair, Sam. But people do strange things."

"Royal has a reputation. But Lucy?" he muttered. "I

don't get it. She's too smart to get involved with somebody like Royal."

"She was obviously involved with him somehow. She
was at his house, right? People don't always do what's
smart."

"Tell me about it."

I guided him to a stop in front of the condiments
and picked out some ketchup. Sam was shaking his
head.

He said, "Don't get that kind. It's runny."

"You're giving me grocery advice?"

"Believe it or not, I know about some things. If it
goes on hot dogs or bratwurst, I know about it."

I wasn't ready to digress into discussing meat on
buns. "What kind of reputation did Royal Peterson
have, Sam? Indefatigable crime fighter? Justice super-
hero?"

Sam laughed before he said, "Cad."

I raised my eyebrows. "Cad?" I wasn't questioning
the concept, just Sam's choice of descriptors.

"It means he screwed around. I think it's a British
thing."

"Screwing around is a British thing?" I said.

Sam hit me on the arm. It hurt.

"You know what I mean."

He waited until I looked up and nodded before he
spoke again. "It's my nature to chew on you about what
you don't tell me, you know that. That doesn't mean
that I'm not grateful for what you do tell me. I'm
guessing that the tip you gave me about the explosive

means you crossed a line that you're not real comfortable crossing. Finding the bomb in Royal's basement will complicate the case against Lucy. I'm grateful to you for that. But"—he smiled in a way that made both of his lips disappear up into his mustache—"I'm not done trying to get you to tell me what else you know. It doesn't stop here, Alan. Friend or no friend, it doesn't stop here."

Ramp flipped among the Denver news channels about a hundred times between the hours of four and six-thirty Friday afternoon. The only breaks he took from thumbing the remote control were to check his computer to see if any of the TV stations had updated their Web sites with fresh information about the explosion in Denver's Dahlia neighborhood.

Two mistakes in one job.

Ramp couldn't figure out what had gone wrong.

When the local news programs were over, he retrieved a Zip disc from its hiding place in a hollowed-out section of the trim that skirted the floor around the perimeter of his small apartment.

He inserted the disc into his computer and retrieved a Microsoft Word document he'd labeled Log 7.

He didn't really need to see the written record; Ramp could have recited the data that was recorded in

Log 7 from memory. But he checked the log anyway. It took him no more than five minutes to review the details of the series of trials he had done at the ranch near Limon.

The device had worked properly all four times that he'd tested it.

All four.

"So what went wrong with number five?" he said out loud. "And why was she driving his car?"

He called Boulder.

"It's me," he said when his call was answered. "You saw the news?"

While he listened to the answer to his question, Ramp stood and moved back to his computer. He linked to the KCNC Web site. It hadn't been updated. He clicked over to KUSA and then to KMGH. Nothing had been added to either site.

You call this news?

Ramp tried to keep the irritation out of his voice when he spoke out loud again. "Like I told you, I followed him twice before I placed it. Both times he was in that car. It was definitely the car he drives to work. I don't know why she was driving it this morning. Bad luck for her is all I can say. I don't feel bad I got her. I only feel bad that I didn't get him and that the message was lost. I'll have to make up for it."

He tucked the phone between his shoulder and his ear as he removed the Zip disc from the drive and tucked it back into its hiding place in the floorboard trim. The trim slid back into place like a hand into a glove.

He shook his head as he said, "No, it was almost all solid state. It shouldn't have shorted. I don't think that's it. I'm thinking it was a rogue radio signal that set it off. The odds are astronomical that another device would be on that frequency in that vicinity, but that's all I can come up with. I've been glued to the news all afternoon. It doesn't look like the police understand the target. And the ATF will waste some time piecing together the device. I'm thinking we're okay. What about the thing at your end? Any fallout from them discovering the bomb in that guy's house?"

Out the front window, Ramp watched a white Denver Police cruiser crawl slowly down the road in front of his Pennsylvania Street apartment. He tracked it with his eyes as it moved south and turned the corner.

"Yeah, I think so, too. Finding the device in Boulder won't point to us at all. I think we're still on track. My guess is that we've had as much bad luck as we're going to get. I say that we both go ahead with tonight's work. You agree? . . . That's right, we should keep the faith."

Ramp pressed the button disconnecting the call. To no one in particular, he said, "Wouldn't it be cool?"

In this phase, Ramp had one more device to place. The schedule called for him to install it that night.

He decided not to alter his plans.

CHAPTER

19

Saturday morning brought Lauren, Grace, and me back to our weekend routine. We left the house early, met our friends Diane and Raoul for breakfast, and did the usual round of errands on North Broadway. During breakfast I tried to maintain a conversation with Raoul, pretending I gave a whit about his newfound passion for fly-fishing while I was simultaneously eavesdropping as Lauren responded to a question about her health from Diane. Raoul was rambling about feathers and string and tying flies; Lauren was saying that she was in less pain and that her brain mud had eased, but that her vertigo was still giving her fits, and, fearing that she might fall, she wouldn't carry Grace more than a few feet. Lauren usually didn't go into such detail about her health with friends.

Or with husbands, for that matter.

When I said "Yes" in answer to a question I didn't really hear from Raoul, he seemed pleased. He said, "Diane didn't think you'd come with me. I told her I thought you would."

I was afraid I'd just agreed to go fly-fishing.

Although April had been warmer and dryer than usual along the Front Range, the weatherpeople were predicting the midday arrival of a cold front from the north preceded by strong winds. It turned out that the meteorologists were wrong by at least a couple of hours. As we were driving home from our errands the winds began to sluice down from Cheyenne with a force that would cause alarm in most places on the North American continent. But not in Boulder. Winds in the fifty- to one-hundred-miles-an-hour range were frequent events in the winter and spring seasons. Only in the upper reaches of the range did the populace seek shelter. In the moderate, fifty- to seventy-five-miles-an-hour range, the primary impact of the winds was inconvenience.

Lauren and I agreed that although these gusts were no stronger than sixty miles an hour, my hopes for a late-morning bicycle ride were shot. As I pulled the car into the garage, Lauren suggested a trip up the turnpike to Flatiron Crossing to buy Grace her first pair of shoes.

"They sell baby shoes in Boulder, don't they?" I asked naively.

"I'd rather go to Flatirons," she replied. Lauren, like many Boulderites, said "Flatirons," not "Flatiron," when referring to the new mall, intentionally refuting all efforts of the huge facility's marketing people to modify the local vernacular. "I want to check out Nordstrom's baby department."

As we entered the house, I was still struggling mightily to find a reason not to go to a suburban shopping mall on a windy weekend morning when everyone else in Boulder County would be looking for an indoor haven to escape the gales. I was actually considering offering to clean the garage when I heard the telephone ringing as we walked in the door.

"I'll get it," I said.

"You're too eager," Lauren said. "If you don't want to go to the Mall, just say so."

I didn't want to go to the Mall. But what I said was "Hello."

"Alan, Sam. Something's come up about Lucy and the bombs. Can you meet me?"

"Now?" I tried to keep the glee out of my voice.

"Yeah, now."

"Sure, where?"

During my drive back downtown to meet Sam, I counted three resounding whacks as the wind lifted rocks and launched them into my windshield. It was one of the reliable melodies of springtime in the Rockies.

The only problem with Sam's plan was that at ten-thirty on Saturday morning the restaurant where we were supposed to meet, the Fourteenth Street Grill on the eastern end of the outdoor Downtown Mall, was closed. I stood for a minute cursing my friend, and had just pulled my cell phone from my pocket to call him when I heard a silky smooth, slightly husky "Thanks for coming."

The voice had no trace of Sam's Minnesota Iron Range accent.

I turned and found myself looking directly into Lucy Tanner's amber eyes. With whatever she was wearing on her feet, she was almost exactly my height. "Lucy," I said, "what a surprise."

"I thought if I called, you'd refuse to meet me, or you'd argue with me or something. Sam said he loved to play around with your head, and he volunteered to make the call."

I was wondering why she thought I would be so resistant to talking with her, when a gust of wind strong enough to cause us both to lean erupted from the north. "Want to get in my car?" I asked. "It's right across the street."

"How about we go someplace and sit down. There's a juice place a couple of doors down from here—it's kind of funky—and there's a Starbucks around the corner. You choose, Alan."

I noted that she hadn't included The Cheesecake Factory, which was right across the street, on her list of possible destinations. I did recall that the Starbucks near the east end of the Mall was the one where Paul Bigg was a barista.

"Starbucks," I said. I hoped there would be someone named Paul behind the counter. I wanted to see if Paul Bigg fit my mental image of the Boulder adolescent Starbucks tender.

Lucy hooked her arm in mine and led me down Pearl Street. Before we made it into the canyon created by the buildings, the wind almost lifted us off our feet. In between gusts, she said, "I'd like a seat that lets me sit with my back to the room, okay? People have been recognizing me."

I led Lucy to a table by the fireplace. She chose the chair facing the wall. "What can I get you?" I asked.

"Chai."

Sometimes I thought I was the last person in Boulder to taste chai—or, considering that Sam Purdy lived in Boulder, too, maybe the second to last. So, although I had no real interest in buying one for myself, I was intrigued at the prospect of at least getting to order one and watch it made. But I was disappointed to see that the baristas at the counter were both young women. One pierced eyebrow and three visible tattoos between the two of them. Impossibly filthy green aprons. No Paul Bigg in sight.

Chai looked to me to be a lot like hot tea and milk. The menu mentioned spices, too. I withheld judgment.

After I paid, I returned to the table with our drinks. Lucy was staring at her hands. Her fingers were long but her nails were trimmed short, and if they were polished, the polish was clear. She looked up and mouthed, "Thank you."

"Why did you think I'd be reluctant to meet with you?" I asked.

She glanced at the occupants of the adjacent tables and leaned into the space between us before she answered. "Sam told me that you were the one who knew about the bomb at Royal's house."

I said, "Shit."

"That's why I thought you'd be reluctant to meet with me."

I shook my head to express my disappointment with Sam. "He shouldn't have told you."

She sat back, narrowed her eyes a little, and she shrugged. "That's one point of view."

"It's mine," I said.

"Is it? You made a decision to tell Sam about the explosives. Are you suggesting that telling one person is okay, but telling two people makes you unprofessional? Sorry, I'm not sure it's a point of view that you can easily defend."

She was right, of course. Pushing Humpty-Dumpty off the wall a second time doesn't make a whole lot of difference to Humpty. It's the first plop that does the irrevocable damage.

"As you can probably guess, Lucy, I can't talk to you about how I suspected that there might be explosives."

Without hesitation she said, "I can help you."

I was taken aback. I expected Lucy to ask for my

assistance, not the other way around. "What do you mean? How can you help me?"

"Sam thinks you've painted yourself into a corner. You know something you'd rather not know. But he says you're someone who can't walk away from what you know. He called it a 'character defect,' by the way." She smiled at me and sipped some of her milky tea. "But he also knows that your problem and my problem may be able to be resolved simultaneously."

"Go ahead."

She lowered her voice to a bedroom whisper. "Whoever planted that bomb probably killed Royal, right?"

"It's likely," I acknowledged.

"I don't think you know who that is. Sam doesn't either. He says you wouldn't leave somebody like that on the street. To me that means only one thing: that you know somebody who may know who planted that bomb. Well, I can help you find the bomber. That's how I can help. Don't forget, I'm a detective, Alan, and right now I have lots and lots of free time on my hands."

"It won't work, Lucy. For you to help me, I'd have to tell you things that I'm not permitted to tell you."

She was prepared for my argument. "And if you don't tell me? Are you ready to live with the consequences of that? People who build explosives don't usually build just one and stop. So what if the one at Royal's house isn't the only bomb? What about that? And what about my situation? Are you ready to sit back and watch me go to jail? Cozy thinks that I'll be arrested within the week."

I didn't answer.

Lucy sat back on her chair and said, "I think you're going to let me help you. Want to know why that is?"

"Sure."

"Because, besides Sam, you're the only one who doesn't look at me like they're wondering whether or not I really did it. Even Cozy's not convinced I didn't kill Royal. Your wife—she's very sweet, Alan—but she's not sure about me, either. I can tell. But you seem to be confident that I didn't do it. And that's why I think you're going to let me help you."

I shifted my gaze outside. A plastic trash can was whistling down the Mall, doing, I guessed, about thirty. Way over the speed limit for rubbish containers.

My espresso cup was empty. I tilted it up to my lips anyway and pondered ordering myself a chai. I said, "Let's go someplace else, Lucy. We shouldn't be talking about this here."

CHAPTER

20

Lucy's place wasn't an option. The media was keeping too close an eye on it. My house wasn't an option, either. Neither Lucy nor I wanted Lauren, and therefore Cozy, to know what we were up to.

We were loitering outside Starbucks trying on alternatives when Lucy said, "We could go to Sam's house."

I considered it. "We shouldn't involve him, Lucy. His position is awkward enough as it is."

"You're right. Can we go to your office?"

"I guess that's okay. You know where it is?" She nodded. I'd forgotten that she'd responded to an emergency there with Sam years before. "There's a back door that opens onto the yard. Why don't you come in that way?"

She shifted her blond hair from her face, held it back with one hand, and smiled at me. "How about . . . I'll park my car around the corner and then I'll come in through the yard, and then come in the back door." She laughed. "That's always kept me out of trouble in the past."

I was impressed by her ability to find irony in her situation.

Lucy and I would be alone at my office. Diane Estevez, my friend and partner, was as likely to be working on Saturday as Boulder was to establish a sister-city relationship with Colorado Springs.

I drove the half-dozen blocks to Walnut Street and parked in back as I always did. I let myself in the French door that opened onto the yard, quieted the alarm system, and waited for Lucy to arrive.

She tapped on one of the glass panels a few minutes later.

"Nice," she said, looking at my office as though she were seeing it for the first time.

"Have a seat, Lucy. I can heat some water for tea, if you'd like. No chai here, I'm afraid."

"No, thank you, I've had enough." She touched the chair. "Is this where your patients sit?"

"There or on the couch."

Lucy was wearing a suede jacket. She took a moment to remove it and lay it on the sofa. Beneath it she was wearing a blue pinstripe shirt that was open halfway to her navel. Beneath that was a thin cotton something.

"Where do we start?" she asked.

"I don't know. I should tell you I'm not comfortable with the position I'm in right now, Lucy."

"I can appreciate that, Alan. I'm not totally comfortable with the position I'm in right now, either."

"Some people—maybe most people—would argue that what I'm about to do is highly unethical."

She sat erect, her hands on her knees. The tendons in her neck had stark definition. For the first time that morning, I got the impression that I was talking with a cop. She said, "Something I've learned working with Sam for so many years is that ethical codes should be written in pencil. Frequently they need revising. When people find new ways to be crooked, that's when it's time to rewrite the rulebook."

The thought sounded like Sam's. The translation was definitely Lucy's. "Maybe that's true, but I've never considered it my job to be the one to do those revisions. I've always been most comfortable with the guidelines that I could read in a book that's already been written."

"But somebody has to rewrite the book. I suspect that none of the authors ever really volunteered. In situations like the one you and I are in, fate determines the authors. Given the predicament, I think you'd have to agree that I'm the lesser of two evils. I'm going to be more discreet with whatever information you give me than the police would be if you called them."

"Lucy, you are the police."

"You know what I mean."

"I've considered going to the police, you know," I said. "Just telling them what I suspect. But realistically, what could they do? Sam might humor me. Maybe he'd go talk to some people. But the people would deny any involvement and say I'm absolutely crazy. I know they would. Nothing would be gained and my professional life would be over for violating confidentiality. That's the only thing that's for sure."

"There are worse things than your professional life being over. Trust me, I know."

I was trying hard not to view Lucy as a cop who was pressuring me to reveal privileged information. "I know that, Lucy. On Friday, I rationalized telling Sam to go look for a bomb at Royal's house. It was highly unlikely that anyone could ever trace that information back to one of my patients. But no matter what I do, I can't think of a way to rationalize what I'm about to tell you."

"Other than that it's the right thing to do?"

"Yeah, other than that." I sighed and said, "There's a guy named Ramp. He lives in Denver. I think he's the key to all of this."

"Ramp? R-a-m-p? Is that what you said?"

"I think that's the spelling. But I don't really know. My experience is that my patients tend to get suspicious when I press them about spelling."

Lucy flashed a grin. "Is that a first name or a last name?"

"Don't know that either."

"What do you know about him?"

"Not much. He's around twenty-one or so, give or take a few years. Like I said, he lives in Denver—city or metro, I don't know—and he's active on the

Internet. He's angry at the criminal justice system because his mother was murdered by somebody who was on probation after an earlier homicide conviction. He apparently talks openly about seeking revenge. He likes explosives. He occasionally hangs out with a high school kid here in Boulder who he met on the Net. The local kid's in a similar situation: feels screwed by the criminal justice system and has all kinds of fantasies about getting even."

"Name of the local kid?"

I hesitated. There was no way around it; I was about to reveal the name of someone I had learned about in psychotherapy, someone whom, maybe, Lucy could track down by checking names in the phone book. "His name is Paul Bigg. He's the one who has the direct beef with Royal Peterson."

Lucy seemed to hesitate a second or two before she asked, "And what do you know about him?"

"He's a senior at Fairview. Actually, he works at that Starbucks we were at this morning, but he wasn't there. From a psychological point of view, he meets just about every one of the criteria the FBI has developed to predict violent acting out by adolescents. These two—Ramp and Paul—have apparently developed a hit list of all the people in the justice system that they feel are responsible for what happened to their families.

"They play this mind game, this 'wouldn't-it-be-cool' game." I explained the game to Lucy in more detail, focusing on the way that Ramp and Paul's game had almost predicted the presence of the bomb in the Peterson home. "Obviously, I concluded that Royal Peterson was definitely on the list of people that these two wanted to harm; that's why I told Sam to figure out a way to search his home for explosives. My problem is that I still don't know who else might be on the would-n't-it-be-cool list." I thought about what I'd just said and concluded, "Unfortunately, that's about all I've learned."

"This Paul Bigg? Is he related to Leo Bigg? That whole mess from a few years ago?"

"Yes. Were you and Sam involved in the original rape investigation? Was it your case?"

Lucy shook her head. "No. But it was one of those cases where the police totally disagreed with the DA's office about the plea. I don't mean we didn't like the plea bargain, I mean we hated it. Everyone who knew anything about the case was convinced that the evidence supported a trial on the charges, or at least a tougher plea bargain. Then when the girl's father ended up doing more time than the rapist . . . Lord. It sucked, what can I say?"

My heart rate was accelerating and my palms were sweaty. I didn't like saying any of this out loud. I forced myself to go on. "There's something else, Lucy. Lauren was involved with the Marin Bigg prosecution. She was helping Nora with the sex crimes unit back then."

Lucy recognized the implication instantly. "Oh, Alan. Oh dear. You haven't told her, have you?"

"No. I keep going back and forth on that. I'm not

sure she's on the list. I'm not sure there really is a list. Her health isn't great right now. I was hoping to learn more from my patient before I brought Lauren in on this."

"And I thought I was the one who was most vulnerable in this situation." Lucy leaned forward, closing the distance between us. She took one of my hands between both of hers. "So Nora's almost definitely on the list. And, maybe, so is Lauren. Who else do you think these two assholes might be targeting?"

"Cozy defended the rapist."

"Great. I take it you haven't said anything to him, either?"

"No. Keep in mind that I don't really know anything, Lucy. I keep weighing the damage I'll do by talking against the damage I'll do by keeping my suspicions to myself. My patient keeps alluding to the Klebolds and the Harrises. Whether they should have known what their kids were up to. Whether they should have talked to the police. That's her big issue. Deciding what her responsibility is. She wants to believe that the kids aren't really planning anything, that this is all just a big fantasy. And they haven't really made any threats that she's heard. Certainly none that I've heard."

Lucy's voice became derisive. "Of course the Klebolds and the Harrises should have known. And they should have talked to the police. There's no doubt about either of those things."

"But at what stage does someone really know enough, Lucy? At what stage do I know enough?

Remember, I still haven't heard any threats. Nothing overt. This is all conjecture."

"The bomb they found yesterday at the Peterson house wasn't conjecture. That was a real bomb, and it was real dangerous. The rest of the people on the hit list are vulnerable, Alan."

"You're right, they are. The problem is that I don't really know the identity of anyone on the list—I'm just guessing at the identity of the people these two might be targeting. I would think it's likely that the list includes the judge who approved the plea agreement. That makes sense, right, that they'd include the judge? But I don't even know who that was."

"That's easy. I'll find out."

I said, "I've given this a lot of thought and I can't think of anyone else who might be targeted in Boulder because of the Bigg case, but I may be missing someone. Ramp apparently has his own list of people who were involved in whatever the situation was with his family in Denver, or wherever it was. I know nothing about that, nothing at all. I think it was his mother's murder. But I don't know the details of the case, where it occurred, even what year it happened."

"That's something I can work on," Lucy said.

I went on. "I am suspicious that the bomb that went off in that car yesterday morning was one of Ramp's. The target doesn't make sense, though. From what I've heard on the news and read in the paper, the woman who was killed in the car bomb has no contact with the criminal justice system. She worked in a children's bookstore. Volunteered at a hospital. She coached her kid's soccer team."

"What about her husband, her family?"

"Her husband works in some store in Larimer Square. Sells some western kitsch or something. Mostly tourist crap." I stood up, walked to the window, and watched the wind whip the last of the beautiful pink flowers from the frail redbud.

"The person who's telling you all of this? Your client? Are you still in touch with that person?"

"Yes."

"So you might learn more?"

"It's possible."

"Let's hope so," Lucy said. "Let's hope so. Tell me who it is, Alan. Who's your client?"

I had a patient once, a man, who routinely visited prostitutes when he was out of town on business trips. He rationalized his trysts as being inconsequential because he never kissed the women. If he actually kissed the prostitutes, he maintained, then the contacts would have been intimate.

I thought of him as I said, "Giving you that name won't help you. I don't want to tell you the name right now. Let's just say it's someone who doesn't want to believe that what they're seeing is true."

Not telling Lucy my patient's name was my way of rationalizing my betrayal of Naomi's confidence. It was my equivalent of not kissing the whore.

Lucy joined me by the window. "What you just said about someone who doesn't want to believe what they're seeing is true? That could be any one of us. It could certainly be me. I think it could be you, too."

I didn't turn to face her. Instead I examined her reflection in the glass. "The biggest reason that I was reluctant to clue Sam in about the bomb and that I'm reluctant to tell Lauren or involve the police—or even to involve you, Lucy—is that I'm terrified that this patient of mine will figure out that I've breached her confidence and then she won't—"

"Come back to see you again."

"Exactly. Then I wouldn't have any way of knowing . . . what kind of danger Lauren might really be in."

Lucy bit her bottom lip, touched me on the shoulder, and said, "You're telling me to be careful?"

"You could say that."

"But you're not going to tell me who your patient is?"

"No."

After a moment, she nodded in resignation. "Then I'll work on discovering who this Ramp guy in Denver is. It's something. Does he use that name online?"

"I don't know."

"I'll also find out what I can about the original Bigg case. See if there are any other potential targets. Maybe somebody in the probation department did an investigation on the rapist and issued a report that the family didn't like. A social worker, someone like that, you never know."

"You never know," I agreed.

CHAPTER
21

That afternoon, while Lauren and Grace napped, I duct-taped a hand mirror to a length of PVC pipe left over from our home remodeling and used the device to check the undercarriage of both of our cars for bombs. I didn't spot anything that didn't match the rather perfect coating of gray-brown grime that was slicked beneath each vehicle, although I did discover a leak in the left front axle boot on my car that I hadn't known about.

When I went back inside the house, I phoned Sam Purdy and asked him for Dorsey's phone number. I could tell that he thought he knew why I wanted it, but he didn't say anything, he just gave it to me. In return for his graciousness, I didn't chew on him about his disclosure to Lucy.

Dorsey couldn't have been kinder when I called. She said that she and Shadow could come by and snoop around that evening around six. I told her that we'd be gone; I didn't want my wife to be home during the search. Before we hung up, I gave Dorsey directions to the house and explained where she could find a key.

When Lauren woke up from her nap, I announced I was treating my girls to an early dinner at Rhumba. Since I didn't want Adrienne wondering why a bomb-sniffing dog was snooping around my house, I invited her and Jonas to come along with us downtown for dinner.

Lauren, of course, wanted to know why I insisted on putting the dogs into the dog run instead of leaving them to roam the house, which is what we would typically do. In response to her question, I said something inane about getting the new litter of fox kits accustomed to the dogs. She looked at me funny but, to my relief, decided not to argue with me. I shushed her out the door ahead of me so that I could lock up the house without setting the burglar alarm.

All the subterfuge and anxiety had left me absolutely exhausted by the time everyone was packed into Adrienne's Suburban for the ride downtown. As she pulled her huge vehicle out onto the lane, Adrienne reminded me, gleefully, that I'd become one of those people who dragged young children along to nice restaurants and ate dinner at five-thirty on weekends.

I smiled at my baby and knew that what my friend was saying was true. Absolutely.

Dorsey had promised me that she would tie something to the front doorknob if Shadow had sensed any explosives on the property. She also said that she would call the bomb squad. Even though I didn't see any emergency vehicles as Adrienne drove back down the lane after dinner, my eyes stayed plastered on the front door.

My relief was palpable as I recognized that the doorknob appeared to be unadorned. The brass handle actually seemed to glow as though Dorsey had polished it.

Adrienne and her son, Jonas, decided to enjoy the sunset and accompany Lauren and Grace and the dogs for a walk through the neighborhood. I pretended that I'd been paged and begged off the evening excursion with the excuse that I had a phone call to return.

I dialed the second I was back in the house. "Dorsey, it's Alan."

"Hi, Alan. Nice house you have, terrific view. And great dogs. What's the big one? Shadow wanted to play with her in the worst way."

"She's a Bouvier des Flandres, a Belgian sheepdog. It's just as well she was in the run—she doesn't always play well with strange dogs." Dorsey may have wanted to chat about the puppies, but I needed to cut to the chase. "The doorknob was empty. I take it you and Shadow didn't find anything?"

"No, your house is clean, so is the garage, so are the cars. I don't know if we were supposed to, but we also did that barn that's a little bit south of your house. It's clean, too."

"The workshop? It actually belongs to our neighbor, but thanks. Can't be too cautious."

"You know," she said, pausing, "Sam didn't really give me much background on all of this."

"I wish I could tell you something, Dorsey. I wish I could."

She paused for a few seconds. I wondered if I heard the wind-whistling-in-the-canyon sound of a deep drag on a joint. "You're a shrink, right?"

"Yeah."

"This has something to do with that?"

"Yeah, it does."

"Okay, well. You let us know if we can be of any more help. Shadow's always looking for training opportunities that involve field trips. She graduates in a couple of weeks and then I'll be dealing with a rookie. If you need help, now's the best time."

CHAPTER

22

Lucy Tanner promised to check in with me on Sunday. She didn't. Grace and I spent the day together as Lauren did her best to cope with the toxic consequences of her weekly interferon injection. She loved the drug almost as much as she hated it. As long as she'd been taking the stuff, it had kept its promise to keep the MS dragons on the other side of the moat. The price for the prophylaxis was that she was sick—sometimes moderately, sometimes severely—for the twenty-four hours after the long needle left her thigh.

Grace and I did what we could to make her comfortable. Whatever it was we did, it felt inadequate. And probably was.

Monday at twelve-fifteen Naomi Bigg showed up right on time for her appointment.

Over the weekend there was virtually no way that she could have avoided the extensive news coverage of the discovery of the explosive device in Royal and Susan Peterson's house. I expected to spend the Monday session dealing with Naomi about my role in the detection of that bomb and rehearsed my arguments as she settled herself on the chair.

Naomi started her session by saying, "What I've been thinking? I've been thinking that there's a big difference between the Klebolds and the Harrises and me—I mean the situation I'm in."

She paused as though she wanted me to ask her what the difference was. I didn't ask. I was too busy trying to spot the ambush that I was sure she was planning about the Peterson bomb.

She went on unprompted. "The difference is that there was no way to defend—to justify—what those two kids were planning. No matter how you look at it, Eric and Dylan were targeting innocent children. They were planning indiscriminate slaughter. They were blaming the world for the way they thought they'd been treated. They wanted blood, they wanted gallons of it, and they wanted it from innocents. If their parents had an inkling of that, there is no excuse for them not acting."

Her words shook me. I stopped plotting my defense to accusations of clueing the police in to look for the bomb. As always, Naomi Bigg had a knack for capturing my attention.

The question that almost jumped out of my

mouth—but didn't—was, *And there is a way to justify what your child and his friend are planning?* I think the reason I didn't actually ask the question out loud was that I feared I was incapable of keeping the incredulousness out of my inflection.

After a few sessions with me, Naomi was growing accustomed to the silences. She didn't hesitate to pick up on her own. "The wouldn't-it-be-cool games that the boys play always target—for want of a better word—perpetrators. People who actually bear responsibility for some serious, serious injustice. That's what's different. So even if Paul and Ramp are actually planning something and not just . . . talking—and I'm not convinced that they are—I think, knowing what I know, that I'm in a different position than the Harrises and the Klebolds. It's a big difference."

What? "It's different because in your circumstances the potential victims . . . deserve what happens to them? Is that it?"

Naomi shrugged. "Want to know what I think? Five years ago, I was somebody who used to think that in this country, justice was equal for everybody. Justice was the courts and the police and the jails. The scales always balanced. What's-her-face never peeked out from beneath her blindfold. But I know now that that's not true. Justice isn't just. Justice isn't like a fresh coat of paint on a wall. It doesn't cover equally. It doesn't spread equally. In our system, justice is more like a line of summer thunderstorms. Some places get soaked. Other places stay bone dry. After going through what

I've been through with my family, can I continue to believe that providing justice should be the sole province of the criminal justice system? For every ten good cops, there's a Royal Peterson. For every office full of passionate prosecutors, there's a rotten cop. And defense attorneys?" She groaned. "Don't even get me started on defense attorneys. Or parole boards? God in heaven. The system is too corrupt to be trusted."

"And the alternative . . . is for people who perceive themselves to be victims of injustice to be free to act on their own?"

She hesitated for only a few seconds. "In certain circumstances, I've concluded that the answer to that might be yes. I couldn't do it myself. But I can understand people doing it."

Was she talking about her husband and his cut-off baseball bat or her son and his friend and their bombs? I couldn't keep myself from asking, "So, if these victims of injustice decide to act as vigilantes based on their own conclusions about events, then their victims deserve what happens to them?"

"Victims?" she scoffed. "Like Royal Peterson? You calling Royal Peterson a victim? Royal Peterson wasn't a victim. He was the poster child of perpetrators. The true victims are the people who suffered because of his plea bargains—and believe me, there are dozens of them that are right now trying to pick up the pieces of their lives all over Boulder County."

As much as I disagreed with some of the prosecutorial decisions that Peterson had made over his long reign in Boulder, I knew the good he had done far out-weighed his mistakes. I could barely contain my impulse to defend him. I said, "And because you dis-agree with some of his plea bargains, because of that, Peterson deserved to die?"

"I've already told you: I don't have any feelings about that. He's dead. I don't grieve him. I don't cele-brate his death."

I struggled to control my breathing. "Let's say, Naomi, just for the sake of argument, that Ramp and Paul were involved in Royal Peterson's death. Your cur-rent feelings are that murdering Peterson was a rea-sonable reaction to what he did to your daughter?"

She shrugged. "Who cries when a child molester is attacked in prison? Huh? Who grieves for that? Peterson ruined lives, too. Hundreds of them. Take a look at his record of plea bargains. Go ahead. Well, let's say someone felt he needed to be punished for that. If that's the case, then, yes, he paid for his sins. Some people might call what happened to him a crime. It feels like justice to me. I'm not going to grieve for that. I am not."

She paused for an extended period, shifting her focus to the windows and the yard beyond. Then she said, "But I don't think they had anything to do with it. I just don't think they did."

Minutes before the session was scheduled to end, Naomi abruptly stopped talking about a staffing problem in her office and said, "The bomb the police found last Friday? At the Petersons'?"

"Yes?" I said, my heart racing.

"Do you wonder how they knew to look for it? Have you wondered about that at all?"

What was I going to say? No? Yes?

"I have," she said, saving me from a lie. "And I'd like to think that you didn't have anything to do with the police deciding to look for it. I'd like to think that I can trust you."

My ensuing silence wasn't strategic. I was absolutely tongue-tied. *Yes, you can trust me, Naomi.*

No, you can't.

"If I can't talk to you about these things, I don't think I'd talk to anyone about them. I certainly wouldn't talk to the police. Even if they knocked at my door, I wouldn't tell them a thing. You know what I mean, don't you? I really need to be able to trust you with all this."

I nodded. I knew exactly what she meant. She was warning me to keep my mouth closed.

Right then I should have heeded her advice. I didn't. I said, "Naomi, it's important that you understand that there are circumstances where I might have an ethical responsibility to reveal certain things that I hear in psychotherapy."

She frowned. "That's obtuse. What are you talking about? What kind of circumstances?"

"If I hear something that indicates to me that someone is being clearly threatened, for instance, I have a responsibility to warn that person or to tell the police about the threat. I have a specific responsibility to protect people from harm."

"So I can't talk to you about these . . . feelings I'm having? About the concerns I have about the boys?"

"Those two questions seem to imply that someone is actually being threatened, Naomi. Is that the case?"

"I've told you already that I don't think anyone's being threatened. I'm trying to understand my feelings. That's all."

"I'm not convinced that's all you're trying to do."

"What do you mean?"

I was ready. "The last few times we've talked, it's felt to me as though you were trying to get me to do something to help you act on your feelings—to get you to do what you know is right. I think you may be trying to back me into the same corner that you feel backed into."

"What corner are you talking about? What is 'right'?"

"The right thing to do would be to protect people from harm. If the boys"—I almost choked as I used her vernacular—"do have a list of people they are thinking of hurting, then those people should be warned. They must be warned. And the boys should be stopped."

"Oh really?"

"Yes."

"Is that what the Boulder DA did with my daughter's case? Putting her rapist in jail for a few months protected the people of Boulder from harm? That was his overriding concern when he made that decision? Protecting people? Innocent girls out on dates? Those kinds of innocent people? I don't think so."

"I think you know what you have to do, Naomi."

"Yeah? What's that?"

"Can you answer that question yourself?"

"Just like a freaking shrink," she scoffed. "Just like a freaking shrink. Ask a question, get a question."

CHAPTER

23

My last session on Monday was over at five-fifteen, so I was surprised when I looked up as the session was ending and noticed that the red light was beaming on the wall.

I gave my patient half a minute to exit the waiting room before I walked out to see whether the light was a mistake or whether I had scheduled another patient and had neglected to note it on my calendar.

I did that sometimes.

The waiting room was empty.

I flicked off the light and moved back to my office to pack up. I walked in to find that Lucy Tanner was sitting in my chair.

"I like this seat better than the other one. This is definitely the power chair in the room."

"Hi, Lucy. How did you get in?" I made a conscious effort to keep my annoyance from my voice. Lucy's presence reminded me of the ethical malignancy that was metastasizing in my treatment of Naomi Bigg. But Lucy also represented my best hope for finding out what Ramp and Paul might be up to.

She tilted her head toward the French door. "That's not much of a lock you have. I can recommend something that's a little harder to pick, if you would like. Sorry. I didn't want to be seen hanging out in your waiting room. How are you holding up?"

I moved to the far end of the sofa and put my feet up. "I'm a wreck. I had a friend of Sam's who trains K-9 dogs come by my house and check for explosives Saturday. I couldn't believe I did it."

"Dorsey? From Westminster?"

I nodded.

"You like her?"

"I do."

I thought Lucy clenched her teeth a little bit. I was about to inquire about her feelings about Dorsey when she distracted me by asking, "She and her dog find anything?"

"Thankfully, no."

"Good. She still smoking dope?"

I swallowed. "I wouldn't know."

"Learn anything new from your 'source'?"

"My *patient*, Lucy. My patient. And no, I didn't learn anything that will help us much. Other than that she is seriously reluctant to believe that her son is plotting anything worrisome. And that if she's approached by the authorities she'll deny everything she told me."

"She's warning you? Does she suspect something?"

"She's suspicious about how the police happened to find the bomb in the Peterson house."

"That's almost like an admission, isn't it?"

"Maybe for a cop, Lucy. It's not enough for me."

She manufactured a small smile. "Sorry I didn't call. I've been pretty busy. When I haven't been with Cozy or his investigator, I've been down in Denver mostly."

"You find Ramp?"

"Not even a trace. I tracked down all sorts of anti-law-enforcement Web sites and scoured the bulletin boards looking for his name. Nothing. Not a first name, not a last name, not a computer name. Asked some friends in the Denver and Aurora PDs if they had anything on anybody with that name, first or last. Nothing. I have a feeler out to someone on the Denver PD bomb squad to see if Ramp's in their database. I'm still waiting to hear.

"Next brainstorm was that I went back ten years and looked at all the murdered women in the Denver metro area. Sorted out all the mothers, then sorted by mothers who had sons, then looked for kids named Ramp.

"I'm working under the assumption that Ramp's a nickname, so I didn't expect to find him on that list, and I didn't. Then I made another list of all the sons of murdered mothers who would be between sixteen and twenty-five years old today. Guess how many that is?"

"Too many. I don't want to know."

"Until I have something else to go on, I'm working

under the assumption that his mother was killed in the metro area. A broader net is just unworkable for me."

"What about the bomb in the Petersons' house? Did that give the bomb squad any clues?"

"Sammy found out what he could for me. But, no. No latents on the bomb. No unusual materials used in the construction. The explosive was commercial dynamite, slightly aged, a little unstable, but not too bad. No recognizable signature. And the architecture of the device didn't draw any hits from the ATF database."

"That's not much."

Lucy said, "I'm left with the phone book."

"Anything there?"

"I've called all the Denver metro Ramps. There aren't that many. I reached two of the listings and ruled them out. A couple more I just got answering machines. Outside Denver metro there are, I think, three more Ramps. I'm going to try them tonight over dinner. It's a good time to reach people."

"So that leaves us where?" I asked.

"We still have the car bomb in Denver. I think—my gut feeling is—that, failing to find Ramp directly, the car bomb in Denver is our best link to him. I have trouble believing that discovering two explosive devices in the metro area on the same day can be isolated events. Sam has a contact with the Denver bomb squad."

"Walter."

"What?"

"Sam's contact's name is Walter. Or at least he calls him Walter."

Lucy laughed. The sound was a refreshing trill. "That means Sam thinks he's reliable. When he doesn't trust sources or snitches, he gives them names that begin with *L*—stands for loser. When he thinks they're reliable, he gives them names that begin with *W*. Those are the winners. So Sam trusts this guy, whoever he is. But until Sam hears more from Walter or something breaks in the news, we're in the dark about the Denver situation."

"That leaves us with Paul or with the mythical Ramp."

"Yes. And the path to Paul leads directly back to your patient, right?"

"Right. But Paul also should eventually lead us to Ramp."

"I agree. That's why Paul is next on my agenda."

I considered the options. If Lucy was discovered following Paul, it would become clear to Naomi that I'd been sharing her information with someone else. That would certainly end the therapy.

"Lucy, I'll follow Paul. If I'm discovered doing it, I have a chance of explaining away my indiscretion. If you get discovered, I'm screwed. My patient would stop talking to me. And I can't risk that."

"You don't know how to do this. This is police work."

"Paul's in school during the day. I know where he works. I know where he lives. I should be able to figure out when he's hanging out with his friend. My patient says they usually get together in Boulder, not Denver."

"And what will you do then?"

"Get a photograph. Get Ramp's license plate number. That should be enough for you to go on, right?"

"Should be," she acknowledged. "Should be."

CHAPTER
24

Cozy's office suite took up a good-sized chunk of the west side—that's the side with the view—of the eighth—that's the top—floor of the Colorado Building on Fourteenth Street near the Pearl Street Mall. After leaving my office, I found a parking place on Walnut, fed the meter, and entered the lobby, which was sized not to impress visitors but rather to maximize leasable square footage for the landlords. One of the building's two elevators was being used for a furniture delivery; the other one—the one I rode in—stopped at five of the eight floors on the way to the top.

I found Cozy and Lauren sitting at each end of a walnut conference table, the surface of which was carpeted with books and papers. Cozy was facing the door and saw me enter. He had a phone to his ear and a file in his other hand. His greeting was a nod.

I walked up behind Lauren and kissed her on her

hair. She reached up and slid her warm fingers across the skin on the back of my neck. I almost asked, "How did you know it was me?" But I didn't. I said, "Hi, how you doing?"

"Tired, but okay."

"You at a place you can stop? We need to get home and rescue Viv. She's had a long day with the baby."

She smiled and said, "Sure."

While she packed up, I examined the overriding reason—hell, the only reason other than its central location—for leasing office space in the Colorado Building: the view.

The streets in downtown Boulder are numbered in ascending order beginning at the base of the foothills of the Rockies. That means that Fourteenth Street is roughly fourteen blocks away from the dramatic incline of the mountains, an almost perfect distance to maximize the view. From Cozy's eighth-floor perch, high above the treetops, Boulder in springtime appeared as a lush landscape of old redbrick and flagstone buildings flanked by gentle rises to the north—Mapleton Hill—to the south—Chautauqua, and barricaded to the west by the vaulting presence of the foothills of the Rockies.

As dusk approached, the vista was glorious.

Lauren and I had almost the same view from our home miles to the east, but ours was wide angle. This was zoom. Every time I saw the close-up perspective from this elevated perch, I was captivated by the difference. Our view from home was mostly sky—the monumental mountains ended up being dwarfed by the infinite western sky. This view was mostly mountains, their sheer mass and grandeur looming over a town that appeared to have been built to the wrong scale.

Lauren took my hand and pulled me away from the windows. We both said good-bye to Cozy. He tucked the phone between his shoulder and his ear and waved good-bye.

In the elevator, Lauren said, "It hasn't been a particularly good afternoon for Lucy, sweets."

I swallowed. "Tell me."

"Over the last hour or so, Cozy and I learned some new things. When Sam and Lucy worked up Royal's house after the murder, one of the pieces of evidence they recovered was unwashed laundry from on top of the washing machine. There was also some laundry in the dryer. Did you know about any of that? I don't remember whether I told you. It hadn't seemed important until today. Anyway, it turns out that a sheet had some stains on it. It now appears that the police suspect that they can link the DNA on the stains to Lucy."

"What kind of stains?"

She sighed. "They think they're vaginal secretions."

"Vaginal secretions?" I said. *Lions and tigers and bears.* "Oh my."

The elevator door opened at the fourth floor. A psychologist, someone I barely knew from some insipid meeting of local psychologists I'd once attended against my better judgment, entered the elevator. I smiled and said, "Hello." She struggled, without apparent success, to place my face before she turned around and stared at the doors. Lauren slid her hand into mine and squeezed. The three of us stood silently and watched the numbers.

It took me only two of the remaining three floors to decide that there weren't very many ways for Lucy Tanner to have left vaginal secretions on sheets in Royal Peterson's house.

In fact, I could only think of one. I wasted a moment considering whether I was being unimaginative.

Outside the building on the Fourteenth Street sidewalk, Lauren asked, "Are you parked nearby?"

"Not too far, over on Walnut. Is your car ready to be picked up?" Her car was in the shop.

She shook her head. "No, they're still waiting for that thing to be delivered. Maybe tomorrow, maybe not." She checked her watch and said, "Let's walk up the Mall for a block or two and circle back to your car. We have time."

The "thing" was a transmission gasket. I took her briefcase and hung it over my shoulder. We held hands. As we turned the corner onto Pearl Street, I said, "Vaginal secretions?"

"Yeah, sorry to say. Apparently the police think they found the whole damn wet spot."

"Semen?"

"No."

"Really?"

"Think condom," she said.

"Oh," I said, feeling stupid. "Did they find that?"

"No."

Wispy clouds hung like smoke above the foothills of the Front Range. The sun was already invisible from our near vantage, though the sky above our heads was still bright. The cloud pattern promised a great finale to sunset, but I knew we wouldn't be home in time to catch it.

Lauren said, "It's too soon to know for sure. But that's the general direction that this is heading. Damned by a wet spot."

While I considered the timelessness of Macbeth, we crossed Thirteenth and moved slowly toward Broadway.

I stated the obvious. "So Lucy and Royal were having an affair?"

"Lucy won't talk about it. She continues to maintain that the details of her relationship to Royal will only serve to solidify the notion that she had a motive to kill him."

I tried to think like a prosecutor. It was not a natural act. "The police think they have means—her fingerprints are on the pottery. They think they have opportunity—a witness places her on the scene. And Lucy basically admits that she had motive. This doesn't look great for your client."

"Tell me about it."

"Lucy was having an affair with Roy and she'd decided to break up with him?" I asked. "Is that what she's saying?"

"She's not saying. But that's what I'm guessing. She's recently engaged, you know?"

"I know, she told me. But the engagement predates the wet spot by a couple of weeks. What's your theory of what happened? One last time with Royal? A good-bye fuck?"

She shook her head. "Nothing fits particularly well, I admit it. Pretty night, isn't it?"

"Lovely. Assume you're right, babe. How do things develop that night so that she ends up whacking him on the head with a lamp?"

"Like I said, nothing fits well."

"Self-defense?"

"Cozy and I would love self-defense. Lucy isn't offering, though. She maintains she had nothing to do with Royal's murder."

"What about Lucy's fiancé? If he found out about the affair, he'd have a motive, too, wouldn't he?"

"We're there already. Cozy's investigator has begun looking into that for us, though Lucy doesn't even know we have an investigator looking at him. I'm sure she'd go nuts if she knew what we were doing."

"And the bomb? What about the bomb? What's the theory as to why Lucy would want to blow up the Peterson house?"

"The bomb is our salvation. It's the only thing keeping Lucy out of jail right now. They can't tie her to it.

If they found a molecule of evidence that put Lucy and that bomb in the same room, she'd be screwed."

I was amazed at how quickly my wife, a lifelong prosecutor, had adopted the vernacular of a defense attorney. People who were her colleagues days before were now "they."

At Broadway, we turned around and traced our steps back down the Mall toward the car. "How do you and Cozy know about the wet spot? There's no required discovery yet, is there? Lucy hasn't been charged."

"No formal discovery, no." She gave my hand a squeeze. "Let's just say that the politics in the DA's office right now are working to our advantage. Everyone's posturing to take Royal's place. Everyone's scrambling to keep this thing from going to a special prosecutor. Keeping us informed is part of . . . someone's strategy."

"Who's feeding you? Mitchell? Elliot? I bet it's not Nora."

She said, "No, of course it's not Nora. And that's all I'm telling you."

On the way home from downtown I slowed to a stop at a red light at the corner of Broadway and University by the Hill. As if to prove to me that Boulder really is a small town, Naomi Bigg pulled up in the lane next to us driving a filthy BMW sedan. She was wearing sunglasses and smoking a cigarette. I don't think she saw me and I said nothing to Lauren about her presence next to us.

Just before the light changed to green, Naomi lowered her window about six inches, took a final deep drag on her cigarette, and tossed the still-lit butt onto the road between our cars.

I didn't get it.

People like Naomi, someone who I suspected wouldn't consider tossing a candy wrapper or a pop can onto the street, thought nothing of discarding cigarette butt after cigarette butt onto public sidewalks and thoroughfares.

Was there some statute I didn't know about that exempted cigarette butts from littering concerns? I suspected that what was more likely was that this was smokers' revenge for society's continuing anticigarette bias.

I also suspected that no matter how successful psychotherapy was, Naomi would still be littering her cigarette butts when we were done.

Later Monday evening I ran into Adrienne while I was taking the dogs outside for them to do their thing at the end of the day. I'd spotted the lights on in her dead husband Peter's old workshop, a barn he'd renovated into a woodworking facility that would leave weekend hobbyists drooling. When the dogs and I walked over we found Adrienne looking futilely for something that she'd put in the workshop in her version of storage, which as far as I'd been able to discern basically involved moving things to a location where she didn't trip over them on a daily basis. So far, nothing she'd moved into the old barn had been labeled, and as far as I could tell, nothing had been organized.

"Hey," she said as I stood in the open doorway. She spoke to me without looking up from the box in which she was rooting around. "You should keep Anvil away from the fields for the foreseeable future. The momma fox just had some new kits, everybody in the family looks hungry, and your poodle, such as he is, looks suspiciously like lunch."

"I know about the kits. They're cute. And Anvil's tough."

She laughed. "Right, and I'm gorgeous." She mumbled a profanity that I think was intended for the box she was trying to open, not for me, before she addressed me again. "I ever tell you that I have a patient who's going through a sex change?"

I raised my eyebrows.

"No, I'm not doing the operation, if that's what you're thinking. Somebody else is actually responsible for remodeling the plumbing."

"Your patient's a guy?" I asked to buy time. The whole topic of sexual transformation made me uncomfortable. Not philosophically, surgically.

"Yeah. You interested?"

"Interested? You mean—"

"Not in trying it, doofus. In helping. You know, professionally. These guys all need psychotherapy. It's part of the protocol. It's required."

"I don't know, Adrienne. How far along is the . . . how do you put it . . . the procedure? Is it like, well—"

"What?"

"Has he, um—"

"You want to know if the hose is still on the fire truck?"

I laughed.

She laughed, too, and returned to rooting in the boxes. She said, "Don't worry, I was just pimping you. I wouldn't send this guy to you. It would make you both crazier than you already are."

"Thanks. I appreciate it more than you know."

She threw a box out of her way and the sound of glass breaking filled the old barn. She ignored the carnage. "So who was the dog snooping around here the other day?"

I'd just recovered from one topic that made me anxious, so I wasn't well prepared for another. "Adrienne," I said. "You know, I disagree with what you said before—you are gorgeous. What, um, dog are you talking about?" Lying isn't one of my best things and I suspected that I'd just succeeded in alerting Adrienne that I was prevaricating.

" 'What, *um,* dog am I talking about?' While we were at dinner the other night, somebody came by with a dog and they walked all around your place, inside and out, and then they came in here."

"What?"

She stood up and faced me. Adrienne was petite. She was holding a folded blanket that she'd pulled from a cardboard box. Next to Emily's bulky mass, she looked like she was a jockey preparing to saddle up for a ride. "Look," she said. "My latest excuse for a nanny came by while we were at dinner and saw some woman and her dog checking out your place like the DEA thinks you're fronting for some drug lord. She said the woman and the dog came in here, too. This place is mine. That makes it my business. So tell me."

Her hands were on her hips.

Adrienne's history with nannies was not illustrious. I tried to distract her with a feint. "You're not happy with your nanny? I didn't know that."

"Let me put it this way: I'll give you ten thousand dollars for the unconditional rights to Viv."

"No way."

"That's what I figured. Now tell me about the drug-sniffing pooch."

I said, "I've been wondering, do you think I'm the right age to start having annual prostate exams?"

"Answer my question or I'll glove up right now and give you one I promise you'll never forget."

I pulled back a dusty canvas tarp and lifted myself up to sit on the edge of one of Peter's old workbench-es. I knew that the fact that the shop was pretty much the way Peter had left it when he died had nothing to do with his wife's attempt to create a shrine. Adrienne wasn't exactly preserving Peter's shop in his memory; she just hadn't gotten around to moving any of his stuff, selling it, or giving it away. I suspected that with the exception of continued additions of boxes and assorted household junk from Adrienne, the barn wouldn't change much in the next decade.

I asked, "Did you know Leo Bigg?"

She lowered herself to the top of a box. The dogs immediately decided that she was prey and surrounded her. Emily sniffed her pockets for treats. Anvil tried to crawl onto her lap.

She asked, "Where on earth is that question coming from?"

"Just curious."

She stared at me. "You're often difficult, Alan, but you're not usually this constipated. If you don't answer at least one of my questions, I swear I'm going to kidnap your dogs."

I smiled. "If the threat of a sadistic prostate exam didn't sway me, you think the threat of moving my dogs across the lane and feeding them too many treats is going to unseal my lips?"

"Talk."

"Leo Bigg's story came up in a therapy session. I just thought that you might have known him."

"Leo's not dead, Alan. He's in prison. And, yes, I do know him. He was a good doc—is a good doc. Everything you'd want in an oncologist. But my suspicion is that that's not what you wanted to know. You want to know about his tragedies, don't you? You want to know whether he was the kind of guy who would do what he did?"

"Yes, I do."

"Everyone who knew him was shocked at what he

did. Everyone. He found something most of us, thank God, never find—he found his breaking point. The weight of his heartbreak must have simply over-whelmed him. I can't explain what he did any other way."

I thought about Marin, the rape, and I nodded. "Did you know his family? His wife?"

"I probably met his wife at parties, but I don't remember her well. Those were the days before Jonas was born, and the Biggs already had kids. Plus the Biggs always floated a few social strata above Peter and me. They wouldn't hang with us. It would have been slumming for them."

"Lauren and I hang with you."

"Like I said, slumming."

Anvil had succeeded in curling up on Adrienne's lap. Emily was still nosing around in search of treats, nudging Adrienne in the flanks as though she were reluctant livestock. Adrienne relented and gave each of the dogs a biscuit from her pocket. She rarely went outside unprepared to indulge the dogs.

She said, "Now tell me about Rin Tin Tin."

Instead of answering I asked, "How's Susan Peterson doing?"

She laughed. "You want me to discuss someone else's bladder control with you? Are you psychotic? Tell me—who's Rin Tin Tin?"

"The woman is someone I met recently. She's a dis-abled police officer who trains K-9 dogs to supplement her income. She likes to take her dogs on what she calls 'field trips' as part of their training. I offered to let her use our place. She came in here by mistake."

"That's the best you can do?"

"Most of it's true."

She laughed loudly.

"The rest I can't tell you."

"Figures. Bet you want me to keep my suspicions from your wife, too, don't you?"

"How'd you guess?"

She stood and returned her attention to the boxes. I asked her if she wanted my help finding something.

She said, "You think I want you to search through my stuff? There're important things in here."

I jumped down from the workbench and started to leave the barn.

Adrienne said, "I ever tell you that being your neighbor is no picnic?"

"Yeah, you've told me. That being the case, it's probably fortunate for me that you love me."

"True. By the by, call my office and set up a time with Phyllis. I think I do want to get a nice slow feel of your prostate."

Under my breath, I said, "Fat chance."

Adrienne said, "I heard that."

CHAPTER
25

Lucy Tanner didn't go home right away after leaving Alan's office.

Shortly after she'd been old enough to drive she'd discovered that nothing she did gave her the succor and peace she felt when she was alone behind the wheel of a car. As a younger woman, she'd required open roads and speed to achieve the contentment she sought from her automobile. During the first few years after she'd graduated from college, she'd thought nothing of driving alone from Colorado to San Diego and back on a long weekend to sneak in a few hours surfing in Encinitas.

The trips were a lark. The surfing was usually a thrill. The driving was a necessity.

Now she could achieve some modicum of solace simply by driving city streets or cruising the narrow canyons that snaked into the foothills above Boulder.

The speed to which she was once addicted was no longer necessary. A dirt lane up Magnolia served her purposes as well as a wide-open interstate on Floyd Hill up I-70. The turbo boost on her cherry-red Volvo was about as essential for her as a box of condoms was to a nun. She was thinking it was time to trade the car in for something else, though she couldn't decide exactly what.

When she left Alan's office, Lucy headed north on Broadway, paralleling the naked hogbacks that ridged Boulder's western rim. Her fiancé, Grant, lived in a townhouse in Niwot, a once-charming rest stop of a village that had grown into an extra bedroom for Boulder's expanding family. She weaved east until she connected with the Diagonal Highway and started the familiar route to her boyfriend's house a few miles down the road. She barely noticed the soft colors that were illuminating the clouds above the hogbacks.

Lucy knew Grant wasn't home. He was in the field, somewhere in central Wyoming, doing a wildlife survey. She'd received an e-mail from him that morning and had sent one back his way, a don't-worry-about-me-I'm-doing-fine pack of lies. Her journey to his home wasn't about seeing him; it was about *driving* to see him. She looped past his house twice, finally parking for a moment in the place beneath the big cottonwood where she usually left her car when she was spending the night.

Her engine running, she listened to Gloria Estefan

sing something in Spanish. The backbeat was invigor-
ating but the tone was lamenting. Gloria obviously
wasn't pleased about something, but Lucy didn't
remember enough of her high school Spanish to know
exactly what. As the song ended and the disc jockey
moved into a commercial for a herbal elixir that he
promised was just as potent as Viagra, Lucy touched a
button to change stations, pulled out from beneath the
cottonwood, and steered her way back onto the
Diagonal, this time heading toward Boulder.

She stayed on the Diagonal until it ended, and then
stayed on Iris until she reached Broadway, where she
turned south. She'd arrived at a decision as she was
stopped at the light at Twenty-eighth Street. Her next
stop was going to be the home of the Bigg family. She'd
already checked their address. They lived south of
Baseline in a cul-de-sac below Chautauqua.

She cruised the cul-de-sac only once. Four houses
on big lots. The garage door was open on one of the
houses on the corner. Somebody was working on an
old motorcycle with a sidecar. A dozen lights were
ablaze in the two-story Bigg home. One car—a six- or
seven-year-old BMW—was parked in the driveway;
two more cars were on the street nearby.

She jotted down the plates on all the vehicles, hoping that she'd happened upon an evening visit by the
man named Ramp. But she didn't think so. Lucy was-
n't feeling particularly lucky.

Sixth took her back toward downtown. But she did-
n't make it all the way downtown. All along she knew

that the Peterson home would be her last stop before heading back to her place.

She cruised Jay Street twice, slowing each time in front of the Peterson house. The lawn had been mowed for the first time that spring. The crime-scene tape was down. The do-not-enter warnings were gone from the front door. The light in one of the upstairs windows was dim, not dark. The ubiquitous flicker of the television screen from Susan Peterson's bedroom, present. She's back home, Lucy thought during her first pass. She felt an urge to park around the corner where she'd always left her car during her prior visits, but resisted, settling instead for permitting herself one more loop past the house.

On her final drive by the house she wondered if she wished things were the same as they always were. As they were a couple of weeks before.

She couldn't decide. She found that interesting, still.

Although she'd promised herself that no matter what she saw in the upstairs window, she absolutely wouldn't stop, she pulled over to the curb and parked her car behind an aging Toyota pickup, killing the engine in the middle of a melancholy ballad by Sinéad O'Connor.

That's one girl, she told herself, who's more confused than I am.

Lucy reached over to the passenger seat and checked her purse to make sure she had everything she might need.

She did.

The air was heavy, the way it is in July when a thunderstorm has just passed. But the April night was dry. A chill permeated her clothing. Lucy kept her head down, counting curb sections, reading the dates imprinted on the borders of the cement work. The oldest section she found had been installed in 1958.

Nineteen fifty-eight must have been a very good year for concrete. The pour was still in good shape. By comparison, some of the newer sections, including one done in 1993, already appeared due for replacement.

She had to cross over Pleasant Street to get to the Peterson home. When she looked up from her reverie to check for traffic, she was almost hit by a bicycle riding on the wrong side of the street.

The walkway that led from the sidewalk to the Petersons' front door was constructed of brick pavers set in a herringbone pattern. The path meandered from start to finish in the elongated shape of a lazy S. Lucy cut the curves, straightening the path into a line.

She had no illusions that she'd find Susan Peterson home alone. She suspected that Susan would have convinced someone—one of her doctors, probably—that her husband's murder had left her in need of a full-time aide. Lucy knew that there was another possibility—that instead of an aide, Susan's caretaker might be one of Susan and Royal's daughters.

Either way, Lucy knew that whomever she discovered in the house would be a woman.

Susan didn't like men close by.

Lucy had never used her key in the front door lock, didn't know if it would even work. Since she'd had the key, she'd always come in through the back door.

She tried the key in the front lock. The thin metal wand slid into the brass slot naturally, as though it belonged. She rotated her hand and the key turned evenly in the lock. She depressed the thumb lever and pushed the heavy door inward. It released with a gentle *whoosh* and Lucy stepped inside the house.

She paused. The living room was to her right. She tried not to think about that night. About Royal.

About Sam.

"You okay, Luce?"

She failed in her attempt to ward off memories of that night; the images flooding her left her feeling a momentary pulse of disorientation. The same almost-vertigo she'd felt when Sam was kneeling over the body.

"Holy shit. You know who this is, Luce?"

She shook her head to clear the slate. Ever since she was a little girl she'd cleared her head the same way she'd erased images from her Etch A Sketch. This time it took two shakes.

The stairs to the second floor were right in front of her.

Lucy heard water running in the kitchen at the rear of the house. That would be the aide or the daughter.

Staying to the far right edge of the staircase because Royal had warned her once that a couple of the treads squeaked, Lucy took the stairs one at a time. She didn't touch the banister.

From the landing at the top of the stairs, she could see that the door to Susan's bedroom was almost closed. Through the narrow opening Lucy could hear the distinct sound of the television.

Martha frigging Stewart.

She paused and thought about Grant.

She was consciously aware that she was looking for a reason to go back down the stairs, back out the door, back into her bright red Volvo. But Grant wasn't going to be that reason. He'd find out everything soon enough and at that point he'd do what he'd do. Lucy thought he'd run like hell, but allowed for the possibility that he might surprise her.

With her left hand Lucy reached into her purse. With her right hand she pushed open the door.

Susan looked up, probably to demand something of the aide.

Lucy said, "Susan. We need to talk."

CHAPTER

26

Lucy e-mailed her fiancé before she scrubbed the makeup from her eyes and slid into bed. She wrote to tell him that she loved him, but she knew in her heart that her words were nothing more than shouting in a canyon.

What she really wanted to hear was the echo.

When the phone rang twenty minutes later, she still wasn't asleep. Wasn't even close to being asleep. She checked the time out of curiosity. The clock read 11:05.

"Hello."

"Lucy Tanner?"

"Yes."

"This is Brett Salomon from the *Daily Camera*."

In a clear voice, a cop voice, Lucy said, "How the

hell did you get this number? I've told you before, Mr. Salomon, I'm not giving interviews. Good night. Please don't call here again."

"Wait, please. Don't hang up. This call is a courtesy for you, Detective Tanner. Hear me out. In tomorrow morning's edition we will be running a story concerning you and the Petersons, and I wanted to give you an opportunity to comment prior to publication. It's up to you, but I suggest you hear me out."

Lucy's heart felt as though it were a new thing in her chest. The suddenly rapid beating got her attention like a loud knock at the door. She swept her hair off her forehead. "Concerning me how? What's the story about?"

When he started talking again, Lucy thought Salomon's inflection had changed, as though he was reading, or reciting something that he'd rehearsed. He said, "Detective Tanner, we will be reporting in tomorrow morning's paper that Susan Peterson is your mother and we will be characterizing your relationship with her. Feel free to comment. I'd like to print your side of the story, as well."

Lucy pressed the mouthpiece of the phone into her right breast and told herself to breathe. The room was dark and the foot of her bed faced the wall. She thought she saw brilliant flashes of light, like flames, erupt in three or four places where she should be seeing nothing but the familiar shadows of her room at night.

She could still hear Brett Salomon's voice. It

sounded disconnected, hollow, distant. But urgent, pressured. He was saying, "Detective? Detective? This is your chance to comment. Detective Tanner? Detective Tanner?"

Lucy hung up the phone and then she vomited all over the sheets.

CHAPTER
27

I misled my wife in order to get out of the house after midnight. An emergency, I said. Lauren, half asleep, assumed that I meant an emergency with my practice. And now, sometime shortly after midnight, I was sneaking down the street, head down, collar up, hoping no photographers' lenses were pointed my way as I hustled into the old house on Pine Street where Lucy Tanner had a second-floor flat.

I was surprised how cold it was outside.

Lucy had been crying. A pile of spent tissues marked the place on the sofa where she'd been awaiting my arrival.

Her flat was dark, a solitary light from the kitchen spilling shadows into the living room. Even in the muted light I could tell that the room was elegant yet comfortable, a pleasant mixture of the modern and the ancient. An alluring step *tansu* filled much of one wall. A gorgeous old highboy secretary marked off the transition to the kitchen. The sofa where she was sitting was covered in a rich tapestry. It was the kind of room that took either serious bucks or an exceptionally high credit limit from Visa.

"Thanks for coming," she said. "I didn't know who else to call." Lucy was wearing a black robe that reached to mid-thigh. As she sat on her sofa, she had to tug the hem of the robe carefully into place to maintain modesty. She grabbed a wadded tissue from beside her and stretched out one corner of it as though she were about to use it to blow her nose. She didn't. She said, "My fiancé is in Wyoming," as though that explained why she'd called me instead of him.

"Sure," I said.

"After I left your office today, I drove around for a while. I do that sometimes. Just drive around. It helps me relax. You ever do that? Just drive around? Does that make me weird?" The last question informed me that she was aware at that moment that she was talking to a mental health professional.

She pulled on a different corner of the tissue, and it ripped. She slipped a fingertip through the hole.

I shifted my weight so that I was leaning forward, closing the space between the chair where I was sitting and Lucy.

She went on. "During my drive I went, well, I went a lot of places, but one of the places I went was the Peterson house. Susan's moved back home. Did you know that? I saw the lights on upstairs. The TV screen was flickering."

I said, "I didn't know she was back home."

"Me neither. I was kind of surprised, actually."

For a split second she lifted her eyes and looked at me. "I don't have many friends, Alan. Did Sam tell you that about me? That I don't get close to very many people?"

"I think he's told me that you're a private person, Lucy. That's all."

"Sam's nice," she said. Here in the dark with something important on her mind, her voice was almost girlish. "My boyfriend says that I seem to love it when he's intimate with me but that I don't want to be intimate with him."

Almost reflexively, I said, "You say that in a way that makes me wonder whether his words make sense to you." It was a shrink phrase. In that room at that time it was as out of place as a bright red clown nose.

She exchanged the ripped tissue for a fresh one and dabbed at her left nostril. "I've heard it before—things like my boyfriend said—from other men. But I always thought that when they were talking about intimacy, they were really talking about sex. That when they complained that I was too distant, they really meant they were unhappy that I wasn't sleeping with them. Or wasn't sleeping with them as often as they wanted."

I wondered where we were heading. I honestly
didn't have a clue. I assumed the reason that I'd been
summoned from my bed was weightier than this. Lucy
had to be warming up for something.

"But it's not that way with Grant. Grant really wants
me to be open—you know, to talk to him." She
laughed. "Don't misunderstand. He wants to sleep
with me, too. But he says that he wants me to tell
him . . . things. What's going on. How I feel about
what's going on. You know."

I didn't want to repeat my mistake. I said, "He
sounds like quite a find, Lucy." It's something I never
would have said in therapy. I know that's why I said it
then—to remind myself that I was meeting with Lucy
as a friend, not as a therapist. Maybe I wanted to
remind her, too.

"He doesn't want me to tell him what's going on
right now, I promise you that. Anyway, he's not
around."

Here it comes, I thought. *The reason I'm not home in
bed.*

She narrowed her eyes and continued. "You know
what that means for you and me? It means that
tonight, instead of being intimate with my fiancé, I'm
going to be intimate with you."

I thought her words carried layers of meaning that
weren't readily apparent, and I wasn't sure Lucy was
even aware that there were stowaways on board whatever trip she was inviting me on.

Again I said something that I would ordinarily say in

psychotherapy, and almost immediately I regretted it. "Intimacy isn't the same as openness, Lucy. It's not that simple."

She looked at me. Her eyes seemed smaller without makeup. She said, "What? What do you mean?"

I debated whether or not I should answer. Finally, I said, "Let's say you go to Denver and you meet somebody in a bar, and let's say they buy you a drink, and you tell them every deep dark secret in your soul—"

She sighed. "For me that would take more than one drink."

"Well, you do that, you open up like that to a stranger—that's not intimate behavior. That's not what intimacy is."

"I don't get it. It sounds like intimacy to me."

"Let me give you another example. You go to that same bar and meet the same guy and without telling him a thing about yourself, about what's in your heart, about what's dear to you, you go home with him. You sleep with him. Then you leave. You don't even know his name. He doesn't know yours. Well, that's not intimacy, either."

She bit her bottom lip. "Okay, I can buy that."

"But put the two experiences together, and you may—you may—have intimacy."

"You've lost me again, Alan. I'm sorry."

I sat back. "I'm not sure this is that important, Lucy. I'm digressing and you have something you need to talk to me about."

"No, go on, please. This is all part of . . . something."

"Intimacy requires two things to happen. Both are necessary. Neither, alone, is sufficient. One is openness. The other is vulnerability. In the first example I gave you, the openness is there, but there's no vulnerability. The guy you meet in the bar can't hurt you. He knows everything about you—every fact—but he can't really touch you in a way that could cause you any pain.

"In the second example, the vulnerability is there, but there's no openness. You're terribly vulnerable to the guy as you have sex with him. But it's anonymous; you never open up to the guy at all."

"What do you call that?"

"I don't know," I said. "Reckless?"

Lucy pulled both her legs beneath her and crossed her arms. For some reason, I chose that moment to scan the room for a cat. Lucy seemed like the type of woman who would have a cat.

She said, "I need to think about this some more."

"Of course."

It was about this time that I would be glancing at my watch and saying, *I'm afraid our time is up.*

Lucy stood and walked to the other side of the room. I could see her reflection in the glass doors. Her legs were exposed from mid-thigh to the floor; her robe was open from her throat to the middle of her chest.

I hoped the exposure was unintentional. But I wondered about her seductiveness. Could she be so unaware of her behavior with men?

Her lips parted as though she was going to speak, then she pressed them together again. Finally, she said, "It's starting to snow. I didn't even know a storm was coming. Did you?"

"I'd heard a front was coming through. But, no, I didn't know it was going to snow."

"I wonder if it will stick," she said.

I didn't reply. I hadn't left my wife in bed to discuss Boulder's springtime climate.

Lucy shifted her weight and lifted one leg from the floor so that it was bent at the knee at ninety degrees, like a stork. She said, "I don't know exactly how to say this. No, that's not true, I do know exactly how to say this. I just don't want to say it." Once more her mouth opened and closed.

"Take your time, Lucy." It was something I said to patients all the time in psychotherapy. For some reason, it usually made them seem to hurry.

"Susan Peterson is my mother, Alan."

I said, "What?" I knew exactly what she had said. My question expressed my befuddlement, not my failure to hear or comprehend.

Lucy returned her weight to both legs and turned and faced me. She'd pulled the robe closed at her throat with one hand. "Susan Peterson is . . . my mother. Or at least she's woman who gave birth to me."

At her pronouncement, I stood. I don't know why. "Lucy, Lucy. My God. I had no idea."

"No one did. We are . . . estranged. That's a good word for it. Estranged. In fact, it couldn't be *es*-stranger."

"Royal knew?"

Again, Lucy spun and faced the glass. She'd released the shawl collar of her black robe. The reflection made it clear that it had again fallen open to the middle of her chest. "Of course Royal knew."

"Cozy and Lauren?"

She shook her head. "No one else in town knows." She found her own words humorous, or ironic, or something. "At least no one in town knew. Until tonight. Now that's about to change."

I tried to make sense of the implications of the news that Lucy had just shared. I had to assume that this was the reason she had been in the Peterson home the night that Royal had been murdered. A visit to her mother would explain all the fingerprints the police had found in the house. Lauren and Cozy could create considerable doubt with that revelation.

But Lucy had also told Cozy and Lauren that if the reason she was in the Peterson home that night was known, everyone would be convinced that she had a motive for Royal's murder.

I couldn't make sense of that.

And, of course, I hadn't heard anything yet that would account for the wet spot.

Lucy turned back toward the room. She wasn't holding the collar of her robe this time.

"We're intimate now, aren't we, Alan?"

I thought, *Whoa*. She saw the puzzlement in my face.

"I've certainly been open with you . . . and, God knows, I've never been more vulnerable in my life than I am right now."

CHAPTER

28

Lucy Tanner was the only child of a man named Charles Tanner and a free-spirited woman he'd met at a sit-in in a bank in Ann Arbor, Michigan, in 1969. The woman's name was Susie Pine. Lucy's conception predated Charles and Susie's subsequent marriage by almost six months. Susie's friends were much more surprised that Susie Pine married at all than they were that she never adopted her husband's last name.

The Tanner-Pine marriage endured, at least as far as the state of Michigan was concerned, for seven years. The reason that Susie gave when she initially left her husband and daughter in Ann Arbor was that she felt she had to go to the bedside of her older sister, who was dying of breast cancer in Tucson. Six weeks later, two days after her sister's Arizona funeral, Susie Pine packed up the things she wanted from her sister's house and moved to Boulder. Within days, she filed for divorce from her husband, Charles.

She never returned to Ann Arbor.

The divorce was uncontested, and custody of the minor child, Lucy, was awarded to Charles Tanner. He remarried two years later and his second attempt at marriage was much more successful than his first.

Lucy's adolescence was less tumultuous than her childhood had been, and she considered herself to be a relatively confident, though shy, young person when she graduated high school near the top of her class and moved west to attend Colorado College in Colorado Springs.

Lucy told me that her move west for school had nothing to do with a desire to reconnect with the mother who had abandoned her during her childhood. She maintained that she chose Colorado College solely because of its unique curriculum.

The psychologist in me noted her resistance, but I wasn't in Lucy's flat to give her a boost up on some eventual psychotherapy, I was there to be her friend. I bit my tongue and kept my thoughts about unconscious motivation to myself.

Susie Pine became Susan Peterson a little more than a year after her divorce from Charles Tanner. She and her new husband, an ambitious thirty-year-old prosecuting attorney named Royal, had two children during the first two years of their marriage, and added a third three years later.

One year after the completion of his family Royal Peterson won his first term as district attorney of Boulder County.

When did you find her for the first time?" I asked.

"I didn't even know if she was still in town when I joined the police department. I figured there was as good a chance that she had moved away as there was that she was still here. I never looked for her. That's not true. I checked the phone book once—does that count? Then I went to a reception when they opened the new coroner's offices in the Justice Center. That was about, I'm not sure, four or five years ago. She was there with Royal."

"You recognized her?"

"Sure. Susan had aged well. But I grew up with lots of photographs of her. My father is quite the amateur photographer and he always wanted me to know who my mother was. But she didn't recognize me. And I didn't talk to her that night. Not at all."

A cuckoo clock chirped once. I'd been wondering what time it was. Now I knew. I was also wondering how people survived living with cuckoo clocks. I still didn't know that.

"I finally went and saw her after I heard rumors about her illness. You know, her MS. I don't know why, exactly. Compassion? More likely pity, I guess. That, or it was just a good excuse to see her so I could try to begin to understand how she could leave her daughter so cavalierly. It was probably a combination."

I was uncomfortable with the way Lucy was referring to herself. "Her daughter was you, Lucy."

"Yeah. Her daughter was me. But, let's face it, I'm not the only kid who's ever been left behind by a parent. I remind myself of that a lot. Being left behind by my mother is not an excuse to let myself be damaged for life. My dad raised me well. My stepmother is a sweetheart. Whatever mistakes my father made with women, he got them out of his system by marrying her."

"Does reminding yourself that you're not the only child who's been left behind by a parent help?"

"Not much." She sighed. "I was terrified that first time that I went to her house to see her. Not that she'd slam the door in my face. My biggest fear? My biggest fear was that I was going to adore her, like instantly, the moment I set my eyes on her. As a girl, I'd idealized her after she left. My father was always kind; he never criticized her and I was left to create this image of her that had almost no basis in reality. She was as pretty as a movie star, as kind as the best mother in the world. Anyway, going to see her that day, I felt that some angel was going to answer the door. And I was afraid that the more it turned out that I adored her, the angrier I was going to be that she'd left me behind. Does that make sense?"

"Of course."

Lucy's voice grew small. "But it didn't turn out that way. I didn't like her. I didn't like her at all. She was critical, belittling, selfish. She wasn't this benevolent soul who'd left me to tend to my ill aunt. She was Susan Peterson. You must have gotten to know her through the DA's office. Didn't you? Lauren worked for her husband for years. You had to have known her at least a little bit."

"I've known her socially, yes."

"Do you like her?"

I managed a complete inhale and exhale before I responded, trying to find an alternative way to answer Lucy's question than the one I ended up with: "She can be difficult."

Lucy shook her head. "Please," she said. "You're being diplomatic. Difficult? That's an understatement if I ever heard one. Susan Peterson is a very unpleasant human being. On her best days, she's a bitch."

I forced a small smile. "At least the problem of adoring her never quite materialized."

Lucy didn't crack a smile. "Right," she said bitterly. "At least there was that."

This was the point where Lucy sat all the way back on the sofa, crossed her legs, folded her arms, and told me that the whole story was going to be printed in the next morning's *Daily Camera*.

A good-sized chunk of an hour later Lucy seemed to have run out of words. It was time for me to head home. I told her so.

She nodded.

I said, "One more thing before I go. Lauren and Cozy were trying to get in touch with you tonight. Did they reach you?"

"I got a message from each of them. I wasn't in any mood to call them back. I'll talk to them in the morning. They'll have a lot of questions about the *Daily Camera* article anyway."

I nodded. If I hadn't been so tired, I would have been thinking more clearly, and I think I would have left things alone at that point. I didn't.

"The reason they were calling? Lauren told me when I went to pick her up after you left my office. The police found some laundry, Lucy, in the Peterson home. Some unwashed laundry, including a sheet—a bedsheet—with a stain on it. The lab has identified the stain as being dried vaginal secretions. They're working under the suspicion that when the DNA analysis finally comes back, they're going to discover that the vaginal secretions are yours."

For some reason I found myself contemplating when I'd last used the phrase "vaginal secretions" in a sentence. I decided that it hadn't been recently.

Her eyes widened. "Oh boy," she said. The words almost disappeared in a rapid inhale.

I waited a moment and stated the obvious. "You're not totally surprised, are you, Lucy?"

She was looking off to the side, into the dark room. "What am I supposed to say? That I can't believe it? That there's no way it's true? Okay, I'll say it: I can't believe it. There's no way it's true."

I'm supposed to be good at reading people and I wasn't sure whether or not she even intended for me to believe her.

She grabbed a pillow from the sofa, hugged it to her chest, and began rocking back and forth from the waist, slowly. "Alan, I'm being careful with you. You're not my attorney and you're not my therapist. There're certain lines I can't cross with you. Do you understand?"

"I understand. Maybe I should have just kept my mouth shut about the sheets, Lucy. I thought you'd want to know what the police had found. But this could have waited till tomorrow. I'm sorry I brought it up. I should have left it to Lauren and Cozy. I apologize."

"Don't. I appreciate it, Alan. I appreciate all you've done. Coming over here tonight was kind."

"I'll tell Lauren I was here, Lucy."

"I know. It makes no difference. By this time tomorrow I won't have many secrets left. You know," she added, "I told you I was going to make the rest of the phone calls to the Ramps that are listed in the phone book. I did, reached three more. Two of them I'm not sure I can rule out, so I'm going to go track them down tomorrow in person. With all that's happened tonight . . . I know I'm going to feel like getting out of Boulder. Maybe I'll get lucky and find the kid."

I knew that everything Lucy was suggesting was true. Whatever scrutiny she had received from the media up until then was only a warm-up to the firestorm she could expect after the news of her relationship to Susan Peterson hit the wires in the morning. And, regardless of the press coverage, one of us did have to continue our efforts to try to find Ramp.

"You'll go in the morning?"

She nodded. "Yeah. One of them lives all the way out near Agate."

"Where's Agate?"

"Out east on I-70, just before you get to Limon."

I blurted, "Limon is where Ramp and Paul played around with the explosives."

She cocked her head. "You didn't tell me that."

"I thought I did."

"Well, you didn't."

"My patient told me that Paul went out to some ranch near Limon and he and Ramp blew up a car or something."

"You didn't tell me any of this." The suffix "you idiot" was understood by both of us.

"I'm sorry."

"There's a listing out near Agate for a man named Herbert Ramp. Herbert's dead, but his widow, Ella, answered the phone. When I asked about a son or grandson, she kind of hung up on me."

"So it may be him?"

"You say the two boys played around with bombs out there? Damn right it may be him. I'm definitely going to go talk to her tomorrow."

"Maybe I should do it instead, Lucy. She may be wary of a cop showing up at her door."

"But a shrink from Boulder won't raise her suspicions at all?"

The tendons in the back of my neck felt like rebar. "I'm not sure what's best, which one of us should meet her. Let me think about it overnight, okay? We'll talk in the morning?"

"Yeah. Call me around nine; I think I'm going to try to sleep in a little bit. Use my cell; I'm not going to be answering my phone."

I stood to leave and opened my arms to give Lucy a hug. First, she dropped the pillow, then she leaned into the embrace with a hunger I didn't expect. When she finally released me, I turned toward the door. My hand on the knob, I stopped and asked, "Lucy, were you having an affair with Royal?"

The silence that followed was eerie. For the first few seconds, I suspected that she wasn't going to respond, and I wasn't surprised. I was already questioning my judgment in asking the question. Finally, I turned my head to look at her to examine the impact of my question.

The cuckoo clock chirped twice.

Lucy had spun away from me. Although I couldn't be sure from the reflection she made in the glass doors, I thought she was crying.

Our eyes met in the black glass. She said, "I wish it was that simple, Alan. I wish it was that simple."

Outside, the snow wasn't sticking to the streets, but the sidewalks were wet. The tree buds and flowers looked as though they'd been frosted.

CHAPTER
29

The alarm clock cracked me awake at six-thirty. Lauren was already up with Grace. Before I climbed in the shower, I wasted a minute trying to decide how many hours of sleep I'd had. Before I reached a number that felt correct, I concluded that the answer was simply "not enough."

After a quick shower and shave I joined my family in the kitchen. I was most of the way through a condensed rendition of the previous night's events for Lauren's benefit when my pager went off. Moments later, I was back in the master bedroom closet trying to simultaneously get dressed and maintain a conversation with Naomi Bigg.

She wasted no time. "Can I see you today? Any time at all. I'll leave work. Please."

"Just a second," I said while I zipped up my trousers

and began to thread a belt around my waist. "I have to go get my calendar." I moved from the closet to the bedroom and retrieved my schedule from beside the bed. I was still undecided about trying to run out to Limon or Agate to see Ella Ramp. I didn't know where I could stick an emergency appointment.

She said, "Please, please. What we've been talking about with the kids? It's come to a head, I think. What you've been—what I've been . . . you know. Anyway, this morning, I found a . . . I found something that's convinced me that I need to . . ." Her voice faded away. "Please," she repeated.

Almost impulsively, I said, "Four-thirty this afternoon. I'm afraid that's all I have, Naomi."

"Four-thirty? Is that right? Okay, okay."

I could feel the pressure building. "Can it wait till then? Do you want to take a minute right now, Naomi, and tell me what—"

She hung up.

"I guess not," I said aloud.

"You guess not what?" Lauren asked from the doorway. Grace was asleep in her arms.

"A patient hung up on me in the middle of our conversation."

"Oh," she said, disinterested. She tilted her head back toward the kitchen. "The story about Lucy's mother is on the news. They make it sound awful. As though the fact that Susan is Lucy's mother gives Lucy a reason to murder Royal. It doesn't make any sense."

"They don't know about the wet spot?"

Lauren covered Grace's ears.

"No, they don't know about the wet spot."

"Well, I'm not surprised the press is making it look bad. That seems to be their job," I said. "I'm late—I need to get downtown. You're okay with Grace until Viv gets here?"

"I'm fine," she replied. She kissed the top of the baby's head. "We're great."

The previous night's snow was history. The faintest reminder of the storm still clung as transparent white frosting feathering the highest reaches of the Flatirons, but otherwise the morning was brilliant and warm and the city bore no evidence of the midnight flurries.

Lucy didn't answer her cell when I tried her a few minutes before nine, nor when I tried again at nine forty-five.

I finished with my nine forty-five patient right on time at ten-thirty. As soon as he was out the door, I checked my voice mail and retrieved two messages. One was a cancellation by my one o'clock, the other another call from Naomi.

"It's me again. I'm sorry I'm so scattered. You said four-thirty, didn't you? If that's not right, call me at the office. I can't tell you how much I need to see you. There's another bomb. That lawyer."

That was it.

There's another bomb. That lawyer.

I replayed the message to assure myself that that was what she had said.

There's another bomb. That lawyer.

Shit. I decided that I couldn't wait any longer to find out what Ramp was up to. I called Lucy one more time. Finally, she answered. She was already far from Boulder—at a diner outside Fort Lupton where she'd stopped to have a late breakfast—on her way to the eastern plains. She didn't argue when I told her that I wanted to meet her. I jotted down directions to Ella Ramp's ranch, which was almost precisely halfway between Limon and Agate, and I hustled out the door. From my car I canceled lunch with a colleague and all my remaining therapy appointments until my four-thirty emergency session with Naomi.

It took me almost an hour to plunge through the northern congestion of Denver's metropolitan area and intersect with Interstate 70 on my journey toward Limon, the little town that is the geographic bull's-eye in the center of Colorado's eastern plains.

Many people who have never visited Colorado have a mental image that the state consists predominantly of mountains. Sharp juvenile peaks, high meadows, glacial faces, deep canyons. Travel magazine stuff.

But if a driver heads east away from the Front Range, especially if he's beyond the boundaries of Denver's metropolitan sprawl, and if he doesn't glance back into his rearview mirror, the state of Colorado is hardly distinguishable from Nebraska or Iowa or Kansas. Less corn, more wheat, but mostly mile after mile of mind-numbing Great Plains high prairie. Some people love it, others don't. Either way, the broad expanse of endless horizon and infinite sky takes up roughly half the state.

I'm convinced that if highway planners hadn't chosen the Limon-to-Agate spur for Interstate 70's northwest traverse across the eastern prairie toward Denver, virtually no one would have any reason to be aware exactly where either Agate or Limon is. Nor would anyone care much. In fact, absent the wide ribbon of interstate, Colorado's eastern plains are geographically pretty close to nowhere, and one look at the map confirms that Limon and Agate are about as close to the middle as is theoretically possible.

I made only one wrong turn as I was navigating the grid of county roads east of Agate, and found the Ramp spread on my first try. As I made the last turn, I spotted Lucy's red Volvo parked in the shadow of a huge stack of hay. The lead-gray color of the straw told me that it hadn't been baled or stacked recently. I stopped and got out of my car.

"You been waiting long?" I asked Lucy.

"Half an hour, forty minutes."

"Sorry, I went as fast as I could."

"It's okay, I'm just killing time today anyway. The house is right down there. Why don't we leave your car here, just take mine. I don't want to spook her any more than we already will."

The Ramp home was a sixties-style suburban ranch house that seemed out of place without a few dozen clones crammed around it on six-thousand-square-foot lots. An uninterrupted line of spreading junipers was the only vegetation around the house. A solitary tree—I thought it was a hackberry—stood at the edge of a field about fifty yards to the east.

Lucy drove past the house once before she doubled back toward the driveway. I wasted a moment trying to decide how nearby Ella Ramp's closest neighbor lived. Distances were great out there, and I guessed it was almost a mile between houses.

An impeccably preserved brown Ford pickup—the vintage was late sixties or early seventies—was parked on the dirt drive, not far from the house. Lucy parked behind the truck and we walked to the front door. She knocked. I was already having second thoughts about being out there; a good-sized part of me wished that I'd instead stayed in Boulder and moved up my appointment with Naomi Bigg.

There's another bomb, she'd said. *That lawyer.*

I nearly jumped when I heard somebody say, "Hell!"

Half a minute or so later the door opened. "What?" squealed the woman who stood in the doorway. She was a wiry woman who'd once been of average height, but her frame was beginning to bow to gravity and osteoporosis. Her hair was as gray as slate and her eyes were a blue that glowed like the ocean in the tropics.

"What?" the woman repeated in the same acidic tone. Despite her posture, I pegged her at only about sixty.

Lucy said, "Hello, I'm, um, Lucy Tanner. I—"

"So what?"

Lucy moved back six or eight inches. "We spoke on the phone. I called about your grandson. Do you remember? May I come in?"

"Are you nuts? No, you can't come in. Didn't your mother ever tell you to wait to be invited? Where are your manners? And of course I remember. How many calls like that do you think I get? I'm not feeble."

At the first hollered "Hell!" I'd shifted into clinical mode. This woman—who answered her door by squealing "What?" and who had just called Lucy nuts—was now questioning her manners. I said, "Hello, I, um—"

She stepped right on my words, ignoring me, instead retaining her focus on Lucy. "You a cop?" she asked.

"Excuse me?" Lucy said.

"On TV, the cops always ask to come in. They never wait till they're invited. Something happen to my boy? Are you a cop?"

"I am actually, but I'm not here today as—"

Ella Ramp pushed out the door and shuffled past us. "Come on. I have to check on the chickens. I bet my ass you've never checked on a chicken in your life. I'm right, ain't I? Never mind, I know I'm right. That," she said, pointing at Lucy's Volvo, "ain't no chicken-checker's car."

The henhouse was about thirty yards away, out back. Lucy and I waited while Ella disappeared inside for about three or four minutes. Because she was stooped over, she fit right inside the coop door.

Lucy whispered, "She's . . . interesting, isn't she?"

"Yes," I said. "She is."

Ella shuffled back out and double-checked the clasp on the fence around the henhouse.

I asked, "Has he been out to visit you lately? Your boy?" I was careful to mimic the language she'd used to describe her grandson.

"What's it to you? And who the hell are you, anyway?" Her tone lightened suddenly as she said, "The chickens are fine, by the way, thanks for asking."

"My name is Alan Gregory, and I'm—"

"Well, whoop-dee-do." She turned to Lucy. "You his new girlfriend, missy? He knock you up? Is that why you've come out here? He's got a thing with the girls. And they certainly have a thing with him. But knocking up a cop? Did he? He didn't. Hell's another."

Hell's another? Hell's a mother? I wasn't sure what Ella had said or what on earth it was supposed to mean.

"No, I'm, um, not pregnant."

Ella stopped. She had to crane her neck to look up at Lucy. "Dearest God, you're tall. You're taller than he is. That'd be awkward in my book. But you're not . . . you and he, you're not . . . ?"

"No, we're not."

"That's for the best, I suppose. But you haven't told me why you are here, have you?"

While Lucy sputtered to find a way to reply, I said, "It's about the explosives, Mrs. Ramp."

"Oh, that," Ella replied in a dismissive voice as she shuffled back toward the house. "I thought he was in trouble or something."

Ella busied herself fixing coffee and I agreed to accept a cup even though I would've preferred a glass of water. Lucy, who despised coffee, took one, too. On the way from the front door to the kitchen, I'd tried to spot a collection of framed family photographs, hoping to see a photo of Ella's grandson. But the living room was spare in its decor and the only photographs in sight were of pets. Mostly horses, but also a dog. A huge dog. I thought it was a mastiff, but I wasn't sure.

Ella's kitchen was as spotless as her truck. The pristine room could have been lifted out of the house in one chunk and installed—intact—in some granite edifice as a museum exhibit about life in 1962. Maybe part of a Dwight-and-Mamie-Eisenhower-at-home exhibit at the Smithsonian. The old refrigerator was a Norge and it hummed at a volume that screamed for someone to clean its coils.

The only modern appliance in the kitchen was a little white color television. Ella had it tuned to one of the Denver stations. She turned the sound down all the way before she served the coffee.

Ella said, "Milk? Sugar? I don't use 'em, but I can find 'em if you want 'em."

"No, thank you," I said.

Lucy added, "Black is fine."

"He came by the explosives legal, by the way. They were Herbert's. I told the boy he could experiment with them the way Herbert taught him. The neighbors don't mind; they're used to it by now. It's been going on for at least a quarter century. You know you're getting old when you hear yourself talking in quarter centuries."

I hesitated a moment to see if Lucy was planning to take the lead. She wasn't. I raised the cup to my lips and tried to sound nonchalant as I replied, "The explosives were Herbert's?"

"Who did you say you were? Are you like her lawyer or something?"

"No, I'm Alan Gregory, Dr. Alan Gregory. I'm a psychologist in Boulder."

"Well, what the hell are you doing out here?"

"The explosives," I said. "We came to talk with you about the explosives."

She harrumphed. "You ever been to Las Vegas?" asked Ella.

Lucy said she had driven through, but never stopped. I added, "I've been there a few times."

"Well, I'm proud to say that my Herbert blew up half that damn town. Maybe more than half."

"He did? He blew up half the town?" I didn't have a clue what she was talking about, but was eager to keep her talking about it.

"You know the company called Demolition Specialists? Doesn't matter whether you do or you don't. They're some of the boys who blow up those big buildings all over the place. You always see 'em on the national news, usually on Sunday. They blow most of the big buildings on Sunday on account of there aren't so many people around. People are drawn to explosions for some reason. Like bugs to light, I think. What they do is they implode the buildings actually, so that they fall in on themselves.

"Herbert was a demolition engineer. He worked for Demolition Specialists for most of our marriage. He traveled the world blowing up buildings. Blew up stuff in Japan and Saudi Arabia. Toward the end he was on the team that did all those big demos in Las Vegas. The old casinos? You see those monsters come down on the news? I flew out with him and watched the Sands Hotel come down. That was some week we had, let me tell you. Fireworks, buffets, slot machines, girls dancing around wearin' nothing over their tits. I joked that they'd all lost their shirts gamblin'. Herbert liked that part best, I think, the girls. That was a weekend." Ella smiled at the memory.

It was easy to smile right back at her. "So that's what Herbert did for a living? He blew up buildings? And he took down those old casinos in Vegas?"

"Not just him. He was a team player. You might not think it, but it takes a mess of people to bring down a skyscraper. Takes weeks to get one ready to come down. He was gone half the time, Herbert."

"And he's dead now, Ella?"

"With the Lord." She touched her heart.

"I'm sorry. And the explosives that your grandson

uses for his experiments? They belonged to Herbert?"
I asked.

"Yes, they did. In between jobs, Herbert did research. His thing was shaped charges. He was always playing around with shaped charges and the best way to cut metal. That was his specialty: cutting metal with shaped charges. Kept material here for his research. Mostly dynamite, I think. But some other things, too. I never paid much attention. We got a shed he had built special. It's more like a vault than a shed, to tell the truth. Herbert had a thing about security of his explosives. Wrong hands, you know?"

I wouldn't have known a shaped charge if I was sitting on one, and now I found myself yearning to have Sam Purdy beside me. Lucy sounded like she was better informed than I when she said, "I always wondered who did the shaped-charge research. That's remarkable about Herbert. And he taught your grandson what he knew?"

"A lot of it, he sure did. Always thought that the boy might follow in his footsteps. Herbert would've loved to have lived long enough to make the boy an apprentice in the company. Can't go to college to learn to do what Herbert knew about bringing down buildings. Herbert always said as long as there are bad architects and worse builders, there'll be a need for people like him. Can I get you all some more coffee?"

I shook my head and pretended to take another sip of coffee. Lucy said, "Do you know how I can reach him? Your grandson? I have some questions for him."

Ella Ramp set her cup on its saucer and stared at her. "You said you're a cop. Now's about the time where you should be getting around to telling me why you want him."

"The truth is, I need to talk with him about the explosives."

Ella stretched her neck from side to side. It appeared that the act caused considerable pain. Midway through the stretch, Ella said, "I'm getting old, I know that. As far as I'm concerned, it's premature, but so be it. Life is what life is. Mine? I live by myself a hundred miles from life as most city people know it. I know more about chickens and horses and dogs than I do about people. I'm stooped over and I'm gray and when I dare myself to look in a mirror I usually conclude that I'm butt ugly. But I'm not particularly stupid. Now stop repeating yourself and tell me what the hell you want with my grandson. What about the damn explosives?"

I took a moment to try to decide how to play this. As a psychologist, I actually adored moments like these. Some of my most memorable conversations with Sam Purdy had been discussions about how to play situations just like this one with Ella.

"Ella," I finally said, "I could bullshit you right now. I could. I'm good at it and despite the fact that I believe you when you say that you are a bright woman, I think I could succeed in bullshitting you. But I won't. So here's the truth: The reason we're trying to find your grandson is that we think he may be responsible for setting some bombs that have hurt some people."

Ella sipped at her coffee. She narrowed her eyes as though she was protecting them from the steam. She asked, "That one in Denver last week? Where that woman died in that car? That's one of 'em?"

"Yes, that's one of them."

She appeared to be puzzled. "Why would he do that? Why would the boy do that?"

Lucy said, "We think he might be angry at law enforcement or the justice system. The courts."

Lucy's words assaulted Ella like a physical blow. Her breath caught in her chest, her eyes closed in a wince, and the fingernails of her right hand cut sharply into the skin of her left arm.

I waited for Ella's next move, which I assumed would be an awkward denial that her grandson was angry at the criminal justice system. But Ella didn't protest. Instead, she narrowed her eyes again and stared at me hard, then glanced over at the TV. "You're that girl who they think killed her momma's husband, aren't you? From up in Boulder? You're the girl from the news this morning?"

Despite her best efforts to maintain her detective's poker face, I could feel Lucy's demeanor change as she tried to process the question.

Ella shook her head in a wide arc. "Well, hell's another. Hell's a—nuh—ther. My own momma always said to wake up looking forward to each day because you never really know what's going to come along with the dawn. But I swear it's been a while since I've had a day quite like this one. A girl from the morning news program sitting right here in my kitchen."

I lifted my cup again but didn't actually get it to my lips before Ella cracked a little smile and said, "So tell me, missy, you have a gun under that jacket? You planning to shoot me if I don't talk?"

Lucy exclaimed, "What?" But she left both hands on the table where Ella could see them. "No, Ella, I'm not going to shoot you."

The tension between the two women was suddenly as thick as butter. I interjected, "But we would like to talk a little bit about how the boy's mother died, Ella. Could we do that?"

Ella burped a tiny burp and covered her mouth. She looked away and closed her eyes, holding them tightly shut.

"Ella?" I said.

"Hell's another," she muttered. "Hell's another."

I never used to curse before she died. Not even in anger. Certainly not just for the hell of it like I do now. The man who killed her stuck one knife in her chest and he stuck another one in my soul."

Hell's another.

I was still unsure what relation Ramp's mother was to Ella. I asked, "His mother was your daughter-in-law, Ella?"

"No, no, no. Denise was our daughter. Herbert and me had one daughter, one son. Our son—that's Brian—he died in a Humvee accident in Somalia. He was a medic in the Marines at the time. It was on the news."

Ella sighed quickly—almost a gasp—before she continued. "Then Denise was murdered in Denver. Bang, bang. Strike one, strike two."

"I didn't know. I'm so sorry."

"Brian—that's our son—he was trying to do good when he died. Humanitarian assistance in Somalia. That's in Africa. He was a peacekeeper. A Marine peacekeeper. Herbert always thought it was an oxy—whaddyacallit?"

"Oxymoron."

"Yeah. Oxymoron. Doesn't matter. Fact is, Brian was a peacekeeper at heart. His death was just one of those things that preachers can't explain no matter how hard they try or how long they talk on Sunday mornings about God's mysterious ways. Herbert was philosophical about it, said it could just as easily have been a pickup truck accident on I-70 that killed Brian. If I'd had a bet to place, I would've rather bet my son's life on the pickup and the interstate, you know what I mean?"

I said I did.

Ella required no further prompting. She said, "But Denise?" She shook her head as though trying to cleanse an image of something she'd rather not recall. "It was four years, five months ago. Two weeks before Christmas. She was living with her husband, Patrick, in Denver, in the neighborhood they call Uptown. You know it?"

"Vaguely," I said. Years before during my first marriage, when I'd spent more time in Denver, the neighborhood was called North Capitol Hill. Now dubbed Uptown on the Hill, the compact urban neighborhood just northeast of downtown was an interesting multiethnic place with a range of residents who varied widely in financial wherewithal. Despite its new name, though, the neighborhood wasn't on much of a hill. Recently refurbished late-nineteenth-century homes sat adjacent to massive redevelopment projects, vacant lots, and old apartment houses gone to seed.

"Denise was a nurse at one of the hospitals nearby. Presbyterian? She liked the neighborhood because she could walk to work and because there were all kinds of people living there. That was her way of telling us that life there was nothing like being out here in Agate. The whole time she and Pat were there, they didn't even know it but three doors down from their old Denver square was a rooming house that was actually a halfway house, you know, a place for released criminals. The ones who've been, whaddyacallit, paroled?"

"Yes," Lucy said, "paroled."

Ella had already shared enough details that I thought I knew the rest of the story. A Denver woman had been stabbed to death by a guy on parole for a previous murder conviction. I remembered the story from news reports and I recalled discussing it in some detail with Sam over a couple of beers one night.

Sam had been especially irate about the crime. The practice of releasing dangerous felons on early parole was an issue that bugged cops more than it bugged anybody else. Except, maybe, the families of the paroled felon's last victims, or the families of his next victims.

"He'd been in the halfway house for a few months," Ella told us. "Luther Smith is his name. He'd served four years, five months, three days for a manslaughter conviction in Commerce City before he was released into a halfway house in Denver. Why there? Why right down the street from my girl? Who knows? But he was living in that halfway house when he began following my Denise to work and deciding that since she worked at a hospital she might be keeping drugs at her house. That's what he told the police anyway; that's the way he explained breaking into her place and ransacking it and waiting for her to come home from work that day.

"Pat—her husband—worked as a pressman at the *Denver Post*. He was gone evenings. Denise thought she was coming home to an empty house. But she wasn't. Luther Smith was there waiting for her and he was mad as hell because he hadn't found any drugs anywhere in the house."

Ella thrust her chin forward. I could see the effort she was using in her attempt to control the quivering that had erupted.

"He began to try to rape my little girl and she fought him like a banshee. That's what the cops said. She fought him as hard as any woman has ever fought off any man. That's what they told me and Herbert.

"So Luther Smith stabbed her. He did it just once. Sliced right through some big artery at the top of her stomach. And my Denise bled to death right there in her own bedroom. It was Jason who found her when he got home from a football game at his high school that night."

Jason, I said to myself. *He has a name. The bomber has a name. It's Jason, but not Jason Ramp. Ramp's his mother's name. It's Jason what?*

To Ella, I said, "I'm so sorry. You've had so much loss."

Lucy added, "I'm so sorry, too. What happened to your daughter is awful. Inexcusable."

Ella frosted her voice with defeat. "He didn't rape her. Coroner said he didn't rape her. I sometimes find myself wishing that he had. Wishing she hadn't fought him so hard so she might be alive."

Her words covered the contours of the irony of rape like upholstery covers an old sofa. "I'm so sorry, Ella," I said again. There should have been better words, but if there were, I didn't know them.

"I still go to church every Sunday, you know. Despite what God allowed to be done to my children. I made a pledge to keep giving Him a chance to explain Himself until the day that I die."

Lucy said, "It's my understanding that your grandson calls himself Ramp, still. That's in honor of his mother?"

"No, our name—his mother's maiden name—is his middle name. The boy's name is Jason Ramp Bass. His friends started calling him Ramp sometime in high school. Something about skateboarding I never understood. There's a lot about skateboarding I never understood." Ella sighed. "You get to be my age, you realize the list of things you never understood is a hell of a long one."

Lucy and I sat at the kitchen table with Ella for quite a while early that afternoon, learning about Denise and Pat, and the boy his grandmother called Jase.

"Pat couldn't manage Jase after Denise died. Boy gave him no end of trouble. So he came out here to live with me and Herbert. Jase didn't like it out here in the country but he adjusted okay. I give Herbert most of the credit for that. When Herbert was in town between demo jobs, the boy and him were inseparable. Always doing things together. Mostly cutting steel with explosives. Herbert said that the boy had a knack with explosives."

From the corner of my eye, I could see the screen on the television set on the counter. A teaser for the evening news was running. I wasn't sure if Lucy saw it, too, but assuming that Lucy's story was about to be featured, I knew that I didn't want Ella to be reminded of Lucy's recent notoriety.

I stood, carrying dishes toward the sink.

"Don't do that," Ella said. "I'll clean up."

"It's not a bother—it's the way I was brought up," I said. I switched the TV off before I stacked the dishes. "I hope you don't mind that I turned it off. It's distracting me."

"Oh, I don't mind. It's only there for company. And I've already got company, today."

"Where's Jase now? In Denver?" Lucy asked.

"Mmm-hmm. Denver. He works for a welding company. It's something else that Herbert taught him. Herbert was always cutting metal and welding metal for his experiments."

"Shaped charges," Lucy said.

"That's right." One side of Ella's mouth elevated in a smile. "You don't know what they are, do you?"

"No," she admitted. "I don't. I don't have a clue what a shaped charge is."

Ella laughed so hard she started to cough from a place deep in the recesses of her lungs. When she finally controlled the spasm, she said, "You two are going to go talk to him now, aren't you? Once you leave here."

Lucy and I both nodded.

"Figured. Well, I'll save you some time and tell you where to find him, but I want to talk to him first. I should also talk to Pat, his father, let him know what you told me. Once I do those two things, I'll tell you where to find Jase. If he really did what you say, well . . . But I want you to remember something, too. I want you to remember that the boy was hurt by his mother's death. You'll remember that? We've all been hurt by what happened."

I said, "Of course."

Lucy wrote her phone numbers on a sheet of paper and gave it to Ella. She said, "That's fair, Ella. You give me a call after you talk to Jason and his father, okay?"

Ella looked back up at me before she spoke to Lucy. "Right now, you're acting like you're going to wait to talk to Jase until I call you. But you won't wait. You're going to go try to find him as soon as you leave here. You're going to go out to your fancy car and get on your cell phone and call your cop friends or you're going to use some computer whizbang and do some magic thing that the police do on TV and you're going to try and find him. Clear as dew, you'd lie to an old woman."

Lucy said, "To track down whoever has been setting those bombs, Ella, I'd lie to every old woman I could find."

Ella opened a drawer that was recessed into the side of the kitchen table. She reached in and slid out a huge revolver. I thought it might be a .45. It was clean and gleamed with fresh oil. Ella rested the weapon on the table, the barrel pointed only slightly away from Lucy.

My heart galloped.

"I like you both," Ella said. "I do."

I thought, *Hell's another.*

CHAPTER
31

Lucy dropped me off back at my car. I would've loved to have had some time to reflect with her over what we'd just learned—or, at the very least, to hear what she thought about Ella's revolver—but I had to rush to Boulder to have a prayer of getting back for my appointment with Naomi.

I held up my watch and said, "If I make it to my office on time, I'm meeting with her this afternoon." I was still reluctant to use my patient's name in conversation.

Lucy wasn't. She said, "You're seeing Naomi?"

"She said she had some news for me, something important. But what we just learned from Ella can't wait for that—Sam needs to know everything we heard right now. So do the Denver Police."

"I'll do that, don't worry," she said. "I know who to

talk to. And maybe the fact that it comes from me will earn me some redemption."

I spent the long drive back to Boulder watching my mirrors for a State Patrol cruiser and trying to prepare myself for what I expected would be a difficult session with Naomi.

When I got to my office and entered through the rear doors, it was only four-twenty but the red light on the far wall was already beaming. Naomi Bigg wasn't only on time for her extra appointment, she was early. And, given what Lucy and I had discovered about Ramp earlier that afternoon, I was more than ready for the meeting. I took a deep breath and made long strides down the hall to greet her.

But the woman I found standing in the middle of the waiting room wasn't Naomi Bigg.

She heard me open the door and barely threw a glance my way before she demanded, "Where is she? Is she back there? Where is she?"

The voice was frantic and distinctly young. The speaker was, too. When I didn't reply right away, she immediately turned back to scan the street, spying at something through the window.

I guessed that she was in her late teens, early twenties. She was blond and overweight. How overweight was hard to tell; her clothes hung on her like curtains. One eyebrow was pierced and adorned with a thin gold ring. Her hair was cut, well, badly, and dyed even worse, though I suspected that the aesthetic impact of the coiffure was intentional. I thought that there was something unusual about her makeup as well but couldn't decide exactly what. Maybe it was the color around her eyes.

"May I help you?" I asked.

"You're her doctor? My mother's doctor? Is she back there? God, this is important! Is she fucking back there yet? I need to talk to her!"

She'd begun screaming at me.

"No, she's not here yet. You're Marin, aren't you?"

She nodded and returned her attention to the window. I could see her shoulders rise and fall with each rapid breath.

I said, "I expect her any minute. You can talk to her then. In the meantime, is there anything that I can do to help you while—"

She raised her arms up above her head and then dropped them quickly past her waist, as though she were signaling the start of a race. "Oh my God, where is she? I can't believe he'd do this. I never thought he'd do this. It's not what she thinks. It isn't what she thinks."

"Who'd do what?" Her terror was infectious. Naomi's message was still echoing in my ears. I was beginning to become aware of pressure building in my chest, my pulse pounding at the veins in my neck.

There's another bomb. That lawyer.

Marin shook her head, exasperated. "Does she park here? In front? Or do you have a parking lot?"

I stared at her, stammering in an effort to start a sentence.

"When she comes to visit you, goddamn it, where the hell does she park her damn car?"

"Patients usually park on the street. But I've never watched where your mother parks her car."

She looked up. "Is that a siren? Oh my God, oh my God. Do you hear that? In the distance. Is that a siren?"

I listened. I didn't hear a siren. I said so.

"What time is it?" she demanded. She seemed to have totally forgotten about the phantom siren.

I looked at my watch. Employing a voice that tried to reflect a pretense that I wasn't talking to a histrionic stranger, I said, "Four twenty-five. A little after."

"Is she late?"

"No. She's not due here for a few more minutes." I had no right to share that information, but I didn't even consider the possibility of not answering Marin Bigg's question.

Marin pointed outside and screamed, "There she is! There's her car. See it? That's it!"

I looked through the glass and saw the BMW that Naomi had been driving when she'd pulled up next to Lauren and me at the stoplight the day before. She was right out front of my building, backing expertly into a parking space that was only a few feet longer than her car. A cigarette dangled from her lips. Even from this distance I could tell that the ash was precariously long.

Marin ran out the door, waving her arms as though

she were intent on bringing a runaway train to a halt. She started yelling, "Mom! Mom! Don't stop the car! Don't stop the car! Get out and leave it running. Mom! Mom!"

I was totally perplexed. I followed her outside.

Marin leapt off the little porch, still waving her arms. "Mom! Mom! Here! Don't stop the car! *Mom!* Don't—"

Naomi stopped the car. The reassuring BMW purr clicked off.

Marin covered her ears.

I exhaled.

Marin had stopped screaming as suddenly as if someone had pulled the plug on her power source.

Her voice now hollow, she said, "It didn't . . . He didn't . . . Mom, Mom. You're okay, Mom."

She may have actually finished those first two sentences, but I was still on the porch, fifteen or twenty feet behind her, and I couldn't hear her well.

Naomi climbed out of the BMW and stood on the street right beside the still-open door of her car. She took a moment to straighten her clothes, tugging down the bottom of a short-sleeved jacket. Her shoulders were stiff. I thought that she wasn't happy to see her daughter. Shaking her head emphatically, she said, "Not now, Marin. We'll talk later. Go on back home— wait for me there. I'm serious about this—wait there."

Marin held her hands out, palms to the sky. "Mom, I . . . I came to warn you. . . ." Her tone grew plaintive.

"About what? About him?" Naomi's tone was

derisive, cutting. I recognized it instantly; she'd certainly used the same tone often enough with me. "It's a little late for that, isn't it? I just talked to him. He came by the office to plead with me, called upstairs and waited outside by my car. I just left him in the parking lot five minutes ago. So I already know what's going on. All of it. The party the two of you have planned is over as of right now, do you understand? I'll do what I can to help you both, I promise. Now go on home. I can't believe you did this. I just can't believe it."

Marin was frozen in place, standing on the sidewalk ten feet from her mother's car. I couldn't see Marin's face, though I could tell from her posture that the tension wasn't quite gone. She said nothing; she didn't seem to have a response for her mother's words.

Naomi leaned back down and reached into the car, grabbed the big Vuitton bag she always carried with her, and slung it over her shoulder. She slammed the car door. The noise it made was a solid, Bavarian thud. "Go home," she told her daughter. "I'll be there in an hour. We'll decide what to do then."

Either Naomi had not seen me eavesdropping on the porch or she was ignoring me. Either way, I was grateful not to have much of a role in this new act of the Bigg family drama.

For a moment, neither woman took a step. When Naomi finally walked with determined strides toward the sidewalk, I decided that the time had come for me to go back into my office and let this scenario between mother and daughter develop however it was going to develop.

I think I turned my head first.

But I'm not sure.

Maybe I'd even completed turning all the way around so that I was facing the door. But the ragged piece of metal that I caught on the outside of my right thigh argued against that.

Regardless, I remember seeing the flash in the periphery of my vision, and I think I heard the boom. Maybe it was the other way around. I know I felt the concussion. The evidence of that was irrefutable. It threw me against the front door of the old brick house with enough force to crack oak.

When I woke up, or cleared my head, or whatever it was that I did, I could finally hear the sirens. I wanted to tell Marin Bigg that I could finally hear the sirens.

I tried to stand up to go find Marin and Naomi, but a young man with a ring between his nostrils and a tattoo of a black flower on his throat kept a firm grip on my shoulders.

He said, "I don't think you should get up, man. Someone's coming to help you. I don't think you should get up, man. I'm serious, here. Come on, now. Cooperate with me."

"Where's Marin? Tell her I hear the sirens."

"Hey, whatever. I'll tell her. I'll tell her."

Up close, his nasal ring captivated me. I wanted to ask him what it had felt like to get that part of his nose pierced. Did they go through the cartilage with the needle or did they slide the metal in front of it in that soft skin that always got so sore when I had a cold? But it didn't seem like an appropriate question to a stranger, so I kept my musings to myself.

Then I recalled Naomi's message.

There's another bomb. That lawyer.

I tried to sit up. I said, "There's another bomb. That lawyer."

He kept his hands on my shoulders. "What? I don't think you should get up, man. You're not real stable."

That understatement was the last thing I recalled until the ambulance ride.

CHAPTER

32

There's another bomb. That lawyer.

I spilled the beans about the wouldn't-it-be-cool games about five minutes after I arrived at the hospital. It took that long for me to collect my wits. Lauren had been called but she wasn't yet at my side, so Sam Purdy was my first confessor. For some reason, he'd been the one elected by the medical staff to inform me that what little was left of Naomi Bigg was dead.

Come to think of it, it was more likely that Sam's position as town crier was self-appointed. At that moment he'd be more concerned with bomb facts than with my feelings.

I asked him about Marin. The nurses and doctors who'd been treating me had been unwilling to tell me her condition.

Sam, on the other hand, didn't blink at my question. Marin Bigg was on her way to surgery. Her condition wasn't critical, though he didn't know the details. He'd let me know when things changed.

I proceeded to tell Sam about Naomi's message. *There's another bomb. That lawyer.* I tried to put it all in context by telling him everything I remembered about Paul and Ramp and the wouldn't-it-be-cool games. When I got around to mentioning Ella Ramp and Jason Ramp Bass and shaped charges and the explosives vault near Limon, he barked, "What?"

"The things that Lucy called you about a few hours ago. Ramp's grandmother is Ella. Jason Ramp Bass is Ramp's real name. Lucy and I met with the grandmother early this afternoon."

Sam's eyes shimmered with a frightening blend of anger and alarm. "I haven't talked to Lucy today, Alan."

"She didn't call you a few hours ago?"

"No."

"You don't know about our trip to Agate?"

"No."

"Oh, shit," I said. I tried to get up. "Oh . . . shit."

I told Sam that I thought Lucy must be out looking for Ramp on her own, and told him everything that she and I had learned that afternoon in Agate. As I related the story, he used his cell phone to repeat the information almost word for word to someone at the police department.

At his urging I offered him my guesses about the list of people that Paul Bigg might have been targeting in

Boulder. Unfortunately, every one of the potential targets was a lawyer, so my list didn't narrow the realm of
potential targets very much. Sam took careful notes
and asked good questions. I made him promise to track
down Lauren and to get Grace and her babysitter over
to Adrienne's house right away. He said to consider it
done.

When I was through with my story about the Biggs
and Ramp and the Agate ranch, he told me in a soft
voice that my judgment was "goofy."

Listening to Sam over the years, I'd learned that
"goofy" is an all-purpose Minnesota word that includes
connotations ranging from "odd" to "totally fucked
up." In these circumstances, I was assuming Sam's
intent fell somewhere at the very profane end of the
spectrum.

Once he was convinced that he'd accumulated all
the salient details about the bombs and the boys, Sam
left me to go confirm that protection was in place for
all the people who might possibly have been targeted
by Paul Bigg in Boulder.

All the lawyers.

I assumed he was also doing whatever had to be
done to make sure that every possible stone was being
turned in the search for the man named Jason Ramp
Bass in Denver.

Adrienne joined me in the ER minutes after Sam
departed. When she saw my name on the ER board,

she had just finished doing some emergency urological procedure that I was sure would make me cross my legs if she shared the details.

She didn't. She merely shook her head at the sight of me.

"Hi," I said.

She actually laughed. From anyone else the reaction would've struck me as inappropriate. From Adrienne, it was comforting.

She said, "You're alive. That's good. The board outside says 'laceration, shrapnel.' Leaves an awful lot to the imagination. I thought my surgical reconstruction skills might be required."

I shuddered at the thought, then told her about the bomb outside my office.

She had a few questions. I answered them before I asked her if she'd heard from Lauren.

She hadn't.

"Will you page her for me?"

"Right now? Sure." She pulled her cell phone from her pocket and entered a long string of digits while she said, "I'm not supposed to use this in here, you know. Could be short-circuiting a heart monitor or screwing up a CAT scan or something. Anything else you want?"

"Call your nanny and have her go get Grace and Viv and take them back to your place. I don't want them in our house. Sam said he'd call, but could you double-check?"

"And the dogs," she said.

"Yes, and the dogs."

She made that call, too.

"*Mi casa es su casa,* and, even better for me, *su* nanny *es mi* nanny. Now, you want to tell me what's going on?"

I nodded and began to tell her about the Biggs and Ramp. Being in a peculiarly confessional mood, I proceeded to fill her in on almost everything that I'd just told Sam Purdy. I was just about to get to the part of the story where I went to Agate with Lucy when Adrienne raised her hand and extended an index finger straight up. She said, "Alan, what did the neurologist tell you?"

"What do you mean?"

"About your . . . mental status?"

"She said I have a minor concussion. I may have headaches for a while. Told me not to exercise for a few days. Said I was real lucky with the leg wound. The shrapnel almost hit a major vessel. But that wasn't the neurologist. That was the guy who sewed me back up. I think it was an ER guy, a new guy, somebody I don't know."

Adrienne nodded knowingly at my comments even though she didn't really know a thing about my condition. I hate it when doctors do that. My patients probably hate it when I do that.

"What?" I demanded. "Don't just nod your head like I'm some imbecile. What are you thinking?"

"This thing you just told me about Paul Bigg? And his friend—what's his name, Ramp?"

"Yes, Ramp."

"You're sure about it?"

"Yes." Suddenly, I wasn't sure.

She nodded again.

"Adrienne, what?"

"I'm afraid that there's no gentle way to put this. But Paul Bigg is dead, Alan. Very dead."

"Oh God," I said. "They found his body, too? Where was it? At their house? The Bigg house?" For some reason, I immediately suspected suicide. After he'd placed the bomb that killed his mother, he'd gone home and killed himself.

Adrienne shook her head and lowered her voice, making it so soft that her northeast accent almost evaporated. "No, hon. Paul Bigg died playing Little League baseball when he was twelve years old. He got hit in the chest by a ball and died from a heart rhythm abnormality."

I felt as though I'd been punched in the gut.

"What?"

"Paul's been dead for, like, five or six years. I told you the other night that Leo's family has had way too many tragedies, even before he went to prison. Don't you remember?"

I stared at her with my mouth in the classic O sign. It took me a few moments to form my next sentence. "That can't be right. No way. She told me he worked at Starbucks. On the Mall, down near Fifteenth Street. Naomi did." I almost argued that Naomi had said that Paul made the best mocha on the planet. I thought she'd said "on the planet." Maybe it was just that he made a "killer mocha." It bothered me that I couldn't remember exactly what she had said. She certainly hadn't said that her son was long dead and that she'd been making everything up.

"He doesn't work at Starbucks, Alan. He probably died before he ever laid eyes on a Starbucks. Paul Bigg is dead." Adrienne was being uncharacteristically gentle, as though she were speaking to somebody with severe mental instability.

Me.

"Adrienne, that can't be true. Naomi just talked with him. A few minutes before she died. I heard her tell Marin about it. She was mad at him about something. He can't be dead."

Adrienne said, "I think you're mistaken."

I protested. "He has this friend. Ramp."

"Maybe he did, Alan, back then. But not now. Paul's dead. Peter and I went to his funeral. I promise you that he's dead."

"I don't understand. I know all about him. His school, his friends. Everything. I know what psychiatrist he went to, Adrienne. What he was treated for, everything."

Adrienne began to nod again, but she caught herself. In retrospect, I'm sure she was fighting an urge to ask me if I knew my name, knew where I was right then, what day it was, who was the current President of the United States.

She didn't ask. She said, "Well, maybe you don't know quite everything that you think you know."

Duh.

CHAPTER
33

Ramp felt the flash from the bomb the same way he experienced the sun as it broke through a thick cloud cover. The light and heat washed over him and warmed him, licking at his exposed skin all at once. He raised his chin an inch or so to greet the energy as it pulsed and engulfed him. Since it was the first time he would be around to see one of his devices go off in public, he desperately wanted to keep his eyes open to record the visual landscape as it settled in the aftermath of his work, but his reflexes overwhelmed him.

The plastic box with the toggle switch in his jacket pocket was moist from the sweat on his hand. He fingered the slick plastic as impulses flooded him. The energy it consumed to control the urges thwarted his enjoyment of the consequences of the blast. He wanted to thrust his hands into the air and yell, "Yes!" He wanted to pull the transmitter from his pocket and thrust it to his lips and display it to the stunned citizens around him.

He didn't.

He monitored his excited breathing by forcing each deep breath to pass through his nose and go deep into his gut. Despite the chaos that was stirring in the aftermath of the explosion, he could hear himself snort and was afraid he sounded like a horse eager to canter.

Ramp had detonated the bomb from where he'd been standing on Walnut in front of the aging house that old-time Boulderites would probably forever consider to be the second home of Nancy's restaurant. As the echoes of the detonation stilled, Ramp heard people in front of Café Louie, the restaurant that had replaced Nancy's, screaming, "Did you hear that?" "What was that?" "Was that a car that blew up?" and "Oh no, oh my God! I think it was a bomb."

The sounds were all on separate tracks in his consciousness, laid down methodically, distinctly. They were the kinds of details that he knew he'd want to remember later.

As people ran past him toward the location of the blast, he wanted to follow them. He wanted to see for himself what havoc the explosive had wreaked. What carnage the metal splinters had wrought. Did he kill one? Or two? Or even three? But he didn't follow the throngs to the source of the damage.

He was sure he didn't want to see the bodies.

There were bodies. He knew that. The bodies meant

casualties. The casualties were necessary, but he feared that each would remind him of the day he discovered his mother's body.

He turned and walked the opposite direction down Walnut, crossing Ninth and moving at a measured pace to cover the short blocks to the Downtown Mall. The plan called for him to linger for a while with the crowds on the Mall before he returned to his car.

He remembered something his grandfather had said about explosives: *Maniacs destroy maniacally. Engineers destroy scientifically. You are the engineer.*

"I am the engineer," he said, barely moving his lips, hardly making a sound.

"And how was it?" he asked himself, adopting a gravelly, deeper voice. The voice of someone who'd inhaled the poisons of way too many Camels. The voice of his grandfather.

"Better than I would have guessed, Granddad. The best, the absolute best. It's so much better when you're there."

The deeper voice responded, "Wait. They only get better. The better you get, the better they get. I liked the last one I did better than I did the first."

"I wasn't really sure I could do it. The first one went off accidentally, you know. So I wasn't sure I could actually detonate one myself. One that counted, I mean."

"I was sure. I was sure."

At the corner of Eleventh, outside the Walrus, a woman approached him on the sidewalk and Ramp ended the conversation he was having. The last thing he wanted to do was draw attention to himself a block and a half from the crime scene.

Another saying from Granddad: *You don't hurry to meet deadlines. You change deadlines so you don't have to hurry.*

Not this time, Ramp thought as he climbed into the driver's seat of his blue RAV 4. Most of what the old man had said was true. But not that, not this time. Ramp knew he'd have to accelerate the whole timetable. He knew that they'd be looking for him now.

Maybe they even knew who he was already.

He had to act now before it was too late. One quick stop at his apartment and he'd be ready to go.

The sign above the workbench in the explosives shed: *Safety is the product of planning, discipline, and control. If you plan well, deploy with discipline, and control your charges, you will be safe.*

But what if you don't care if you're safe? What if you're willing to go out with the blast?

The old man couldn't have imagined it, so he had never had an aphorism for that.

Ramp started the car.

He tuned the radio to AM and hit the scan button, listening for the sound of breaking news.

Before he made it to the edge of town, he was gripped with a hunger that was as tight as a choke chain. He stopped at the McDonald's on Baseline and ordered a Big Mac Extra Value Meal. As he pulled forward to the pick-up window, a young kid in the required bad clothes and polyester hat asked him if he'd heard about the explosion downtown.

"No," Ramp said. "What happened?"

"Don't know, but somebody got smoked. Did you say you wanted a Coke with that?"

Somebody got smoked. Ramp had trouble finding the skills necessary to continue to breathe. "Yes, I want a Coke with that."

He'd wanted to demand the facts. He'd wanted to ask the kid if only one somebody had been smoked. But he didn't.

Ramp stayed east on Baseline, pulling french fries from their red cardboard sleeve one by one, feeding them into his mouth like severed branches into a shredder, finally turning onto the Foothills Parkway toward the turnpike that would return him to Denver.

He continued to scan the radio stations for news. He was halfway to Denver, driving through a speed trap on Highway 36 in Westminster, before he heard the first bulletin about the explosion. Initial reports listed one victim dead from the explosion in downtown Boulder, three injured.

Three meant at least one innocent bystander.

Ramp shrugged and took a long draw from his Coke.

"Shit!" he said suddenly and yanked the wheel hard to make the exit at Federal Boulevard. He steered with one hand and began patting furiously at the pocket of his jacket with the other.

There it was. He still had it with him. What if he'd been stopped? What if a cop had found an excuse to search him?

He heard the words in his head as clearly as he'd heard them the first time his grandfather had spoken them to him: *Careless is just another word for failure.*

"Shit!" he repeated before silently repeating the old man's mantra over and over again, using it as a way to flog himself back into control.

He drove around the back of the bowling alley that was adjacent to the freeway on the southwest side of the Federal off-ramp and pulled up next to a row of three Dumpsters. He stepped out of the car, pulled the radio controller from his pocket, dropped it to the asphalt, and crushed the plastic box with one sharp thrust of his heel. He divided the shattered electronic remains between the three Dumpsters, saving the tiny joystick as a souvenir.

Ramp spent the next couple of miles on the road trying to devise a way to attach the joystick to his key ring.

Fifteen minutes later he was turning into the alley that ran behind his apartment building. The building had six alley parking spaces for twelve apartments. Ramp was shocked to find one available. He let himself in the back door and climbed the three flights of stairs to his fourth-floor unit.

The first thing he did once inside was to boot up his

computer and check the Internet for fresh news of the Boulder bombing. Not much had been added to the radio bulletin. The three living victims had been taken to Community Hospital; one was in critical condition. Police weren't commenting on a possible link to the explosive device that had been found hidden in District Attorney Royal Peterson's house.

"Let them comment all they want," Ramp said aloud. "They won't find a single similarity in materials or design. Signatures are for fools."

Done with the Internet connection, he began the series of keystrokes that would format the hard drive of his computer, erasing all his digital tracks. Getting the process started took him less than a minute. He'd practiced the procedure before. None of it was new to him.

Another sign above the workbench in the explosives shed: *Novelty creates confusion. Practice eliminates novelty.*

"Right on, Granddad," Ramp said.

He collected three radio transmitters from the kitchen cupboard above the dishwasher. The three devices were dissimilar. One was a garage door opener. One had operated a remote-control children's car. The third had been designed to operate a model airplane. He placed them in a leather dopp kit that was already provisioned with fresh batteries for the transmitters.

He pried the floorboard away from the wall and pocketed the Zip disc that he'd stashed there. His work clothes and the other supplies were already packed in a duffel bag that he'd used to carry his soccer clothes when he was in high school.

Last, he retrieved a fresh battery for his cell phone, dumped everything into the duffel with his clothes, locked up his apartment, and descended the stairs toward his car.

CHAPTER

34

Before I was allowed to leave the hospital, a lot of people wanted to talk to me. Almost all of them were from law enforcement.

Lauren, I think, wanted only to yell at me. But she didn't. She was overtly kind to me the way that I knew I would someday be overtly kind to Grace after she cut herself or broke a bone solely because of *her* poor judgment and stupidity.

Lauren could afford to be kind to me because she knew that I knew how stupid I'd been. She knew it because I reminded her of it every few minutes.

The first few repetitive apologies took place while I was still at the hospital. The neurologist who was assessing me for closed head injuries actually expressed concern to Lauren that my perseveration might be ample evidence that I'd suffered brain trauma. Soon, however, my wife concluded that my refrain was merely a recurring prayer seeking psychological absolution for my mortal sins against good judgment.

As the shadows were fading and darkness was sealing the end of the day, Lauren drove me home. On the way down North Broadway, I heard birds singing that had probably been singing the evening before and smelled flowers that had certainly smelled just as sweet that morning. But, after surviving the explosion, my senses felt sharper. I wanted to test the hypothesis further and taste my wife's kiss, but she was in no mood to indulge me. As we cruised past the new Bureau of Standards building on South Broadway near Table Mesa, Lauren used an oh-by-the-way tone to caution me that serious discussions were probably ongoing in the district attorney's office about whether or not I could be charged with a crime. Something about withholding evidence.

Like what? I wondered, though not aloud. For some reason, Lauren's warning didn't particularly alarm me. What were they going to do to me?

Maybe I'd be arrested for not blowing the whistle on a kid who had been dead for six years.

I decided that it would almost be worth going to trial just to hear the opening statements on that one.

Prior to making Ella Ramp's acquaintance in Agate that afternoon, the act of rationalizing my willingness to disclose confidential information to the Boulder

Police had taken some significant gymnastics. Because patient privilege survives patient death, even the fact that Naomi was now dead wasn't actually enough to free me from my legal restrictions to keep quiet. What finally liberated me to open my mouth to the authorities about all the things I'd learned from Naomi in psychotherapy was the now undeniable reality that Naomi's fears about bombs and explosives weren't the product of her imagination, and my near one-hundred-percent assurance that the bomber was a kid in Denver named Jason Ramp Bass. My assurance that Jason Bass had set a bomb off in the Louis Vuitton bag that Naomi always carried slung from her shoulder was as close to one hundred percent as it could get.

The leap from those realizations to the acceptance that other people were still in danger from other bombs was all that I needed to free myself from the bounds of confidentiality. Lawyers and practitioners could argue whether the circumstances actually constituted legally enforceable *Tarasoff* conditions, but the truth was that I had lost any remaining interest I'd had in debating the finer legal and ethical threads.

I ran my belated rationalizations by Lauren. She made it clear that she thought I'd jumped through the progression of ethical hoops in a peculiarly tardy fashion. Although it was clear she was admonishing me, I was relieved that she was at least trying to be nice about it.

Sam **called around** nine o'clock that evening. He had news. The Boulder Police had discovered an "explosive device" during a sweep of the home of the woman who ran the District Attorney's Sex Crimes Unit. The bomb was found in Nora Doyle's garage, well hidden among some gardening supplies that were stored directly opposite the driver's side door of her Honda Accord. Had the bomb gone off, Nora might have been impaled on a hoe.

The bomb squad thought the initiator was radio controlled. Sam promised to tell me more when he knew more.

There's another bomb. That lawyer.

Cozier Maitlin's office, car, and Mapleton Hill home had been swept with extreme care, with negative results. The evacuation of the Colorado Building on Fourteenth Street had apparently been quite an inconvenience for quite a lot of people. Sam reported that at least one passerby voiced her hope that if there was indeed a bomb, she was praying it was big enough to bring the damn ugly place down.

The home and chambers of Superior Court Judge Richard Bates Leventhal, who had approved the plea bargain in Marin Bigg's rape, were swept, too. No bombs were discovered.

Lauren and I already knew, of course, that our property had been re-searched without result before I'd left the hospital that afternoon.

At times of stress, I ride my bike. The more stress I feel, the harder I ride. The amount of stress I was feeling the day Naomi died would have necessitated a fierce climb—a muscle-burning, ass-never-touches-the-saddle ascent that few mountain ranges in the world can offer on paved roads. But the eleven stitches high on the back of my leg near the imaginary line where butt becomes hip and my quasi-concussion conspired to keep me housebound and off my bicycle. My stress relief would have to come from baby Grace, who, bless her heart, handled the job effortlessly, and from the dogs, who, though generally amusing, weren't quite as reliable a tranquilizer as Xanax.

I tried to read. Couldn't concentrate. I tried to nap. Couldn't sleep. Mostly I spent the evening thinking.

Pondering.

Okay, perseverating.

Patients lie to me all the time.

All the time.

Most of the time I accept the mistruths as being part of the process that people go through while they're coming to terms with the myriad of ways that they are lying to themselves. I don't, as a rule, take it personally when I learn that I've been served untruths by patients. And I'm usually not even embarrassed when I discover that I've fallen hook, line, and sinker for the prevarications.

I've heard colleagues say that they know when their

patients are lying to them. I find the contention preposterous. I can't usually tell, and even when I think I can tell, I'm not usually sure. And I'm almost always unconvinced that it matters. I try to make it my job to learn as much from my patients' lies as I do from the truth. Either way, the therapy benefits.

But Naomi Bigg had *lied* to me.

She'd really, really lied to me. And I'd fallen for her creative story like a four-year-old stuffing a tooth beneath his pillow believes in visions of an impending visit from a dental fairy carrying a twinkling wand and dressed in white organza.

Paul Bigg, Naomi's living, breathing, wouldn't-it-be-cool, green-apron-wearing kid, was dead.

Or was he?

I was rapidly approaching a conclusion that Paul hadn't ever really been dead for his mother. Although I'd probably never know for sure, I suspected that Naomi hadn't resurrected Paul solely for my benefit; I suspected that Naomi had never really buried her son at all. In the psychotherapy I'd been doing with Naomi, I wondered if I'd just been hanging out on the bank of the pond, witnessing the ripples of her unsettled grief.

The psychological process Naomi had been engaged in was either crafty as hell or it was delusional as hell. My money was on delusional, on some kind of narrowly defined psychotic process.

If I was right, it meant that, as Naomi's therapist, I'd totally missed the presence of her psychotic symptoms.

There was no escaping the fact that my care of

Naomi Bigg had not been one of my better clinical moments.

Lauren put Grace to bed while I watched the local TV news accounts of the bombing death of Naomi Bigg. Marin, according to all reports, was out of surgery but remained in serious condition.

Reading between the lines, I assumed she was still uncommunicative with the police.

The other big story of the day was the *Daily Camera*'s revelation about Lucy Tanner's parentage. The local legal analysts made it clear that the Boulder prosecutors were getting perilously close to believing that they had a motive that would firmly tie Lucy to the Royal Peterson murder.

Sam called again just as I was about to learn what the weather was going to be the next day in the Carolinas.

"Hey," he said.

"Hi," I replied. "Any word on Lucy?"

"No, not yet. Certain people aren't convinced he's got her. There's a consensus developing that she's just hiding from what was in the paper this morning. Guess where I am."

I wasn't in the mood. "Sam, I'm not in the mood."

"Okay, I'll just tell you. I'm sitting on the stairs that go up to the second floor in Naomi Bigg's house. We're executing a search warrant."

"Oh," I said. I wasn't surprised about anything but

that it had taken so long for the search to begin. I assumed the delay was a paperwork/convince-the-judge kind of problem. I doubted that any evidence of the explosives would be discovered at the Bigg home. Whatever law enforcement personnel ended up searching the Ramp ranch between Agate and Limon were the ones who would find the explosive residue.

"Finding anything?" My feelings about Sam's errand were more than a little confused. Maybe it was the minor concussion. But I wasn't exactly sure whether I wanted Sam to answer my question "Yes" or to answer it "No."

He made a nasal sound that I couldn't interpret. "Who knows? We just got here and we're still looking. I tell you, it's going to take all night to go over this place. Rich people's houses have lots of rooms and they own lots of shit. You ever notice that? This house has a little room that seems to be set aside just for wrapping presents. Like a gift-wrap room. Who has a gift-wrap room? Well, the Biggs do. I look at some of the stuff in this place and I wonder how somebody could be standing in a store somewhere and ever convince themselves that they actually needed one of those. You know the kind of stuff that I mean?"

I did, and I didn't. "You wanted something, Sam?"

"You're okay, right? Just the bump on your head and the cut on your butt?"

"Upper leg, Sam. That, and a dead patient whose daughter is still in serious condition in the hospital. And Lucy." I let the words hang.

He said, "Every cop in the state is looking for Ramp. I'm hoping there's something here that helps us find him. We find him, I think we find her. Anyway, I was telling you what I discovered here. Right at the top of the stairs, first door on the left, is the kid's room. You know, Paul? The one who died playing Little League? The one you thought was busy planning his own little Columbine?"

Regardless of the fact that I'd almost been killed by a bomb earlier that day, my friend Sam wasn't above a well-placed dig. I tried to deflect it. "Paul's room is still there?" I was thinking out loud; I knew that I was still struggling to understand the extent of Naomi's delusions.

Sam, of course, seized on the opportunity to take me literally. "Sure. That happens when kids die. Parents aren't ready to let go. They preserve stuff. Bedroom is often high on the list. This shouldn't be news to you, Alan. It's like your field, you know? Human behavior?"

"Yeah."

"Anyway, I thought I'd call you because I thought it was interesting what's plastered all over the kid's door. Outside of the door, facing the hallway. It's kind of goofy."

"What?"

"Little signs. Maybe fifty of 'em. Maybe more, who knows. I'm sure somebody will end up counting them. They're all lined up in neat rows and columns. The signs are all different designs—no two of 'em match—

but they all say one of two things. Though some are in languages I don't even want to know. Want to guess?"

"No."

"About half of them say 'Do not disturb.' The other half say 'Be right back.' You being a shrink, I thought you'd get a kick out of that."

"Little 'Do not disturb' signs and 'Be right back' signs? All over his door?"

"Yeah, just like the ones you hang from the door-knob when you're staying at a Ramada. Though you probably don't stay at Ramada, do you? Those kinds of signs. The kid must have collected them."

"I don't know about that. I wonder if it was Paul or his mother who put them on the door. What does the room look like?"

"Like a kid's room. It does have a certain time-warp quality. Kid liked the old Dallas Cowboys. Lots of Troy Aikman and Emmett what's-his-face. Good stuff, expensive. Autographed jerseys. Signed pictures. Emmett Smith? Is that it? I think that's right, Smith. I should know that. He sure gave my Vikings enough grief over the years, didn't he?"

I didn't know. "But nothing unusual?"

"Not at first glance. Just the signs. I thought those were unusual, that's why I called."

Although I didn't believe what I was about to say, I said, "They could just be a preadolescent boy putting up a 'No trespassing' sign."

"Doesn't feel that way. I'll get a picture of the door to show you. This is something."

While I was considering the discovery, I said, "Is there someplace in the house where somebody could have made a bomb, Sam?"

"Not at first glance. There's no obvious workshop and we haven't identified any explosives. We'll swab for residue, but I'm betting that we'll come up with jack."

"Then what?"

"Everybody's looking for Ramp. That's where the money is. We're hoping to find an address or phone number here. Other than pointing us toward the Internet and to his grandparents' ranch, you don't know where to send us to find him, right? No recovered memories since this afternoon?"

The "recovered memories" comment was another dig.

"Has anyone talked to Marin, Sam? Is she awake? Maybe she knows something about Ramp."

"Scott Malloy's standing by over at the hospital to talk to her the moment she's able."

"How bad are her injuries?"

"To quote one of the docs, the wounds are uglier than they are serious. Her mom absorbed most of the blast. They think Marin will be fine—if her luck is bad she may lose use of an eye."

"Poor kid."

"Poor kid was mixed up with somebody who made bombs. For all we know right now, she was helping him."

CHAPTER
35

It took Lucy more than a thimbleful of patience, but she'd waited until she was in Agate before she made her next move. She'd allowed Alan to pull out ahead of her and watched him turn onto the interstate as he headed west toward Boulder. She turned into a gas station adjacent to I-70, filled the Volvo's tank, and bought a carton of chocolate milk and a tasteless sandwich filled with milky-white slices of something masquerading as turkey.

She didn't call Sam Purdy.

Instead, she made a phone call to a police department colleague who'd made no secret of the fact that he was eager to get into her pants, and asked him for help tracking down Jason Ramp Bass's current address in Denver. She didn't tell the man why she wanted the address. And he didn't ask.

As she killed the call she figured that she'd know

exactly where to find Ramp before she was done with her sandwich.

She was wrong. The return call with Ramp's address didn't come for almost two and a half hours. Her contact had been yanked into a meeting before he'd been able to get back to her with the information. When he finally did phone, he dangled the address like a carrot at the end of a stick until she agreed to have a drink with him after work. She picked a day for the rendezvous that was almost a week away. It left her plenty of time to cancel.

Once she had the address, she thought once more about calling Sam Purdy with the day's news. If she called him, he'd make her back off, wouldn't even let her close to the case. That wasn't okay.

She reached the same decision she'd reached every other time she'd pondered the problem since Agate. She decided to find Ramp by herself.

Capitol Hill in Denver is just south of the Uptown neighborhood where Jason Ramp Bass once lived with his parents. Although it bears some resemblance to Uptown, Capitol Hill is more densely populated, is even more diverse, and suffers from fewer pockets of acute gentrification than does its northern neighbor.

The apartment building where Lucy thought Ramp lived was in no danger of going condo, and nobody in their right mind was ever going to mistake it for a loft.

It was a postwar brick rectangle that looked as though it had been modeled after a shoebox. It was flanked on each side by gorgeous stone mansions.

She parked her car just down from Ramp's building on Pennsylvania Avenue and walked back toward it. The doorbell to apartment 3B was marked "Bass." Lucy smiled and shook her head. All day long, given the kind of day she'd expected to have, it had all been too easy. It was just about time, she thought, where something should go wrong.

To ring or not to ring, that was the next question.

She rings and he's not home, nothing's lost.

She rings and he's home—that's when things could get complicated. What would she say to him? Sam Purdy had always taught her to walk into any interview she conducted with the cards stacked in her favor. And with at least one ace tucked up her sleeve. Her favorite ace in the hole was her detective shield, and she'd had to give that up when she was suspended.

What else did she have?

Her wits. And her personal handgun. That was about it.

She backed down the concrete steps and started strolling away from the building to give herself time to rethink her options. She considered calling Cozy to see how bad the fallout had been from the *Daily Camera* story about her and Susan Peterson but decided that she could wait to learn about that. No matter how bad it had been, she was sure it had been bad enough. She also second-guessed her decision not to call Sam until she was absolutely certain that Jason Ramp Bass was the man they were looking for.

She reminded herself to think like a cop. There was no way she should approach Jason Bass alone without notifying somebody what she was up to. Ella Ramp may have already called her grandson and warned him that Lucy was on his tail. The young man could be armed.

Lucy stopped and used her cell phone to call Alan. She got his voice mail. "Alan, listen, it's Lucy. I think I found Ramp. He lives in Capitol Hill in Denver." She recited the address on Pennsylvania. "I'm heading up to his apartment to try and talk to him now. If for some reason I don't get back to you later today or this evening, call Sam and tell him what I was up to."

She hung up, squeezed her left triceps against her rib cage to feel the reassuring pressure of her holstered weapon, returned to the front door of the apartment building, and hit the bell marked "Bass."

No answer.

She tried the knob on the front door of the building. Locked.

One more time she tried the bell. As she waited for a response she backed away from the door and stared up at the fourth floor, trying to guess which apartment was Ramp's.

CHAPTER

36

Ramp was halfway to the Water Street location of the welding supply company where he worked when he realized that he'd forgotten his inspiration. He turned his car around and headed back to his apartment.

The elusive alley parking spot was filled. He double-parked and ran up the back stairs. He retrieved the framed photograph of his mother from on top of the bookcase and was just about out the door when the buzzer sounded from downstairs.

Ramp froze momentarily, then slowly walked to his front windows. The buzzer sounded again.

He waited. Half a minute or so later he watched a blond woman back slowly away from the door, looking up toward the fourth floor.

Who is she?

Ramp said, "Shit," and stepped away from the

window. "Here or there?" he asked himself. "Up here or down there?"

If I let her up here, he thought, whatever happens will leave evidence. Trace. Can't have that. Out loud, he said, "The correct answer, therefore, is down there." He bounded out the door of his apartment and flew down the stairs like a kid afraid to miss something. Only slightly winded, he grabbed his bag from his car, stuffed the photograph of his mother inside, circled his building, and was on the sidewalk behind the blond woman before she got all the way back to her car.

The red Volvo had the old, traditional, white-sky-over-green-mountains style Colorado license plates. The lettering on the plates read "MST." Ramp knew that designation meant the car was registered in Boulder County. The new green-over-white plates lacked a county code; you couldn't tell where the car was from.

Who the hell would be visiting him from Boulder? Nobody he wanted to see, that's who.

He noted the absence of a uniform and the presence of the leather blazer the woman was wearing on a warm afternoon. If the cops were after him, they wouldn't send a patrol officer. They'd send a detective, he thought. Probably two. He wondered about a gun under the blazer. He wondered about a partner. He couldn't spot anyone.

If she was a cop, she had a gun. Either under her blazer or in that purse. But why would they send a solitary cop?

Ramp was five feet behind her when he said, "Detective?"

She turned to face him.

He saw the look of resignation on her face when she realized she'd been duped. He smiled, and he said, "Thank you. That was easy. Go ahead and get in your car, Detective, but slide all the way across to the driver's side. I'll be right behind you. Once you're in the car, put your hands under your thighs. I'll take that purse, now, if you don't mind."

Ramp recognized the woman from the news. She was the Boulder cop who was the prime suspect in killing the Boulder DA. She was on leave from the police force. There'd been something in the news all day long about her mother, too. Ramp hadn't really paid attention.

She didn't seem frightened. Certainly wasn't jumping to obey him.

He said, "Do what I say. Hand me the purse, please, then slide into the car." He lifted the satchel he'd just retrieved from his apartment. "I have a weapon in this bag—actually, it's an explosive device—a bomb—that will kill both of us instantly. Although I'm willing to set it off, I'd really rather not do that."

He watched intently as the cop began to lower herself onto the car seat. When she was seated on the passenger's side, Ramp said, "Stop there for a second." He leaned in toward her and with his left hand pulled back the lapel of her blazer, exposing the butt of her handgun. Careful not to brush her body with his fingers, he removed the weapon and added it to the bag. "Now scoot over to the other side."

She did.

She noted that he wasn't using her weapon against her and asked, "Can I use my hands to raise myself over the console?"

"Sure," he replied. "Thanks for asking. I don't think either of us wants to be surprised right now."

She said, "You're Jason?"

"I am. You're the cop from the news?"

"Yeah, that's me."

"Nice to meet you," he said.

Despite herself, Lucy thought that Jason Ramp Bass was charming. She also thought that the fact that he was charming explained a lot.

CHAPTER

37

Lauren waited until we were in bed to ask me who I thought had killed Naomi Bigg and severely injured Marin. Her question came after I filled her in about my conversation with Sam.

I'd been thinking about that exact question—who had set off the bomb?—all day long, of course. Prior to the moment when Adrienne informed me that Paul Bigg had been dead for six years, I'd been assuming that it was Paul who had placed the bomb that had killed his mother and maimed his sister. I figured that he'd somehow managed to slip the device into Naomi's Vuitton bag during their confrontation in the parking lot outside her office.

I said, "Before my visit to that ranch today I would've thought it was Paul. After I met Ella Ramp, I would've guessed that it could've been either Ramp or Paul."

"But it wasn't Paul." Lauren spoke gently, wary perhaps of the unpredictability of the reaction of someone with closed head trauma. "We know that. Why do you think Naomi did that? Why did she keep Paul alive the way she did?"

"I don't know. I'm not convinced that Naomi actually lied—not in the sense that she was trying to fool me by creating a grown-up version of her son. I think Naomi was just inviting me into her delusions. Maybe she'd split Marin in two and given half her daughter's life to her son in order to keep him alive. I'm not sure. But we know that Ramp is real and that he's connected to Marin in some way that's not clear.

"I am convinced that before Naomi came over to my office, she had just spoken with somebody in her office parking lot."

"Ramp?"

"Yes, has to be."

"And you think he placed the bomb then, right?"

"She carried this big Vuitton bag around with her all the time. It always looked like it weighed a ton. I think he met with her at her office and managed to get the device into her bag."

"Why?"

"I'm not sure. Maybe Ramp wanted to kill her because he found out she was talking to me about her fears about the wouldn't-it-be-cool games. She'd called me and implied that she was about to do just that. So Ramp met her at her office, and he placed the bomb. The alternative is that Naomi was carrying the thing around on her own. I don't see that."

"Maybe the person who put the bomb in there was trying to kill both Naomi and Marin," Lauren suggested.

"If Marin recovers, maybe we'll know the answer to that. She was terrified that her mother was in danger. She'd come to my office to warn Naomi about something. Marin was frantic, hysterical. She yelled at her mother not to turn off her car. It makes me think that she expected that the car was wired with an explosive."

She asked, "Did Sam say how the bomb was set off?"

"No, he didn't say. Hopefully the police can figure that out from examining the debris. The one they found in Nora's garage had a radio control. They blew it apart with that thing, that—"

"Disruptor. The bomb squad calls it a disruptor. And it will be ATF and CBI doing the figuring, not the police." Lauren gazed at me warily, watching my reaction. I think she was still unconvinced that the condition of my brain would permit me to recognize either the acronym of the Alcohol, Tobacco and Firearms Administration, the federal agency responsible for investigating bombings, or that of the Colorado Bureau of Investigation.

"I know what the letters stand for," I said.

"I heard from Elliot that the ATF is mobilizing a Special Response Team. That means that they're taking this seriously. A forensic chemist deploys as part of the team, so we should know something soon about the explosive residue. I've been thinking, from the way the bomb went off outside your office the fuse had to be connected to either a timer or a radio signal. Do you see it that way?"

I'd considered the options, of course. "That, or some kind of motion switch. She'd just thrown the bag over her shoulder when the explosion happened. Aren't there switches that respond to that kind of thing?"

"I'm sure there are. But it seems like a risky way to set off a bomb to me, don't you think?"

She was right, of course. I shuddered at the thought of the alternative. "If it was a radio switch, whoever set it off had to be close to Naomi. Close enough to see what she was doing, right?"

Lauren said, "Yes."

We both grew quiet as we digested the image of the bomber witnessing the carnage. Finally, I said, "Sam said every cop in the state is looking for Ramp."

She allowed my words to dissipate like smoke and began caressing my neck. The taut muscles that stretched up from my back barely yielded to her touch. She said, "Alan?"

"Mmmm?"

"Did you think Grace and I were in danger?"

"I was never really sure. Naomi hinted at things, but she was never really clear about what she knew. I tried to make decisions . . . as though you were at some risk."

"I don't get it. What do you mean? If you thought we

were in danger, why didn't you tell me what was going on? Why didn't you go to the police?"

There was no mistaking her words. They were an accusation. She was asking how I could put my family at risk.

I made sure she was looking at me. "Like I said, I was reading between the lines. And Naomi warned me that if I told anybody about her concerns, she'd stop talking to me, and then I would have never known whether you were really at risk or not. And I wouldn't have known what the two boys were planning or how to protect you. Or anybody else."

"Even after they found the bomb at Royal's house?"

"While we were at dinner the other night with Adrienne, I had a cop friend of Sam's bring her K-9 over here to check for explosives. She had the dog search the house and your car."

"You did?"

"Yes. She didn't find anything, obviously."

"Why didn't you tell me?"

I didn't want to answer that question, but I did. "One, privilege, which, given what happened today, is lame, I admit. But yesterday, it made some sense. Two, I thought you'd insist on going to the police, and then Naomi would stop talking to me. Three, your health. Although I was afraid, I really didn't know that you were at risk and I didn't want to add stress to your life by alarming you. I've been worried about an exacerbation of your MS."

She digested my words. "And now?"

"I'm still worried about an exacerbation. But now Naomi's dead. She won't be giving me any more clues. The police are all we have."

Silence settled on the room like a comforter snapped over a bed.

I broke the silence. "I didn't have any good choices, Lauren. I did what I thought was best. I thought I was protecting us."

"I know," she said.

"Maybe I blew it. Maybe I made the wrong call," I said.

"Somebody's dead," she said. The words were her way of agreeing that perhaps I had made the wrong call.

"Yes. But I'm still not convinced that things would have been better if I had opened my mouth." I didn't know what else to say. "What exactly would you have wanted me to do, Lauren?"

"I'm not sure. I'll think about it, okay?"

For some reason I thought of Lucy Tanner just then. I was eager to change the subject anyway, so I asked, "Did you and Cozy hear from Lucy today?"

"You mean about Susan?"

"Yes. How she feels about all the news coverage about . . . Susan being her mother."

"Cozy got a message this morning. Lucy said she was planning to spend the day in Denver—I suspected to try to avoid the media—and she was going to get back in touch with him this evening. The last time I spoke with him was a couple of hours ago, and he hadn't heard from her again.

"Before the bomb went off, Alan, I was thinking of calling Susan. Just to see how she was. This has to be terrible for her, too—all the stress. But the day sort of got away from me, you know?"

"Yes," I said. "I know."

The phone beside the bed rang. For the third time that night, Sam Purdy was calling.

CHAPTER
38

Sam picked me up at our house around eleven-thirty. It took me twice as long as it should have to climb into his Cherokee. When we arrived across town at the Peterson house on Jay Street, it took me at least a minute to pull myself back out of the car. The shrapnel wound on my butt had tightened up as though the sutures were contracting like rubber bands, and pain was pulsing across my hindquarters like the backbeat of some hellacious tune.

Watching me, Sam said, "You should really be home in bed."

"Yes, I should be home in bed. But you said this might help find Lucy. There are times you have to play hurt."

A lilt of mirth in his tone, he said, "My, my. You're talking like a hockey player." From Sam, this was the ultimate compliment and expression of appreciation.

I laughed. It hurt, I winced. "Hardly," I said.

Sam arrived at Susan Peterson's threshold long before I did. I was still trying to mount the single step in the walk without having to bend my leg. He turned and looked back down the walk and said, "By the way, I decided not to tell her I was bringing you with me. Thought the surprise factor might work in my favor."

"Whatever."

"Your role inside? In case you're wondering, it's lubricant. That's your job. If the bolt seems stuck, you're the WD-40. Otherwise let me do my thing. Got it? I may be nice to her, I may not. I don't plan these things out. But don't interfere unless things get squeaky."

I nodded. I had a pretty good idea what to expect. In my experience, Sam was almost always the good cop and the bad cop all rolled up into one tasty package.

He waited for me to join him on the landing. "Why don't you ring the bell? She might be happy to see you."

"Sam, the last time I saw her, Susan was bedridden. She's not going to answer her own door. And anyway, it's almost midnight and it's Susan Peterson. She's not going to be happy to see anybody. Go ahead and ring the damn bell."

He did.

Susan's home-health-care worker pulled open the door after twenty or thirty seconds. She was a middle-aged woman with a big smile and bright green eyes. No makeup, wild curly brown hair, peasant blouse. I felt certain she'd been a hippie thirty years earlier.

"I'm Detective Purdy," Sam said, holding out his badge. "I phoned a little while ago."

"Alan Gregory," I added. "I'm a friend of Susan's."

She eyed me suspiciously, as though she was finding it hard to believe that Susan actually had friends. "Hello, hello, we've been expecting you. Come on in. I'm Crystal. Susan's upstairs waiting. Let me show you."

Sam said, "That's not necessary. I know the way." His voice was less than pleasant. I was placing my bet that he was going to start this process in the bad-cop persona.

I said, "The detective has been here before." What I didn't tell Crystal was that Sam's previous visit to this house was the night that Susan's husband was murdered.

My ass throbbing, I gazed longingly at the electric lift that had been installed to assist Susan up and down the staircase. I was tempted to ask Crystal how to use it. I didn't. Sam waited at the top of the stairs while I took the steps one at a time, dragging my wounded leg behind me.

"You're quite a gimp, you know?" He'd lowered his voice to a semblance of a whisper.

"Yeah, I know." After what felt like a technical climb in Eldorado Canyon, I joined him on the upstairs landing.

"You ready? You go first. Go lubricate."

I knocked and walked in. Susan had a hospital bed in her room. Although a bedside lamp was on, she appeared to be sleeping. "Susan? It's Alan Gregory. I came along with that detective who wants to talk with you."

She opened her eyes halfway and said my name. She appeared medicated. I wondered if she was taking something for pain or for sleep.

"Susan, how are you doing?"

"Oh, the pain. I'm having some pain."

"You took something for it?"

"I take things, but they can't find anything that really works. Doctors, doctors. The girl who's here—she's, she's—oh, let's just say she tries to help. I suppose they all try, don't they?" The aroma of her condescension and self-pity filled the room like a tuna sandwich left behind in the trash.

"This is Detective Purdy." I pointed behind me at Sam.

I'd seen Sam interview children before. He had a magical way of folding in on himself to disguise his size and appear less threatening. He managed the same transformation right then with Susan as he approached her bed. He became a big friendly gnome.

"Pleased to meet you," he told her. "I'm so sorry about your husband. I admired his work."

Admired his work? Sam was a private but vocal critic of the dead district attorney's proclivity toward plea bargains—on more than one occasion, I'd heard Sam call Royal Peterson "feckless"—though I didn't think it would be consistent with my role as a can of WD-40 to remind him of that at that moment.

"Yes," she murmured, sighing. "Thank you. It's been a hardship."

The closest chair was across the room. A stack of old newspapers covered the seat. It was apparent that Susan wasn't accustomed to welcoming visitors to her bedside. I cleared off the chair and carried it across the room. I moved an aluminum walker and a fancy carved cane out of the way to make space for Sam before I retreated into the shadows.

"I wish my children were closer," Susan said. "I really shouldn't be alone at a time like this. . . ."

I thought the obvious, that Susan's children had moved from her vicinity as soon as they were able—and that Susan bore some significant responsibility for their migration.

"It has to be hard having them so far away," Sam said. "Especially during a time as difficult as this."

I should have warned Sam to use a light hand when offering sympathy—that Susan was capable of sucking up compassion like a big tornado in Oklahoma sucks up trailer homes.

"I feel like I've been deserted. I'm so alone here."

Her words were weepy. My own compassion reserves were running dry and I didn't plan on using what I had remaining in the tank on Susan Peterson. I wondered if it would be considered rude to go back out the door and check out the operation of the lift on the staircase. But I reminded myself of my role as a can of WD-40.

Sam was searching for words. I chimed in. "Susan? It's funny that you're thinking about your children tonight, because that's what Detective Purdy needs to discuss with you. He has some questions about your first child, your daughter Lucy. From your first marriage."

Susan paled.

She looked away from Sam and me before she spoke again. "All day the phone is ringing. All day. People have questions, questions, questions. They don't even ask how I am. I'm a sick woman who has just lost her husband, lying here in the bed where I'm probably going to die, and everyone has questions about something that happened so long ago. It makes no sense to me. None."

Sam jumped right back in. "The questions I have aren't about long ago, Mrs. Peterson. That's your business. My questions are about the last few days. I'm just wondering if you've spoken to your daughter Lucy recently, if maybe she called you after the story came out in the newspaper."

Susan hesitated before she said, "No. You'd think a daughter would, wouldn't you? I mean call her own mother after something like that shows up in the newspapers." With each word, she sounded older.

Sam straightened up on his chair. The gnome was gone. Sam was now as big as Shaq. "That answer covers today, Mrs. Peterson. What about yesterday? Did you speak to your daughter yesterday?"

"Well, um, let me think. No, no, she didn't call

yesterday either." Susan actually smiled, as though she was proud of her answer. I felt myself cringe. I was riding shotgun with Sam now, and saw the transparency of Susan's protestations. If Susan thought she could play Sam for a fool, she was in for a surprise.

She probably couldn't recognize the signs, but I could. She'd pissed him off. Sam pressed her without mercy. His voice was now as intimidating as his posture. "She didn't call. That means she came by, doesn't it? Lucy came by to see you, Mrs. Peterson? When was that, exactly?"

She lifted a bell from beside her bed and shook it vigorously. I imagined it was an effort to summon Crystal. Susan winced and moaned like an old dog sighs. "The pain . . . I'm not sure, I'm not sure."

Sam stood. "When was she here?"

"I take a lot of medicine."

"And I eat too much food. When was she here?"

Her eyes flashed at Sam, the message behind them volatile. "Last night, about this time. It was the first time I'd seen her in a long time."

Sam ignored her threat. "How long a time?"

She hesitated. I couldn't decide whether she spent the moment trying to remember or whether she used it up manufacturing a lie. "Over a year."

Crystal walked in the door, smiling, and said, "Yes, dear?"

I said, "We'll just be a little while longer, Crystal. Susan will be fine until we leave."

Susan looked as though she wanted to disagree, but

after a glance at Sam she wisely chose not to protest. She just looked pitiful.

Crystal was unsure what to do.

"Really," I told her, "it's fine. I'll let you know when we're leaving. If she needs anything I'll come find you."

Crystal retreated out the door. I closed it behind her.

Sam hadn't turned away from Susan. He asked, "And what did Lucy say when she was here?"

"She warned me."

"Yes?"

"She warned me not to talk to anyone about . . . the family. About her, or me, or Royal. Or her father."

"Did she threaten you?"

"No. Well, kind of. Maybe."

"How did she threaten you?"

Susan considered her answer before she said, "It's not important."

"Then tell me what she didn't want you to tell anyone."

With no hesitation, Susan said, "No." She added, "You can't make me, Detective. I know my rights. My husband was the district attorney."

Sam stepped closer, eliminating the space between him and the edge of the bed. If I'd been the one gazing into his eyes at that moment, I would have told him exactly where the treasure was buried.

Sam said, "Mrs. Peterson, your daughter is missing. I'm trying to find her. I need your help."

"My daughter? You mean Lucy? Sorry, you're going

to have to do better than that, Detective. She's been missing most of my life. She's a worse daughter than I am a mother. Regardless, I don't know anything that will help you find her. She's probably hiding somewhere. I know I would have if I'd done what she did."

"What's that? What did she do?"

Susan smiled. "No, Detective. I'm done talking to you. Alan, please ask that girl to come back in here."

Before Sam had a chance to voice his opinion about Susan Peterson, his cell phone beeped in his pocket. We were standing on the sidewalk in front of the Peterson home as he flipped it open.

"Purdy," he said.

For about a minute he listened, nodding, occasionally saying, "Yeah." Once he said, "They did that?"

He closed up the phone and said, "That was one of my buddies at the department. He just got a call from the Denver Police. They think they found Ramp's car. It was towed out of the alley behind his apartment building after six o'clock tonight. He'd left it double-parked for some reason. They're still busy getting warrants to search his apartment and to search the car, and they're still trying to get one to search that damn ranch out in God-knows-where."

"Agate."

"Yeah. Agate."

"Lucy's car? Anything there?"

"No, no sign of Lucy's car. Thing's as bright as a fire

truck, you'd think it would show up on someone's radar."

"What do you think of Susan's theory that Lucy's just gone into hiding to avoid the press?"

"I don't buy it. She called me this morning, told me she'd be back in touch early this evening. If she went into hiding, she'd call and tell me where she was. I'm sure as hell not going to tell the press. And that message she left for you? Why would she have left that message if she was going into hiding?"

I limped back toward the Cherokee. Sam was next to me. I said, "You guys finish the search at the Bigg home, Sam?"

"Mostly."

"Did you find anything?"

He shrugged. He wasn't sure he wanted to answer my question.

I said, "I don't like this, Sam."

"I don't either. Come on, I'll take you home." He stopped. "Did you know Lucy had visited Susan here?"

"No, Sam, I didn't. She didn't tell me."

He studied my face in a way that left me convinced that he was deciding whether to believe me or not.

I said, "What do you think of Mrs. Peterson?"

"I have trouble believing she's related to Lucy. I now know exactly where I come down on the whole nature/nurture debate. That's what I think. How's your ass holding up?"

"Not too good. I think maybe I should've borrowed some of Susan's pain meds."

"That's a felony. I would've had to take you in for it. Come on, I'll drive you home."

Before he had a chance to fire the car's ignition, Sam's phone sounded again. He flipped it open and said, "Purdy."

I shifted my weight to take the pressure off my wound. It didn't help.

Sam's eyes were open wide as he listened to the phone call. After about a minute, he said, "Be right there."

"Be right where?"

"Marin Bigg is awake and talking. We're going to Community, see if she has any insight into anything."

"Like who murdered her mother?"

"Yeah, like that."

"Drop me off at the Boulderado on the way. I'll get a cab home."

"Sorry, this game has gone into overtime and you're still in the lineup. I want your opinion of her. We're still not sure if she's part of Ramp's crew or if she's a victim."

CHAPTER
39

Lucy spent the night in a filthy construction trailer in Denver's Central Platte Valley, not too far from the REI that had taken over the old Forney Train Museum. A quick glance at the painting on the sign that graced the entrance to the construction site left her thinking that the building that was being framed was going to be some overpriced loft development.

Her hands and ankles were bound by plastic handcuffs that Ramp had discovered in the trunk of her Volvo after he'd parked it in a big shed in an industrial neighborhood on Denver's west side, somewhere between Broadway and Interstate 25. Ramp waited until after dark before he drove them in a gray Ford truck a mile or two to the construction site.

Since they'd arrived he'd only removed the bindings on Lucy's wrists and ankles twice, each time to allow her to use the portable toilet outside the construction trailer. He'd covered her with her own handgun the whole time. When she was done in the toilet, he'd had her rebind her own ankles and then lie prone on her abdomen before he recinched her wrists. Each step he prefaced with "please" and closed with "thank you."

Ramp fed Lucy a dinner of Slim Jims and Dr Pepper. She declined dessert, which was Little Debbie's oatmeal cookies, even though she'd adored their supersweetness when her dad had given them to her as a kid. Ramp allowed Lucy the small sofa that was tucked into one end of the trailer while he curled up on an army-surplus cot ten feet away. The sofa smelled. When Lucy commented on the odor, he told her that he'd smelled it, too, and thought the aroma was from construction adhesive.

Some kind of radio transmitting device—it looked to Lucy like a garage door opener—was taped to the inside of Ramp's left wrist. He demonstrated how he could hit the button with either hand at any time he wanted.

She'd asked him where the bomb was.

"Close by," he'd responded.

"A shaped charge?"

His eyes twinkled. "You've been talking to my grandma," he said. "She's a piece of work. I love that woman to death."

Lucy said, "Yes, I talked to her this morning."

"She tell you where to find me?"

"No. She didn't. I asked, but she wouldn't tell me. She wanted to talk to you and your dad first."

"That sounds like her." He ran the fingers of his right hand through his hair. "She's gotten bitter. It's been hard to watch."

"Your grandmother's had a lot of loss recently. Her husband, your uncle, your mom—it's a lot for someone to deal with."

"I know," he acknowledged. "It's still been hard to watch. When you love somebody, it's hard to watch."

She noted the empathy. Lucy hadn't yet heard a word of malice from Jason Ramp Bass. Not one.

He was a cute kid with tousled blond-brown hair, good skin, and a single silver earring in his right ear. He was also blessed with his grandmother's dazzling blue eyes and the kind of fetching smile that probably opened a lot of doors with girls while he was in high school, which Lucy figured wasn't too long ago.

"What do you like to be called?" she asked him after he told her it was time to get some sleep, that tomorrow was going to be a busy day.

"Jason. I like that best."

"Not Ramp?"

"Nah. My friends hung it on me, but I never loved it."

"Is tomorrow going to be busy for me, or just for you?"

"Both of us. I didn't originally plan on it, but I'm beginning to see how having a hostage might be helpful."

The word sent chills through Lucy. She was the hostage. "What's going to happen? What are your plans, Jason?"

He didn't have to think long before he answered her question. "My plans? I want to get a dialogue going."

"A dialogue?"

"A dialogue. About justice in America. The way it works, the way it doesn't. I have a friend—he's black, a guy I went to high school with—who's doing more time for selling speed than the murderer who killed my mom got for killing his first victim. Is that right? I want a dialogue about stuff like that. I think it's time that we had a dialogue about that. As a society. About sentences and judges and courts and parole. About protecting innocent people. About malpractice in courts the same way we talk about malpractice in hospitals."

"The inequities," Lucy said.

"Yeah, the inequities," he repeated. Lucy thought he seemed pleased at her choice of words.

He stood and moved across the room to the sofa. "I'm going to have to tape you down so I can get some rest without worrying about you trying to get away. What position do you want to be in?"

She thought about it. "On my back, I guess." She could only imagine how sore she would be by morning.

"You want to go to the Super Bowl first?"

"What?"

"The plastic head outside. It's called the Super Bowl. You want to go again before I tie you down?"

"I just went."

"Whatever."

He grabbed a huge roll of duct tape and wound it individually around her ankles and then under and around the sofa. He repeated the procedure twice more and moved up her torso. She could tell that the proximity to her breasts made him uncomfortable. With her manacled hands she held them up and out of the way so that he could wrap her around her rib cage.

"Not too tight, please. I need to breathe."

"I'll be careful," he said.

"Thanks."

He returned to his cot. "Don't know if you noticed, but there was an actual dialogue for a while after the shootings at Columbine, and again for a little while after the thing at Santana, that high school near San Diego. About bullying, and cliques, and jocks and freaks, and insiders and outsiders in high school, how destructive it all is. It got drowned out by all the hoopla because those kids were so angry and so stupid about what they did, so the dialogue didn't do enough or last long enough to accomplish what it could've. The Columbine kids and that boy at Santana were more interested in the killing than the talking. I'm more interested in the talking. I want this dialogue to last longer. And I think it will. I hope it makes a difference, though I doubt I'll be around to see it when it does."

Lucy had a hard time finding a position where she could see her captor across the narrow trailer. But she knew she'd just heard him predict that he wasn't likely to survive whatever was about to happen. "You're sure that you're not just trying to get even? To get some retribution for what happened to your mother?"

His hands were locked behind his head and he was

staring up at the trailer's ceiling. "You ever notice how this country doesn't seem to pay much attention to anything important until somebody dies? It's the funniest thing. Whether it's putting in a traffic light after a kid gets killed on the way to school or something like Columbine or the terrorists who blew up that ship— what was it, the *Cole*? Then it seems we forget about it just as fast as we remembered. Is that human nature, you think? I wonder about that a lot. The more spectacular way somebody dies, though, the longer we seem to talk about it. It's a peculiar thing in this country but I'm willing to take advantage of it. That's for sure.

"Tomorrow's going to be spectacular. There's no doubt about it. People will talk for a while. I just hope it's the right kind of dialogue."

Lucy was aware of parallel instincts. The part of her that was the hostage wanted the captor to fall asleep. The part of her that was a detective wanted to burst from her bonds, overwhelm him, and interrogate the bastard to find out his plans.

Ramp continued. "I don't feel good about what I did today, in case you're wondering. I didn't know how I'd feel if it came to that. But I do, now. I don't feel good about it."

Lucy wondered if he was talking about kidnapping her or if he was talking about something else.

"You mean kidnapping me?"

"No, no, no. I mean, I haven't even thought about how I feel about that. Not yet. I don't know if I will think about it for a while. I'm talking about the bomb in Boulder. Killing Marin's mom."

Lucy's heart felt like it hiccupped. "Marin's mom? You killed Naomi Bigg with a bomb?"

He sat up on his elbows. "You hadn't heard? It's been all over the news since this afternoon."

Her voice was fragile. "I hadn't heard anything about it. I've been avoiding the news because of . . ."

He finished her sentence. "The thing with your mother."

"Yeah, the thing with my mother."

"What is that? I don't understand. What is that thing with your mother? You've been like ignoring her or something? Pretending she wasn't your mom? I can't . . . imagine it. I'd give anything for a chance to spend another day with my mom. Anything."

"I envy you that. That she was so special to you."

"Your mom wasn't?"

"She left me and my dad when I was little."

"She just left?"

"I didn't see her or even hear from her for years, then I tracked her down when I was an adult, hoping for a reconciliation. But it didn't work out the way I wanted. We never got along. The police think that the fact that she and I had such a difficult relationship might have given me a motive to kill her husband. He was the Boulder County district attorney." Lucy suspected that Ramp knew all about the murder of Royal Peterson, but she kept her suspicions to herself.

Ramp lowered himself back down on the cot. "That

doesn't make sense. Why would you kill him for that?"

Lucy sighed. "They think I was sleeping with my mother's husband. That maybe I killed him to shut him up or something, you know, so that she wouldn't find out about the affair."

Ramp was silent for a long stretch before he asked, "Were you? Were you sleeping with him?"

To Lucy, his words sounded reluctant, as though he didn't want to find out that it was true. She wasn't sure how to answer but didn't want to lie. "Yes," Lucy said. "I was. It's funny to say it. I haven't admitted that to anyone before right now. Not even my friends or my lawyers."

"But you didn't kill him."

"No, I didn't kill him."

Lucy recalled the conversation she had recently had with Alan Gregory and what he had said about intimacy. That true intimacy required not only disclosure, but also vulnerability.

Jason had just admitted a murder and she'd just admitted an affair with her mother's husband. That was disclosure.

If she got away, Jason Ramp Bass was on his way to life in prison or even death row in Cañon City. If she didn't get away, Ramp was probably going to kill her.

That was vulnerability.

She looked over at Ramp and thought that they were so intimate at that moment that they may as well have been sleeping naked in the same cot.

Ramp said, "In a way, we both lost our moms."

Lucy felt a flutter in her heart and thought that he'd made the words sound like the lyrics for a song.

He murmured, "Good night, Lucy. Get some sleep."

And she knew she was going to cry. But she wasn't sure why. Just that it had something to do with mothers.

The night before, when Lucy had walked unannounced into the master bedroom of the Peterson house on Jay Street, she'd said, "Susan, we need to talk."

Susan had looked up and greeted her without surprise. She'd said, "What? You think things have changed? Just because Royal's dead?"

"Everything's changed, Susan. You know that."

"You still call me Susan, not Mother. That hasn't changed. I still have this damn disease. That hasn't changed. Royal's not here anymore—that's all that's changed."

Lucy didn't bite. "I haven't told the police that you're my mother, Susan. I came here to talk with you because I think we should leave it that way."

Susan scoffed back. "Why? So your life isn't complicated by the fact that you have a disabled mother? Sorry, if they ask me, I'll tell them. I don't care who knows. I just lost my husband—nobody will care what happened with us, Lucy. They'll forgive me for what I did to you. They might not understand why you're so callous now, but they'll forgive *me*."

"Susan, what do you want from me?"

She straightened the sheets on her bed and hit the mute button on the remote control before she said, "Just do what's right, Lucy. Isn't that what I always taught you?"

CHAPTER

40

I can't sleep. Can you?"

Lucy's eyes had been tracking the linear shadows that were making a picket fence of light appear across the ceiling of the construction trailer. She was wide-awake. In response to Jason Ramp's question, she said, "No."

For a moment both were silent. Lucy finally stammered, "Is it because you killed somebody today?"

"Yeah," Ramp said. "That, and I keep going over what's going to happen tomorrow."

"You want to talk about it?"

"Maybe, I'm not sure. I don't know if I do. More people are going to die tomorrow. I'm sure of that much. So I'm not sure why I'm so weirded out by Marin's mom dying today."

"Maybe that's it—that she was somebody's mom."

"Whoa, I hadn't thought about that. That's something to think about, isn't it?"

"Why did you do it, Jason? Blow her up?"

"She figured out what we were up to. I'm not exactly sure how. I think probably Marin left some stuff around the house or was careless on the Net or something. Doesn't matter now, I suppose. Marin said that her mom was going to tell everything to that shrink she was seeing. I had to keep her from doing that. One more day, that's all we needed. One more day."

Lucy sensed a vulnerability. She tried to exploit it. "You ever kill anyone before?"

"That woman who died in the car bomb in Denver? I caused that. She wasn't the intended victim. Her husband was. I guess you could say I killed her. But the bomb I put under their car went off by accident. I wasn't going to set it off until . . . until the right time came. Her husband should have been driving, not her."

"Why him?"

He ignored her question.

Lucy spoke into the darkness. "Maybe you feel troubled because you knew Marin's mother. I imagine that it makes a difference, killing someone you know."

He parried with his own question. "Have you been angry enough to kill your mother?"

The question felt like a physical blow to Lucy. She had trouble catching her breath. "I've never thought about it."

"Think about it now. Please."

"I don't know, Jason. I don't know. My God, what a question."

"You might be surprised what you can do when you've been hurt enough. You might be surprised."

"Have you been hurt enough?"

"Have you?" he countered.

Lucy looked away from him. "Are the others all going to be strangers?"

"What others?"

"The ones who are going to die tomorrow."

Ramp's voice softened. "I don't know them, not personally, if that's what you mean. I know who they are. I picked them because of who they are, but I don't know them. Others will get hurt or die, too. Unintended victims. No matter how careful you are, bombs tend to be a little indiscriminate when they go off around people. I've accepted that risk."

"So what is it then?" She was trying to feed his self-doubt.

Ramp stood up and crossed the distance between them slowly, his body emerging from the shadows the way a lover might approach the bed. He straddled a metal desk chair three feet from her.

"I'm telling you a lot. You tell me something about you. Something personal, private."

Lucy almost laughed. She looked up at the grimy ceiling before staring into his cool eyes. "I already told you I was sleeping with my mother's husband. How much more private you want me to get?"

She could only see half his face. The eyelid that she

could see was heavy, and a soft beard had emerged on his chin. She thought she recognized something unexpected in his glare.

She double-checked her impressions and decided to take a chance. Lucy said, "My boobs are two different sizes."

He laughed and pounded a boot on the dirty carpet.

She joined him laughing.

"My mom told me that all girls' boobs are two different sizes. That's not a big deal."

"Mine aren't a little different, they're a lot different. More than a whole cup size different."

"That's a lot?"

"Yeah, that's a lot. It made for some tough times in the locker room at school. And it complicates shopping for lingerie." She said the final word wistfully, hoped it hung in the room like perfume.

He crossed his arms on top of the chair back and sprawled his legs out in front of him, smiling to himself. "Which one do you like more?"

She laughed with him again, trying to draw him along. "What kind of question is that?"

"If you could have them both be the same size, which one would you choose?"

"The left one."

He looked down at her chest and laughed again. "That's a good answer."

His appraisal of her chest left her questioning her decision to flirt with him. She said, "Thank you."

"You know," he said, "when I was like nine or ten, I

used to think they had bones in them. Boobs. Breasts. I didn't know they were soft. I thought they had like a cone of little bones holding them in shape. One time I was in a swimming pool playing some game and I accidentally kicked a girl in her chest and her breast just squished underneath my foot. I remember that I thought I'd broken it."

"So how did you find out the truth about boobs?"

"Personal research."

"Seriously."

"My mom. She told me. She'd tell me anything. Never made me feel stupid. Then she died."

Lucy felt the flirtation that was developing between them evaporate like water splashed on a griddle. She knew that the strategic advantage she'd been nurturing evaporated along with the teasing. She said, "I'm so sorry, Jason. About what happened to your mom. It sounds like you two were very close."

He leaned over the edge of the cot and said, "Thanks for saying that. I'm sorry about what happened with you and your mom, too. At least I got a lot of memories with mine. You don't even have that."

"No, I don't even have that."

"Lots of wives and sisters and daughters die because of the stupid way the system works. So this . . . thing I'm doing, it's really about lots of moms. Everyone has to remember that. It's not just about my mom."

"It's about sons and brothers and fathers, too?"

"Yeah."

Lucy said, "What was she like? Your mom?"

"I don't think I want to talk about her."

"You know, I'm no expert on mothers, that's for sure," Lucy said. "But she sounds very special."

Ramp's jaw took on a tight set. He said, "They won't find you here. In case that's what you're hoping. They might be looking for you, but . . ." His voice faded away.

"Oh," Lucy said.

"Nobody knows that I'm here. That we're here, in this trailer. Not even Marin knows where I'm planning to spend the night. The truck I'm using won't be missed for a couple of days. My company thinks it's in the shop with transmission trouble."

Lucy fought a fresh flush of despair. She needed to keep him talking. "How did you know her? Marin?"

"We met on the Web. In a chat room."

"Complaining about the justice system?"

"Yeah."

"You recruit her?"

"I guess. Didn't take much effort. It was more like I invited her. She was as angry as I was. You know what happened to her a few years ago?"

"Yes, I do. I didn't work the case but I knew a lot about it. Are you two like boyfriend and girlfriend?"

"At first, kind of. But no. Not now. I don't stay with girls very long. Not that way, anyway. I'm not ready for a real relationship."

Lucy couldn't tell whether she heard some disappointment or longing lurking in his words.

A siren erupted nearby. Its insistent wail filled the

trailer like a sour stench. Lucy and Jason both waited to discover whether the sound would approach them or recede into the distance.

It faded.

"Told you. They won't find you here."

"Is she part of what's going to happen tomorrow?"

"You mean Marin?"

Lucy nodded.

"She was going to be. Now she's in the hospital, so I guess not. The whole thing was planned so that we would operate independently. Just in case one of us was caught. Either one of us can make our half of the plan work on our own."

Lucy watched Ramp stand and move to the trailer's window. The thick layer of dust on the glass turned the night sky behind him pasty and sick.

"Were you trying to hurt Marin today? Or was that an accident?"

"You know, I'm not really sure. At the moment I touched the button, I wasn't sure whose side she was on. Mine or her mother's."

"Wow," Lucy said. "You're not even sure whether you were trying to hurt her. What a thing to say."

"Yeah."

Lucy pressed. "The bomb at the district attorney's house in Boulder? That was one of yours?"

"Yes. It was. That was going to be part of Marin's route."

"Route?"

"Tomorrow, we each have a route. There will be a

series of bombs. The bombs in Boulder are designed differently from the ones in Denver so that they can't be tied together. And I have something special planned at the end, like a finale at a fireworks show."

"Who's going to die tomorrow?"

The silence that followed her question allowed the hum of I-25 to infiltrate the trailer. An eighteen-wheeler was having trouble with a low gear. The whine of air brakes sounded.

"A lot of people."

"You don't want to tell me who?"

"People who've had a hand in the bullshit. That's all I'll say."

"Regarding your mother? That bullshit?"

"Not just that. Remember, I'm talking about the whole system. I want people to talk about every last place where the system is broken. The problem with Columbine, even with McVeigh in Oklahoma City, was that . . ."

Ramp's words faded into the darkness as he suddenly refocused his attention out the trailer's window.

"Was what, Jason? What was the problem?"

"Shhh." He waved an open hand from his shoulder to near his waist. "Shhh. Don't speak."

She watched the reflexive movement as his fingers curled toward the switch that was taped to his wrist.

Lucy whispered, "Is there someone here?"

Calmly, he said, "I said shut up. I meant it."

Lucy considered the opportunity that was being presented to her. She wasn't gagged. She could scream and maybe get the attention of whomever Ramp was tracking outside the trailer. At this hour, she assumed it would either be a security patrol or a trespasser.

She forced her heart to still so she could hope to hear whatever it was that was going on outside. She heard nothing. No tires on gravel. No voices. No music from a car radio.

Ramp straightened at the window and moved his fingertips away from the switch on his wrist.

Her moment was gone. She felt a tear form in the corner of one eye. "You were telling me what the problem was with McVeigh and with Columbine. What was the problem?"

"Not just one. A few. The main one was their rage. But also the randomness of what they did. And the fact that they targeted innocent people. Those things changed the debate. If the bully steals your lunch and you respond by blowing up the whole damn cafeteria, nobody ends up paying attention to what the bully did to you. They focus on your rage, and on the innocent victims you killed by how you retaliated. That was the problem with Columbine. What they did—killing so many innocent people—changed the debate forever, and their message was diluted to the point that nobody really paid any attention to their motives. Not in the end, anyway. I won't allow that to happen tomorrow."

"You want the debate?"

"I want the debate."

"But you already said that there will be unintended victims from what you're planning."

"Yes, but they're not targets. That's the difference. They will prove one of my points, however."

"I don't understand."

"My mother was the unintended victim of the justice system's decision to free a murderer and put him back on the street. My plan will duplicate that. There's some irony there, I think. The ones who are responsible will suffer losses, and so will some innocent people. The justice system didn't target my mother. But they allowed her to be killed. They were callous to her safety."

"And you'll do the same tomorrow?"

"Yes."

"What gives you the right?"

He laughed, a tight sound that seemed to catch in his throat. "Revolution always begins with an act of anarchy. By definition, no one has the right to be an anarchist. I'm hoping to start a little revolution. So by definition, I'm assuming the right to be an anarchist."

"You can call it anarchy but it sounds like revenge to me. Vengeance. I don't see how what you're doing is any different. You'll be just another pissed-off kid with blood on his hands. You don't have to do this."

"I don't want the blood. I want the dialogue. That's what's different. The blood will get everyone's attention."

She implored him, "Don't do it."

"It's too late."

Lucy felt herself sinking into the sofa. The cogency of Ramp's argument was exhausting her. She wanted to ask him to use his energy differently. To beg him to find another way. But she knew he wasn't remotely interested. Her desperation caused her to play a card she wasn't sure she should play.

"The shrink that Marin's mother was going to see when you killed her today? I know him. His name is Dr. Gregory. He already knows a lot about what you and Marin are planning."

His pale eyes narrowed, the tips of his brows curling down toward the bridge of his nose. "How do you know that?"

"We're friends. He was worried about his wife's safety, so he came to me. I thought he might be able to help me figure out who killed Royal Peterson. We've been helping each other."

"Are you lying?"

"You still have my cell phone?"

"Yeah."

"Hit redial. You'll see his number. He's the last person I called. Or check caller ID. His number's in there."

Ramp retrieved the cell phone from his duffel and hit the redial button. He read the number that came up and then killed the call.

Lucy asked, "You know how to work it? Check the directory and you can match the name and number."

"Yes," he said, touching a series of buttons. "There it is. Alan Gregory."

"See?"

"He could be anybody. You could be playing me right now. How do I know you're not lying?"

Lucy said, "He knows about Paul."

Ramp smiled in a way that seemed full of compassion and something else. She wasn't sure about the something else. "You think Naomi told this Alan Gregory what the plans were?"

"I know he knows some things. I also know he was reluctant to tell me some other things."

"But he knows about the bombs?"

"Yes. And that you're angry at the justice system."

His jaws tightened. "She told him that?"

"Yes."

"What else? Tell me."

"He knows about the wouldn't-it-be-cool games."

"God, really? The man might really know something."

Lucy's phone suddenly came alive, chirping in his hand.

Ramp stared down at the phone. Didn't answer it.

He asked Lucy, "Who do you think was trying to call you?"

She hesitated a heartbeat or two. "My partner. His name is Sam Purdy. He's a detective in Boulder. And he's my friend."

"You were trying to decide whether to lie to me right then, weren't you? What did you decide?"

"I decided to tell you the truth." She paused. "Mostly because you can check for yourself on caller ID."

She waited for him to check the caller ID log. He didn't. "So your friend, this detective, he makes a habit of calling you in the middle of the night?"

"Sam knows I'm missing by now. I told him I'd check in with him when I got back from seeing your grandmother."

"What will he do if he thinks you're missing?"

"Whatever he can think of to find me. Sam's relentless and he's pretty resourceful."

"What does he know?"

"Whatever Alan Gregory knows, Sam knows. They're good friends."

"You making this whole thing up as you go along? You're pretty good if you are."

"It's all true, Jason."

"Do they know about the bombs?"

"For sure? No. But they're the ones who found the bomb at Royal Peterson's house, and Dr. Gregory was so worried that you might have targeted his wife with a bomb that he brought an explosive-sniffing dog into his house and to check his cars."

"Really? You mentioned his wife already. Who is she?"

"She's a deputy DA in Boulder who was tangentially involved in Marin's rape case."

"Her name?"

"Lauren Crowder."

"Doesn't ring a bell. I don't think Marin mentioned her."

Lucy shrugged to hide her sense of relief.

Ramp was flipping the phone into the air, catching it again as it completed one end-to-end rotation.

She said, "The special part you mentioned that would be coming at the end of the day. That's part of your route?"

"It is."

"What good am I in all this?"

"So far you're just good company. I appreciate that. I'm still considering what else you'll do."

"You're going to kill me, aren't you, Jason?" The use of his name was intentional. She even emphasized it.

He stepped back from the window and moved halfway into a shadowed place close to the wall. "I don't think I'll have to. I really hope not."

"I don't understand."

"If I'm still standing at the end of the day, your job is over. I won't have to kill you."

"But if they catch up with you before that?"

"That's up to them, of course. Your presence is to ensure that I get to keep going. To finish what I started."

"But there will be bombs close by all day long. Who knows what will happen? That's what you're saying?"

Ramp's hand flashed toward his right hip as though he'd been stung there by a yellow jacket.

The swift movement of his hand caused Lucy's breath to catch in the middle of her chest as though she'd suddenly been dipped in ice water.

He lifted a beeper from his belt and lit the screen.

"Wow," he said. "What a surprise. I have to go make a call. I'm going to have to gag you. I'm sorry."

"Please, no."

"I said I'm sorry. You want something to drink first?"

CHAPTER

41

They wheeled her to X-ray. She went out a back door when the tech went to get something."

A young detective whom I'd never met was the one doing the I-can't-believe-it-but-we-lost-her shuffle. Even without glancing at his face, I could tell that Sam Purdy wanted to take someone's head off and was considering whether this young man's noggin would be a good place to start.

Sam said, "We were watching her, right?"

"Yeah, we had someone outside her door for her protection. He followed her wheelchair down to X-ray and checked out the room. He thought the other door in the room went to a place for developing the X-ray film or something. Didn't know it led to a hallway."

"So she went out that other door? That's how she got away from him? She just walked away?"

"Yes."

"What's she wearing? One of those hospital gowns?"

"Probably not. There's a supply closet close by where scrubs are stored. We found a gown on the floor by the scrubs. We think it was hers. So she's probably wearing scrubs. Light purple. You know, like lavender."

Sam glared. My guess was that he was reacting to the detective's use of "lavender."

"She's barefoot?"

"She's wearing a pair of those little foam hospital slippers, as far as we know. They weren't with the gown."

"What kind of head start did she get?"

"A few minutes. Maybe five."

"The building get sealed?"

"Not for another five or so minutes after that."

"Maybe ten?"

"Yeah, maybe ten. Seven or eight, you know."

"She's ambulatory?"

"Unfortunately, yeah. Injuries from the bomb were to her upper body. Worst damage is to her left hand, from shrapnel. That's what she was in surgery for earlier. Her face is cut up, too. She has a bandage on her cheek right here, between her ear and her eye." He touched his own face to demonstrate the spot. "Got patched up by a plastic surgeon."

"So she's ambulatory and she has a ten- to fifteen-minute head start. She could be somewhere in this big hospital or she could be out on the street."

"That's the situation."

"What did you get before she ran?"

"Not much. Her surgeon only gave me about five minutes with her at first. She was still pretty groggy from the anesthesia and the painkillers, said she didn't remember anything at all about the bombing. Kept asking me about her mom as though she couldn't believe she was dead."

"But she knew?"

"She knew."

Sam inhaled like he was about to blow up a balloon. Then he sighed. "Nothing at all about this guy Ramp?"

"I asked, Sam. Said she didn't even know him. Didn't know what the hell I was talking about."

A uniformed officer approached us and waited until Sam said, "What do you want, Officer?"

"Sorry to interrupt but we just discovered that a purse is missing. One of the X-ray techs is telling us that her purse is gone along with her denim jacket. The purse was in a little room where the staff hangs out sometimes at the back of radiology. Kind of like a little lounge."

"What was in the purse?"

"What you'd expect. Wallet, ID, about fifty bucks."

"And the denim? Blue, faded, what?"

"Blue, not too old. From The Gap."

"Great," Sam said. "Just fucking great. Now she has money and street clothes. Has anybody called RTD or the taxi companies?"

"We're on that."

Sam stuck his hands in his pockets, probably to

quell his impulse to place them around somebody's neck.

I couldn't see the point in sticking around any longer. I'd been able to convince myself that I might be of some assistance in helping Sam evaluate Marin Bigg. But I didn't see a thing that I could contribute now that the task had evolved into searching for her. Anyway, my ass hurt.

I said, "I'm going to get a cab home, Sam. Call me if there's something else that I can do."

"Yeah," he said.

Reading between the lines, I realized that his words were kind of like "Thanks for your help."

"Wait a second. Before you go, give me your take on all this. She's hurt, she's on the run. Her mother's dead. Her house is surrounded by the good guys. Where would she go? The girl? Where do you think she'd go?"

"That's a tough one. She's young. I'm not sure she'd do anything that you or I might consider predictable."

"Think."

"Assuming that this kid Ramp set off the bomb that killed her mother, she'd try and find him, I think."

"To get even?"

"Possibly. But maybe to join back up with him. It all depends where her allegiance was strongest."

"You mean to him or to her mother?"

"Yes, that's exactly what I mean. She didn't seem that tight with her mother when I saw her yesterday."

"She could forgive Ramp for killing her mother?" Sam looked a little incredulous at the thought.

"Naomi was about to turn her in to the police. Or at least turn her in to me. Marin may be part of this whole conspiracy with Ramp. She may feel that she was betrayed by her mother. Teenagers make strong alliances with their friends, Sam. Stronger than with their families sometimes."

"So you think that if we find her in the next little while, she could lead us to Ramp?"

I knew Sam was thinking that leading him to Ramp meant leading him to Lucy. "I suppose."

"But you're not sure when she finds this Ramp whether she wants to kill him or kiss him?"

"She may not be sure, either." I was so tired that I wanted to sit down, but my butt screamed at the thought of having weight on it. "The only thing we know for sure is that one of them is going to eventually show up at Nora's house," I said. "To set off that bomb that they left there. That's your best bet of finding one of them. Stake out Nora's house and wait."

"It's not going to happen. Those damn Fox News people have the story about the bomb at Nora's house already. They ran with it on their nine o'clock news. If the kids are paying any attention at all, they'll know we found that bomb."

There's another bomb. That lawyer.

As the echo of Naomi's warning sounded in my head, a new question surfaced. Was the bomb at Nora's house the one that Naomi was warning me about? The hospital hallway felt cold in the way that only hospital hallways can. I wished I had a sweater.

"Go ahead and go home," Sam told me. "If you hear from Lucy . . ."

"Of course."

I turned to leave, stopped. "Sam? What if there's another bomb? One that you guys didn't find this afternoon? What if the one at Nora's wasn't even the one that Naomi was telling me about?"

He snapped at me as though he was irritated that I wasn't already gone. "What are you saying?"

"I don't know exactly. It's just that—I'm thinking that maybe there might be someone at risk that we haven't thought about. Maybe there are some people on the wouldn't-it-be-cool list that we haven't even considered."

"More lawyers?"

"I guess. Naomi said, 'That lawyer.' "

There's another bomb. That lawyer.

"You mean besides Nora and Royal?"

"That's what I'm thinking."

Sam's voice took on the timbre of debate. "We checked for bombs around the judge who accepted the plea on Marin's rape. Negative. We checked Cozy Maitlin's house and office. He was the rapist's defense attorney. Negative. We checked everything on Lauren, who was assisting Nora with the prosecution. Negative. We checked and found devices at Nora's and at Royal Peterson's home. So who's left?"

"Maybe Lauren and Nora can answer that. I don't know the system well enough to know who else might have been involved."

He took a step away from me before he stopped and faced me again. "How come every time I think you're going to bring clarity to a process, you end up clouding everything up like a damn fog machine? Why do you think that is?"

CHAPTER

42

She didn't like being bound.

She despised being gagged.

It was obvious that he hadn't planned for this step, either. The gag he fashioned was a clean white sock stuffed partway into her mouth and held in place by a long strip of duct tape.

The ambivalence she was feeling when he left the trailer ambushed her. She found herself wavering back and forth between wishing that Ramp wouldn't be gone long and hoping that the next person she saw walk through the door of the construction trailer would be the job site foreman stumbling in shortly after the eastern sky was streaked with bands of orange and blue. He'd be carrying a cardboard cup of gas station coffee and his brain would be brimming with the assorted headaches that he'd have to solve before lunch. Lucy imagined that he'd drop the coffee at the sight of the woman duct-taped to his sofa.

But Lucy was also hoping that Ramp wouldn't be gone long.

There was a name for what she was feeling. She tried to remember what she'd read about it. It was something Scandinavian. The Copenhagen Effect? No. The Stockholm Syndrome? Yes, that was it. The Stockholm Syndrome. Something about a train hijacking. The psychological phenomenon where hostages begin identifying with their captors.

Was she identifying with him? Lucy didn't think so. His rationalizations for the next day's terror rang hollow for her.

But she liked Jason Ramp Bass. She liked his charm. She liked his respectful manner. She liked the fact that he adored his mother. She even admired the way he'd managed to subvert his rage into something concise and, well, neat.

She wished she could see a clock. She wished she could roll onto her side. She wished she could empty her bladder. Mostly she wished she could call Sam and tell him to send in the cavalry.

People were going to die tomorrow. Nobody knew but her. And she couldn't do a thing about it.

Lucy had dozed off and didn't realize the door to the trailer was opening again. She didn't even hear Ramp enter or approach her.

He touched her gently on the cheek and said, "Hey, gotta get up. Plans have changed. Lucy, Lucy."

When she opened her eyelids, the soft blue of his eyes filled her vision like the sunlight fills the morning sky. Behind him the room was dark but the picket fence shadows still lined the ceiling.

"Hi," she said into the gag. Her heart pounded in her chest and the tape around her body suddenly seemed too tight to allow her to draw a breath.

Part of her response, she knew, was terror about what was going to happen next.

Part of it wasn't.

He removed the duct tape but not the gag and neither the wrist nor the ankle restraints, and he helped her to her feet.

"I'm going to carry you outside to the truck. You want to use the bathroom first?"

She nodded definitively.

She guessed he was only five ten or five eleven, maybe one hundred sixty pounds, but he lifted her effortlessly and carried her out the door the way a new husband lifts his bride over the threshold. She would have hooked an arm around his neck if she could, but she couldn't.

He stood her up outside the chemical toilet and opened the door. She held out her wrists for him to cut her plastic cuffs. Instead, he grabbed her around the waist and lifted her inside the plastic door. "I don't have time to free your restraints. You want help or can you do this yourself?"

She spoke into her gag and nodded her head. He reached up and stretched the sock away from her lips. She spit cotton before she said, "Undo my pants and pull them over my hips."

He hesitated.

"I can do the rest. Do that much." She held up her bound wrists. "I'm not going to slap you, don't worry."

He fumbled with the belt on her pants and had even more trouble with the button. The zipper he mastered quickly.

She wriggled her hips to help him get the tight pants over her butt and hips and stood still while he yanked the waistband all the way down to her upper thighs. Even through the gag, she figured he could tell that at that point she said, "Okay. That's enough."

She thought she saw his gaze focus momentarily on the lime-green triangle of her exposed underwear before he stepped back and gently closed the door of the chemical toilet.

A minute or so later she knocked the door back open with her shoulder. The top of her pants was at mid-thigh, as high as she could get them on her own. "Help me," she said.

She watched as he moved his eyes quickly from her upper legs and crotch to her face, and then back down.

He didn't hesitate this time. As he tugged her pants into place, his fingers grazed the soft skin that was exposed below the hem of her underwear. She felt his knuckles press against her belly as he buttoned her jeans, and she found herself holding her breath as he pulled up the zipper and closed the belt.

With an arm around her waist, he lifted her from the toilet and carried her to a different truck than the one she'd ridden in a few hours before.

This one was a small flatbed with welding supplies strapped into place in the back. The sign on the driver's door read "JT Welding Supplies."

"You're going to have to curl up on the floor. Can you do that? The alternative is that box in the back of the truck. But that will get hot tomorrow, I promise."

Lucy tilted her head at the cab. More despair. Tomorrow seemed like a long way away.

"Good choice," he said.

Once she was curled up on the floor of the cab, Ramp said, "While I was gone, I talked to your doctor friend. I think we're cool. And, for what it's worth, I think he's worried about you."

CHAPTER

43

Cruising taxicabs are rare at any hour in Boulder. Past midnight there was no hope I would find a cab prowling the streets, so I used my cell phone to request that a taxi be sent to the emergency entrance of the hospital. The dispatcher yawned twice before he responded by asking for my phone number and telling me to watch for a car within five minutes, maybe less.

The cell phone rang a few seconds after I ended the call with Yellow Cab. I guessed it was the dispatcher phoning back to ascertain that I was someone who really wanted a ride.

I said, "Hello."

A male voice said, "Is this Alan Gregory?"

I thought the voice was young, and immediately recognized that it wasn't the bored dispatcher with whom I'd just spoken. "Yes, it is. Who's this?"

"Never mind. Tell me what you know about Paul Bigg. I want to hear everything."

My ass suddenly stopped hurting. My ass actually stopped existing. I repeated, "Who is this?"

"Use your imagination and you'll know who this is. Now tell me what you know about Paul Bigg. This is a test, by the way. It's pass/fail. You get one chance. There are no retests."

My mouth felt as though I'd just tried to swallow a dirt clod and failed. I almost coughed out the answer to his question. "He died in a Little League accident about six years ago. A heart rhythm problem, I think."

"Go on."

I assumed I was talking to the infamous Ramp. I couldn't begin to guess what he wanted or how he'd managed to reach me on this number. "His mother, her name is Naomi, acts—acted—as though he were alive sometimes. She talked about him as though he'd never died."

"You passed," Ramp said.

"Good," I said. I suspected my trials weren't complete.

"You have a tall blond friend?"

God. He had Lucy. That's how he got my number. He was holding Lucy. "Yes," I said, "I do. Is she okay?"

Sam, I knew, was going to want to know every word, so I began to chart the conversation in my head to help me remember the details.

"As far as I know, she is."

"Do you have her? Is she with you?"

"I'd prefer to be the one asking the questions, if you don't mind."

"How can I help you?" I said. It was a variation on the line I used to start therapy sessions with new patients. It was similar to the line I'd used with Naomi Bigg only a couple of weeks before. I don't know why I used it right then.

"What have you told the police?"

"I've been talking to them ever since the bomb went off outside my office. I've told them a lot."

"Are they with you right now?"

"No. I'm standing by myself waiting for a taxi to take me home."

"Where?"

"I'm at the hospital in Boulder. Community Hospital."

"Were you hurt today? By the bomb?"

"Yes. I got a piece of shrapnel in my butt and had a minor concussion. I banged my head on the door."

"I'm sorry you were hurt. What do the police know?"

I hesitated. "I'd like to answer your question. But I've told them a lot of things. Do you want me to try to—"

He sighed. "Just tell me about the wouldn't-it-be-cool games. What do they know about those? Before you begin your answer, a reminder: Please don't forget about your tall blond friend."

I hadn't forgotten. "I told them everything Naomi told me about the games. They've put together a list of the people who they think might be on Marin's list and they've already searched all of those people's homes and offices for explosives." I remembered what Sam had said about Fox News letting the cat out of the bag about the bomb at Nora's house. "The police have already found one device. It was in a prosecutor's garage. They've disarmed it."

"They don't actually disarm them. They disrupt them. They blow them apart with water cannons."

"I'm sorry," I said. "I knew that. I'll try to be more specific."

"Did you say 'one device'?"

Did he sound relieved? I wasn't sure. "One," I repeated.

"What about any other wouldn't-it-be-cool lists? Besides Marin's?"

"To the best of my knowledge, they're still working on compiling the . . . other list."

I actually thought I could hear him smile over the phone.

"See you," he said, and the line went dead.

Sam wasn't officially directing the search for Marin Bigg. He wasn't actually officially investigating anything that had to do with any of the Biggs, or anything to do with Ramp, or with the explosion outside my office.

Sam was freelancing.

He was at Community Hospital in the middle of the night because he was looking for Lucy. In his mind, this gave him a platinum-plated invitation to stick his bulbous nose anyplace he felt like sticking it. When I tracked him down inside the hospital, he was in a first-floor corridor pacing on the periphery of a conversation other cops were having about the search of the interior of the hospital that was taking place in an attempt to find Marin.

I caught his eye and mouthed, "Come here."

He apparently saw something in my face that

indicated he should heed my invitation. He walked right over. I led him around the corner into an empty hallway that was lined with closed doors.

"What? I'm busy. I can't give you a ride."

I held up my cell phone. "Ramp just called me, Sam. I was standing outside waiting for a cab and he called me."

Sam grabbed me by the wrist and dragged me down the hall, checking knobs until he found an unlocked door. Once he closed it behind us, he blurted, "Tell me everything."

"He asked me about my 'tall blond friend.' He said it twice. I think he has Lucy."

He leaned his face within six inches of mine and froze me with his glare. "Did he say that?"

"No. But he knows things that I told Lucy. Things about Naomi and Marin and Paul Bigg. And he knew my cell number. Almost no one knows my cell number. But Lucy does."

I watched the tendons at the junctions of Sam's jaw-bones squirm like fat worms under his skin. "Have you tried her cell phone number?"

"No."

He yanked his phone from his belt and speed-dialed Lucy.

No answer.

He returned his focus to me. "Now tell me every last fucking word of your conversation."

I sat down on a flimsy plastic chair, hanging my wounded buttock over the edge.

I said, "This whole conversation with Ramp is crystal clear in my head. You want to take notes?"

My relating the details of the phone call and Sam's subsequent questions consumed about five minutes. He scribbled details in a notebook for the first sixty seconds or so.

After I was done and he'd asked his last question, he said, "Give me your cell phone."

At moments like this, Sam's intensity overwhelmed his civility, and the rules of polite discourse tended to escape him. I watched as he retrieved the number of the last person who had called me. In this case, that would be Ramp. He then pulled his own phone from a holster on his belt, called the department, and asked somebody to get a reverse listing for the number he'd taken from my phone. He waited for almost a minute before he said, "Figured. Thanks."

"Pay phone?" I said.

"At a 7-Eleven on Speer Boulevard near Federal in Denver. That was a mistake on the kid's part; it's a public place. Maybe there's a wit, somebody who saw him there a few minutes ago."

I couldn't see how that would help us much, unless the witness had thought that the guy talking on the phone had been so suspicious that the witness also decided to scribble down a license plate number or follow Ramp wherever he went after he made the call. I didn't share those thoughts with Sam. Although he was talking out loud, he was really talking to himself, and he was less than not interested in my opinion.

Sam handed me back the phone. "How's the battery on that thing?"

I looked down and checked. "Okay, maybe half charged. Why?"

" 'Cause we have to go to Denver. And when he calls again, I want to make sure the damn phone works."

"Sam, think. Think." I tapped my temple. "What are we going to do in Denver at this hour? We don't know anything."

"For starters, we're going to talk to the guy at the 7-Eleven. See what he can tell us about Ramp."

"What guy? You don't even know that there is a guy. You're guessing about there being a witness. You shouldn't be driving to west Denver on a wild-goose chase, you should be using your time arguing with your colleagues about ways to find Lucy."

With a defeated tone that I wasn't accustomed to hearing in his voice, he said, "I don't expect them to listen to me. There's a search on, but nobody wants to go out on a limb for her right now. Some cops are doing what they can, but to tell you the truth there are more people who believe she's hiding than there are that believe she's been kidnapped."

"You have to try to convince them, then. Tell them about the phone call I got from Ramp."

He stood up, towering over me. "You're right. Even though they're going to think I'm just trying to help Lucy with her defense, I need to try to convince them that Ramp has her." He reached down for the door-knob and added, "There's another bomb hidden some-place here in Boulder, isn't there? That's how you read what Ramp was saying to you?"

"Yeah. That's how I read it. At least one more."

"I agree. Somebody needs to find Marin. She's prob-ably getting into position to set off another bomb."

"The question is, who's the target?"

There's another bomb. That lawyer.

He held the door for me, an act of graciousness that was quite unexpected given the circumstances.

I was a single step past him when it suddenly struck me what Ramp hadn't asked me.

"Sam, Ramp never asked me how Marin's doing."

I turned in time to watch his eyelids drift closed. He said, "Shit."

"That means that when I talked to him on the phone, he either already knew that she'd run from the hospital or he didn't care about her condition. I don't think he doesn't care."

"Shit," Sam repeated. "He's already talked to her." He pounded the doorframe with the blunt side of his closed fist. "What on earth have the two of them got cooked up for us?"

I was about to say, *More bombs,* but I didn't. Sam didn't often wax rhetorical, but I suspected right then that that was exactly what he was doing.

CHAPTER
45

I kissed my sleeping daughter, inhaling her freshness, before I crawled into bed next to Lauren. I accomplished it all without glancing at a clock. It was a conscious effort to avoid learning the time—I didn't want to know how little sleep I was going to get. I did consider waking Lauren and telling her that I thought her one and only client had been kidnapped and was being held hostage by a mad bomber. But I quickly decided that would accomplish nothing.

My wounds and aching head combined to prohibit me from finding a comfortable place in the bed. The telephone conversation with Ramp kept playing in my brain as though it were on an endless loop of tape.

In the shallow water of my dreams the bomb in Naomi's bag didn't explode.

Grace woke up with both nostrils plugged with green snot that appeared to have been mixed with Portland cement before it was spread in a thick layer across both of her rosy cheeks. She was as cranky as I was tired. I changed her diaper while I explained the natural history of colds and generic upper respiratory infections, though it didn't seem to placate her, especially when I used a suction bulb to aspirate the volcanic flows from her tiny nostrils. We moved to the kitchen and I mixed her cereal and warmed her formula while Lauren showered. When Lauren was done getting dressed, we would trade places. In between I gave her the headlines about Lucy, then I showered while Lauren fed the baby.

We were rushing. Though my first patient wasn't until nine, Lauren needed to meet Cozy in his downtown office at eight-thirty. Since her car was still in the shop, I was her ride.

Viv arrived right on time at eight-fifteen. Fortunately, Grace's copious snot didn't faze her. Lauren and I each kissed our baby before we headed downtown. Finding a comfortable way to sit on the driver's seat took some considerable imagination on my part. I was grateful I didn't have to deal with a clutch. On the way to work we finally had a chance to talk about the night before, about Marin leaving the hospital, about the call from Ramp, and my fears about Lucy's safety.

She listened with surprising patience. "God, I hope you're wrong about Lucy."

"Me, too."

"You know, Cozy's going to hate this. This morning's meeting? We're trying to figure out a way to control the damage from the story in the *Camera* about Susan Peterson being Lucy's mother. Now this. God, I hope she's okay. She should never have gone to Denver by herself."

I nodded agreement. "Sam said he'd stay in touch. I'm sure half the Denver Police force is looking for her by now. I promise I'll call if I hear anything." We were stopped at the light on Arapahoe at Twenty-eighth. An ancient Corvair idled in front of us, belching fumes that left me wondering what toxin it was burning for fuel. Lauren was fussing with her eye makeup in the vanity mirror. I decided to risk asking a question that frightened me every time it neared my lips. "You're feeling a little better, aren't you?"

She didn't look over. "Yeah, a little bit. The brain mud is better. I'm hoping it was a false alarm."

I swallowed. "But you're not sure?"

"Am I sure? With this disease? Sorry, sweetie. Hopeful is as optimistic as it gets, I'm afraid. The light's green."

After I'd heard the words I'd been praying for, my heart felt lighter as I ignored the horns honking behind me. A couple of minutes later I pulled into an empty parking space twenty or thirty feet from the lobby door of the Colorado Building.

Lauren kissed me and said, "I wish we had time for coffee. I'd love to talk more about last night."

"I have time for coffee. Starbucks is right around the corner. You know, it's the one where Paul Bigg never worked."

"I don't have time, babe, I'm sorry." She cracked open the door and added, "My car should be ready today."

"I'll give you a ride later to pick it up."

"Don't worry," she told me. "I'll get a ride from Cozy or I'll call a cab."

I spotted Cozy approaching from the north, taking long strides down the sidewalk on Fourteenth from the Pearl Street Mall. He had the kind of chin-in-the-air posture and regal gait that would have looked perfectly natural had he been tapping the sharp end of an umbrella on the sidewalk beside him. I pointed at him. "Cozy's hoofing it today," I told my wife.

We kissed again. "A cab, then. We'll talk later," she said, and hopped out of the car with her briefcase.

She waited for Cozy to join her on the sidewalk.

I checked the time and watched Lauren and Cozy disappear into the front door of the Colorado Building.

I adjusted the volume on the radio and slid the gearshift into reverse. When I looked up to check my rearview mirror again, a bakery truck that had been idling behind me was pulling forward a few feet so that I could get out.

Before I started backing up, I noticed with amazement and wonder that red bricks had begun raining off the side of the Colorado Building, about halfway up its eight-story height.

The glass doors at the lobby entrance blew apart and a muffled roar reached my ears. The car rocked gently as though a passerby had bumped against the fender.

A second or two passed before the thought careened into my head like a drunk turning a corner at high speed:

There's another bomb. That lawyer.

Lauren. Cozy.

Those lawyers.

I threw the gearshift into park and popped out of the car in a single motion.

There's another bomb. That lawyer.

Lauren.

Two steps toward the main doors. Frosty kernels of safety glass sprinkled the sidewalk in front of the building. The brick veneer that had adorned the sheer wall high above the lobby continued to tumble to the concrete alley, falling like bloody hail.

What I noticed from the corner of my eye was the bandage. If it weren't for the bandage, I don't think the fact that a young woman with her head down was walking from the lobby of the building would have registered in my consciousness. The bandaged person climbed into the driver's seat of a white Dodge Neon. She was wearing a floppy hat and sunglasses, and the steel-blue reflection of the lenses mirrored the cold terror I'd begun feeling in my soul.

The fresh white bandage had a tiny stain at the lower edge, close to her nose. The stain was rusty-red and shaped like a crescent moon.

Marin Bigg.

Almost without thinking, I slowed my run to a gentle walk and retreated between the cars toward the street. I climbed into the bakery truck, slid behind the wheel, and dropped it into gear, allowing the big van to roll forward about twenty-five feet until it blocked the rear end of the white Dodge Neon. Pocketing the keys, I climbed down from the truck, and jogged back to the sidewalk.

Sirens had begun to fill the air in downtown Boulder, the shrill squeals reflecting off the faces of the taller buildings until the urgent sounds were squeezed tighter and tighter.

The sirens were apparently Marin's cue to exit the scene. I watched her begin to back up her car. She was still leaning forward on her seat, gazing skyward, watching to see if the fat red bricks would continue to rain from the sky, so she wasn't looking behind her as she backed up. She ran smack into the bakery truck. The impact rocked both vehicles. She'd hit it pretty good.

The impact stunned her. She pulled off her reflective shades and stuffed one of the earpieces between her teeth while she shook her head. Shock and panic bubbled up into her eyes.

Solitary cop cars were approaching down the alley from both the east and the west. The cop coming in from Thirteenth skidded to a stop before his vehicle was directly below the slowing cascade of tumbling bricks. A cop hopped out of the passenger side waving his arms at me. He yelled for me to get farther away from the building.

Marin, too, was climbing out of her car. I walked three steps until I blocked her path to the sidewalk and said, "I don't think you're going anywhere, Marin."

She looked at me as though she didn't quite remember me. I wanted to reintroduce myself by hitting her in the face with my fist. I didn't. She tried to run past me. With malicious intent I grabbed her on her bandaged hand and squeezed until she screamed at a pitch that began to cause me pain.

She stopped running.

The cop approached us with his gun drawn, the barrel pointed at the sky. His eyes betrayed his confusion at the circumstances. Before he could decide what to bark at me, I said, "This woman set off the bomb that just exploded. Her name is Marin Bigg. I think you guys are looking for her."

The cop was busy deciding whether or not to believe me when Marin said, "Fuck you," and spit on the cop.

It ended his indecision. He reached behind his back for his cuffs. As soon as he stepped forward I sprinted toward the lobby of the Colorado Building.

CHAPTER

46

The dust was silky and light, the color of fresh concrete after a rain. It hung in the air like a gentle fog.

Dust or no dust, I'd been in the lobby of the Colorado Building often enough to know where I was heading. The lobby was small, maybe fifteen feet by thirty feet, and it was unfurnished. The only two elevators were side-by-side in the northwest corner, far from the front doors.

One of the mantras of my psych ER training days entered my head as I scanned the space. *The first thing to do during an emergency is to take your own pulse.* Heeding the dictum, I tried to stay calm and was surprised that the chaos in front of me was offering an insistent conclusion about what had occurred.

The two pairs of elevator doors had been blown outward in the center like envelope flaps puffed out by a sharp burst of air. Across the lobby, the glass wall of the brokerage was decimated, the shattered glass fragments blown into the offices, not back into the lobby. The doorway that led to the fire stairs and the lobby's alley exit seemed undamaged.

My conclusion? The direct force of the bomb blast had blown into the lobby from the thick reinforced concrete of the elevator shaft, which focused its explosive intensity like a lens. The bomb had not been placed in the lobby.

I remembered the cascading bricks tumbling from what appeared to be four or five stories up. The bomb had exploded about halfway up the elevator shaft of the eight-story building.

I poked my head through the opening that was created by the damaged elevator doors. One of the two elevator cars, the left one, was below me, in the building's only basement level. The other car had to be somewhere high above me, invisible in the lingering dust. I sniffed the air in the shaft, recognizing nothing but the nasty tang of hot electrical motors. The air was unusually pungent with an odor that wasn't familiar. The explosive?

I glanced down again. The elevator car that was below me sat cockeyed in its concrete channel, the top collapsed on one side, its cable curled on top of it like a sleeping snake.

I listened for motion in the shaft, but heard nothing.

The elevator on the right side was still somewhere high up the concrete cavern.

I yelled down to the damaged car that was in the basement, "Lauren! Cozy!"

I didn't hear a reply.

I yelled up into the darkness.

Nothing.

Behind me someone said, "Hey!" Through the dust I could see a firefighter in full regalia. An ax in one hand, he stood silhouetted against the morning brightness on Fourteenth Street.

The firefighter would soon see what I'd just seen and he would either evacuate the building until the bomb squad checked it out, or he would participate in an immediate effort to rescue anyone caught in the car that had fallen into the basement. I didn't know which option he would choose. If Lauren and Cozy were in the fallen car, I could only pray that the firefighters would get down there as soon as they could. But if Lauren and Cozy were still in the other elevator car, the one high in the shaft, I knew that I had work to do.

I spun and pushed open the door to the stairs. Inside the stairwell, a locked door blocked my path to the basement. Another steel door led directly outside to the alley, and safety.

The firefighter called after me, "Sir? This way out! This way! We need to evacuate the building. Sir!"

Ignoring him and the pain in my butt, I took off up the stairs, taking the treads two at a time. At the landing between the first and second floors, I met two women descending furiously toward the exit. One of them carried her high heels in her right hand while her left was gripping the handrail. The two women were so focused on their retreat from danger that they paid no attention to me as I raced past them.

I passed no one else in the stairwell as I climbed. The other people working in the building must have been using good judgment and exiting the building down the south stairs, as far as possible from the site of the explosion.

At the fifth floor I ran from the stairwell to the elevator lobby. The damage to the elevator doors was much worse than I'd witnessed downstairs. They were peeled back from the center like flower petals seeking the morning sun.

A number of psychologists and social workers I knew and liked had offices down the hall on the fifth floor. I prayed none of them had been arriving at work when the bomb went off.

It took some effort to get close enough to the shaft to try to find the location of the elevator car in the right side of the concrete tower. From that vantage, I spotted the car easily. It was above me, maybe fifteen or twenty feet. I yelled, "Lauren! Cozy!" but heard no reply.

I sprinted back into the stairwell. My destination was the seventh-floor elevator lobby.

From there, it was clearly apparent that the top of the elevator car was about eight or ten feet down the shaft, somewhere between the sixth and seventh floors.

A series of steel treads formed a ladder on the east side of the shaft. I stepped gingerly through the opening in the damaged doors and balanced myself on the narrow stainless-steel threshold above the shaft. Four or six inches at a time I shuffled sideways closer to the steel treads that would lead me down to the car. When I reached the far end of the threshold, with little room for error, I lurched for the closest tread and sealed my fingers around it, allowing my feet to swing down and find purchase below.

It was at that moment that I began to worry what would happen if the elevator suddenly began to rise.

I was down to the roof of the car in seconds. I paused before I left the relative safety of the ladder to check the cable for obvious signs of instability. I couldn't see any, but then, if the thick cable wasn't cut or frayed, I didn't have a clue what I was looking for, nor did I know whether the elevator was operated by counterweights or hydraulics or both.

Gingerly, I stepped to the roof of the car and made my way to the hatch that led to the inside. It took me a moment to free the latch and lift the cover.

A dim light bathed the interior of the car in a glow that reminded me of the lighting inside an aquarium at night. At first all I saw below me was a tableau composed of six legs and five shoes. I counted two wingtips, two New Balance athletic shoes, and one black Cole Haan sandal.

My heart jostled my soul. The sandal was Lauren's.

"Lauren," I said. "Cozy?"

The wingtips had to be Cozy's.

I lowered my head into the hatch.

Cozy was on his back, his head propped unnaturally against the wall of the car, a trail of blood running from one ear down his neck and disappearing below the collar of his perfectly starched shirt.

A woman dressed in cut-off carpenter's pants and a tight sleeveless T-shirt was resting on her side. At first I thought she was covered with blood, but I spotted a pressed cardboard tray and three toppled cups and realized she was covered with spilled coffee.

She squirmed on the floor and a brief grimace spasmed across her face. Her eyes were open and she appeared dazed.

Lauren was against a back corner in a position that approximated sitting, but her left hand and wrist were caught in the elevator's railing at an angle that was painfully unnatural.

None of the three people looked coherent. Only the other woman's eyes were open.

I didn't know what to do.

I heard a faint moan and prayed it was Lauren's.

Fighting every instinct that made me want to drop down into the car to be with my wife, I made my way back to the ladder and climbed away from her. I don't know exactly how I managed to get from the ladder to the elevator lobby. I'm pretty sure I set a world record for descending stairs before I literally ran into three firefighters near the second-floor landing.

I grabbed one of them on his arms and much too

loudly, much too breathlessly, I stammered, "The east elevator—the one on the right—it's caught just below the seventh floor. There are three people in it. They're all hurt. Please help them."

47

Sam Purdy found me almost instantly after one of the firefighters escorted me from the building.

"You okay?"

I nodded. "I'm fine. Lauren and Cozy are hurt, Sam. They're trapped in an elevator near the seventh floor."

Sam put a hand on my shoulder and nodded. He didn't bother with platitudes. He didn't tell me that he was sure Lauren and Cozy would be fine. I barely noticed the fact that he was leading me down the sidewalk on Fourteenth toward the Mall. We stopped just beyond two parked ambulances, just outside the record store, still well within the confines of the yellow tape that had been stretched far beyond the north side of the Mall.

"Where's Marin?" I asked.

"She's still here. Couple of detectives are putting some pressure on her to find out what's coming next.

We really need to know if there's a secondary in there."

"What's a secondary?"

"A second explosive device. Sometimes these assholes set off one device to draw cops and firefighters close, then they set off a second device to kill them."

I kept looking back at the lobby entrance, hoping to see Lauren emerge through the doorway. I wanted to see her walking out with a firefighter at each of her elbows. I was willing to see her being wheeled out on a stretcher.

But I wanted to see her.

"It's started, Alan. The bomb here. Another one already this morning in Denver. She and Ramp have started their spree."

"What about Lucy?"

"No sign of her yet. Not a trace."

"What happened in Denver this morning?"

"It's kind of baffling. Some ride at Elitch's. Don't see how it has anything to do with the criminal justice system, unless the kid is trying to be metaphorical in some way I'm too tired to comprehend. I don't get it."

I wasn't looking for metaphor. I asked, "Somebody was hurt in the Denver explosion, weren't they?"

"It only happened half an hour ago. They've just started to sift through the mess."

Sam stepped away from me and stopped a patrol officer who was hurrying toward one of the ambulances. I stayed a step behind Sam.

He asked the officer, "What's up?"

"Hey, Detective. One of the elevators had its cable severed by the explosion. They just found a body in the car in the basement."

"Dead?"

"Yeah."

I thought about my friends on the fifth floor.

Sam asked what I was too stunned to ask. "Who is it?"

The officer said, "It's some guy named Bob. He's like the super, the maintenance guy in the building. He fell from fifty, sixty feet up, maybe more. Apparently everybody knows him."

"I don't," I said.

Sam's phone tweeted in his pocket. He pulled it out, hit a button with his fat thumb, and said, "Purdy."

A few seconds later he turned his head away from me and said, "Yeah, of course. What's up, Walter?"

I waited until Sam shut off the call before I asked, "What did Walter have to say?"

He flashed a how-the-hell-do-you-know-about-Walter look until he recalled our conversation wandering the aisles of the grocery store. He said, "The Denver Police just found an apparent explosive device in the center of the stage at Red Rocks. Bomb squad is responding."

I was focusing most of my attention on the lobby entrance to the Colorado Building, waiting for Lauren and Cozy to emerge. What could be taking the rescuers so long? Sam's words registered on the boundaries of my awareness. I said, "What?"

"There's a bomb, or something that looks like a bomb, right in the center of the stage at Red Rocks."

"The amphitheater?" Red Rocks was Denver's world-famous outdoor concert venue. It was set in a gorgeous sandstone bowl in the foothills west of the city. Although totally surrounded by Jefferson County, Red Rocks was technically a Denver city park facility.

"Yeah. The bomb squad's on the way to evaluate it. It doesn't look good; they want to X-ray it."

"Is there a concert or something up there?" I asked.

"On a weekday morning at this hour? Hardly."

A yellow-suited firefighter emerged from the front of the Colorado Building, waving one arm back and forth across his chest to clear a wide path from the lobby to the ambulances waiting nearby. I started toward the doorway as though I were on a moving sidewalk.

The end of a stretcher broke the plane at the front of the building. Thick rubber wheels. Tubular aluminum frame.

I saw sneakers. The woman who had been carrying the coffee.

An eternity passed before a second stretcher breached the doorway.

Wingtips the size of dinghies.

Even from thirty feet away, I could almost count the little holes in the leather.

Cozy.

Sam's fingers curled over my left shoulder. He was

providing comfort. He was also preparing to keep me from rushing the door.

A third stretcher began to emerge from the door as though the building were giving birth to it.

Triplets.

I held my breath and waited to see one black Cole Haan sandal and one elegant, very pretty, bare foot. Lauren's toenails were painted. I tried to recall what color she'd used. I couldn't.

The stretcher came out the door empty.

A sound emerged from somewhere deep in my tissues. Somewhere that knows no sound. It was part groan, part yelp, part plea.

Sam's fingers tightened on my shoulder. He said, "Wait."

It was an order.

I didn't know it at the time, but Sam's eyes were flitting between the doorway and Scott Truscott, the Boulder County coroner's assistant. Scott's vehicle was across the street and Scott was waiting to be invited inside the building to assess the casualties whose injuries were so monumental that they didn't require an ambulance ride to anywhere.

"Where is she?" I said to God.

Another stretcher began to come into view.

I saw black hair and I started to cry.

CHAPTER

48

The long trip from Denver's Platte Valley to the foothills near Morrison perplexed Lucy. She was able to track the journey from her cramped lair on the floor of the welding supply truck by reading the overhead highway signs on the Sixth Avenue Freeway.

When Ramp stopped the truck, he didn't bother to restrain her further. He told her he wouldn't be gone long and that she shouldn't move. She could feel the truck shudder as he did something in the back. The movement stopped; she guessed that Ramp had moved away.

She considered her options. Despite the restraints on her wrists and ankles, she thought that she could manage to get the truck door open, tumble outside, and try to hop away. It was possible that Ramp had parked the truck in a location that would allow a passerby to see her and come to her rescue. Possible, but not likely.

`Not at that hour.

She raised herself up from the floor and, bracing her bound wrists on the seat, lifted herself up high enough to look out the back window of the truck. Eight or ten tall green oxygen tanks almost completely blocked her view. She looked out to the side and was thrilled that what she was seeing was slightly familiar.

She couldn't quite place it. The huge rocks. The dust. The flat-roofed building. Wait, wait, wait. Could this be Red Rocks?

"I told you not to move."

Ramp's voice was admonishing but not angry, the kind of tone someone might use to correct a curious puppy.

"Get back down. We're leaving."

Lucy thought, *No explosion?* She fell heavily to the floor of the cab.

As though he'd read her mind, he said, "This one's different from all of the others."

The highway signs told her they were going back into Denver. The noise told her that traffic was starting to accumulate. Ramp played a Dave Matthews CD, not the news, and didn't seem at all concerned about his rearview mirrors.

The light to the east told her it was dawn.

The next place that the truck stopped was somewhere near Sixth and Santa Fe, and Lucy's promise to stay down—the alternative was having her wrists duct-taped to the center console—earned her coffee and an egg-and-chorizo burrito. She wasn't hungry but she forced herself to eat a few bites.

While the gag was still off her mouth, she asked him, "What exactly are you doing?"

"Making this memorable. I want people to talk, remember?"

"Dialogue."

"That's right."

"So you're going to blow up Red Rocks?"

He smiled at her. "That would piss people off, wouldn't it?" She couldn't read his eyes.

He replaced the gag, pausing when he was done to caress the soft skin below her temple. "Don't worry, I don't have enough explosives to blow up Red Rocks. Anyway, I like Red Rocks."

Santa Fe all the way to Speer, Speer north toward I-25. As soon as they were on the freeway, southbound Lucy thought, they exited again. She wished she knew Denver's geography better. She thought that they must have been somewhere near the Children's Museum.

Only thirty seconds or so after they turned off the freeway, they turned again. Soon the truck came to a stop.

Ramp put the truck in park and killed the engine. He said, "I like this view. You want to see it?"

She nodded. He leaned over and helped her pull herself up onto the passenger seat.

She looked out the windshield. Ramp had parked in one of the big lots flanking the banks of the South Platte River just east of Denver's new aquarium, Colorado's Ocean Journey. On the river, a couple of hardy early-season kayakers were slicing across the abbreviated rapids at the confluence of the South Platte and Cherry Creek. On the other side of the river was Six Flags Elitch Gardens, and beyond it, the downtown skyline.

Ramp lifted some binoculars from the floor in front of his seat and raised them to his eyes. To Lucy, it appeared he was examining something in the sky that was just above the jagged profile of the amusement park. In the early-morning light the park looked forlorn and insincere, the way a saloon looks afterhours when the cleaning floods are on bright.

He sighed. "There he is. Right on time. My grandfather loved punctuality more than he loved almost anything in the world other than me and my grandma. He would have loved this guy; he's always on time."

"What guy?" Lucy mumbled into the cotton sock. Lucy thought he was pointing at the Ferris wheel.

Again Ramp reached down to the floor in front of his seat. He raised a complicated black plastic device and extended an antenna from the top. Without looking toward Lucy, he said, "It's for model airplanes. Good range."

He placed the transmitter on his lap and raised the binoculars to his eyes. He held them in place while he studied a narrow slice of the Colorado sky. When he lowered the glasses, he said, "He's getting pretty high up there. It'll be just a couple more minutes."

She wanted to ask, *Till what?* but didn't bother. She knew. Or at least she thought she knew.

He mused, "You know how easy it was to get what I needed for all this? Anything I can't get at Toys 'R' Us, I can get at Radio Shack. Except for the explosives, of course. For that, you need a relative in the demolitions business."

He raised the binoculars once more, held them in place for only a few seconds, and said, "My guy's up there. Here goes. It took me three trips to get all these charges in place. I used more explosives here than everywhere else put together."

He fingered one of the levers on the black plastic box and raised his eyes to a spot just above the horizon. Lucy tried to follow the line of his gaze.

"Three," he whispered, "two . . . one."

At first, Lucy didn't see anything change in her field of vision and wondered if Ramp's device had failed. Then, barely to the right of where she was focusing her attention, she glimpsed a puff of smoke, like a flare from a campfire. It had emerged from a spot close to the ground in the middle of the amusement park.

Rapidly—close by the first—another puff of smoke followed. Lucy's eyes trailed up from the source to the elaborate superstructure of a loop-the-loop thrill ride. The highest part of the metal structure started to lean, she thought, just a little.

Another puff of smoke erupted from the base of the

ride—this one was slightly larger and a little higher off the ground. Lucy thought she could hear the concussion of a blast, too. But she wasn't sure that her mind wasn't just filling in the blanks.

Ramp said, "It's called The Sidewinder. Ever been on it? It's an okay ride. It *was* an okay ride. I don't think it's going to be too much fun anymore."

Lucy watched the single spiral of steel lean farther and farther to the west. Then it steadied and hung in the sky in defiance. She glanced over at Ramp. He touched another switch on the black plastic console.

One more puff exploded near the base of The Sidewinder, and the temporarily reluctant steel structure continued its fall to the west.

"Wow," Ramp said as the structure disappeared into the fabric of the amusement park. "I did it. It fell right where I wanted it to fall."

He stared at the empty sky and the rising cloud of dust for more than a minute before he started the truck and eased away from the bluff above the river. "The guy who was climbing the ride just then? He was the twin brother of the defense attorney who represented the man who killed my mom."

As they circled underneath the viaduct and drove past the big REI store that had been built inside the old Forney Museum, Ramp said, "Things will start to happen fast now. If they go well, you should be free in a couple of hours."

CHAPTER
49

Cozy's injuries were the most severe.

The elevator car had been ascending between the seventh and eighth floors when the explosion rocked the concrete elevator tower. The car came to an abrupt halt, throwing both Lauren and the woman who had been carrying the coffee to the floor. The woman with the coffee broke her right wrist, and Lauren's head slammed against the side of the car. Cozy somehow maintained his balance. The fact that he was still standing made him much more vulnerable when the car dropped precipitously. He flew headfirst up into the ceiling of the car and crashed back to the floor when the car jammed to a stop where I found it in between the sixth and seventh floors.

Lauren's violet eyes were open as I ran to her side

at the rear of the ambulance. She was strapped to a backboard, and huge cushioned cervical braces immobilized her head and upper body.

She asked, "How's Grace?"

What?

"The baby's great," I said. "How are you?"

"I'm okay," she said. They lifted her into the back of the ambulance and closed the doors.

An hour later, Cozy was in surgery. The woman with the coffee had been released from the hospital with her arm in a cast. Lauren was in observation. My own observation was that she was looking pretty good, considering.

During our few minutes together, Lauren had told me what happened.

Bob, the building handyman who'd died in the elevator crash, had been waiting in the lobby when Cozy and Lauren walked in that morning. He'd been puzzling over a sign that had been placed on one elevator declaring it out of service for a furniture delivery. Bob complained to Lauren and Cozy that no one had permission to reserve an elevator without talking to him, certainly not at that hour of the day. He told them to go ahead and use the reserved elevator, which was waiting on the first floor. He'd take the other one and find out who was responsible for the sign.

Lauren said they stopped once on the third floor and the young woman with the coffee joined them.

Moments later the explosion rocked the elevator tower.

Adrienne somehow created enough of a hole in her day to sit with me while I held a cup of hospital coffee in my hand. The coffee was too foul to actually drink, but I got some comfort from holding it. Adrienne was acting unnaturally, saying pacifying things like "You know that you did everything you could." And "It's lucky you told the firefighters where to go." I think I would have actually felt better if she had just lovingly berated me like she usually did.

I said, "Based on my recent experience, I think if you have to be in the emergency room, it's easier being the patient than being the one waiting to hear news about someone you love."

Before she could respond to my comment, the phone in my pocket rang. Initially, the sound meant nothing to me. It simply didn't register. Finally, Adrienne said, "That's your phone. It may be Viv. Let's take it outside. They don't like cells in here."

I followed her out the sliding glass doors of the emergency department, hit a button on the phone, and said, "Alan Gregory." We were standing on the edge of the driveway with three people who were sucking nicotine in smoker's Siberia.

I heard music playing through the phone, a song by Everclear that Lauren liked. I'd never understood how she could like it. I said, "Hello."

The song ended; a commercial jingle started. Something about why I should buy my next car at Burt Chevrolet. Then a man's voice said, "I'm going to try and find the news." The voice was in the background, as though the speaker wasn't talking directly into the microphone.

The voice I'd heard wasn't Viv's, but it was vaguely familiar. I said, "Hello, who is this?"

I was about to hang up when the same voice sounded again. Clearly. "I need to find out if they sent the bomb squad to Red Rocks. I don't think they have two mobile X-ray units. And I don't think they have two robots."

Adrienne asked, "Is it Viv?"

I shook my head. The sound in my ear was of stations changing quickly on a radio. Music, commercial, talk. The channel lottery stopped abruptly with a perky female voice prattling on about the explosion earlier that morning at Elitch's. I wouldn't exactly call what she was doing "news."

Adrienne said, "Who is it?"

I held up a finger, asking for her patience. She squished up one eye and shook her head at me to remind me that patience wasn't one of her best things.

As though I might have forgotten.

I covered the mouthpiece again. "Nobody's talking to me, but I hear a voice talking about the bomb at Red Rocks."

"What?"

That's when I heard a muffled sound of protest.

Oddly, it was the most distinct sound that had yet come through the phone.

Again I covered the mouthpiece. "Adrienne, you have your phone with you?"

It was clear from her expression that it was like asking her whether she had her nose with her.

"Call Sam Purdy. I need to keep this call going." Even Adrienne could recognize the urgency in my voice when I told her the number.

She yanked her phone from her belt and punched at the buttons.

I handed her my phone and took hers. "Adrienne?" I spoke her name to see if she was on my wavelength. She was. "Keep the microphone covered," I told her. "I don't want whoever is on the other end of that call to hear anything from us. Is that clear? If you hear anything interesting, let me know."

She made a face to communicate how unhappy she was about how perplexed she was, but she placed her index finger over the microphone, leaned her head to the side, and slid the phone below her hair.

I waited until I heard Sam's bored voice before I turned my back on Adrienne and spoke. "Sam, it's Alan. Listen—my cell phone just rang. Nobody's actually talking to me but the line is live and I can hear part of a conversation going on in the background. Somebody is talking about the bomb that they found at Red Rocks. I don't know what to make of it."

I counted to three before he responded. "What exactly did you hear?"

"It's a guy talking. He's in a car, I think. He said some-thing to someone about needing to find out whether they sent the bomb squad to Red Rocks. And I'm pretty sure he said that he thought the Denver Bomb Squad only had one mobile X-ray unit and one robot."

"Really? He said that? He talked about mobile X-rays and robots?"

"Yes."

"And this is all just like conversation in the back-ground? He's not talking to you?"

"That's right."

"What else?"

"He's punching buttons on a radio, trying to find the news."

"That's it?"

"And there was a muffled sound like a groan."

"Muffled?"

"Yeah."

"A groan?"

"Yeah."

"The call's still going?"

"Just a sec." I turned to Adrienne. "It's still going?"

She nodded. I saw some magic flicker like a jewel in the corner of her eyes. I knew she wasn't bored.

"Still going, Sam."

"Where are you?"

"Outside the ER entrance at Community."

"I'll be there in three minutes."

I ended the call. When I looked up again, Adrienne's eyes were as big and bright as marbles.

She was almost breathless. "The guy? He just said he would take that off if somebody promised not to scream."

"Take what off?"

"I don't know. There was some funny moaning noise. Then he went, 'I'll take that off if you promise not to scream.' That's all he said. Jesus, Alan, do you really think—"

"Yes," I said. "I really do."

CHAPTER

50

The route into Lower Downtown was familiar to Lucy for two reasons. She was a Rockies fan and she was a young single woman. Being a Rockies fan meant Coors Field. Being a single woman meant way too many regrettable first dates in the clubs and restaurants of LoDo.

After Ramp circled along the Platte past the REI store, he went down Fifteenth Street to Wynkoop, turned left past Union Station, and then made a loop that brought the truck to the corner that was opposite the old Student Movers Building that had been incorporated into the structure of Coors Field. The ground floor of the renovated building was used for the Sandlot Brewery.

"This will work. We can park here for a while," he said. "But you need to stay down." He displayed his wrist, the one with the transmitter button taped to it.

She wondered if he was planning on trying to bring down the baseball stadium and immediately decided that it was impossible. She protested loudly into her gag. He ignored her.

They sat. She couldn't see a clock but she guessed that they sat for at least half an hour.

Finally, he said, "There she is."

Lucy had no idea which woman Ramp was identifying.

He started the truck and turned and circled back around until they came out a block away at the corner of Twentieth and Blake, directly across from the main entrance to the ballpark. Again, Ramp parked the truck on the street. This time, he hopped out of the cab and fed the meter.

When he climbed back into the truck, he said, "I'm going to try and find the news."

Lucy tried to talk into her gag. She couldn't even understand herself. The effort was futile.

Ramp said, "I need to find out if they sent the bomb squad to Red Rocks. I don't think they have two mobile X-ray units. And I don't think they have two robots." He reached out and started punching buttons on the radio.

Lucy tried to understand what was going on. Why did it matter to Ramp what was happening up at Red Rocks? Why was it important how many mobile X-ray units and robots the Denver Bomb Squad had?

She screamed into the gag.

Ramp raised his wrist and lifted an index finger to his lips to warn her to be quiet.

A minute or so passed. He said, "I'll take that off if you promise not to scream."

She nodded urgently.

He reached down and lowered the sock so that it was resting on her chin, not her mouth. Almost involuntarily she said, "Thank you." It came out in a cotton-mouthed whisper.

He was looking out the windshield.

"You're welcome. It's time." He reached down to the floor in front of his seat and lifted a device that looked like a controller for a child's electronic toy. "I thought you wanted to say something."

"Ramp, stop. Please. Don't do it. Don't set off any more bombs."

"That's it? That's all you wanted to say?" He reached over and lifted the sock back into place in Lucy's mouth.

She closed her eyes and shook her head in despair. She tugged at her wrist restraints until the plastic bit into her flesh. It was futile.

"I'll be back in a minute. I need to get closer for this thing to work. It doesn't have great range. Stay down or things will get worse for you. I'll be in sight of you the whole time. Do you understand?"

She didn't look at him.

"I'm telling you that you'll be within range." He raised his arm, the one with the transmitter taped to it.

She nodded.

His voice still even, he said, "I know this isn't any fun. But tell me you understand."

She nodded again.

Twenty or thirty seconds after Ramp exited the car, Lucy heard the reverberation of an explosion. It wasn't loud, or sharp. If she didn't know he was setting off a bomb, she would have believed the sound was caused by something else, something less sinister.

She started to cry.

It wasn't long before Ramp climbed back into the truck. A distant peal of sirens began to pierce through the benign blanket of sounds that covered the city in the morning.

"In case you're wondering, that was for a woman who worked for the Rockies—she was the wife of the judge who approved the sentence of the man who killed my mom. Time to go," he said. "Time to go."

CHAPTER
51

Sam pulled down Balsam from the east. I imagined that he was still at the Colorado Building when I called him, and guessed that he must have come across town on Thirteenth, avoiding Broadway. He was driving his city car, not his old Cherokee, and I didn't recognize him until he turned into the entry drive for the ER. I waved at him, careful to keep one finger planted on the mouthpiece of the phone.

As he pulled into the ambulance-only zone, I ran to his car, pointing to the phone at my ear. "I think I just heard a woman's voice."

"You're sure?"

"The guy said, 'I thought you wanted to say something.' Then the woman's voice said, 'Ramp, stop, please don't do it. Don't set off any more bombs.' Then the guy said, 'That's it?'"

"Anything else?"

"A car door slammed."

"And now?"

"Nothing."

Sam sighed.

Under my breath, I said, "Oh no. Oh my God!"

Sam threw open the door to his car and started to climb out. He barked, "What? What?"

"I think I just heard an explosion, Sam. A bang. No, more like a deep rumble. Now nothing."

"You're not imagining this? You're sure it wasn't like a car backfiring or something?"

"I don't think so."

Sam fell back down onto the seat and pulled his radio to his lips. He asked the dispatcher to check to see if there were any reports of an explosion in Denver in the last couple of minutes.

"Sam? The car door slammed shut again. Then the guy said, 'Time to go. Time to go.'"

Sam nodded at me. Into the radio, he said, "It's okay, I'll wait as long as I have to wait."

Half a minute passed, then a minute. I couldn't understand the reply when it finally squawked back to him through the radio.

"What?" I asked.

"A bomb just went off at Coors Field. There are casualties. The half of the Denver Police force that isn't at Elitch's is responding right now."

"I can hear the sirens," I said, for the first time realizing that I'd heard the explosion live. I pointed at the phone. "I'm listening to Ramp, Sam. He has Lucy with him."

"Let me have the phone."

He listened for maybe fifteen seconds. "I don't hear anything. You sure it's still live?"

I nodded. "It was a few seconds ago."

He handed the phone back to me. "Keep listening. I have to get the location of this call identified somehow. There's no reason to think this kid is done blowing things up."

An out-of-tune diesel delivery truck plowed up Balsam. I turned away from Sam to escape the noise. The call went dead.

I checked the screen of my phone to be sure. I even shook the handset as though that would restore the connection.

"Sam, we lost it."

"Don't tell me that."

"It's gone."

"Check your caller ID. Find out who the hell called you."

I did. Lucy's cell phone number popped up on the little screen. "It was Lucy, Sam."

He buried his lower lip in his mustache and pondered the cards in his hand. "Here's what I think's happening: She speed-dialed you and Ramp doesn't know that her phone is on. She can't risk saying anything but she wants us to hear everything that's going on. When she realizes that the call got dropped, she'll do it all again. Let's be ready."

I asked, "How do we get ready?"

"I don't know." Sam looked exhausted. "How's Lauren doing?"

"It looks like she'll be okay. She sprained her wrist and she banged her head pretty good. They have her in observation now. Cozy broke a bone in his neck. He's in surgery."

"Damn. Fusion?"

"I don't know, maybe."

"The other girl?"

"Broke her wrist, got burned a little from the coffee. She's home already. Is Marin talking?"

"Not yet. She said she'll tell us whatever we want later in the day. Believe it or not, she lawyered up. Is that ironic or what?"

I didn't want to get lost thinking about the Biggs. "What do we do about Lucy, Sam?"

"I'm not sure. I need to call all this in. Why don't you go back inside and check on your wife."

"What's Denver going to do? Evacuate the whole city until this kid runs out of explosives?"

"We have to find them."

"What about the phone?"

"If it rings again, run back out here like someone's life depends on it."

I consciously placed one foot in front of the other and was mildly surprised when the automatic door sensed my presence on my way back inside the hospital.

Sam fiddled with the radio on the dashboard before he asked, "What's the pattern here? Red Rocks is an amphitheater, Elitch Gardens is an amusement park, Coors Field is a baseball stadium. What's the pattern? Where does he go next? The new football stadium? The Pepsi Center? What?" He grunted. "If this asshole does anything to the Pepsi Center and I have to miss any Avalanche games, I swear . . ."

He left the threat unfinished.

We were on the Boulder Turnpike, heading southeast toward Denver, just opposite the Interlocken office park. The morning rush hour was over and the traffic on 36 was merely heavy. Sam was driving his detective mobile. A red beacon on the dash flashed notice of our presence to other cars. I thought the strobe was an inadequate herald, considering our obvious haste. Sam was speeding mercilessly and changing lanes a lot and his driving was making me nervous.

It had been my idea to turn down the offer of a ride to Denver in the Denver Police helicopter. I'd argued that the noise in the chopper would interfere with our ability to hear what was going on if Lucy was able to make another cell phone call. So we were speeding to Denver in Sam's car and I was having second thoughts about not taking the chopper.

I was feeling many things; one of the most prominent was discomfort about leaving Lauren in Boulder.

When I'd told her what was going on with the bombs in Denver and with Lucy and Ramp and the cell phone, she told me to do whatever I had to do, that she'd be fine. I told her Sam wanted me to accompany him to Denver. She encouraged me to go. Adrienne promised to drive Lauren home whenever she was released from the ER, and Viv promised to stay at our house until I got home.

My bases were covered, but my ambivalence was pronounced.

As Sam used the right lane and a good chunk of the shoulder to pass an eighteen-wheeler full of Mercedes SUVs, I said, "I don't think what Ramp's doing is about the buildings, Sam. I think it's about the people. The wouldn't-it-be-cool games that Naomi described were always about people."

Sam scoffed. "He's hit, or tried to hit, three of the most identifiable landmarks in Denver, Alan. You think that's an accident?"

"Not accidental, Sam. But maybe it's incidental."

"I'm too tired. What?"

"He's not after buildings. He's not after body count, either. He could have done any of those buildings when they were full of people, right?"

Sam touched a button on his radio before he replied, "Right. I thought of that, too."

"Well, he didn't. All the venues were basically empty. The bomb he set at Coors Field was actually in an office, not in the stadium itself."

Sam argued, "But people died both times that a bomb went off."

"Exactly. And those are the people we should be paying attention to. I would guess that they were the targets. He's using these bombs to kill specific people, not random people."

Sam looked at his notepad and steered with his knees. I prayed he wasn't going to try to change lanes again, not with his knees. When he looked back up, we were closing on the butt end of a cement mixer. Sam steered around it as though he'd expected it would be in his way. His voice betrayed his skepticism about the hypothesis I was making as he said, "Let's see, three dead so far. And who are they? A couple of ride testers at Elitch Gardens. A bookkeeper for the Rockies and her boyfriend, a . . ." He flipped a page in his notebook. "The boyfriend was an assistant manager in group ticket sales."

"One more, Sam. Don't forget the woman who died in the car explosion last week."

"Okay, four dead. I'll throw in the housewife from last week. I don't care. Look at the list, Alan; these aren't the kind of people that terrorists usually salivate over eliminating."

"Then we're missing something."

Sam rubbed his eye with his knuckle. "There's no doubt about that. How's your phone?"

My cell was resting in my lap. "What do you mean?"

"The battery."

I didn't even have to look. "It's fine."

"Check."

I checked. "It's fine."

Sam said, "You're thinking about something, aren't you?" He made it sound like an accusation.

I said, "Somebody needs to cross-check the list of people involved with letting Ramp's mother's murderer out on parole with the list of the casualties of the explosions so far."

In a monotone, he replied, "Ride checker, bookkeeper, assistant manager, housewife. Those people don't make decisions about sentences and parole. That dog don't hunt."

His argument was academic. He was a professor trying to keep a debate going in a seminar. I was happy to play along. I said, "Look at Marin's list, Sam. The first bomb was found in Royal Peterson's house. He was the DA who signed off on the plea bargain on her rape. Second was in Nora's garage. She was the prosecutor who negotiated the deal. Third was in Cozy's office. He was the defense attorney who represented

Marin's rapist. The progression is purely logical. The wouldn't-it-be-cool games targeted people directly involved with the decision to offer Marin's rapist the plea bargain. Why would Ramp proceed differently? Everything we know tells us that he's the brains behind this thing."

He argued, "It's not that complicated. The brain obviously decided to do landmarks instead of people."

"I don't buy it. It's inconsistent."

Sam shrugged. The shrug said, "Tough." But I surmised he didn't want me to stop arguing with him. I held my breath as we whizzed past a Ford Taurus being driven by someone whose head looked like it was all felt hat and gray hair.

I said, "Humor me. You're already in touch with someone at the Denver Police Department, right? I mean, this morning—whoever it was who offered to send the helicopter for us."

"Yeah."

"Walter?"

"Don't go there."

"Whatever. Call whoever it is and find out where the husband of the woman who was killed in the car bomb last week worked and where he parked his car. Will you do that?"

"Why?"

"Just make the call. You certainly aren't using much of your attention driving this car."

I expected resistance but he flipped open his phone and made the call. I closed my eyes. I didn't want to see how he was going to maneuver the interchange at I-25 one-handed. Or no-handed.

I feared it would involve the steering wheel and Sam's fat knees.

When he was done talking to Denver, he turned to me and said, "Her husband owns a tourist shop in Larimer Square. Sells western shit. He parks right behind his store."

We were merging onto I-25. "See, there you go," I said. "He was the target, not her. That keeps the pattern intact. He was the one who was supposed to get killed in the explosion. It should have gone off this morning while he was parking his car behind his store in Larimer Square."

"Seems to support the landmark theory, not the wouldn't-it-be-cool-to-kill-people theory. We're talking Larimer Square, tourist central. Assuming you're right, and he was the target, and assuming the bomb hadn't gone off prematurely, there would have been one more blown Denver landmark this morning. That's how I read it."

I couldn't believe how fast we were approaching the Mousetrap, the legendary bottleneck interchange of Interstates 70 and 25. I chanced a glance at the speedometer. We were doing over ninety. My pulse was doing twice that, easy. The scariest part was that there were a couple of cars going so fast that we had trouble passing them.

"It's the people, Sam. Don't get distracted by the landmarks. Columbine was about the kids, not the building."

That last comment quieted him. He slowed as we approached the exit that would take us to Coors Field.

He said, "Then why the landmarks?"

"To confuse the situation. To exaggerate the press coverage. I don't know. There could be a dozen reasons. To get the cops to waste time having arguments like the one we're having."

Sam said, "I'll ask them to cross-check the list."

A Denver patrol car was waiting to escort us down the viaduct to the baseball stadium. Sam fell in behind the car while he chatted on the radio with someone about the cross-check. A minute later we pulled to a stop along the curb on Blake Street. We were right in front of the brick walkway beside Coors Field. The Denver Police had established a wide perimeter. The TV stations' microwave trucks were sequestered at least a block away.

Sam threw the phone onto his lap. He said, "The Denver cops are already there. The bomb squad detectives are working under the assumption that the victims were targeted because they were relatives of people involved with Ramp's mother's case. You're smarter than you look."

I said, "One relative worked at Elitch's. Another for the Rockies. What about Red Rocks?"

"No connection they know of. They're still looking."

"And the guy who managed the store in Larimer Square? The one whose wife died in the car bombing?"

"His father is on the parole board. Let's go talk to the people in charge. Compare some notes."

I got out of the car.

Sam asked me, "Why relatives?" This time he seemed genuinely curious about my opinion.

I felt confident about my answer. "Ramp wants the people he believes are responsible to know how it feels to see a loved one killed. It completes the circle for him. The people he wants to hurt now will know exactly what it's like to feel what he felt when his mother died."

"Killing them would be too easy?" Sam was edging close to sarcasm. Close, but not quite there.

"Killing them would spare them the pain they're feeling right now. Ramp doesn't want to do that. He wants them to suffer his pain. The loss he feels."

Sam grunted. This time I translated the grunt to mean that he approved of my argument.

"How's your phone?" he asked.

I glanced down at the battery meter. "It's fine. No problem. It has hours left. Stop worrying."

"You see Lucy sitting pretty anywhere around here? Until you do, I don't stop worrying."

A Denver patrol officer was pointing Sam down the sidewalk, indicating a stocky man with a starched blue shirt and a navy blue tie. The shirt was unbuttoned at the collar, the tie was far from tight, and the shirt-sleeves were folded up near the man's elbows. The shoes were polished like a Marine's dress pair.

"You Purdy?" the man asked as we approached.

Sam said, "Yeah. This is Alan Gregory, the guy with the phone."

"That's the phone?" He pointed at my hand.

"Yes," I said.

Without asking permission he took it from my hand and plugged a small tape recorder into it. "It'll kick on automatically. It's a backup in case the phone company doesn't capture the call. Notify me the second it rings.

"I'm Rivera, by the way. You're not going to believe this, but we just took a nonemergency call from somebody warning us about some bombs at East High School."

Sam said, "East High School? Bombs? It's in session, right? The school's full of kids, right?"

"Yeah, it's full of kids. They've started evacuating the buildings. We're sending as many people out there as we can and we've asked the surrounding cities and counties for help from their bomb squads and SWAT teams. The way this morning is developing, we need five bomb squads."

Sam asked, "You getting all the cooperation you want?"

"Anything we need. Except from Boulder. They seem to need help almost as much as we do."

"Did you ID the caller on the warning?"

"The call came in on a nonemergency line, so we didn't get an automatic ID. Anyway, it was blocked, and it was too short a call to trace. We have a tape of the entire call; it's like ten seconds. I'm sure the RP was the kid. They played it for me over the phone. I'm sure it was the same kid. East High School. Damn."

Ramp was "the kid."

My phone rang. I almost dropped it. At first I gaped at it as though it had given me an electrical shock.

Sam stopped in his tracks. He looked at me like he'd just discovered he was standing in the center of a minefield.

Recovering my wits, I hit a button and listened for a count of two before I whispered, "Hello, this is Alan Gregory."

I didn't really expect a reply.

CHAPTER
53

Ramp's gesture as he climbed back into the truck after initiating the explosion at Coors Field was both nonchalant and innocuous, but it was sufficient to fracture the fragile skeleton of hope that Lucy had been constructing.

He removed the windbreaker he'd been wearing and tossed it over the center console of the truck, burying Lucy's cell phone below it.

She wanted to cry. She'd already noticed that her earlier call to Alan Gregory, although live for a while, had been dropped. She'd been waiting for an opportunity to hit the redial button once again. To get a chance, she knew that she'd have to wait for Ramp to make another sojourn from the truck. With the jacket covering the phone, she didn't know how she was going to get her bound hands to the button quickly and she wasn't at all confident that the phone's microphone would pick up sound through the insulation of the jacket's fabric, anyway.

She wondered if Alan had figured out anything from her earlier call. Maybe he hadn't even bothered to listen when he'd discovered that there wasn't anyone at the other end of the line.

Ramp headed down Blake across Broadway into the part of Denver's old warehouse district that hadn't yet been converted into lofts, restaurants, and galleries. He stopped the truck in the middle of a block that was swarming with trucks making pickups and deliveries. He told Lucy, "I have a little time to kill. Try to get some rest."

She watched him lean back in his seat and settle a baseball cap over his eyes. As though he could read her mind, he added, "Don't try anything, Lucy. I'm tense. Try to relax."

She yelled at him into her gag. He slid the hat away from his eyes and glanced down at her. She raised her bound hands as though she were going to remove the gag herself.

He said, "I told you, if you touch that, I'll move your arms behind your back. You won't like that."

She screamed again.

He stared at her for a moment, then lowered the gag so that it rested on her chin. The tape tore at the skin on her jaw. She spit fragments of cotton into the air and tried to speak. The first attempt came out in a rasp.

Finally, she managed, "Why are you blowing up those buildings?"

He didn't answer right away. "I used a lot of explosives to knock down the ride at Elitch's, but the rest of the bombs aren't that powerful. All I'm doing is creating chaos. When the dust settles, hopefully people will wonder why. Dialogue will fill that void. The more people care about the buildings, the more they will wonder why I blew them up. That's why I chose people who work in buildings that people might care about. That's why I didn't do it at their homes. Believe me, that would have been much, much easier."

"You're not just bombing buildings, though. You're killing people, too, aren't you?"

"Yes."

"Why?"

"So that . . . some people, particular people . . . will know how it feels to lose someone they love to stupidity."

"You're not done?"

"No."

"Why?"

"So the people in power will care."

"I don't get it."

"For this to be effective, it has to get personal. People, especially powerful people, have to realize that they are just as vulnerable as I was. They have to believe that in their hearts. Deep in their hearts. There's no other way for me to be certain that I'm getting my message across and that they'll pay attention.

You cause somebody enough pain, you get their attention. Trust me, I know. The people in power have to know that, too."

She fought a swell of compassion for him. She said, "Jason, stop. Please, stop now."

He scoffed. "Why?"

"I'll help you."

"I don't need your help, Lucy. Unless they catch up with me before I'm done, I don't need your help."

"I know a good lawyer."

He laughed. "I know you do. Your lawyer's the one who got Marin's rapist a slap on the wrist. For me, he's part of the problem, not part of the solution. Anyway, it's irrelevant. Your lawyer's dead, too. He was on Marin's list this morning. I set a charge against the counterweight cable in his building's elevator. Marin was supposed to wait until he climbed into the elevator, then she was going to set it off."

She vaulted to her knees. "You little—"

He raised his wrist, curling his fingers so that the tips rested on the switch that was taped to his arm.

She stilled. He pushed the gag back into place. "Why don't you get some rest? Please don't make me sorry I brought you along."

After twenty minutes or so, Ramp exited the truck without a word. Lucy couldn't see which way he went, and didn't know how long he would be gone. She fought the temptation to go for the phone, but suspected that he was testing her, so she remained in place.

He was back in a minute, maybe two. "Just a little diversion," he told her. "I'm sending the bomb squad over to East High School. I have some surprises planted there that should get everyone's attention for a little while. Oh shit, I left the number sitting by the phone. Be right back."

She screamed into her gag and almost choked with the effort. *Not a high school. Please, God, not a high school. Not in Colorado. Not again.*

Ramp climbed out of the truck.

She scrambled to get some balance, threw back the windbreaker, fumbled with the phone until she identified the tiny redial button, and pressed it. She could hear Ramp's footsteps approaching the truck as she tossed the jacket back into place and dropped back onto the floor.

He climbed into the cab and said, "We're off again. Short drive this time. But fasten your seat belt anyway." He looked at her and said, "Just kidding."

She protested into her gag, hoping to create enough noise to alert Alan to what was going on.

He said, "You know, you're cute."

She said, "Fuck you."

He shook his head dismissively, as though he might have actually understood her mumbles.

He started the engine and pulled back onto the street, retracing his route down Blake, crossing Broadway, and heading right back into the heart of LoDo.

CHAPTER

54

I don't think I hear anything, Sam. Maybe some background noise, but I'm not sure. Is there someplace more quiet we could go?"

Rivera led us into the main entrance of the ballpark, near the ticket turnstiles. We were away from the street noise, but I still couldn't make out much on the phone. In my other ear, I heard Rivera tell Sam that the explosion had been right upstairs in the ball club's office suite.

Again, I said, "I don't hear anything."

Sam said, "Give it to me."

I handed him the phone and the attached recorder.

He listened for ten seconds and shook his head. Finally, he said, "Wait, wait. Maybe a voice in the background. Everything's muted. I wonder if she's losing her battery."

He turned to Rivera. He had a phone to his ear, too.

Sam asked, "Can we trace this? Triangulate it?"

"They're trying. The technology's tough apparently. But they're trying. I hope this call doesn't die."

A young woman wearing a bomb squad windbreaker walked toward us and waited until she had Rivera's attention before she said, "Detectives feel confident that the device was under the woman's desk. Or maybe in her desk, in a drawer or something. But she was definitely the target."

Rivera said, "The woman in accounting?"

The young cop nodded. "And we don't think there's a secondary. We did a quick search along with the Rockies people."

"You don't *think* there's a secondary?"

She grinned just the slightest bit. "That's right. In case you haven't noticed, this is a very big building. Your people can go inside anytime. Detective said to remind you that we're handling the detonation investigation."

Rivera said, "I know. We're merely looking for a terrorist who's holding a cop hostage. I'll stay out of your way." They were interrupted by a young black woman who didn't seem to appreciate Rivera's tone. I couldn't hear what she told him but his reply was clear: "What did you say? Dear Jesus."

Sam asked, "What's going on?"

Rivera answered, "The bomb threat at East High School? They just found a device. He wasn't kidding."

Columbine images flooded my consciousness. Everyone's.

Sam was shaking his head slowly. "I'm picking up a siren. Rivera, you recognize it?"

Rivera took the phone from Sam and covered the microphone with his fingers. He closed his eyes as though he were appreciating some good jazz. "I'd say it's the fire department, but I'm not sure. I wonder how fast we can find out where they have trucks running with sirens right now. Shouldn't be that hard to do."

Sam narrowed his eyes and said, "Damn," under his breath. I followed him as he hustled outside onto the wide sidewalk in front of the stadium. He fixed his eyes to the left. A big pumper, lights flashing, siren blaring, was two blocks away, approaching down Blake from the east. He turned to me. "They're here, Alan. I can smell them. Ramp and Lucy. They're right around here."

The truck killed its siren and glided to a stop a hundred feet away. Rivera walked outside to join us. Bomb squad personnel were running past us and jumping into their vehicles to respond to the fresh threat at East High School.

Sam said, "The siren stopped, didn't it?"

Rivera nodded.

Sam pointed at the electric-green pumper. The dirty-yellow-suited firefighters clustered around it, tugging at equipment. Sam said, "That was the truck, Rivera. They're right around here. Damn."

Rivera gave Sam the phone. Immediately, he handed it to me, ordering, "Tell me if you hear anything important."

Sam stared at the streets while he huddled with Rivera. I shuffled close to the building to mute as much traffic noise as I could.

As I listened hard to the tiny speaker at my ear, there were moments when I was convinced that I could hear faint voices, other moments when I was sure that I was hearing nothing more than the desperate pulses of my hope. The whole time, I watched the traffic funneling down the viaduct from I-25 and the traffic being diverted from Blake Street up to Market and Larimer. Did I expect to see Lucy waving to me from the passenger seat of a passing car?

Not really.

But if she was waving, I wanted to be watching. That was the nature of my hope's persistence.

CHAPTER

55

Ramp slowed as a cop waved him away from Blake Street, then he followed the detour up Twenty-second to Larimer, before turning back down Twentieth all the way to Wynkoop.

A little over ten years before, Wynkoop Street had been ground zero for the rejuvenation of Denver's old warehouse district into the trendy center now called LoDo. The very first renovations in the decrepit section of Denver that bordered the railroad tracks of the Santa Fe and the Union Pacific had been in the brick warehouses that faced Denver's 120-year-old Union Station. The arrival of Coors Field in the mid-1990s had cemented the reincarnation, and the new LoDo was crowded with vibrant businesses, overpriced lofts, and the kind of sidewalk bustle that the Chamber of Commerce coveted.

After turning left onto Wynkoop, Ramp passed one

of the most recent renovations, the stately old Beatrice Foods Ice House, and turned into the drive that led to the front entrance of Union Station. The neoclassical railroad hub consisted of a huge stone building that was constructed between the two original 1881 wings after a 1914 fire. From her position on the floor of the truck, Lucy could clearly see the trio of huge arched windows that graced the lobby, and the garish neon "Travel by Train" sign high above the building's stone cornice.

She screamed *"No!"* into her gag.

Ramp turned up the radio in response to her protest, before pulling the truck to a stop on the far left side of the entrance drive. He reached down to the floor in front of his seat and lifted yet another transmitter. The device was bright yellow. "This one's from a model boat. Decent range," he said for Lucy's benefit. "Listen carefully, you might be able to hear it go off. Maybe not—the walls of this place are really thick. You should feel something in your bones, though. Try."

He lowered the volume on the radio. Lucy screamed again.

He looked askance at her. "You want to know who it is?" Ramp asked.

Lucy nodded vociferously.

"A photographer. She has her studio in there. She's the wife of the guy who was head of the parole board when the guy who killed my mom got out of prison."

Lucy's eyes softened and Ramp pressed straight ahead on a lever on the plastic console.

She heard a muted thud that felt like nothing more to her than an extra heartbeat.

Ramp raised an eyebrow as two huge double-hung windows burst outward on the upper floor of the train station and said, "That's it. The cake is baked. All that's left now is the frosting."

I heard some music in my ear. Not clearly enough that I could recognize the artist or the song, but clearly enough to know that the phone call was still alive. I ran over to Sam and Rivera. "I hear music."

Sam said, "That's it? Just music?"

"Yeah. Maybe some voices in the background. I'm not sure."

He turned back to Rivera.

"And I heard a little pop. A little boom."

"An explosion?" Rivera asked.

I said, "I don't know."

"Give me that thing," he said.

I did. Rivera turned his back, pressed the phone against one ear, and stuck an index finger into the other one.

Two bomb squad members came flying out the front door of the Rockies' offices. "Another explosion. This one's at Union Station," one of them said as he passed by. He directed the words at Rivera's back.

Sam said, "What did he say?"

"He said there was just an explosion at Union Station."

Sam grabbed my arm. "Shit. How far away is that?"

"Maybe three blocks."

He released my arm and tapped Rivera on the shoulder. Rivera lowered the phone and took the finger out of his ear. "I don't hear shit," he reported.

Sam pointed at the activity at the curb. "A bomb just went off at Union Station."

The Denver cop shook his head. In disbelief? Disgust? I couldn't tell. He said, "Union Station? Not East High School? Are you sure?"

"That's what they said."

"How bad is it?"

Sam shrugged. His face was the color of the winter sky.

Rivera pointed to a brown sedan at the curb. "That's mine. Let's go."

Ramp exited the drive in front of Union Station and pulled the truck across Wynkoop and then straight down Seventeenth past the Oxford Hotel into Denver's downtown business district. After a few blocks, the wail of sirens began to echo in the canyons between the blunt faces of Denver's skyscrapers. Seventeenth was a one-way street leading away from Union Station, and Ramp's truck was unimpeded by approaching emergency vehicles as it headed toward Broadway.

While he waited for a light to change, he lifted his windbreaker and threw it behind the seat of the truck. He fumbled for some coins on the console. "I'll need some quarters for the parking meter. Don't want to draw any attention prematurely this morning."

Lucy prayed that he wouldn't see the red light that glowed on her phone. To her, it looked as bright as a streetlight on a dark night. She screamed again to distract him.

He looked at her. "What?"

She screamed again. She was trying to say, "Take this off! Take this off!" She kicked at the floor.

The light changed. He said, "I'll take it off in a minute. We're almost at our next stop."

She pounded the console with her closed fists.

He raised his wrist, displaying the transmitter that was taped to his arm. "I said wait."

From the backseat of Rivera's car, I said, "Voices. Sam, I hear voices."

Sam spun on his seat.

I held up my finger, asking for quiet.

"The guy just said, 'What?' Then there were a couple of muffled screams."

Rivera stared at me in the rearview mirror.

"Now the guy said, 'Wait a second. I'll take it off in a minute. We're almost at our next stop.' And then another muffled scream, and . . . and some pounding.

"Wait. It's him talking again. He said, 'I said wait.' " I continued to listen intently. "Silence now, Sam. Just background noise."

I looked up. We'd pulled to a stop in front of Union

Station. Uniformed cops were directing pedestrians and traffic away from the building. By now I knew the drill. The bomb squad would be evacuating the building prior to beginning a search for secondary devices. I couldn't shake the feeling that we were a step behind Ramp and that that was exactly where he wanted us to be.

Rivera ordered me to "Stay put and keep listening." He got out of the car and huddled in front of the train station entrance with a black man in a brown sport coat. Sam nodded his head in their direction. "The guy with Rivera? That's Walter. My friend Walter." For the first time all morning, Sam smiled.

I said, "The one whose name isn't really Walter?"

"Yeah, that Walter."

He pointed at the phone. "Anything?"

I mouthed, "No."

Sam said, "We're wasting our time here. Going from bomb to bomb after they go off isn't going to get us where we need to be."

"I was thinking the same thing." I raised one index finger. "They're talking again. I think I hear Lucy, Sam. I do. She's still alive."

He exhaled as though he'd been holding his breath for most of the morning. "What'd she say? Give me that thing."

CHAPTER

56

Ramp stayed southbound on Broadway until he was just past Fourteenth. He pulled to a stop by the curb opposite the plaza of the block-long complex housing the Colorado History Museum and the Judicial Heritage Center. He hopped out of the cab, fed the parking meter, and jumped right back in.

He stared at Lucy for a few seconds before he reached down and lowered her gag to her chin.

"Stop," she pleaded. "Please, stop. No more bombs, Ramp."

He smiled an ingratiating smile. "Don't worry. This is the last stop. This is where the day ends. If all goes well here, you'll be free."

She couldn't tell where they were parked. The landmarks she could see weren't familiar to her. He placed a nylon windshield screen across the inside of the windshield and pushed a piece of cardboard against the glass of the window above her seat.

"Where are we?"

He chuckled. "We're at the principal's office."

She was amazed at Ramp's calm demeanor. He was like a kid confident that he was about to ace a test. It was as though he already had all the answers.

She said, "What does that mean?"

"One of the many mistakes that Klebold and Harris made is that they failed to target the boss man. They went randomly after kids, and they didn't seem to care who they killed as long as they killed someone. That's unproductive rage. That's not my style. I've identified specific targets, deserving targets. And the final target on my list is the principal, the one who is ultimately responsible for the culture that took my mother from me."

"You're not even in school. Who's the principal? I don't get it."

"My problem is with the judicial system, right? Who makes those rules? Who's the boss?"

He was playing with her. "I don't know—the governor?" Were they parked outside the governor's mansion? From her position on the floor she couldn't tell where they were.

"Wrong. The head of the judiciary in this state is the Colorado Supreme Court. For me, that's the equivalent of the principal's office. That's where it all begins and that's where it will end."

"You're going to kill the Supreme Court justices?"

He reached down between his legs to the floor on the seat in front of him. "I know I won't get them all. But I should be able to get a few."

She had trouble grasping his threat. *Kill the justices?* "Wouldn't you have to kill all the legislators? They make the laws. They write the sentencing statutes."

"No, no. It's too late to change. It's going to be the justices." His hand held a thick roll of duct tape. "I don't trust you not to interfere. I need a few minutes to get set up, and I can't risk you doing anything to draw attention."

She said, "I'll be good. I will."

"Sorry."

Ramp reached down below his seat one more time and came up with a neat package wrapped in brown paper. The package was about the size and shape of a roll of paper towels that had been sliced in half lengthwise. A loop of insulated wire emerged from the package and a slender antenna extended up from the top about three inches.

"What is that?" Lucy demanded. She already knew what it was. She just didn't know what Ramp planned to do with it.

He leaned across the console and placed the flat side of the package against her upper abdomen and chest, pressing down hard, separating her breasts. With economical motions, he affixed the package in place with duct tape, concluding with three quick bands of tape all the way around her back.

He raised his wrist, displaying the switch that was

taped to his arm. With a magician's flourish, he reached behind the switch and touched something. A tiny red light began to glow on the plastic case, a light so small Lucy hadn't even noticed it before.

She knew that he'd just armed the damn thing. And she knew that it hadn't been armed until then.

She mumbled, "Shaped charge?"

"Again?" he said.

"Shaped charge," she repeated. It was no longer a question.

He smiled. "Yes, Lucy. A shaped charge. The energy of the blast is largely directed at your spinal column. But don't worry about paralysis. Before the blast ever gets to your spinal cord, it will liquefy your heart and lungs."

He saw a new level of fear spread across her eyes. It seemed to kill something healthy as it swelled, like a plague.

"I'll be in the back of the truck for a few minutes, getting ready. I'll be able to see you through the rear window the whole time. Do you understand?"

She nodded enthusiastically.

"You get off the floor, you're dead. You try to speak to anyone or get their attention, you're dead. Do you understand me?"

His voice told Lucy that he didn't want to kill her. Not that he wasn't willing to. Only that he didn't want to.

Ramp's eyes moved from Lucy's and rested briefly on the console. She felt certain he could see the status of the cell phone.

He moved his face to within a foot of hers. "Let me tell you something else, okay?" With an awkward motion, he sat back and crossed his left leg over his right knee, exposing the bottom of his hiking boot to Lucy. He pointed a finger at a tiny silver button taped to the sole of the shoe. "See that?"

A thin wire snaked through the treads. The wire was taped to the side of the boot and disappeared under Ramp's trousers.

She nodded. She saw it.

He uncrossed his legs, planting his left foot firmly on the floor of the truck. "It's a pressure switch. A dead-man switch. As long as I have weight on the switch, the circuit's closed. If I don't have weight on the switch for ten seconds, the circuit opens. When the circuit opens, the device on your chest will explode. If the police shoot me before I'm done, and I fall over, you will die ten seconds later. You won't believe how long those ten seconds will last, Lucy. It'll be a whole lifetime."

Involuntarily, she glanced at the cell phone. She regretted the act as soon as she did it.

Without hesitation, he lifted the phone to his face. "You guys get that? I hope so. Now pay attention to this, too. There are a series of explosive devices hidden in the chambers and courtrooms of the Colorado Supreme Court. The staircases and the elevators are wired. So are the fire exits. I want everyone in the building to get ready to come out through the front doors. You have ten minutes to get everyone organized.

But no one leaves until I say so. The justices will come out last. I want them in their robes. No switches. I know exactly what they look like. Got it? Good."

He pressed the "end" button.

CHAPTER
57

I was relieved that Sam had the phone. I was terrified by what he was reporting to Rivera.

"Listen to this, listen to this. Ramp's at the Supreme Court Building. He says he's going to kill them, the justices. He says he won't get them all, but that he should get a few. That's his last stand. This is where it's going to end."

Sam made a perplexed face, then nodded to himself as he listened intently to the phone. When he winced, I did, too.

"Jesus. He's taped a shaped charge to Lucy's chest. He says he'll set it off if she does anything. . . . They're in a truck. He's going to the back of the truck to do something. He can see her through the window. He's in a truck, Rivera. Tell them he's in a truck, okay? Do that."

Sam stopped talking for a moment, then his mouth fell open.

"Oh my God. He says he has a dead-man switch on the bottom of one shoe. We shoot him and Lucy dies ten seconds later." He raised his voice. "Ten seconds. Rivera, tell them a cop is wired with explosives. You tell them that, you hear me? Tell them that if they hurt him, a cop dies. You hear me?"

Rivera waved at Sam in a manner even I found dismissive. I assumed that the gesture left Sam homicidal.

Sam's eyes closed in an effort to shut out the chaos that was growing around us. He mumbled, "Oh no, oh *no*. Fuck me. No, no, no." He faced Rivera one more time. "He knows that we're listening to him, Rivera. He's been feeding us all this stuff. Who knows if it's true."

Rivera hustled next to Sam.

Sam went on with his report. "He's talking to us now. He says that the Supreme Court Building's wired. Chambers, courtrooms, elevators, staircases, exits. The whole thing. He wants everyone to evacuate through the front doors. Justices have to come out last, wearing their robes. We have ten minutes to get everybody organized, but nobody comes out until he says so. That's it. Ten minutes."

Rivera stared at Sam. Finally, he said, "Ten minutes?"

"Ten minutes to get everyone organized. Justices have to exit last. In their robes, Rivera."

Five seconds passed. Ten.

Sam's eyes burned into his colleague. "That's a cop in that truck with him, Rivera. You understand? She dies if we shoot him. You understand what I'm saying?"

Rivera's face was impassive.

Sam handed me the phone. "Line's gone dead. Where the hell's the Colorado Supreme Court Building? Anybody know?"

The motorcade of emergency vehicles plowed up Seventeenth Street like the leading edge of an assaulting battalion. Rivera's gray sedan was behind a phalanx of motorcycle officers. I was alone in the backseat; Sam was up front next to Rivera. Traffic cleared in front of us like delicate fish fleeing a school of sharks.

The sirens were deafening. Every sound reflected a thousand times off the glass, aluminum, and stone towers of the central business district. We weren't trying to sneak up on Ramp. That much was certain.

The procession headed south on Broadway before stopping at Fourteenth. Six or seven Denver Police cruisers and at least one fire-rescue vehicle were already in place at the corner. Rivera screeched to a stop and we popped out of the car.

The Colorado Supreme Court was housed in a modern, six-story building at the corner of Fourteenth and Lincoln, across the street from Denver's new main library and a block away from the state capitol. A wide plaza separated the building from the Colorado

History Museum. I'd driven past the complex many times without realizing that the chambers and court-rooms of the Colorado Supreme Court were inside one of the two buildings.

Everyone's attention was locked on a flatbed truck parked against the curb on Broadway. The truck was relatively new. There was an emblem on the door that I couldn't read. A man was standing on the bed in the back. He was partially obscured by a large metal equipment box and a steel rack filled with tall green gas cylinders. The tanks appeared to have been placed into the rack upside down.

The windshield on the truck was screened by a sun-shade. I wondered if Lucy was inside the cab.

Someone with binoculars walked up to Rivera and said, "Everyone's concerned that he could have a big device—a fertilizer and fuel-oil type thing—in that equipment box that's on the back of that truck. He may be planning an Oklahoma City rerun. We need to move this perimeter back."

"Do it," snapped Rivera. "And get me somebody from the bomb squad to advise me."

"I'm trying. They're spread all over the city chasing the other bombs. A bunch are on their way to East High School. Some are still at Elitch's and Coors Field. And some are still searching for secondary devices at the train station."

"Damn it," Rivera cursed. "Screw Elitch's and Coors

Field. Screw the train station. Get everybody who's not at the high school back down here. I want the containment vehicle here, everything." Rivera lifted binoculars to his eyes. "It's a kid. Just a kid. The truck is from a company called JT Welding Supplies. Somebody call them. The kid's wired from head to toe. He has something taped to his wrist. Looks like a garage-door opener. And some other switch-type thing at his waist. We have to take him out while we have a chance."

Sam said, "You can't. You shoot him and a cop gets blown to bits. You can't do that, Rivera."

"The alternative? He kills half the justices of the Colorado Supreme Court? It's a tough call, Purdy, but I'm not afraid to make it. Sorry. Columbine taught us all the consequences of waiting too long to go after the bad guys."

Ramp leaned over and briefly disappeared from view. The rack of gas cylinders on the back of the truck slowly pivoted forty-five degrees so that the bottoms of the tanks were directed toward the entrance doors of the Supreme Court Building. I was still wondering why the tanks were upside down.

Sam said, "What the . . . ? What's he doing with that thing? How many tanks are on that rack?"

I counted the blunt ends that were pointing toward the plaza. I said, "Nine."

"What's in them? Anything toxic? Explosive?"

I said, "If they're for welders, they could be a lot of things. Oxygen, acetylene, helium. I don't know. What's weird is that the tanks are loaded into the rack upside down, Sam. Does that mean they're empty?"

"I don't know anything about welding. What's he doing? I need some binoculars."

Rivera handed his field glasses to Sam. Sam stared at the truck. "What the hell is that kid up to?"

"Can you see Lucy?" I asked.

"No. I bet she's in the cab."

Rivera was busy listening to a report on the readiness of his sharpshooters. It sounded to me as though the snipers were ready.

My phone rang.

Sam had the binoculars glued to his eyes. I could tell he was staring at Ramp. Loud enough for everyone to hear, Sam told me, "Answer it, Alan. It's him."

CHAPTER

58

"D r. Gregory," Ramp said to me. I recognized his voice from our conversation the night before.

"Yes. You want to talk to one of the police officers?"

"No, I want you. They'll lie to me without hesitation. You'll hesitate."

Ramp and I were appraising each other over a distance that I guessed was about fifty yards. His body was mostly blocked by the equipment box and the rack of gas cylinders, but I could see him clearly from the chest up. He was holding a phone to his left ear.

The Denver Police helicopter hovered high above him. The *thwack, thwack, thwack* reverberated like the muted pulse of the city's racing heart.

"How's Lucy?" I asked.

"So far, fine. You ready to relay my demands?"

"If that's what you want me to do."

"It is."

"I'm ready."

"Tell them this. If they shoot me, Lucy dies. I'm not kidding about the switch on my boot. In case that's not enough deterrence, have them try this on instead. See this button?" He raised his free hand.

Sam continued to stare through the binoculars. He said, "He's showing us a red box with a button on it."

"Yes," I said. "I can see your hand. And it does appear that there is something in it."

"Every time I touch this button, it resets a time switch for the explosives inside the building. If I don't hit the button, the switch isn't reset, and the explosives go off in ten seconds. Therefore I have to hit the button every ten seconds. If I hold it down for three seconds continuously, the devices in the building will go off instantly. Do you get it?"

"Yes."

"Explain it to those cops. Talk loudly so I can hear what you say. I want to make sure they get it."

I tried to repeat what Ramp had explained to me. It didn't help my concentration to note that Sam was breathing heavily through his nose and that Rivera's dark brow was dotted with sweat, like old macadam after a gentle rain.

When I was through with the explanation, Ramp said, "You did good. I'm going to be sitting down now between the tanks and the equipment box. In about a minute, I'll give the okay to start the evacuation from the building. I want to remind everyone that the justices come out last, wearing their robes. Remind the cops."

I did.

"Now tell them to get the chopper out of here. It's bothering me."

I said, "Rivera? He wants the chopper out of here."

Rivera stared at me malevolently, as though moving the helicopter had been my idea. Within ten seconds, the helicopter departed in the direction of the state capitol building.

Rivera said, "I want a guarantee he's not going to harm the evacuees."

My mouth was as dry as insulation. "The police are concerned that you're planning to hurt the evacuees as they come out of the building. They want your word that you won't."

"They're assholes. Have I spent my day trying to kill innocent people? Let me talk to the cop, the one you keep talking to."

I handed the phone to Rivera. "He wants to talk to you."

Sam asked me, "How does he sound?"

"Less nervous than me."

"Did he say anything about Lucy?"

"No."

Sam said, "He's smart. Where he's sitting now, the sharpshooters would have a hard time hitting him."

"Could they risk it? The way he has the explosives wired it seems too risky to shoot him."

"Rivera thinks he's bluffing."

I tried to swallow that news and ended up almost choking with the effort. "Rivera thinks the kid is bluffing? After all that's happened this morning?"

"I don't envy him; he's in a tough spot. He doesn't want to be accused of waiting to act, the way the sheriff in Jefferson County did during Columbine."

I asked, "What do you think?"

"Lucy's in that truck. That's what I think."

Rivera handed me back the phone. "He wants you again."

"Yes?"

Ramp's voice was harder now. "Change in plans. Let's see if you guys were planning to play fair. I want the justices outside on the plaza within thirty seconds. In their robes. I'm counting, starting now."

I snapped at Rivera: "He's changed his mind. He wants the justices outside on the plaza in their robes within thirty seconds."

"Shit!" Rivera barked a command into his radio. "We can't do it. We can't do it in time. We have state cops in their robes. Buy some time." He began running down the sidewalk to some of his colleagues who were hidden behind patrol cars in front of the library.

Sam and I followed Rivera as I said, "Ramp! Ramp!" into the phone. I was wondering how the hell I was going to buy some time, but when I looked back over to the truck, Ramp was holding the cell phone high in the air, far from his ear. He wasn't prepared to listen to Rivera's excuses.

Sam broke the news. "Rivera, look. He's got the phone in the air. He's not even listening."

The seconds ticked away. I stared at my watch as

three became two became one and then . . . a sharp *craaack* filled the air and glass and stone flew out onto the Broadway sidewalk as at least three windows blew out from the third floor.

In my ear, I heard Ramp's voice. "That one was a warning from an empty office. Thirty more seconds. The next one's going to take some people with it. Tell him."

I did.

Rivera yelled commands into the radio. After twenty-two more seconds leaked away, the justices began to exit the building. One by one they walked to the center of the plaza. Their robes swayed gently in the morning breeze. I couldn't see their faces but I could feel their terror, even from this distance.

Ramp said, "The one in back is not a justice. The tall guy. If he doesn't leave that group in five seconds, you assholes will have some blood on your hands. Tell him that. Do it."

I repeated Ramp's message word for word.

Rivera cursed and spoke into his microphone.

A heartbeat later, one tall, robed figure walked backward away from the clustered judges.

"Tell the cop not to screw with me again. I'm not in the mood."

I held the phone a few inches from my mouth and told Rivera what Ramp had just said.

"Now I want the justices to back up against the wall of the History Museum and get on their knees."

Rivera used a megaphone. The justices moved back

slowly, reluctantly. The building on the other side of the plaza was the Colorado History Museum. Its wall rose from the stone at an unconventional forty-five-degree angle.

"Now, have the people who are still inside the court building begin a single file evacuation. They should exit to Lincoln, then south. No running. No hands in the air. Just have them walk out. The justices stay put."

Rivera eagerly gave those commands.

Sam had the binoculars to his eyes. He said, "He's been moving that rack of tanks on the back of the truck. He's doing it real slowly, but the bottoms of the tanks are pointing directly at the plaza now. The base of the rack is solid metal, not an open grid. That's not usual, is it? What the hell's he doing?"

I said, "The hostages are coming out, Sam."

One by one, stepping quickly, seemingly fighting an urge to run, a steady stream of men and women began walking from the entrance of the building, across the plaza, down to the sidewalk, and then south on Lincoln.

Rivera touched me on the arm. "Cover the microphone on that cell phone."

I did.

He spoke into his radio. "Give me a status report from the sharpshooters. We're taking him out as soon as anyone is ready. On my order."

CHAPTER

59

Without warning, Ramp jumped off the back of the truck and hopped into the cab with Lucy. Within seconds, the driver's-side window was blocked with a sheet of cardboard.

Rivera's order to the sharpshooters had been seconds too late.

I thought he looked like a kid who'd missed Christmas and was trying to figure out how to lure the fat man back down the chimney.

"Shit. Now what?" he asked.

Sam pointed at the plaza. "The justices are moving away. Look."

They were. The whole pack of them was squatting in their robes and edging down the angled wall away from Ramp toward Lincoln Street. From this distance, they looked like a pack of nuns trying to walk away on their knees.

Ramp noticed, too. He barked at me, "Tell them to stop moving. Tell the cop, *now!*"

I said, "Rivera? He wants the justices to stop moving."

Rivera looked to make sure I'd covered the microphone with my finger. "Screw him. They're almost away."

As though he'd read Rivera's lips, Ramp reacted. An audible little boom sounded and a tiny puff of smoke emerged from the steel rack on the back of the truck.

Sam, the binoculars still at his eyes, said, "Oh shit."

One of the tall green tanks began spewing its pressurized contents with an immense hiss and roar. The volume of the noise of the escaping gas was incredible.

As they heard the blast and the subsequent roar, the justices stopped their progression from the plaza and dropped back down to the ground.

Blunt end first, a green tank lifted from the steel rack on the back of the truck like a missile leaving its launcher.

I held my breath.

Another small explosion followed, and then came the roar of additional escaping gases. A second tank immediately lifted from the rack.

Rivera screamed into a megaphone, urging the hostages to run. I'm sure they couldn't hear him. I was five feet from him and I could barely discern his words above the hiss of the ruptured tanks.

Although the first of the tanks launched into the air like a slow-motion rocket, it returned to the ground no more than thirty feet from the truck. It bounced off the stone plaza like a smooth rock on a glass lake, hopping across the wide expanse with a speed and ferocity that should have belonged only to objects launched by the Marines. A stone bench slightly changed the tank's trajectory: It skidded up the angled wall about twenty feet from the huddled Supreme Court justices before it vanished over the top of the roof.

The second tank stayed airborne at least twice as far as the first one had before crashing blunt end first into the plaza. From there it tumbled once end over end like a child's jack, finally bouncing high and disappearing into the second floor of the building, demolishing all the windows in its path. The destruction was only fifteen feet above the huddled hostages.

As the hissing died away, I could hear screams. I could also hear Rivera yelling for someone to take Ramp out.

A third puff of smoke emerged from the back of the truck and a third tank launched into the air with an enormous swoosh. A fourth tank followed two or three seconds later.

My eyes followed the two new hurtling tanks until Sam—Rivera's binoculars still glued to his eyes— screamed into my ear, "He just busted out the back window of the truck. Watch him!"

Ramp dove athletically through the empty space where the window had been and immediately disappeared into the void between the big equipment box and the steel rack full of tanks.

I didn't hear any shots from sharpshooters' rifles.

I looked over in time to see one of the newly fired tanks skittering through the justices like a bowling ball through a fresh stand of pins. Black-robed bodies went flying into the air.

I didn't know where the other tank had gone.

The binoculars still at his eyes, Sam yelled, "He's turning the rack this way. Everybody run!"

The steel rack was now pointing right at us, the blunt end of the remaining tanks shining brightly like polished coins.

Boom! Boom! Boom!

Ramp launched three tanks in rapid succession. Cops, firefighters, and paramedics scattered like ants. I was pinned by two Denver Police patrol cars. My only route to safety was following Sam across the road toward the front end of the parked flatbed truck. Ramp couldn't rotate the rack that far—if he did, the cab would interfere with the launch of any more tanks.

I could feel the impact of one of the newly launched tanks as it crashed into a patrol car behind me. The concussion was so intense that I almost fell to the asphalt as I sprinted after Sam.

The patrol car burst into flames. A second or two later the whole thing ignited like a bomb as the fire reached the fuel in the gas tank.

Sam and I were enveloped in heat; the force of the explosion threw us to the ground. We crawled the rest of the way across the street and crouched out of sight in front of Ramp's truck. I looked back to discover that the other two tanks had made it all the way across Broadway and impaled themselves in the façade of the Philip Johnson-designed Denver Public Library.

I tried to find Rivera in the chaos. I couldn't spot him.

Sam said, "He only has two tanks left."

A new roar filled the air and another rocket left the launcher. Sam held up his index finger and mouthed, "One."

My instinct was to turn my head to follow the trajectory of the missile as it lifted from the back of the truck. But Sam held my face firmly with both his hands, forcing me to stare into his eyes. As the roar of the newly launched tank diminished, he said, "I'm going to shoot him, then I'm going to compress the switch on his foot. You're going to press the button on his hand every five seconds until the bomb squad tells you to stop. You are not going to hold it down. Every five seconds. You got it?"

I nodded.

"You're sure?"

I nodded again.

He moved around to the passenger side of the truck. I followed him.

Ramp turned just as Sam was leveling his weapon. Ramp's eyes were soft and inviting, at once disbelieving and trusting. I sensed that he knew what was about to happen, and that he welcomed it. My ears were so overwhelmed by the hissing gases and the fomenting chaos that I'm not sure I even heard the explosion from Sam's handgun. But I think I saw a dark hole emerge three inches below the collar line and two inches left of center on Ramp's chest.

Ramp's face registered no surprise before he fell.

Sam screamed, "Alan, now! Every five seconds. Count out loud so I can hear you."

Ramp had collapsed into an awkward heap in the confined space between the steel rack that had been full of tanks and the big metal equipment box. Sam and I were bumping into each other, clawing at Ramp's limbs, desperate to find the correct hand and the correct foot.

Sam yelled, "I got his foot! I have the switch."

Ramp's right hand was pinned beneath his body, which seemed to weigh a thousand pounds. I yanked at his elbow. It didn't free his hand.

"You got it?" cried Sam.

I didn't answer. I put all my weight into another tug on Ramp's elbow. In my head I was counting to ten and was already at eleven.

Ramp's hand came free.

I traced down his wrist, turned his hand palm up, and pressed maniacally with my thumb.

The red button was gone.

"It's gone."

"What do you mean it's gone?"

"It's gone."

"Get Lucy and get out of here. Do it! *Now!*"

Sixteen, seventeen, eighteen.

I crawled backward off of Ramp's body and almost fell before I ripped open the door to the truck. Lucy was huddled in the footwell on the passenger side. Her eyes were streaked red and tears stained her cheeks. As she saw me, she pushed herself up onto the seat. I raised her over my shoulder in a fireman's carry and ran north on Broadway, waiting for an explosion to sever Lucy's body and end my life.

I screamed, "Bomb squad! Bomb squad! Over here! Bomb squad!" until Lucy and I were just inside the taped perimeter near Fourteenth Street. But when I arrived at that spot and looked around, I realized we were alone.

The aftermath of the impact of the last few tanks that Ramp had launched and the destruction caused by the exploding patrol car had created enough carnage and confusion to occupy all the emergency personnel on the scene.

I stood Lucy on the sidewalk at Fourteenth and Broadway and stared at her restraints. She was yelling something at me as I tugged at her gag.

She coughed. "That's a shaped charge on my chest. It's not wired to me. It takes a radio signal to set it off. Get it off of me!"

I examined the bulky pack on her chest.

She implored me, "It's just taped on. Take it off! Take it off of me!"

I looked around once again for someone wearing a windbreaker that said "Bomb Squad." No one was coming to help us.

I thought of Sam, contorted in the truck, firmly maintaining pressure on the button on the bottom of Ramp's boot.

Then I began to unwrap the duct tape that secured the package on Lucy's chest. Of course, my fingers shook. Of course, the tape tore where it shouldn't. Of course, I heard ticking even though my head knew that this device wasn't timed.

I could barely see through the images of Grace that were flooding my consciousness and the sweat that was dripping into my eyes.

Finally I had the thing in my hands. It was heavy for its size. My instinct was to twirl into a discus thrower's motion and throw the thing as far away as I could. Instead, I sat it gingerly onto the concrete as though it were a sleeping baby. Then I lifted Lucy into my arms and ran north down Broadway. I put her down in the shadows of the Veteran's Memorial and sprinted back toward Sam, making a wide arc around the shaped charge on the sidewalk.

A hundred feet from him, I yelled, "She's safe, Sam! The bomb is off her chest."

"I can let go?"

"Yeah. The device is back there, on the far corner. But stay down. It's a big thing."

"That's it? There?"

"Yes."

"Nobody's near it?"

"No."

He held his hands high in the air so I could see that he'd released the switch on Ramp's boot.

I counted to ten. When I got to fourteen, the charge on the corner exploded.

CHAPTER
61

The three of us didn't have much to do.

By the time Sam and I had freed Lucy from her restraints and the three of us checked each other for injury and hugged each other about twenty times, the volume of emergency personnel on Broadway made our presence superfluous.

We sat on the lawn in front of the state capitol. Across from us the distant Rockies peeked out above Civic Center Park. Ambulances were streaming from the plaza in front of the Supreme Court Building in the direction of Denver Health Medical Center and Presbyterian St. Luke's Hospital.

A small group of cops hovered around the flatbed truck. They'd found Ramp's body.

"How did Ramp do it?" I asked. "Launch all those tanks? Does either of you know how he did it?"

"He had small charges on the valves," Lucy said. "When he set them off, the valves blew off the tanks and the compressed gases started to escape out the opening. It was just like a rocket nozzle. He modified the rack himself. When he came back inside the truck, he told me all about it."

"The tanks are under that much pressure?"

She shrugged. "He told me that he had them pressurized to almost three thousand pounds per square inch. Think of the air coming out of a balloon."

Sam shook his head at the thought. "Those tanks weigh a ton. It would be like being hit by a truck on the freeway."

I still had my cell phone. I used it to call Lauren to see how she was doing—fine—and to tell her that the three of us were safe. She was near panic, having watched the morning's events unroll on television. Sam asked me to have Lauren call his wife, too.

When Lauren and I were through, I offered the phone to Lucy. "Want to call your fiancé?"

In a quick flash something important transpired in her thinking. In another circumstance I might have asked her about it. But not then. She shook her head. "No, thanks." To Sam, she said, "They probably aren't going to let me go home, are they?"

Sam said, "The Denver cops?"

Lucy nodded.

"No. I doubt it, Luce. I doubt it. They're going to want to talk to you about your time with that kid. Given your circumstances, you should probably have a lawyer with you. They're going to want to talk to us, too, Alan."

Lucy asked, "Why?"

Sam seemed to have trouble forcing his lips apart to say, "I'm the one who shot him over there. The kid."

Lucy said, "Oh." Her eyes widened. "I thought it was a sharpshooter." She lowered her face and rested her chin on her fists. I thought she looked like she was about to cry. "It's kind of crazy, I know, but I . . . liked him. Jason. I liked him. If there was more time, I think I could've talked him out of it. He wasn't evil, Sam. He wasn't crazy, he was . . ."

Sam said, "He killed people, Lucy. He murdered innocent people. What he did was senseless and vicious."

"He had reasons, Sam. He—"

"I don't care about his reasons. He murdered innocent people. That's all we need to know."

"I know what he did, Sam. And I guess that means I should hate him. We're not supposed to have sympathy for kids who do what he did. But I don't hate him. I'm sorry he's dead."

Sam opened his mouth to argue with her some more. She saw it coming and reached out and touched his lips with her index finger. He swallowed his words. I could tell that they didn't go down easily.

She turned toward me and her face fell into shadow. "Is Cozy dead, too, Alan? Ramp told me that the girl set off a bomb at his office this morning."

"Last we heard, he was getting out of surgery," I

said. "Broken bone in his neck. Lauren was there, too, in the building. She's okay, a concussion."

Lucy looked at Sam, not me. "Will Cozy be all right?"

Sam lifted his shoulders and shook his head. He didn't know. I was thinking that he hadn't totally given up arguing with Lucy about Ramp.

Again, I offered the phone to Lucy. I said, "You know, you don't have to cooperate with them. Maybe you should talk to Lauren and get some legal advice before you go over there."

Sam glared at me.

"No," she said. "I don't need a lawyer with me. I'm a cop, right? I was a hostage, right?" She stood up. "I need to pee. Then let's go find somebody in charge. I want to get this over with and go home."

The three of us walked in the direction of the smoldering patrol car. Sam held his shield out in front of him the whole way.

Lucy took my hand. She leaned over and her lips were so close to my ear I could feel the air moving between us as she said, "I liked him a lot."

CHAPTER
62

Over the next couple of days, Sam kept me informed about the progress of the investigation in Denver. I didn't know whether he was getting his information from Rivera or from Walter or from somebody named Lou. I didn't ask, and I didn't really care. I appreciated not having to rely on the reports on the local news.

Ramp, it turned out, had been out of explosives. The explosives vault at his grandmother's ranch near Agate was totally cleaned out.

Much of what he had threatened at the Supreme Court Building was a ruse. The Denver Police Bomb Squad found no additional devices hidden in the building. In fact, the second device that was discovered at Red Rocks turned out to be a fake that was intended to draw bomb disposal resources away from the city. No secondary devices were found at any of the earlier bomb sites. All three devices that were recovered at East High School were dummies.

The gas cylinders that Ramp had launched at the Supreme Court had done a lot of damage. One justice had died, two others had been severely injured. The exploding patrol car had killed one cop and burned three others. A woman watching the drama from a Denver Public Library window had been badly injured by debris sent flying by the tank that had impacted there.

The earlier bombs had mostly hit their marks. Two were dead in the amusement ride at Elitch's; two more were dead in the offices at Coors Field. The target at Union Station had escaped injury because she was down the hall in the bathroom when the bomb went off in her second-floor studio.

It was still unclear whether Ramp would get his wish about public dialogue.

At first, the attention of the media was mostly on the carnage. The seemingly endless news footage of the final conflagration on Broadway proved to be enough of a magnet to attract temporary nonstop national and local coverage of Ramp's Rampage. That's what the event had been nicknamed by the loud blond guy who did *Hardball* on cable, and the moniker had stuck to the events like a bad cold.

Marin's rape, Leo Bigg's retaliation on the rapist, and Ramp's mother's tragic death were all chronicled and rechronicled. Herbert Ramp's role in the demolition of Las Vegas was broadcast and rebroadcast for no other reason, it seemed, than that the tape was available and that it was pretty spectacular to watch the hotels fall down all over again.

CHAPTER
63

Lucy was holding two pine twigs like chopsticks to scratch at the rough granite boulder that we were sitting on. She said, "There are some things in life that Sam can't forgive. I suspect this is one."

"He's a good friend, Lucy. I think you can trust him."

"It's not about trust, Alan," she explained. "You know him. Sammy has a simple view of the world. Simple in a good way. Uncomplicated. He's not an imaginative person. He still gets surprised at what's up on the screen when he goes to the movies. On his own, his mind would never travel down the road where I would have to take him. Not on his own, no way. And the truth is, he doesn't belong there. He'd try to understand what I did, why I did it. He'd try to make sense of it because he's a good guy. But he wouldn't be able to understand, not really. As much as he's been exposed to in life, he's still an innocent in some ways. To forgive me he'd have to find a way to understand what I did. And he could never ever do that."

I still didn't know what it was that Lucy had done, nor was I sure she was planning on telling me. I suspected that her secret had to do with Royal Peterson's murder, but I didn't know whether it was as simple as explaining why she had been at his house that night or whether it was as complicated as explaining why she had killed him. I did know that I was maximally ambivalent about hearing it, whatever it was. My recent experience had taught me that some confidences of this nature, maybe most confidences of this nature, weren't worth knowing. The burden of the knowledge was often greater than any benefit that accrued from harboring the private facts.

Lucy and I had run into each other while visiting Cozy as he was recuperating at his Victorian on Maxwell Street. It was just before noon a couple of days after the morning of bombs in Denver, and Cozy was home from the hospital, though he was still far from agile. His neck was immobilized in a plastic structure that looked as though it had once been part of an architectural model for a single-span suspension bridge.

As we left the house together, Lucy told me she would like to talk and asked if I had a few minutes for her. When I said I did, she led me to her red Volvo and drove us up Flagstaff, taking the sharp curves up the mountainside carefully, as though she was fearful that a tire on her car was about to blow.

The extension of Baseline that twisted up Flagstaff Mountain was the steepest and most curvaceous paved route out of Boulder. Vehicles over thirty feet in length were banned because they couldn't maneuver the curves. The upside was that a minute after passing the Chautauqua complex on Baseline, Lucy and I were afforded the kind of views that in most environs were available only to birds.

"You come up here often?" she asked me.

I shook my head and was going to leave it at that until I realized that Lucy would have to take her eyes from the road to read my head motion. I quickly added, "No, but maybe I should." The truth was that I found the view from the high foothills disconcerting. The perspective from the mountains toward the east was too infinite for my comfort, the Great Plains spreading out like a petrified ocean. I preferred the view from my house toward the west, believing that, visually, Colorado was a place that should be experienced either in the mountains or toward the mountains, but not away from the mountains. This vista, from peaks to plains, was too much like looking at the state from the rear-facing third seat in my parents' old station wagon.

"I do," she said. "Sometimes I like to be above it all."

She continued to drive, taking us high above the

Flagstaff House Restaurant. I was beginning to suspect that our destination was the summer 2000 burn near Gross Reservoir until she pulled the car to a stop in a clearing off the shoulder of the narrow road, touched me on the leg, and said, "Come on, this way."

I followed her out of the car and down a dusty path that wound around sharp rock outcroppings and dodged rugged ponderosa pines.

An old-timer had once told me that Boulder had been named by the first pioneer who ever tried to put a shovel into the dirt. The old-timer then laughed and said he knew the story was apocryphal because if it had really happened that way, the town would be called Oh Shit.

He hadn't actually said "apocryphal." He'd said "bullcrap."

I joined Lucy as she scrambled across a rough slab of granite and perched on the edge of a boulder the size of a two-car garage. As she lowered herself to a squat, I examined the position she'd assumed and knew that I hadn't managed that particular posture in about ten years. Maybe fifteen. I sat on my butt and side-by-side we gazed at the oasis that the city of Boulder forms on the border of the endless prairie. We were a little too close to the edge of the cliff for my comfort. My thoughts were rarely far from my daughter anymore, and I was thinking that I wouldn't allow Grace to sit as close to the edge as we were.

That's when Lucy began to tell me about Sam's lack of imagination.

Remember what you told me about intimacy?" she asked me.

"Of course," I said, but my radar was tweaked and I was wary of where we were going.

"There are natural limits, aren't there? With some people, I mean. Like with Sammy, he doesn't really want me to open up to him. He doesn't really want to know my secrets. He gives me lots of signals that tell me when to stop."

I shot a quick glance toward Lucy. She was looking east. A split second before, I'd been looking in the same direction, busy imagining that I could perceive the gentle curvature of the earth on the horizon.

I replied, "In a relationship, intimacy can be restricted, or enhanced, by either person." My words sounded banal. "Sorry, Lucy. That sounds trite. I don't mean it to. What you're saying is true. At least it is about Sam. He draws lines in the sand sometimes. We all do."

She waved a hand, dismissing my apology. "No, it's fine."

Wind whistled through the pines in a short burst. It wasn't a melodic tune—it was more acid than sugar. The sound reminded me of the first gasp of gas escaping the green cylinders on the back of Ramp's truck. Though the day was warm, I felt a chill as the memory hissed at me.

Lucy stood. She towered over me. From our precipice she appeared to be a diver contemplating the degree of difficulty of her next jump. The image troubled me. I didn't stand beside her.

I wondered about Lucy's recklessness, about what despair could have fueled her compulsion to be taunting fate. I knew I wouldn't have let Grace stand there—when she could stand, anyway. I got lost temporarily contemplating how many more weeks that might be and wished I'd paid more attention during the human development class I'd taken as an undergraduate.

"I told Ramp I was sleeping with Royal," she said. "He asked me, so I told him. I spent much of the rest of the time I was with him wondering whether or not it was an act of intimacy on my part."

At Lucy's admission about her relationship with Royal, I felt my breath catch just a little in my chest. The hesitation was not over learning that she'd slept with him, but rather at hearing her admit it. My mind flashed back to Lucy's oddly provocative behavior the night I visited her home, and I tried to put her confession about Royal in that context. Ever since I'd learned about the wet spot, I'd been preparing myself for the likelihood that Lucy had been intimate with the DA. Still, hearing her confirm the fact was far from comforting.

I asked, "Whether what was an act of intimacy? The sex with Royal? Or telling Ramp?"

"Good question. The telling. The sex with Royal wasn't intimacy. I don't have any doubts about that now." She kicked at something on the granite boulder. "How do you do that so easily? You didn't even hiccup when I told you that I'd slept with Royal. Weren't you surprised?"

Although I hadn't really been surprised by Lucy's revelation, at some level I knew that my sensibilities were offended, but years of clinical work had left me practiced at not revealing that kind of reaction. I said, "I suspected, and the truth is, I don't surprise easily anyway. Maybe I'm not as innocent as Sam. Maybe it's the work I do—I hear a lot of things."

"You don't care that I was sleeping with Royal?"

I chose my reply with care. "You mean do I judge you?"

"I guess that's what I mean."

"I'm in no position to do that. Knowing you slept with him is like skipping to the back of a book to find out how it ends. It's dangerous to make assumptions from there. I don't know what came before. What your motivations were."

"Are you curious?"

Good question. "We're both in difficult positions, Lucy."

"Does it make sense why I wouldn't tell Lauren and Cozy?"

"Sure. If you were having an affair with Royal, it wouldn't be hard for someone to extrapolate that maybe you had a motive to kill him." I, for instance, was having no trouble making that precise extrapolation. None. I added, "But they are your lawyers, Lucy."

Almost coyly, she asked, "Do you want to know about it? What happened between Royal and me?"

"I'm not sure. I don't want to be in a position to compromise your position."

"You mean legally?"

"Yes."

"It's not like that. With what I'd like to tell you, you could hurt me, but not legally."

I finally guessed where she was going. "But you would be vulnerable? Psychologically?"

"Yes. I would be very, very vulnerable. To you, certainly." She spread her arms to the side and closed her eyes. She held her position with the assurance of a yogi. "Stand up with me," she said.

Reluctantly, I did. Inches from my toes, the canyon dropped at least a hundred yards—okay, maybe fifty—almost straight down. If I fell, I counted at least two or three sharp outcroppings of rock that would crack my skull and my bones on the way to the bottom.

Lucy looked at me. I turned my head to her slowly, afraid that a more rapid motion would disturb my precarious balance.

She said, "I think Susan wanted me to."

I said, "What?"

"I think she wanted me to be . . . involved with Royal. It served her purposes."

Fortunately, she caught me before I keeled over.

"A little less than a year ago—it was early last summer—she called me one day, out of the blue, and asked me to come over to her house. I thought it was odd, but I did. I went. She said her illness had finally taken its toll on Royal, and that he was planning on leaving her. He wasn't going to run for DA in the next election. He didn't love her anymore and he was going to divorce her and move on with his life.

"She blamed the illness, of course. It never crossed her mind that Royal might have grown to despise her even had she been healthy."

I opened my mouth to speak but reconsidered. I needed to listen, not talk. Lucy had just admitted that she'd been sleeping with her mother's husband, and yet she was choosing to talk not about her own behavior but about her mother's. My antennae were twitching.

Lucy continued. "She said she'd need someone to care for her." I watched as Lucy lifted her right foot from the uneven stone and bent that leg ninety degrees at the knee, finally resting the foot against the inside of her left thigh. "She meant me, of course."

She maintained the position for a count of about twenty. I held my breath until she lowered her leg again. Both feet firmly on the rock, she reached out and grabbed my hand. The breezes were shoving insistently at our backs, nudging us toward something.

"I didn't even let her ask. I told her no, that I wouldn't take care of her. No way. Not a chance."

Lucy grew silent for a while. I was aware that we'd started to sway in unison. I really wanted to sit down.

"She acted surprised, almost offended, that I could think she would ask me to take care of her. But I knew where she was going before she got there. I don't know why, or how, but I just did. Sitting with her then, I felt like you feel right now. On the edge of something dangerous. Unsure of my balance, what I should do next."

She knew I was nervous.

"And she . . . I thought she was kind of threatening me. She was subtle, but I got the message anyway. She told me that she always thought that she could count on her daughters for help if circumstances . . . demanded. Me, I was one of her daughters. What she was doing was she was letting me know she'd be willing to tell people that she was my mother. She actually said she was beyond humiliation. She didn't care if the whole town knew she'd abandoned her daughter."

"She said all that?"

"She didn't have to say it all."

"But it felt like a threat to you?"

"It felt pitiful. It made me despise her more."

"So what do you think she was doing? Why did she invite you over?"

"I don't know. Maybe she was trying to play on my guilt. She knew I didn't want to have anything to do with her. And I'm sure she knew I didn't even want to be associated with her publicly. She was letting me know that she could make living in Boulder uncomfortable for me, and she was offering me an alternative."

"Taking care of her?"

She nodded. The wind stilled temporarily and Lucy seemed to be pondering her next words. I told myself to wait her out. The wait was prolonged. She didn't speak until the wind returned to accompany her tale.

"A week or two later Royal called and asked me to come over to discuss 'things.' That's what he said—'things.' But I didn't want to go to Susan's house, so I asked him to meet me at my place. It was a Saturday afternoon that he came over. The Broncos were playing a preseason game. I don't even remember against who." Her voice brightened as she asked, "Did you ever get a chance to spend time alone with him?"

"With Royal?"

She nodded.

"I only knew him socially, Lucy. The smallest group I ever saw him in was probably a dinner party."

Her gaze seemed to fall out of focus. "You missed something special. Royal was charming when you got him alone. Truly charming. That day he came over to my house I liked him right away. He was nothing like what I'd expected based on seeing him on the news."

Lucy liked Royal. I tried to process that data.

"Nothing happened that day. We talked about life with Susan. He told me about his plans, what life might bring after he left the DA's office. We talked about the Broncos and cars and being a cop."

And, I wondered, *what bridges to intimacy did you cross?*

"The next move was mine. I called him a week later, asking if we could talk again. Neither of us wanted to be seen out together in public, so he suggested I come by his house after Susan was in bed.

"I did. That's the night we made love for the first time." Her head lolled back and she stared at the sky.

"I almost didn't do it because, in some sick way, I knew right from the start that I was doing it partially for Susan. Like a gift. But I really liked Royal, so I knew I was doing it for me, too. I was having my cake and eating it, too. I can't think of another time when that's been true in my life. Not one."

"I don't think I understand how it was a gift for Susan." Whether or not I understood wasn't particularly relevant. What I was really saying was that I suspected that Lucy didn't truly understand how it was a gift for Susan.

"As long as Royal and I were involved, he wouldn't have a reason to leave her right away. Susan had told me that she thought their youngest daughter could help her out when she got out of school the following spring. My relationship with Royal bought Susan time."

Using my office voice, a voice that sounded foreign to me out here among the rocks and pines, I said, "So you convinced yourself that having sex with Royal was an act of generosity to your mother?"

She registered my change in tone. She stilled and asked, "What do you mean?"

I allowed the vinegar of incredulousness to seep into my words. "By sleeping with her husband you thought you were being generous to her?"

"As long as I was involved with him, I didn't think he'd leave her."

I could hardly believe the level of denial that I was hearing. It bordered on hysteria or dissociation. But if

Lucy's denial were doing its job protecting her ego from the rage she obviously found so intolerable, she would be almost immune to gentle confrontation from me. Part of me felt I should turn and walk away from Lucy's defenses, leaving the thick insulation undisturbed.

Part of me—maybe unfortunately—didn't. I wouldn't put it past Susan to snare Lucy into some kind of evil, but I truly doubted that Susan's motivation would have anything to do with prolonging the Petersons' marriage. I said, "And you believed . . . that what you were doing was . . . uncomplicated? Just a favor to your mother? Like bringing her hot meals occasionally?"

My words were more generous than my thoughts. In my head I was thinking that Lucy had been sticking a dagger into her mother's heart and had somehow convinced herself that the act was bypass surgery.

Could she have performed a similar operation on Royal? I wasn't sure. I just wasn't sure.

"No, of course not. I knew it was weird, that part of it. But the other side of it was that . . . Royal was special to me. I knew that I was getting what I wanted from him. That came first. I'm not blind about all this. If it was just about Susan, I wouldn't have done it."

I sighed involuntarily, and ratcheted up the confrontation. "I think maybe you've been kidding yourself, Lucy." I was eager to be certain that my words had registered, but she didn't look back at me. I continued. "I don't think your decision to sleep with Royal was anywhere near as uncomplicated as you would like to think."

I gave her a chance to reply. She passed on the opportunity. I went on. "If—and it's a big 'if'—Susan was really inviting you to get involved with her husband, what she was really inviting—Look at me please, Lucy." I was mildly surprised that she turned toward me. "What she was really inviting was your hostility, and you fell right into her trap and complied. She held out a noose and you agreed to close it around her neck."

I watched Lucy's jaw tighten, watched her eyes narrow. A gust of wind blew her hair across her face. She threaded it away with her long fingers. "You think that's what I did? I did this to . . . hurt her?"

She looked baffled, almost disoriented, as she recognized with alarm that I'd been busy setting up an ambush on her denial.

I decided to give understatement a chance. "I think you may want to look at it, Lucy."

"She wanted me to punish her?" The question was naive. This was virgin territory for Lucy. I continued to fight astonishment that, despite the events that had transpired since the night Royal was killed, Lucy's defenses were so resilient.

I shrugged. "That's part of it. Assuming she knew what was going on, the other part is that she also wanted to injure you as well. The hostility cut both ways. I'm afraid she accomplished that, too. Didn't she?"

Lucy shook her head as though my words stunned

her, but when she spoke again she ignored my question, returning instead to the issue of her own rage. Her cheeks drained of color as though they'd suddenly been bleached. "That makes me what? Sadistic? To my own mother? Is that what I am—a sadist?"

"I don't think the label is necessary or helpful."

"What, then? What is necessary?"

"The awareness of how furious you've been at her. Maybe that's a good place to start. That's precisely what she took advantage of, Lucy—your anger. She knew all about your anger."

Her shoulders hunched upward and her body began to sway back and forth like a sapling against the breeze.

I put a hand on her upper arm and told her that I needed to sit. She sat with me. Still way too close to the edge for my comfort, but at least we were sitting.

Lucy's sobs were almost drowned out by the gusting wind. I had to struggle to make out her next words. "I could've fallen in love with him. Maybe I did. It wasn't all about Susan."

I weighed her thoughts for further evidence of rationalization. But I knew I'd been witnessing evidence of something else, something more pathological than a garden-variety ego defense. Could it have been possible that her rage at her mother was really as isolated as it appeared? Had she been so incapable of seeing how Susan had been hurting her all over again? So out of touch with her own agony? And so unwilling to see her own vicious response toward her mother?

It seemed like time for me to say something. I said, "This wasn't about Royal, Lucy."

"It wasn't?" The sound of her question was so puerile it was as though I were watching a child move from doubts about immense bunnies to recognition of the fact that Easter morning was a fiction.

I shook my head. "No, it wasn't."

Lucy said, "I wondered if she knew."

I didn't respond.

Lucy went on. "I don't know if she knew. Royal thought she suspected, but I didn't see how she could really know. We met at their house. He'd give her some sleeping medicine before I came over. That was the arrangement. I'd park on the next block and come in through the backyard. Royal and I would get a few hours together." She wiped her eyes with her fingertips and wet her lips with her tongue as she scanned the sky.

Reality was settling the way that dust coats a mirror.

"God, it was hostile, wasn't it? What I did."

I replied, "And what she did. And what Royal did."

In a quick motion she popped to her feet and circled me on the rock. The abyss in front of me felt as though it was pulling at us with the force of a vacuum. For a fleeting moment the image of a bloody confrontation between Royal and Lucy filled my awareness. I considered the possibility that she was intending to jump off the rock, and I wondered if I was strong enough to stop her. I knew I wasn't.

Before I could decide what to do, she stopped wandering around the rock and lowered herself to a squat again. She was slightly in front of me, inches from the edge. "Am I crazy, Alan? How crazy do you have to be to do what I did?"

I thought, *What did you do?* I said, "You're not crazy, Lucy."

"But I have problems, don't I?"

I revisited understatement. "Yes, Lucy. I think you could use some help."

After a few minutes of silence she said, "After I went out with Grant for a while, I decided what I was doing with Royal was crazy and I decided to break it off. The night Royal was killed, I'd told him it was the last time."

"That was it?"

"He wasn't happy about it but I don't think he was surprised. It wasn't like we argued about it or anything. He was . . . rather gracious . . . and he said I didn't have to worry about Susan, that when he moved out he'd make arrangements for her, that he had some long-term-care insurance she didn't know about, and that he'd been looking into assisted-living facilities. He told me that he'd already talked to their kids and none of them was in a position to live with Susan. And that was it.

"I was relieved I wasn't going to have to take care of her. I felt guilty about that, but I was more feeling sad that the thing with Royal was over. We said good-bye and I left."

"Royal was still alive?"

She squeezed my hand. I read no offense in her voice as she murmured, "Of course he was." She squeezed harder. "You know what Royal said right at the end, as I was leaving that last time?"

I shook my head.

"He said, 'I wondered which one of us would come to our senses first. I'm glad it was you.' At the time, I didn't know what he meant."

"And now?"

"Right now? I think he knew what Susan and I were doing. How we were hurting each other."

I added, "But he was willing to participate anyway."

"That's sick, too, isn't it?" she asked.

I didn't have to answer.

She stood up and took a step away from me.

I opened my mouth to ask another question, then closed it. She said, "Go ahead, ask me."

"No, I was going to change the subject."

"Ask."

"Your fingerprints were on the pottery, Lucy. The piece that was used to bash Royal in the head."

She nodded. "The pottery was a new acquisition of Royal's. He was proud of it; it was by some artist he really liked from New York City. He'd found it on eBay and was thrilled that he had won the auction. He showed it to me when I first got there that night."

"That's it?" I asked. "You touched it when he showed it to you?"

She shrugged. "What was it Freud said about cigars?" she asked.

I managed a weak grin for her benefit, but was thinking that Lucy was in no position to make a decision whether or not this cigar was really just a cigar. I also knew that she hadn't shared all her secrets.

CHAPTER

64

Was Ramp there that night, Lucy? Did Royal discover him placing the bomb? Is that what happened?"

She shook her head. "I asked Ramp about it. He said that he and Marin placed the bomb in the Peterson home at least a week before Royal was murdered. He said they were real careful to make sure no one was home. They were in and out of the house in ten minutes and didn't see anyone."

"You believed him?"

"Of course. And I still do. What possible reason would he have had to lie?"

She seemed surprisingly sanguine.

Not really sure why I was asking, I said, "You know who killed Royal, don't you?"

"Any cop will tell you that knowing who did it is sometimes the easy part. Proving who did it, that's the hard part. This town learned that lesson the hardest possible way."

I figured she was alluding to JonBenét Ramsey's murder. The old homicide was a stray dog that followed Boulder cops everywhere they went. No way was I going to comment on that mutt.

She hadn't answered my question. I said, "But you know, don't you?"

"Sure I do. So do you."

She actually smiled.

"What do you mean?" I asked.

She shook her head.

"Sorry," she said. "The hostility has to end somewhere."

CHAPTER

65

Susan Peterson killed herself the next morning.

Sam and I were sitting downstairs at her kitchen table while she did it. I still think that I was more surprised than Sam was, which gives you some idea about how much to rely on a psychologist's ability to predict suicide.

Since Sam wasn't an active part of the investigation of Royal Peterson's murder and had no official reason to visit Susan again, he'd asked if he could accompany me on my next visit to see her.

After my conversation the day before with Lucy about Susan, I wasn't at all certain I would ever choose to see Susan again. When I told Sam that I had absolutely no plans to make another visit to the

Peterson home, he looked at me with mocking condescension and asked me if I was getting thicker with
age.

I replied by wondering aloud if there was any alternative. He said no, that it was important.

I made the necessary calls and we drove to Jay
Street together around eight-thirty the next morning.
Susan's health aide, Crystal, answered the door and
ambushed me by greeting Sam as though they were old
friends, even giving him a little peck on the cheek. She
stepped out onto the porch wearing a cable-knit
sweater. She was carrying a macramé bag over her
shoulder that I guessed functioned as her purse.

To Sam, she said, "An hour, you think?"

He replied, "That should be plenty of time. It's
enough for you?"

"If there's not too bad a line over there, it should be
great for me. You're an angel, Detective, an angel." She
glanced back over her shoulder. "I imagine she'll be
waking up soon enough. Her food's in the fridge all
ready to go."

As Crystal meandered down the walk toward the
street, Sam explained, "She needs to get her driver's
license renewed. I told her we'd keep an eye on things
here for an hour or so."

"You two are tight?"

"We had a beer last night. She likes hockey, actually
knows what she's talking about. I told her if this works
out I might be able to get her some Avs tickets. She's
from Wisconsin, but Crystal's okay."

I'd never understood the nature of the relationship between the residents of Wisconsin and Minnesota, but decided not to pursue an explanation at that moment. "If what works out? What did she tell you?"

I thought he almost grinned as he said, "You'll see."

I followed Sam inside the Peterson home and watched as he squatted down and opened the housing on the underside of the electric lift that Susan used to get up and down the stairs. I was instantly suspicious—if Susan was upstairs sleeping, as Crystal had just implied, the chair should have been at the top of the stairs, not the bottom. Sam flicked a red switch before he shut the cover back tight onto the housing.

A large oval piece of pottery sat smack in the middle of the third step on the staircase. Sam touched it to make sure it wasn't balanced too precariously. He whispered, "Recognize it? This is from Royal's collection downstairs. With that hole in it, though, I don't know what you'd actually use it for, but it's kind of nice to look at."

I assumed he wasn't planning on telling me what he was up to, so, sotto voce, I asked, "You turned the lift off?"

He nodded. "Crystal promised to leave some coffee and things for us. Come on."

We walked into the kitchen. Sam poured us each a mug of coffee and dragged a plate of muffins across the table so that it was smack in front of him. I smelled apples and spice. Morning light drenched the kitchen and from our perch on the sloping foothills of the Front Range the budding leaves on the trees in the Boulder Valley gave the beautiful view a lime-green aura.

I could have pressed him to divulge his strategy, but it would have been futile. Sam was directing this play and act two would come after act one. That was the natural order of things. Sam liked natural order.

After ten minutes or so talking about our kids and hockey, Sam said, without segue, "Lucy says that Royal told her that he was going to leave Susan. Was thinking about putting her in a nursing home. Did you know that? He had some insurance or something that would help pay."

"Lucy told me the same thing, Sam. Just yesterday." I didn't tell Sam what else Lucy had told me the day before.

He nodded as though he knew exactly what Lucy had revealed to me. But I knew he didn't know. Lucy would never tell Sam what she'd told me on Flagstaff Mountain.

Never.

With the fat edge of his hand, Sam scraped muffin crumbs into a little pile in front of him and then pressed them into a tiny orb that he tossed into his mouth. He said, "Even though I really shouldn't be here, I can't sit and wait around for this investigation to go on any longer. I don't ever want to know what the lab says about the stain on the sheet, you know? Not today, not tomorrow." He began to break apart another muffin. "Remember a cop named Manes? Brian Manes?"

I shook my head.

"Couple of years back, he was accused of coercing women to have sex with him on traffic stops?"

"I remember now."

"He went to my church. Has a kid Simon's age. He coached the kids' soccer team. His wife is a sweetheart. And, until the first woman filed a complaint against him, he had a perfect record as a cop."

I sensed where he was going. "Sometimes you just can't see what's going on below the surface with people, can you?"

"I could never figure out why, what was going on in his head, how he could risk so much for so little."

Were we talking about Brian Manes or were we talking about Lucy? I decided Sam didn't really want me to know for sure. "Sometimes people don't even recognize what they're doing, let alone why they're doing it."

"That's what keeps you in business? The fact that people fuck up their lives and don't have a clue what the hell they were doing or why the hell they were doing it?"

"What do they say, Sam? Denial's not a river in Egypt."

Sam adjusted his ample weight on the chair. He didn't move any of the crumbled muffin pieces toward his mouth. "Anyway, I don't want to know how the stain on the sheet got there. Not a bit. And I don't really want anybody else to know, either." He forced his chin forward. "I suspect there's a good possibility that it wouldn't be good news for Lucy. All in all, I'd rather not confront that possibility."

Sam was wrapping himself in his denial as though he were bundling up in a parka to go out in a blizzard. I wondered if the gesture was intended to be an ironic charade on his part. I said, "I can understand that, Sam. But remember, Brian Manes abused his office. If Lucy screwed anything up, it was only her personal life."

"That's what I tell myself, too, that everybody has dirty laundry." He smiled at the inadvertent allusion. "But there's something else," he said. "Something that doesn't really have to do with my deep level of disappointment in my fellow man. I've had trouble with the whole laundry thing right from the beginning. Not the sheet with the stain on it so much. That wakes me up in the middle of the night, sure, but that's not what I mean. I mean the laundry that was already in the dryer. You may remember that the first officer in the house heard the dryer running when she went in. I asked Lucy about it. She says that Royal was as likely to do a load of laundry as he was to change the oil on the space shuttle. So I wondered who it was who put that load in the dryer."

"It wasn't Lucy?"

"She says not."

The intercom erupted across the room, Susan's voice emerging from the speaker. I found the sound irritating, like the grainy feeling in my sinuses when I'm warding off a sneeze.

She said, "Crystal, I'm awake. I'm ready anytime."

To me, Sam whispered, "Crystal says that despite how it appears, Susan's strong enough to do laundry. So I'm doing a little experiment. You know me, I like to be empirical."

I wondered how Sam was planning on tricking Susan into doing a load of whites. But I didn't say anything. Sam had asked for an hour or two. I had time.

A minute later, after the plumbing announced the flush of a toilet, Susan repeated her entreaty to Crystal, her voice a decibel or two higher.

Sam asked me if I wanted more coffee.

I didn't.

Susan's patience was diminishing. When she called for Crystal again, she sounded closer. She seemed to be screaming down from the top of the stairs, apparently suspicious that the problem she was experiencing might be with the intercom and not with her health aide.

She finished her little tirade with, "I can smell the coffee down there, Crystal, damn it."

Sam raised his index finger to his lips to keep me silent. Seconds later we could hear Susan fumbling with the switch that, had Sam not disabled it, would have called the seat of the lift from the bottom of the stairs to the top. Susan cursed at the machinery when it didn't budge.

Sam raised his eyebrows in mock surprise and mouthed, "Such language."

We listened to two or three minutes of shuffling and

huffing and puffing and cursing and mumbling before Susan muttered, "Who left this thing on the stairs?" More profanity, then a final, "Crystal, did you turn this off? Crystal! Where are you, woman?"

A few seconds later, Susan Peterson walked into the kitchen looking like she'd spent the last eight hours sleeping with the devil. Her pajamas were creased. Her hair was a mess, her face was devoid of makeup, and her eyes had the glaze of someone with a narcotic hangover. She supported herself with one hand on a cane that was carved to resemble a stack of tiny turtles.

In the other hand she held the large oval ceramic that had been on the stairs. She held it up easily, naturally, as though she were about to waggle it at Crystal and demand to know what it had been doing on the stairs.

Her mouth hung open when she saw us sitting at the kitchen table.

The silence in the room was stunning.

Susan's eyes darted from Sam to me and then back to Sam before they came to rest on the heavy piece of pottery that she was holding in her hand. Finally, she said, "Oh."

Sam said, "Crystal will be back in a bit. She had an errand to run. I see you made it down the stairs all right. I wondered how you'd manage with the lift not working. It seems I needn't have worried; you managed just fine."

Susan shook her head, as though she were disagreeing with something Sam had said. Or perhaps she was trying to clear her thoughts. The gesture caused me to have an uncomfortable association to Lucy.

Sam went on. "Crystal said your arms are stronger than your legs. The way you're holding that heavy piece of pottery, it looks like she was right. But apparently your legs are strong enough to get down the stairs."

"And . . . what's your point?" Susan asked defiantly, but I could tell that her heart wasn't really in her protest.

Sam placed his hands palm-down on the smooth surface of the table. He said, "Why don't you go get dressed, Susan? I'd like you to come with me over to Thirty-third Street."

Her voice cracked as she asked, "Why?"

He paused, inhaling a thin stream of air through pursed lips, tasting his words the way my friend Peter used to taste wine before he pronounced it palatable. "I think you killed your husband. The detectives who are investigating his murder will have some questions for you." He somehow managed to make the declaration sound mundane.

His words reeled me back to a recollection of my recent afternoon visit up Flagstaff Mountain with Lucy. I thought of her almost intractable denial about her strange ménage à trois, and about the way she was able to wall off her hostility toward her mother. And then I realized that perhaps she wasn't alone—that my own denial of the events that had taken place in this house had been as impenetrable as blackout curtains.

I wasn't in denial that Susan might have killed

Royal—at some suburb of my awareness I'd been entertaining that possibility for a while. No, my denial had been about Susan Peterson's ultimate expression of hostility. As I sat watching Sam's production I was finally beginning to accept the obvious: *From the moment she descended the stairs to kill her husband, Susan had been setting up her own daughter to take the fall.*

Evil, I realized, had many faces. It was becoming increasingly obvious that Susan Peterson wore most of them.

Susan made a noise. It seemed to come from deep in her throat, but it wasn't exactly a groan. I thought that she appeared to be weighing Sam's directive that they head across town to the police department. As though she'd reached a conclusion, her eyelids closed slowly, like a curtain descending at the end of an evening at the theater.

There was no applause.

I watched as she shifted the bulk of her weight onto the arm supported by the cane. She mumbled, "I'm not well."

I didn't think the words were intended for Sam or me. I think she spoke them because she found them palliative.

Sam said, "Mrs. Peterson? Susan?" When she didn't respond, he repeated her name twice more until she reopened her eyes. The moment she did, he recited Miranda to her, the familiar words somehow as lyrical as Whitman.

I was still thinking about the faces of evil as I heard the hum of the lift carrying her up the stairs.

The roar of the gunshot came about three or four minutes later. I jumped up at the sharp clap, knocking my coffee mug off the edge of the table.

Sam winced and shook his head. He said, "I wondered if she'd do that. Actually thought she might take some pills. Didn't really think about Royal having a gun in the house, but I have to admit that I wondered whether she'd do something." He stood up and sighed. "I guess I have to go upstairs and see how good a shot she is. Or was."

I intertwined my fingers to quiet the tremor that had erupted in my hands.

"Want to come with?" Sam asked.

An extract from Stephen White's
exciting new thriller

THE BEST REVENGE

Available in Little, Brown hardback
from 3 July 2003

PROLOGUE

1997

If Kelda James hadn't been wearing inch-and-a-half heels and the toilet paper roll hadn't been empty, Rosa Alija would probably be dead.

At about ten-twenty that morning Kelda had excused herself from her fellow FBI agents and followed directions to the rest room – down the long hall, go left, last door on the right. The bathroom was a step up from what she had expected to find, given the tacky condition of the rest of the building. She was relieved to see that the sink was reasonably clean and the toilet seat wasn't stained with yellow coins of urine. The only problem was that there was no toilet paper on the cardboard roll.

Kelda stepped back out into the hall to retrace her route and retrieve her shoulder bag and its stash of tissues, but noticed a closet marked 'Utility' adjacent to the bathroom. The knob on the door wasn't locked and she found herself staring into a space about six feet square. A window was mounted high on the wall, dividing the small room in half. A jumble of brooms and mops leaned against a cracked porcelain sink on one side; the opposite side was stacked with particleboard shelves piled high with what appeared to be a lifetime supply of paper towels, soap, disinfectants, and toilet paper. Kelda reached onto an upper shelf for a fresh roll of toilet tissue and reflexively glanced over the sill and out the window as she rotated back toward the door.

The window overlooked the alley behind the building. Across the alley was the back of a single-story light-industrial building not noticeably different from the one that Kelda and her FBI colleagues had just raided.

Except for the hand.

Kelda was sure that for a split second she had glimpsed a hand in a window of the building across the alley. In her mind she was already considering it to have been a tiny hand, a child's hand.

She approached the utility closet window, stood on her toes, and peered again at the building across the alley. No hand. She raised her fingers to the sill to hold herself up and examined the distant window in detail. The bottom edge of the cloudy pane was streaked with parallel vertical lines that could have been made by fingers.

Tiny fingers. Child's fingers.

'Oh my God,' she said.

Fresh out of the FBI Academy, Special Agent Kelda James had been in the Denver, Colorado, field office for all of five weeks. Her initial assignment was to a squad that investigated white-collar crime, and that morning she had been ordered to accompany three other agents — all male, all senior to her, all somewhere between significantly and maximally apprehensive of her skills — to serve a federal warrant and raid a company called Account Assistants, Inc., on Delaware Street in Denver's Golden Triangle neighborhood. The company did contract billing for medical practices, and the raid was intended to collect evidence of suspected Medicare fraud.

For an FBI white-collar crime squad, this was routine stuff.

Prior to entering the FBI Academy, Kelda had earned her credentials as a certified public accountant and had spent a few years investigating fraud for an international insurance company. Her role in the raid of Account Assistants, Inc., was to cover the back door as the raid started and, later, to use her forensic accounting background to help make certain that the agents didn't fail to retrieve any records that they might ultimately need to press their case against the firm.

Most important, though, she knew that her primary

responsibility was to remember at all times that she was the new guy, or in FBI parlance, 'the fucking new guy.' Her primary responsibility was not to screw up.

Later in the day, after she and the other agents had finished collecting the evidence and had transported the boxes back to the Denver Field Office, Kelda figured that she – the fucking new guy – would be the one who would be assigned to spend the next few weeks sitting at her Bureau desk examining the mind-numbing details of the service and billing records, trying to use Account Assistants, Inc.'s own numbers to prove the fraud case that had spawned the warrant and the raid.

It's what she did. And she knew she did it well.

That was what she was contemplating when she saw the hand flash across the window a second time. But as swiftly as it appeared in the window, the little hand disappeared again.

A more experienced agent might have gone back to her squad, reported what she'd seen, and asked one of her colleagues to accompany her across the alley to investigate the fleeting hand. A more experienced agent – one who wasn't a bookish young woman with an accounting degree whose colleagues called her Clarice behind her back – would have been less concerned about the scorn she would suffer if she pulled a fellow agent – or two, or three – away from important work to search the back of an adjacent building because she *thought that maybe* she had seen a child's hand in the bottom of a window.

Kelda could only imagine the relentless ridicule she would endure from her fellow agents after word spread in the field office that she had begged for assistance in checking out what would probably turn out to be nothing more nefarious than an unlicensed day-care facility.

Kelda moved out of the utility closet, closed the door, and took three steps farther down the hall to a door that was marked 'Exit.' An hour and a half earlier she'd stood in the alley on the other side of this very door in case any of the principals of Account Assistants, Inc., tried to flee out the back as the FBI team announced the raid and the warrant was served by the agents who entered the building through the door at the front.

She checked the inside of the exit door for an alarm: She couldn't spot any electronic devices attached to the heavy door that would announce that she had opened it. She stepped outside, propped the door open with a softball-sized piece of concrete, and then jogged across the alley to the window with the streaky glass and the disappearing tiny hand.

Two days before, six-year-old Rosa Alija had vanished from the playground of her elementary school's summer day camp near Thirty-second and Federal on Denver's near west side. The other children on the playground told police conflicting tales of a van or truck that was gray or brown and one man who was white or two men who were black or two men and a woman who were all kinds of different combinations of races and colors who had waited for a child to chase a ball into the field adjacent to the school and then, when Rosa Alija had been that child, had scooped her up, covered her mouth, and carried her away in the van or truck.

Some of the child witnesses reported that Rosa had kicked her legs and cried. Others maintained she was already dead by the time she got to the van.

No adult reported seeing a thing.

And no one had seen Rosa since. The girl's frantic parents, an independent landscaper named José Alija and his receptionist wife, Maria, waited in vain for a ransom demand. But neither the police nor the local FBI office expected to hear from Rosa's abductors. The Alijas weren't the type of family who were chosen for a kidnapping for ransom.

Rosa Alija had been taken for some other purpose.

Denver mobilized in an unprecedented fashion to find the girl. Hundreds of citizens – Hispanic, white, black, Native American, Asian – searched the city for little Rosa. Posses of private citizens scoured the banks of the South Platte River and Cherry Creek. The huge expanse of rail yard between her school and Lower Downtown was searched, and the interior of every last boxcar in the yard was examined. Her picture was featured on the front page of both daily papers, and the quest to find her dominated the local TV and radio news.

Bloodhounds tracked her route away from the school. The dogs seemed confident that her abductor had taken her down Speer Boulevard after the kidnapping, but the hounds lost the scent near the spot where Speer intersected with Interstate 25. The cops knew that once Rosa's abductors had her on Denver's main freeway, they could have taken her anywhere.

Anywhere. The Rocky Mountains, the Great Plains, the Great Basin. North to Wyoming, south to New Mexico. Anywhere.

Even into the back room of a light-industrial building in one of Denver's transitional urban neighborhoods.

The bottom of the window in the building across the alley was level with the top of Kelda's head. She listened for the sounds of children playing, but all she heard was the sough of distant traffic on Speer Boulevard; she heard nothing to convince herself that she'd stumbled onto a day-care facility. A moment's contemplation failed to suggest any other good reason that a small child would be scratching at the glass in a back room in a building in this neighborhood.

Kelda grabbed a discarded plastic milk crate from the alley and carried it back toward the window to check and see what was inside the building.

Before she had a chance to step onto the crate, she saw the hand again. It was reaching, groping, the fingers extended against the bottom edge of the pane, but they could only stay there for a second or two. Kelda imagined that every time the girl lifted her hand someone else was yanking it right back down.

Most of the doubt about what she had discovered evaporated from Kelda's mind. *Rosa Alija*, she was hoping. *It's Rosa Alija.* But even in her head, the thought was only a whisper. If hope was the balloon, reality was the ballast.

What if it's not?

For the first time since Kelda had graduated from the Academy, she withdrew her handgun from its holster with the clear understanding that she might be about to fire it. The Sig Sauer felt almost weightless in her hand as she stepped up onto the crate. Her confidence grew; Kelda's best days in training at Quantico were the days that her Sig weighed about as much as a glove. She knew instantly that this was going to be one of those days.

The filth on the glass and the dark interior of the room kept Kelda from peering inside. For a split second she considered returning to Account Assistants to collect her colleagues, but she was already fearing what would happen if she left the little girl alone for another minute. She decided that she would use her radio to summon the other agents the moment she was absolutely certain that she had indeed found the abducted child.

The building had a small loading dock that faced the alley. She pulled herself onto the narrow cement shelf of the dock and tried the big door. It was locked tight. She hopped back down and moved to the side of the building. The long cinder-block wall was interrupted by a solitary steel door that was secured by a hasp and padlock. Around the front, two old newspapers still in their delivery bags littered the sidewalk at the main entrance. A big 'For Lease' sign hung in the window, and three or four flyers were stuffed in the mail slot. Kelda put pressure on the handle of the glass entrance door. It didn't give.

Whatever this place once was, it wasn't in business anymore.

She returned to the side door. The bolt on the lock was in place, but the hasp seemed to be beginning to break free of whatever was holding it to the cinder block. She searched the weeds behind her and found a rusty length of angle iron, jammed it behind the hasp, and began to pry the steel hasp away from the wall.

After two minutes of constant pressure, the fasteners securing the hasp gave way and the door creaked inward half an inch.

Kelda had made a hundred armed entries into buildings during her training at Quantico. Maybe two hundred. She knew the drill. She knew where to look, what to say, how to hold her weapon.

She also knew not to do it alone.

In one minute, she promised herself, she'd call for help. Right after she was sure that Rosa Alija was safe and that her kidnapper couldn't spirit her away to some new location before the cavalry arrived.

Once inside the door, Kelda turned left toward the back of the building and stopped. Her gun was in her hand. It was not pointed at the ceiling; it was pointed in front of her. Why? Because that's what the FBI had taught her. Why? Because, as one instructor had shouted at a classmate during a drill, 'very few fucking UNSUBs are going to be waiting on the ceiling.'

She listened for any indication that the building was occupied. She heard nothing, and the stale air she was breathing confirmed her impression that the building was probably not being used.

She paced silently across the empty loading area until she confronted a closed door. The door, she figured, should lead to the room with the window. With the same gentle squeeze she would use to compress a trigger, she put pressure on the knob. It was locked.

She thought she heard a whimper.

Kelda's heart was cleaving. *She thinks he's coming back, that's why she's crying.* Kelda swallowed, checked her breathing.

He could come back any second.

Any second.

Her breathing grew faster, shallower. She realized there was a possibility she hadn't considered: *Maybe he's already in there with her.*

Kelda retreated across the loading area and backed into the hallway. She keyed her handheld radio. She'd decided not to communicate any doubt about her discovery: she'd already wasted too much time – she couldn't afford to give the other agents a reason to delay.

'Gary?' Gary Cross was the supervising agent of her squad. He was a fifty-year-old black man who seemed sincerely interested in helping her adjust to the curious culture of the FBI. He also seemed sincerely interested

in making certain that no one else recognized how helpful he was being to her.

'Gary?' she repeated.

'Yeah? Where the hell are you? Get back here. We
need you to look at something.'

In a throaty whisper she said, 'I've just stumbled on
Rosa Alija. You know, the little girl who was kidnapped?
I'm in the building directly across the back alley from
you. The door on the west side is open. The girl's in a
room that faces the alley. I need backup. Hot.'

'What? You found Rosa Alija?'

His reply had been too loud. Cursing silently, Kelda
fumbled with the volume on the radio. 'Gary, please
confirm. I have a feeling I'm not alone here.'

She actually heard a clatter of footsteps before she
heard him say, 'We're on our way.'

The door that led from the loading area to the adjacent room opened slowly. Kelda could hear it squeak.
She couldn't see the doorway, though, from where she
was standing; she had melded herself against the
cheap walnut paneling that lined the hallway.

A male voice called out, 'Who is it? Who's there?' He
was breathing loudly through his mouth. She listened to
his footfalls and knew that the man had taken two steps
before he repeated, 'Who is it? Is somebody there?'

She tried to analyze the accent. *What is it? A little
bit of East Texas? Or is that more Louisiana?*

The man took another step. One more, she figured,
and he'd be able to see her where she was standing in
the hall.

Kelda turned to face where he'd be after his next step, slid her left foot forward into an ideal shooting stance, and said, crisply, 'Federal agent! Get down! Drop your weapon!' Before the last words had passed her lips, a gunshot pierced the seam of the paneling across the hall from her. The hole in the wood was at chest height. After a half-a-heartbeat delay, two more shots followed. One was higher, the other was lower, inches from her waist. The shooter was covering his bases, bracketing his shots like a photographer unsure of the light.

She heard a shuffled step; she interpreted the noise to mean that he'd moved away from her, not toward her.

Intuitively, she was sure that he was retreating now, intent on barricading himself in the room with little Rosa. Kelda knew she couldn't permit that. The situation she'd walked into would be exponentially more difficult if the UNSUB could use the little girl as a hostage.

Staying low, she sprang forward, dove, and rolled across the loading area, finally coming to rest in a prone position eight feet away from where she'd been hiding in the hall. As she moved she heard more shots – two, three, four. She wasn't sure exactly how many. She did feel confident that none of them had entered her body.

Rolling to a stop, Kelda jammed her elbows against the floor, the 9mm poised and ready. Within a fraction of a second she fixed the man's torso in her sight and in rapid succession fired three times into the black and white target that she imagined was pinned to the center of his chest.

Each impact caused him to jerk a little, as though he'd hiccupped. He didn't drop his gun right away. She released a fourth round and kept light pressure on the trigger until he fell. It took every bit of discipline she'd acquired in her training to refrain from emptying her clip into him.

The room, she thought, smelled like the range at Quantico.

It was as comforting as the aroma of a lover's sweat.

Two or three seconds passed. Through the haze of what she had just done she saw the silhouettes of two of her colleagues as they entered the building through the side door. She held up her left hand to them to tell them to wait where they were. 'I'm okay, Gary,' she called. 'The UNSUB is down. Let me go in and get the girl.' The reverberation of the gunshots still echoed in her head, so she couldn't hear her own words as she spoke, and wondered if she'd said them loudly enough for Gary to hear her.

Kelda stood and stepped over to the man she'd shot, keeping the Sig pointed at his head until she was able to kick his weapon farther away from his hand. The handgun the man had fired at her was a monstrous .45; she shuddered at the thought of being hit by one of the gun's slugs.

The UNSUB on the floor was slight. He wore new Adidas, a clean pair of jeans, and a white shirt with the sleeves rolled up to his elbows. His shirt was untucked and his belt was undone.

The man had fallen on his side, facing away from

her, and she couldn't detect any sign that he was still breathing. His rimless eyeglasses sat cockeyed on his head. She didn't see much blood, just three dark circles on the back of his shirt. She wondered if she'd somehow lost the fourth round that she'd fired, though she couldn't imagine how that could have happened.

Her Sig at the ready, she crouched beside him and checked his pulse.

Nothing.

Standing erect over him, she said, 'Damn you. Don't die, asshole. Don't you dare die.'

In order to control an impulse to kick him in the face, she stepped back away from the man. Then she inhaled twice to quiet the echo of the exact same impulse. In her peripheral vision she saw Gary move into the room like a bishop striking from the corner of a chessboard.

'Get the girl,' he said. His voice competed unsuccessfully with the echoes of the gunshot; he sounded as though he was trying to get her attention across a crowded bar. But she knew what he had said.

Three quick steps forward took her into the room with the window that faced the alley.

Rosa was kneeling sideways on a mattress, wearing only a pink T-shirt with a filthy picture of Big Bird on it. The little girl's face was wound with duct tape. One of her skinny arms was manacled to a chain that was bolted to a D-ring that was anchored to the wall.

She was weeping.

'Hi, baby,' Kelda said. 'I'm here to take you home.'

Kelda was weeping, too.

GIDEON
Russell Andrews

When they asked him to be a ghost writer, he didn't realise they wanted him dead.

Struggling writer Carl Granville is hired to turn an old diary, articles and letters – in which all names and locations have been blanked out – into compelling fiction. But Carl soon realises that the book is more than just a potential bestseller. It is a revelation of chilling evil and a decades-long cover-up by someone with far-reaching power. He begins to wonder how his book will be used, and just who is the true storyteller.

Then – suddenly, brutally – two people close to Carl are murdered, his apartment is ransacked, his computer stolen, and he himself is the chief suspect. With no alibi and no proof of his shadowy assignment, Carl becomes a man on the run. He knows too much – but not enough to save himself . . .

'A fast-moving thriller in the Grisham genre'
Sunday Telegraph

HARD LANDING
Lynne Heitman

Her departure time was closer than she thought . . .

On a cold afternoon on the North Shore of Massachusetts, the body of Ellen Shepard is found. She leaves no family. She leaves no note. And she leaves vacant her position as the general manager of the notoriously brutal Majestic Airlines operation at Boston's Logan Airport.

From the moment Alex Shanahan takes over control of the Boston operation, she is pulled into the menacing intrigue of her predecessor's death. She is welcomed by an obscene depiction of Ellen's dead body – a warning that secrets can kill, and the threat that once she knows them it will already be too late.

But Alex wants to know the truth. She follows the trail of corruption and betrayal from the loading ramp to the airline's executive suites. What she uncovers could bring down the company and destroy the lives and careers of everyone involved. It could also cost Alex her life . . .

UNHOLY TRINITY
Paul Adam

Death, politics and the eternal city.

The murder of the Red Priest seemed like the beginning . . . Rome foreign correspondent, Andy Chapman, investigates the brutal killing of a controversial left-wing priest and discovers evidence which appears to implicate the Vatican in the death. He turns his information over to the investigating magistrate, the beautiful Elena Fiorini, and together they begin a hunt for the killers. Probing deeper, they find themselves up against the might of the Catholic Church and a sinister network of neo-Fascist fanatics. Their quest leads them to the very heart of the Vatican and back to the last days of Mussolini's dictatorship, when people changed their identities but not their allegiances.

The murder of the Red Priest was not the beginning. It was merely another link in a conspiracy which powerful, unseen forces will go to unimaginable lengths to conceal . . .

CONFLICT OF INTEREST
David Michie

When he was head-hunted he didn't realise
they wanted his life . . .

It's the job offer of a lifetime: £120,000 a year,
a top-of-the-range BMW, and the chance to
work with charismatic sportswear billionaire
Nathan Strauss. But on the very day that
Chris Trieger celebrates his new job with
Britain's most powerful PR firm, Nathan
Strauss stuns the corporate world by falling off
the balcony of his ninth-floor hotel suite.

Chris now finds himself reporting to Nathan's
brother, Jacob, and his sinister spin doctor – a
man whose loyalty borders on the obsessive.
Meanwhile, investigating the bizarre death of
a leading financial analyst, Chris's former
lover Judith Laing discovers he was on the
point of revealing damaging evidence about
Chris's new bosses. Chris refuses to believe
her – until another death occurs . . .

'When it comes to writing about the world of
PR skulduggery, Michie is an insider
trading on his strengths'
The Times

Other bestselling Time Warner Paperback titles available by mail: